THE 24-HOUR
DATING AGENCY

Mary Jayne Baker

An Aria Book

First published in the UK in 2022 by Head of Zeus Ltd,
part of Bloomsbury Publishing Plc.

9 7 5 3 1 2 4 6 8

A catalogue record for this book is available from the British Library.

ISBN (PB): 9781803282893
ISBN (E): 9781803282879

Cover design: Sophie Melissa
Typeset by Siliconchips Services Ltd UK

To my best little writing buddy, Millie the border collie pup, without whose input this book would have been finished in half the time...

Saffie fixed on a professional smile as she accepted a cup of tea from Councillor Jameson, the newest elected member of Braybrook Town Council.

'Thanks for seeing me, Councillor.'

'Please, call me Daphne.' The councillor's businesslike expression flickered briefly into warmth as she took a seat behind her desk. 'Now, what publication did you say you were with? *Lifestyle North?* I've had so many requests for interviews since my election that I'm finding it hard to keep track.'

'No.' Saffie fumbled with her Dictaphone. 'It's, um… *The Throstle's Nest.*'

'Curious name. Is that a newspaper or a magazine?' Daphne groaned. 'Please don't tell me it's a blog. I specifically told my assistant I wouldn't waste my time on websites. Nobody reads community news blogs.'

'No, we're print. Officially I'm supposed to describe us as a periodical.'

'How is that different to a magazine?'

'I'm not entirely sure. Fran Cook, our company director, has the idea that if we refer to ourselves as a periodical then we're more likely to be taken seriously.'

'Is that something you struggle with?'

'Oh, not at all,' Saffie lied. 'We're one of the oldest magazines in the country, and still family-owned. Fran's father founded us back in 1939, and his great-granddaughter is the current editor. We've just got a reputation for being... unusual, I suppose. Quirky.'

Once when she was out on a date, Saffie had described the publication she worked for as follows: 'You know that bit at the end of the news where there's a waterskiing squirrel or whatever? Well, *The Throstler* is one hundred pages of waterskiing squirrels.'

The councillor looked Saffie up and down, taking in her denim dungarees, her butterfly wrist tattoo and blue hair. 'You seem to encapsulate that profile yourself, Miss Ackroyd. No offence, but for this interview I would have expected a writer who was rather more...'

'Conservative?' Saffie asked, raising an eyebrow.

'Mature, I was going to say. Someone with experience of the political world.'

Saffie wondered whether to confess that she was, in fact, *The Throstler*'s only writer (well, aside from Tamara, her perpetually flustered editor). She was also its only sub-editor, webmaster, photocopier repair person and wielder of the official company spatula, which they used to jam the door closed on the ancient office microwave.

'Don't be fooled by the hair. I'm older than I look,' she said instead, flashing Daphne a tight smile.

Honestly, politicians. Saffie had experienced this attitude before. She was thirty-five years old; she was an NQJ-qualified journalist and she'd been doing this job for the best part of a decade, but if you were under fifty and dressed in anything that wasn't tweed, they treated you like you were doing an interview for the school paper.

'What is a throstle?' Daphne asked. 'Some sort of bird?'

'It's an old word for a thrush,' Saffie said as she flicked through her notebook.

'And you only cover Braybrook?'

'Yes, but we've got subscribers from all over the world. Our readers call us *The Throstler* for short; sort of a nickname.'

'Why would people overseas want to read a magazine about a small town in North Yorkshire?'

'I suppose because… there's nothing else quite like us.' Saffie waggled her Dictaphone. 'You don't mind if I record this, do you?'

Daphne nodded graciously. 'Go ahead.'

Saffie turned the device on and scanned her list of questions.

'You'll want to talk about the pedestrianisation of Braybrook high street, I suppose,' Daphne said. 'It's been generating a lot of debate.'

'Um, no.' Saffie coughed. 'I mean, yes, I'll be asking about that in due course. But first I wanted to talk about, um… about Glondu.'

Daphne frowned. 'Glondu?'

'Yes,' Saffie said, seriously hoping she'd been sent to interview the right councillor. If not then she was about to make a proper tit of herself. 'Your husband?'

'Ah. You heard about that, did you?' Daphne sipped her tea calmly. 'Well, I try not to let my work and home lives mix. It seems to unnerve people when I tell them I'm married to an extra-terrestrial being from the Kepler star system. Suffice to say, Glon's been very supportive of my plans for the town centre.'

Saffie was at her desk transcribing her interview notes when Milo waltzed into the office, late as usual. He flung himself into his swivel chair and stretched his long legs out on the desk.

'Another exciting day at *The Quibbler*,' he said, yawning. 'How was the little green councillor from Mars, Saf?'

'Actually, she's from Leeds. It's her husband who's from Mars. Well, Kepler-62.' Saffie glanced at Tamara's office door. 'And you'd better not let your sister hear you calling us *The Quibbler* again.'

'She's not in yet, she's taking Willow to the dentist's. Anyway, it's a compliment. It's like I always say: we're not weird. We're cult.'

'All that means is that only a handful of oddballs like us.'

'Yeah, but they're our oddballs.' Milo pushed his glasses up and went to peer over Saffie's shoulder at her notes. 'Was this Councillor Jameson as barmy as she sounds?'

'Actually she seemed quite with it, aside from the obvious.'

'I still can't believe she got elected. It's like when Hartlepool voted in that bloke in the monkey suit as mayor.'

'He was a novelty candidate though,' Saffie pointed out. 'He didn't think he was an actual monkey, did he? Whereas Councillor Jameson very much believes she's married to an alien from Kepler-62.'

'Why do people vote for these guys?'

Saffie shrugged. 'If the news has taught us anything, it's

that a high percentage of our public servants are narcissistic Machiavellian pricks who'd deport their own granny if they thought it'd buy them a few votes. Is Daphne Jameson's belief in close encounters of the sexy kind so much worse? As long as their elected representatives get the potholes filled in, I suppose people will put up with a certain amount of eccentricity.'

'Yeah, but there's eccentricity and there's believing you're married to an alien from Kepler-62.'

'Maybe she really is married to an alien from Kepler-62; you never know. There are more things in heaven and earth, Horatio.'

Milo snorted. 'You what? I thought you were the office sceptic.'

Saffie massaged her temples. 'I blame all those pieces I've been writing for the "Stranger Than Fiction" page. You can't help wondering if there might be something in these things.'

'Shame we couldn't get the exclusive on Councillor Jameson,' Milo said. 'This has got *Throstler* all over it. Did you meet Kal-El or whatever he's called?'

'Glondu,' Saffie said. 'No, he lives on Kepler-62. Apparently he just pops back every once in a while for a home-cooked meal and a cheeky anal probe with the missus.' She nodded to the red beanie her best friend was wearing. 'What's with the hat? You got a bald spot developing?'

He shrugged. 'Just keeping my ears cosy.'

'Milo, it's May. It's twenty degrees outside.'

He gestured to her coffee mug. 'My turn to get the brews in, isn't it?'

'OK, that was the least subtle subject-change ever.' She

pointed at his head. 'Come on, get it off. I've got a tenner that says bald spot.'

'Saffie, there is no bald spot.'

'Yeah? Prove it then, and win yourself a tenner.'

'I don't need to prove it. I'm your oldest friend, you should take it on trust.'

She nudged him. 'Hey, I've got a Sharpie in my desk. Want me to colour it in for you before Tam gets in?'

'Saf, I swear to you I am not going bald,' Milo said, putting one hand on his heart. 'I'll get the kettle on.'

Saffie carried on typing up her notes while a still be-beanied Milo went to the kitchen area at the back of their office to make drinks. He came back with three mugs steaming on a tray.

'One each for us, one for Tam when she gets here,' he said. 'It's nice not having the boss in so we can catch up on gossip, isn't it?'

'She's not your boss. She's my boss. She's your sister.'

'She's my big sister. That automatically makes her the boss of me. At least, she thinks it does.' Milo took a sip of the sickly-smelling herbal concoction that had been his regular drink ever since he'd started going out with West. 'That's why Fran trained Tamara up as editor. I'm too much of a sexily irresponsible, devil-may-care scamp to be trusted with the precious family business.'

'You mean you're a lazy git.'

'Oi. Graphic design's a tough job.'

'Not the way you do it.' Saffie nodded to the feature notes on her monitor. 'Where in the running order do you think this ought to go? The "Believe It or Not" page or the local news roundup?'

'Definitely "Believe It or Not". As interesting as Councillor Jameson's pedestrianisation plans might be to the people of Braybrook, it's her old man who's the real hook.'

Saffie sucked the end of her biro. 'No. No, I think we should put it with the news: Jameson'll like that. Does no harm to keep her sweet in case we want to do a follow-up. And what do you think of this for a strap? "I married ET – but when it comes to local issues, I won't be phoning home."'

'Christ, that's *National Enquirer*-level cheesy.' Milo sipped his drink and pulled a face at the taste. 'Tam's going to love it.'

Saffie sighed. 'I'm not exactly rivalling Jeremy Paxman here, am I? Even Councillor Jameson struggled to take me seriously, and she spends her evenings necking with goggly-eyed spacemen.'

'Why didn't she take you seriously?'

'Oh, she was all "are you sure you're mature enough to do this interview?", just like when I interviewed that MP last year.' Saffie ran her fingers through her blue locks. 'Maybe I should change my hair colour. Although I'm not sure "mature" isn't actually a euphemism for "male".'

'You'll never change your hair to anything Councillor Jameson's going to approve of,' Milo said. 'You've been murdering it with synthetic dyes for so long, I can't even remember what colour it is naturally. Still no luck pitching the freelance feature that's going to propel you into the big time?'

'Just a load more rejections for my already bulging collection,' Saffie said gloomily. 'Whenever I dig up a really juicy story, I always get scooped before I can sell it.'

'The country's been stricken by a plague of freelance feature writers, that's why,' Milo said. 'Ex-national press, a lot of them.'

'Like your cousin wossname – the one your grandmother's always raving about? He used to be on one of the nationals, didn't he?'

'Russell, yeah. Lost his job due to downsizing, started his own regional lifestyle magazine with his missus, now it's the second biggest-selling publication in Yorkshire. No wonder he's Fran's golden boy.' Milo sloshed his drink around, showing no intention of taking a further sip. 'That just goes to show it can be done, Saf.'

'If you're him it can, sure. I've never worked for a national paper. I've only worked at this place.' Saffie cast a morose look at a wall display of past *Throstle's Nest* covers, with their twee chocolate-box illustrations of local scenes. 'You're right, Milo. Mags and newspapers all over the country are laying people off, and the first thing these unemployed journos do is buy themselves a fedora with a bit of paper saying "PRESS" in the hatband and start scouring the streets for stories. Print's dying in the online era and there are hundreds of experienced, talented freelancers fighting each other for what few paid gigs are out there. Where the hell does a glorified Newsround Presspacker like me fit in?'

'Now, come on.' Milo rested a soothing hand on her shoulder. 'You're a great writer.'

'What does it matter how good I am, if I'm competing with freelancers who came from *The Times* or the *Guardian*? All I've got under my belt is a decade's worth of *Throstler* features about batty town councillors, Yorkshire's tallest octogenarian and local farmers who've trained their cockerels to herd sheep. I'm a joke, Mile.'

'No you're not, you're a hard-working, talented young woman with a portfolio that shows she can write about anything. Your time will come, Saffie Ackroyd.'

'At the rate my features are getting rejected, the editors of the world would beg to differ. But thanks for trying to chivvy me up.' She nodded to his stinky tea. 'Your rhubarb infusion's going cold.'

'Is it? Thank God for that.'

'Milo, just have a coffee. I promise I won't tell West on you.'

Milo sank back into his chair. 'But I'll know I drank it, won't I? And if I know, he'll know. He can always tell when I'm hiding something. He can probably smell my unaligned chakras.'

'Then tell him. He's your boyfriend, not your mum.'

'I'll only get his lecture about my body being a temple. He might even make me do extra yoga as a penance. No thanks.'

'Look, if you and West have got such different views on how you want to live your lives, why not call it a day?'

'Saffie, I'm thirty-six years old, I can count the number of long-term relationships I've had on the fingers of... on three fingers, and I've been through four depressing breakups in the last six months.' Milo took a sip of the tepid rhubarb infusion and wrinkled his nose. 'My inner romantic might hate me for saying it, but there comes a time in every thirtysomething's life when "finding Mr Right" has to give way to "settling for Mr OK".'

Saffie grimaced. 'That's a depressing thought. I'm only four months younger than you.'

'I know you're sick of the dating game. The creeps, the bores, the endless disappointments. Don't you ever wish you could just rest?'

'Well yeah, but I'm not going to commit to life with the wrong person just because I'm tired. I only narrowly avoided making that mistake with Kieran. I'd rather stay single, thanks.'

'Well, I wouldn't,' Milo said firmly. 'If there's any possibility of not dying alone, then I'm going to jump on that. Even if it does mean a lifetime of rhubarb infusions and arthouse all-female performances of *Antigone*.'

Saffie pulled a face. 'West's making you go see *Antigone*?'

Milo nodded miserably. 'In the original Greek.'

'Ouch.'

Tamara came in, wearing an outfit that was a far cry from her usual skirt and blouse combo. She was in a faded pink tracksuit, her unbrushed hair pushed into a hasty bun, no make-up on and scowling like someone had just run over her cat. Her gaze skimmed over them to settle on the cup of coffee perched on the edge of Milo's desk.

'Oh God, is that for me?'

Her brother nodded. 'It might be a bit cool now.'

'Don't care.' She seized it and swallowed a mouthful.

'Half-term blues, Tam?' Saffie asked. 'You look pissed off.'

'I'll say I am. As if I didn't have my hands full getting Willow off to holiday club every day, sorting out everything the twins need for uni in October, keeping this place running and generally trying to keep a roof over all our heads, I got a text from Satan Incarnate this morning.'

Milo frowned. 'What, Andy?'

'Who else?'

'What did that bastard want? It's three years since you split; he can't suddenly have remembered some CDs he forgot.'

'Actually, it's four,' Tamara muttered. 'Four years since he walked out on his family, and now suddenly he's remembered he's got three children. Oh, and you'll never guess what else.'

'What?'

'He's getting married again. Some poor cow he met through work. She's only seven years older than Marcie and Dale, for Christ's sake.'

'Does Andy not see the kids at all now?' Saffie asked.

Tamara snorted. 'He sends the twins presents at Christmas, but he's only actually *seen* them about three times since the divorce. He told them he'd been working overseas, which I'm convinced is complete bollocks. Now all of a sudden he wants to make an access arrangement with me; set up regular visits.'

'What will you do?'

'Marcie and Dale are eighteen: it's up to them if they want their dad back in their lives. But Willow...' Her frown deepened. 'Every time I think about it I feel like punching something. He walked out on all of us, but Willow wasn't even a year old. Said he was too old at forty-one to go through the toddler years again and he needed "space" to "find himself", like some fucking teen off on their gap year. Willow wouldn't know her dad now if she bumped into him in the street.'

'Did you text him back?' Milo asked.

'I wrote a reply, but it was mostly four-letter words.

Marcie talked me into ringing him later instead, when I was calmer.' Tamara nodded to her brother's head. 'What's with the hat, Mile?'

'He doesn't want us to know he's going bald,' Saffie said.

'Oi. I told you, I am not going bald. Please try not to contribute further to my premature midlife crisis, thank you, Saffie.'

'Well, then what is the hat in aid of?'

Milo sighed. 'I suppose I'll have to come clean to the pair of you eventually.' He yanked off his beanie. 'Go on, laugh. I'm too miserable to care.'

Tamara stared. Then she snorted.

'Milo, you look like Annie Lennox.'

'Sod off, Tam.'

Saffie shielded her eyes as she gazed at her best friend's suddenly peroxide-blond hair.

'What the hell made you bleach your hair?'

Milo propped his chin on his fists. 'West said it'd suit me.'

Tamara shook her head. 'Mile, if West told you to jump off a cliff, would you do it?'

'Honest answer? Probably.' He glared at Saffie, who was fighting the giggles. 'I don't know what you're laughing at, Smurfette. You're not the only one entitled to go a bit punk.'

'It really doesn't suit you though,' Saffie said. 'Sorry, Milo, but it doesn't. With the specs, you just look a bit…'

'Milkybar Kid,' Tamara supplied helpfully.

'I know that, don't I?' Milo took his glasses off and wiped them on his T-shirt. 'Hence the hat. I tried to object, but West said it was empowering to reinvent yourself occasionally. Then he stood over me giving me his "have we learnt nothing from Lady Gaga?" speech until I cracked.'

'Why are you still with him?' Tamara asked. 'You've got nothing in common, he's forever trying to make you into someone you're not, and I know you secretly think he's a pretentious wanker with daft facial hair. Move on, Mile. He'll never make you happy.'

'He makes me... not alone,' Milo said quietly. 'I'm starting to think that after all these years, that's the best I can hope for.'

2

Saffie finished putting the next issue of *The Throstle's Nest* to bed at half past five. Milo had long since shut down his computer and was currently trying to beat his office record for wastepaper-bin basketball. Tamara was in her office with some cover options for the August issue, but Saffie could see through the glass door that she wasn't working: just scowling into space.

'Right, that's the July issue done,' Saffie said to Milo. 'It's a pretty good one. We've got the piece I wrote today on Councillor Jameson and hubby, plus there's that artist who makes models of Yorkshire cricketers out of Fimo, the interview Tam did with the Ripon town crier and my feature on the comic book series reimagining the works of James Herriot in manga. I reckon we've earned ourselves a drink.'

'Don't you have to go work on your latest pitch?'

Saffie swept her notepad and Dictaphone into her bag. 'I'm actually supposed to be going out with some bloke off Bumble, but after your depressing anti-pep talk this morning I can't face a date. I'm going to message him with an excuse. How about the pub? I'll buy you a pint, or whatever it is West lets you drink these days.'

Milo sighed. 'Wish I could. He's cooking me a meal tonight. Cauliflower rice and tofu, or something equally unappealing.'

'He's still got you on the vegan diet then?'

'Worse. We're doing keto now too.' Milo groaned. 'God, I wish I could just go to the pub and mainline beer and pork scratchings until my heart explodes.'

'Then do,' Saffie said. 'I mean, don't make your heart explode. But do come to the pub.'

'No.' Milo got to his feet and slung his jacket over his shoulder. 'I can't let him down. I'll see you tomorrow, Saf.'

'Yeah, all right. Have fun then.'

'Unlikely when there are no carbs involved, but thanks.'

Milo headed off to his unappetising-sounding date and Saffie went to knock on Tamara's office door.

'Mag's gone to the printer's,' she said when Tamara called her in. 'Fancy a wine at the Duck? Milo's gone to meet West so it can be just the girls.'

'Hmm?'

'Have you got time for a drink to celebrate putting the next issue to bed?' Saffie took in her friend's tired, anxious expression. 'You look like you could use one.'

Tamara had evident longing in her eyes, but she shook her head. 'I'd better not. Marcie's going over to her boyfriend's later and I promised Mum's Taxi would be available.' She fell silent, staring out of the window. 'Saf, have you got any grey?'

Saffie blinked. 'Sorry?'

'If your hair wasn't blue, would it have any grey in it?'

'Er, no. I'm sure it can't be far away though.'

'I was about your age when I got my first grey hair,'

Tamara said, talking half to herself. 'Mid-thirties. It doesn't seem so very long ago.' She ran her fingers through her silvering curls. 'Now look at me. Forty-five and I look like one of the zombie backing dancers from *Thriller*.'

Saffie took a seat. 'You don't at all. You're a silver fox, Tam.'

'Men get to be silver foxes. Women get to be dried-up old hags. That's what happens when you let them make the rules.'

'Still dwelling on Andy's message?' Saffie said gently.

'How can I not? He walks out on me, tells me he's too old to deal with a new baby and leaves me to go grey coping with Willow plus two hormonal teens, and now he's starting again with a woman twenty years my junior. That's not something I can just push to the back of my mind.'

'I know it isn't.' Saffie patted her hand. 'You're sure you don't want to come to the pub? I'm sure Willow's fine being looked after by the twins for half an hour, and you can always make it a spritzer if you have to drive.'

'No, I'd better get back. Stuff to do.' Tamara closed her eyes. 'I need to call my arsehole of an ex-husband, for a start.'

When Tamara got home, she found Dale glued to his phone as usual. His sisters were on the carpet playing Willow's current favourite game of 'Mummy's Work'.

'Marcie, you're doing it wrong,' the little girl was telling her big sister. 'You have to colour in the pictures before you write under them. That's called *capshuns*.'

'Don't be so bossy, Will.'

'I'm allowed to be bossy in the game though because I'm the editor, like Mummy.'

Tamara smiled and went to sit down with them. 'Hi kids.'

Marcie glanced up. 'Hiya Mum.'

Tamara tapped her cheek and Marcie planted a reluctant kiss there before Willow hopped on to her mum's lap to give her a smacker on the forehead.

'What about you, Dale? Got a kiss for Mummy?' Tamara asked. Her son responded with a grunt.

'All right, then I'll settle for a hello.'

'Hey bruh,' Dale muttered, his attention still on his phone.

'I still prefer Mum, Dale.'

'Hey, Mum bruh.'

'Best I'm going to get, I suppose.' Tamara picked up one of the sheets of A4 spread out in front of her daughters, covered with a combination of eighteen-year-old Marcie's tidy, rounded writing and five-year-old Willow's enthusiastic but indecipherable scribbles. 'So what's the crack, chaps? Is the latest issue of *The Willow* ready to go to bed?' It was fantastic that Willow was already shaping up as a potential successor to the family business, but Tamara hoped it wasn't a sign of developing egomania that she refused to name her first publication after anything but herself.

Marcie rolled her eyes. 'Whoever says "what's the crack", Mum? Even other old people don't say that.'

'That's because they're not free-thinking rebels like your dear old mum. Did you guys eat yet?'

'I gave Will her fishcakes and beans but we were waiting for you.'

'Oh yeah. Mum, I'm having tea at Olivia's after my

driving lesson so don't make me anything, OK?' Dale said, not looking up.

'I already made you something. I did pasta bake before work; it's in the fridge.' Tamara frowned. 'Hang on. Who's Olivia when she's at home?'

'He's finally managed to get a girlfriend,' Marcie told her with a smirk.

Willow giggled. 'Dale's got a girlfriend. They're getting married.'

'She's not my girlfriend,' Dale said, his cheeks flushing crimson. 'She's just a girl who's a friend. We're going to try out the new skate ramp in the park.'

'And did you think to check with me first?' Tamara asked. 'I know you're technically an adult, Dale, but since I'm providing your room and board, it'd be nice to get a heads up that I'm wasting my precious time preparing meals for you.'

'I'm checking now, aren't I?' He finally looked up. 'It's OK, right?'

Tamara sighed. 'I suppose. Just be back by eleven and don't stay in the park after dark, and—'

'—carry my keys between my fingers and don't take sweets off strangers, I know,' he said, rolling his eyes. 'I'm eighteen, Mum.'

'Yes, yes, all right. Just be careful.'

'Did you call Dad back yet?' Marcie asked.

Dale was suddenly alert. 'What? Did Dad ring?'

'He texted Mum this morning,' Marcie told him. 'He wants to talk to her about seeing us.'

'He can eff off then,' Dale said, going back to his phone. 'Tell him we don't want to see him, Mum.'

Tamara smiled grimly. 'I fully intend to.'

'Well, did you call him?' Marcie asked her.

Tamara cast a cautious look at Willow, who was carefully arranging the pages of *The Willow* into publication order. 'Not yet. I was going to do it after I'd driven you to Ashley's.'

'Do it now. Otherwise you'll only put it off.'

Willow looked up. 'Marcie, is your dad my dad too?'

'That's right, Will. He's all of our dads.'

'Then how come you know him and I don't?'

Marcie looked to her mother for help.

'Well, because… he's been working away,' Tamara said tactfully. 'That's one reason.'

'And another is because he's a total deadbeat who hates us,' Dale muttered.

Tamara frowned. 'Not helpful, Dale.'

'Well, he is. You shouldn't lie to her about it just because she's a little kid.'

'Does he hate us?' Willow asked her mum. Tamara pulled her youngest child closer and kissed the black hair combed into a long plait.

'No, sweetheart,' she said gently. 'He doesn't even know you. That's why I need to speak to him.'

Willow looked afraid now. 'But I won't have to go see him, will I?'

'Not if you don't want to.'

'Can he make me live with him instead of you, if he's my dad?'

'Certainly not. He can't make you do anything you don't want to do.'

But Willow wasn't to be reassured so easily. 'What if you were poorly?' she demanded. 'Like, what if your legs were broken, or you had that thing where your hair falls out like Evie's mummy?'

'Cancer,' Tamara murmured.

'Yeah, that thing. Then could he?'

Marcie leaned over to give her sister a hug. 'Don't worry, Will. If Mum couldn't do it then me and Dale would look after you.'

Willow's lip was wobbling. 'I don't want to see him though, Marcie. I don't! He's not really my dad anyway. I haven't got a dad. I told everyone in my class I hadn't, and Jesse Ghosh said I had to because of sex, but I said I didn't and I cried so he stopped saying stuff about it.' She looked up mournfully at Tamara. 'I haven't, Mummy, have I?'

'Well, yes and… and no,' Tamara said weakly. 'There are lots of different types of families, Will. Some have a mum and a dad, some have two mums or two dads, some have just one or the other.'

'But what type are we?'

'We're the type with a mum and… well, your dad lives somewhere else so I suppose that's the type we are. A family with a mum, and a Willow and a Marcie and a Dale. But all the same he is your father, and I do need to talk to him.'

'Do it now, Mum,' Marcie said. 'We want to know what he says.'

'Yes.' Tamara stood up. 'I'll do it upstairs. Make sure you cover your sister's ears, since I'm probably about to start turning the air blue.'

Tamara headed to her bedroom. She scowled as she reread Andy's text message.

I really need to talk to you, Tam. I want to set up regular access to the kids, OK? I know that'll come as a surprise, but I've changed, honestly. I'm getting married again. Her name's Natalie; we met through work. She's young, only twenty-five, and she's helped me see my life in a new light. Mainly she's made me realise how important it is that I reconnect with my children and make peace with my role as a father. Just please, call me when you can.

Tamara muttered a string of expletives. The gall of the man! Giving her all this new-age claptrap about making 'peace' with himself as a 'father'. When had Andy ever been one of those? He'd been the ultimate in hands-off dads even when he'd been here. Tamara still remembered the look of trauma on his face when she'd arrived home from the shops once and discovered he'd tried to change Marcie's nappy on his own. Christ, you'd think he'd just returned from the trenches. And now he had the nerve to waltz back into all their lives trying to play the loving dad!

Even that phrase 'hands-off dad' pissed her off. Dads came in two flavours: hands-off or hands-on (the heroes!). But mums were just mums, weren't they? Picking up the slack for partners who felt that having contributed their genetic matter, everything else was optional. Partners like Andy fucking Horan: king of the double standard.

Well, the kids didn't want to see him. Willow had looked terrified at the very idea – as well she might, when her father was more of a stranger to her than the man who drove the neighbourhood ice cream van. Dale thought his dad was a feckless deadbeat, and even Marcie, the child Andy had been closest to, curled her lip when she spoke about him.

Tamara would tell him how things stood, then he could crawl back under his rock.

What was the worst-case scenario? Andy could hire a lawyer to try to get access to Willow. So what? No court in the land was going to grant that. He hadn't seen his daughter since she was a year old, and Willow sure as hell didn't want to see him.

Tamara had been playing the 'worst-case scenario' game all her adult life. Milo called her a pessimist, but that was because he didn't understand. In Tamara's mind it was a positive thing, helping her cope with whatever life threw at her. If you knew what the worst outcome would be, then you knew you could deal with it. You were prepared for whatever followed, worst case or not.

Except... except that sometimes a totally unexpected worst-case scenario came hurtling out of the ether to blindside you. Like an unexpected pregnancy at thirty-nine, and your husband walking out on you shortly after the baby arrived.

Or cancer. It had made Tamara shudder when Willow had said that. The little girl had a knack of throwing worst cases at Tamara that she'd never considered. What would happen to her youngest child if she were to become ill or... or to die? Andy was Willow's father, but that didn't give him any claim to guardianship given his absence from her life. And yes, the twins were adults by law, but they were really children still, with their own young lives to live. Tamara's parents were in their sixties and living in a retirement complex down south: they couldn't cope with a primary-schooler. Who'd be responsible for Willow if her mother wasn't around? Marcie? Milo?

Tamara tried to snap out of it. She might be an older parent – she had nearly twenty years on some of the playground mums – but she wasn't, so far as she was aware, ill. There was no need to torture herself thinking about things that would probably never happen.

Although that's what Willow's friend Evie's mum had probably thought before her breast cancer diagnosis. And she was only thirty-two...

Mentally, Tamara gave herself a slap. She needed to stop dwelling on this morbid stuff and focus on the job at hand. She sat down on her bed, trying not to catch sight of her gaunt face and greying hair in the mirror, then pulled up Andy's number.

'Tamara,' Andy said when he answered, his tone eager. 'I wasn't sure you'd call me back. How've you been?'

'Cut the small talk, Andy,' she said in a low voice. 'Do you want to tell me what the hell that message was about?'

'Well, what it said. I've been doing a lot of thinking, and...' He took a deep breath. 'Look, Tam, I know I haven't been there for you and the kids. I know you think I'm a waste of space, a useless father and a pretty pointless human being, and every insult you fling at me is more than deserved. I can't make it right, but I do want to make it better.'

'Well, you can't. It's too late: the kids don't want to see you. Marcie and Dale have made their views quite clear, and Willow almost cried when I told her she had a dad as well as a mum.'

'Did she?' he said quietly.

'Yes she did. It's distressing to discover you've got a parent you don't remember who couldn't pick you out of a crowd.'

Andy was silent for a moment.

'Are they… how are they doing?' he asked at last.

'Dale's bright, shy and monosyllabic. Marcie's confident, kind and mature. And Willow's just a wonderful bundle of bossiness, bounce and joy.' Tamara smiled tightly. 'But you'd know all that if you'd spent any time actually being a father to them in the past eighteen years.'

'I know. I know that. I've got a right to see them though, haven't I? I am their dad, for all my failings.'

'Whether they see you is up to them. The twins are adults. If you want to have more contact with them, ask them yourself. I'm not acting as a go-between.'

'Marcie and Dale aren't eighteen yet, are they?'

Tamara laughed. 'Yes, Andy! They turned eighteen last month. They're going to uni in the autumn. Did you think they'd been frozen at fourteen years old, waiting until their dad remembered they existed?'

'I suppose I deserved that,' he murmured. 'What about the little one? Will you let me see her?'

'She doesn't want to see you. The very idea of it distresses her. So no, I don't think I will.'

'She's my daughter, Tam.'

'Barely,' Tamara said. 'Willow isn't something you can drop and pick up when you feel like it. Especially given that you all but blamed her for driving you away.'

She could practically hear him wince down the phone. 'It wasn't like that. To start again with a new baby after fourteen years… it felt like such a mountain to climb. The stress was unbearable. Can't you understand that?'

'*Your* stress was unbearable?' She laughed. 'And so you left me to climb the mountain alone. Well, Andy, I did climb it, and I don't intend to be fed to the huskies right when I'm nearing the summit. Which is a fancy way of telling you to knob off.'

'You know I wanted to terminate. Then when you insisted on going ahead I just couldn't... Tamara, look, I'm sorry. I'm really, truly sorry.'

'Good for you. Now, if you've quite done—'

'Wait! Don't hang up.' Andy took a deep breath. 'This isn't just about me.'

She snorted. 'Andy, all your life it's been just about you.'

'Not this time.' He paused. 'It's just that, me and Natalie... well, there's no easy way to put this. We're having a baby.'

And there it was: the worst-case scenario that was worse than the worst-case scenario. The one Tamara had never seen coming.

Suddenly, it felt as though all the colour drained out of her world. Her eyes fixed on the mirror, and she saw her own horror-struck gaze staring back at her.

'What?' she whispered.

'We're having a baby. A little boy. Nat's six months gone.' The pride in Andy's voice was like a knife.

'You mean... on purpose?' was all Tamara could say.

'We planned it, yes. Nat's young, Tam. I knew that if I wanted to be with her then I'd have to think about doing it all again – I couldn't deny her a family of her own just because I'd been through it once before. And when I got to thinking about being a dad again, doing it right this time, it... well, it felt kind of exciting.'

'So you... you mean after me and you... Willow...'

'We never intended to have Willow, and I wasn't ready then to start again. Now I am. I've grown – perhaps I've finally grown up. I really want to be a dad to my kids again, Tamara: the ones I've got and the son who's on the way. I know I'll have to work for it, but I'm ready to do that.'

'You're having a baby. After you blamed *me* for having a baby, for making you… making you…'

'You're angry. I get that,' he said in the soothing, patronising voice she loathed. 'But like I said, it's not just about me. Don't you think Willow and the twins have the right to a relationship with their little brother?'

'You bastard,' she whispered. She swallowed hard, willing herself not to cry.

'Look, I'll leave you to think it over. I guess you'll want to sit down with the kids and… just ring me when you're ready to talk, OK, Tam?'

He hung up. Tamara threw her phone to the floor, fell back on the bed and sobbed.

3

'Hey, Milo,' West said in his affected quasi-American drawl when he opened the door of his flat. 'Namaste, bro.'

'Hi.' Milo handed him the bottle he'd brought. 'My contribution.'

West eyed it warily. 'You know I don't drink.'

'It's not wine, it's Kombucha. Virtually non-alcoholic, plus it's supposed to boost your immune system.' He smiled awkwardly. 'I thought you'd like it.'

'Well, I'm watching my sugars but I suppose I could have one glass,' West said, in the tone of one offering a huge favour. 'Come in.'

He stood aside, and Milo walked into the large apartment.

Decor-wise the place felt a lot like West himself: very sleek, very clean, with a sterile hospital-ward feel. Everything was white, and there was no clutter at all, not even a book. There was nothing alive either – pets were out of the question, and West had views about houseplants that Milo couldn't recall other than that he wasn't in favour of them. Something to do with moisture and oxidisation. It was a far cry from Milo's cosy, untidy terrace with its overgrown garden.

'Sit,' West said, gesturing to a curved white table. Milo

did so, and West put an unappetising-smelling concoction in front of him. It looked all right – West had obviously taken pains with the presentation – but it smelt disturbingly like cat wee.

There was a painful silence as they each pushed food around their plate, waiting for the other to start the conversation.

'Good day at work?' West asked.

'Pretty productive. Saf wrote a feature about that new town councillor who thinks her husband's an eight-foot-tall extra-terrestrial, I sent out all the outstanding ad proofs, then we put the July issue to bed.'

'Mm.' West sounded like he wasn't really taking this in. 'Think you'll stick around that place?'

'Well, yeah. I mean, it's the family business.'

'Yes, but it's a bit…'

'What?'

'Well, a bit… *rural*, isn't it?'

'We are rural. We're in the middle of the Yorkshire Dales.'

'You know what I mean. Sort of… small-time. I always thought it was only farmers and old men who read that thing.'

'It isn't just old men,' Milo said, trying not to sound defensive. 'Lots of people love *The Throstler*.'

'I could get you an in at our place if you wanted to aim higher. I've seen your work. You could do better for yourself.'

'I'm flattered you think so,' Milo said. 'I'll, um… think about it.'

He wouldn't though. The last thing Milo wanted was a job at the ultra-modern IT company West worked for. For all his eye-rolling about *The Throstle's Nest*, Milo loved that little mag.

He looked up from his tofu to examine his boyfriend of two months. West was well-groomed as always, dressed in clothes that were smart, tasteful and discreetly expensive. His dark hair was shaven down one side, then swept across and gelled. His short beard was painstakingly manscaped, like all of the hair he allowed to remain on his body.

Milo guessed it suited him. OK, West's style might come across a bit... well, *TOWIE*, but he was fashionable, good-looking, and he kept himself in shape. Milo often wondered what someone like West was doing with an ordinary, run-of-the-mill scruffbag like him.

'This is delicious,' Milo said to fill the silence, nodding to his barely touched food. West smiled lazily, but he didn't speak.

Milo tried again. 'What even is tofu? A mushroom?'

'Bean curd,' West said without making eye contact. 'Very high in protein.'

'How do you curdle a bean?'

'By coagulating soy milk.'

'Oh.' Milo looked at the cube of tofu on his fork. 'Yum. I've always thought there ought to be more coagulated food in the world.'

As he forced the meal down, Milo thought back to his conversation with Saffie and Tamara earlier that day – one of many that always left him with the same West-themed questions knocking around his brain. Could he do this? Was it what he wanted?

During their dates, Milo frequently found himself questioning whether he and West could work together as a lifelong thing. He badly wanted to believe they could – after his disaster of a love life so far, and with the clock ticking inexorably towards middle age, he needed to believe it. Milo had a mental list he liked to run through to remind himself of everything he'd gained from being with West, and everything he stood to lose if they broke up.

Number one: West was sexy, buff, and he had an actual, real-life six-pack. The best Milo had experienced with a previous partner was a two-pack, and he wasn't sure that what he'd thought was muscle definition hadn't actually been an appendix scar. He definitely fancied West, even if his boyfriend's insistence on them showering both before and after sex tended to kill the spontaneity.

Number two: West was cultured. He'd introduced Milo to a whole world of obscure theatre and subtitled black-and-white films that no one else had heard of. The fact they bored Milo shitless didn't mean they weren't good for him. Like West always said, it was broadening his mind.

Number three: West was healthy. Milo was sure he'd added years to his life in the two months they'd been seeing each other. With his boyfriend's encouragement, he'd totally overhauled his lifestyle. Yoga every morning; a 5K run four times a week. No more meat, dairy, chocolate, beer, coffee or processed, sugary crap. He was in better shape than he'd ever been. Yes, some might say that giving up those things had sucked what little joy there was from his life, but Milo's body was certainly thanking him for it.

West was good for him. Milo had been stuck in a rut before: not exercising, eating rubbish, going on repetitive, tedious dates with people he neither liked nor fancied. In a lot of ways, West had saved him. He really wanted to make this work, because if he didn't... well, it was like he'd said to Saffie. There comes a time when you realise you have to accept what's wrong for you about a person so you can enjoy all the things about them that are right. And there was so much about West that was right.

Milo smiled at him with renewed fondness.

'So the new hair was a hit in the office today,' he lied. 'Saffie said I look like Ryan Gosling.'

'Yeah?' West regarded him doubtfully. 'What about Tamsin?'

'Tamara. Well, she said I looked like a cross between Annie Lennox and the Milkybar Kid. But she's my sister so she has to be a dick about these things.' Milo put down his fork. 'Listen, West, I've been thinking. We've been seeing each other for two months now, and I... I thought it might be time for you to meet them. They're two of the most important people in my life, and now you're part of my life too it seems...' He trailed off when he clocked the look of panic on West's face. 'I mean, not like some big important thing or whatever,' he said airily. 'Just a fruit juice down the pub or something.'

'Actually, Milo, I've been doing some thinking myself. I didn't ask you over tonight just to eat.' West sighed. 'Look, we need to talk.'

Saffie swilled her margarita around the glass as she listened to the man opposite her. In her head, she was reciting the lyrics to Don McLean's 'American Pie', a technique she'd developed for maintaining an expression of focused concentration while being bored to death on dates.

God, why hadn't she blown this off like she'd told Milo she was going to? Since her friends had plans, she'd thought she might as well go on a date as not. But now she was here she couldn't help thinking of home, where her comfiest lounge pants and Netflix were calling her name.

Tonight's Bumble match was nice enough: not one for the creep files. He was called Jack, which Saffie had felt was a good, solid name for a date. He had a good, solid job too: a carpenter, which sounded kind of sexy. Saffie had idly imagined him turning up in an open lumberjack-style shirt to show off his toned abs, a toolbelt slouching round his waist.

Unfortunately, Jack didn't have a toolbelt, and Saffie was pretty sure there were no abs lurking under his plain white shirt. Not that she'd hold that against him; he looked rather cuddly, which she also liked. There was a total lack of chemistry, but Saffie was a big believer in the idea that chemistry could materialise as a result of finding out more about each other.

The major problem was that they had nothing in common. Saffie couldn't see herself getting into Jack's hobbies no matter how much she tried, and he'd shown no glimmer of interest when she'd talked about classic movies and other things she enjoyed.

'Saffie?'

She pulled up short just as Don was driving his Chevy to the levee. 'Sorry, what did you just say?'

'I asked if you'd ever been to a re-enactment.'

This was Jack's big thing. Whenever he wasn't whittling

spice racks or mucking about with lathes, he apparently enjoyed nothing more than getting kitted out as a roundhead and waving a mace around.

'What, a battle re-enactment?'

Jack looked annoyed. 'That's what we've been talking about for the past half an hour, isn't it?'

It was what *he'd* been talking about. Obviously her complete lack of engagement had been mistaken by Jack for rapt interest.

Shit, Milo had been right. If you were chronically single then the mid-thirties were where your dreams of romance went to die. They were where you had to make a choice between spending your life alone or settling for a West or a Jack: someone you had nothing in common with but who was unobjectionable enough to share your bed for the rest of your time on earth. Maybe she should just buy some chainmail and accept that this was her life now.

'Er, yeah, once,' she said. 'I wrote a feature on a re-creation of the Battle of Towton.'

Jack brightened. 'Did you like it?'

'It was, um... long. The costumes were impressive though.'

Jack seemed thrilled. 'Aren't they? Hey, Saffie, my group are actually staging a battle this Saturday. I could arrange a spare costume if you wanted to—'

Saffie sagged with relief as her phone started ringing.

She took it out. It was Milo.

'Sorry,' she said to Jack. 'It's my fr– printer. I guess there's a problem with the issue we uploaded today.'

'Right.' Jack looked put out, but he summoned a gracious smile. 'Well, take it if you have to. I'll nip to the loo.'

When Jack had gone, she swiped to answer.

'Mile, what's up?'

'Is that offer to buy me a pint still open?' he asked.

'I'm out on my Bumble date. Thought I might as well go.' She frowned as his tone registered. 'What's up, love? You sound choked.'

'I am a bit.' He swallowed. 'West dumped me.'

'Oh... God.' She sighed. 'Milo, I'm so sorry. What happened?'

'He said he just couldn't see it working long-term for us. That we didn't have enough in common, and that...' Milo gave a wet laugh. '...that he doubted my commitment to veganism and the principles of Iyengar yoga.'

'Well, I hate to say it but he's right. You don't give a flying chuff about Iyengar yoga, or chakras or kale and ginger smoothies or any of that stuff he's been trying to get you into.' She glanced towards the wine bar toilets, where Jack was re-emerging. 'My date's coming back. Sorry, Mile, but I'll have to go in a minute.'

'What's this one like?'

'He's into historical re-enactments, but he's pleasant enough. Jack the carpenter.'

'A carpenter? That's a bit strange, isn't it?'

'Why is it? A career in carpentry was good enough for Jesus Christ, Milo.'

'I just meant it's an unusual job. No need to be so touchy about it, you're not married to the guy.' He swallowed a sob. 'God, Saf, I really hoped I could make this one work. Do you reckon you'll go home with this carpenter, or is there the chance of a shoulder to cry on?'

Saffie sighed. 'All right, hang on.' She raised her voice as

Jack approached. 'You're kidding me! He's sent the wrong centre spread?'

'Eh?' Milo said.

'I am so sorry, Tim.'

'Tim? Have you gone completely bats?'

'The distributors will go ape if the mags aren't there on time,' Saffie went on, ignoring him. She put her hand over the microphone. 'Jack, I'm so sorry about this. Milo, our designer, somehow managed to upload last month's centre pages instead of the July ones. Honestly, he's such a useless git.'

'You know, I can still hear you,' Milo said. 'So, meet you in the Mucky Duck?'

'All right. Give me fifteen minutes.' She hung up.

'You're not shooting off, are you?' Jack said. 'They can't expect you to go into work now.'

She summoned her best apologetic grimace. 'Deadlines are deadlines. Our company director prides herself on the fact we've never missed one in the history of the mag, not even during wartime. I have to get the right pages emailed ASAP or the printer won't be able to set the presses running overnight.' She finished her margarita and stood up. 'I'm sorry, Jack. Thanks for tonight though, it's been... an experience.'

'What about Saturday?' Jack asked. 'We're recreating a siege from the War of the Roses.'

'Er... I'll WhatsApp you.' She grabbed her handbag and hurried out.

4

Tamara took a cigarette from the packet she kept hidden in the basement utility room and lit it with trembling fingers.

She'd sneaked down here after her phone call with Andy, badly in need of a timeout before she faced her kids. She could hear Marcie calling for her. Tamara was due to drive the girl to her boyfriend's in forty-five minutes, and Dale was about to leave for his driving lesson. Tea was still uncooked in the fridge.

She fumbled for her mobile and put on her favourite Judy Garland playlist, turning it up as loud as she dared. Then she put her head between her knees, like one of the diagrams showing you what to do during a plane crash, and stared at the stone flags while she took deep drags on her cigarette.

The moment she'd told Andy she'd taken a positive pregnancy test was playing in her head. Her initial excitement, quickly fading when she registered his appalled expression. Him pleading with her to get an abortion, using every weapon in his arsenal to convince her. The timeshare they'd been planning to get in Provence – a new baby meant no money for luxuries like that, he'd reminded her. His job as an event planner, and the recent increase in his responsibilities that meant he couldn't cope with the additional stress a baby would bring. Their social life, the nights out with friends that they'd been able to start enjoying now the twins were older: suddenly off the cards for another fourteen years. But Tamara had stood firm, determined that this would be a loved baby even if it hadn't been a planned one.

That was when the trouble started. Andy couldn't help resenting her for going ahead with the pregnancy, and what was worse, he'd resented their baby. Present-day Tamara took the cigarette from her mouth to let out a sob.

Andy hadn't even been present at the birth. He'd been at work when Tamara went into labour, and although he'd rushed to the hospital through heavy traffic – or so he claimed – he'd been too late. Tamara had always been suspicious he'd deliberately dragged his feet in the hope of avoiding being with his wife when the baby came.

There'd been no bonding between father and daughter. When he'd held Willow's tiny fingers, there'd been no light in his eyes as there had been for the twins; just irritation and sadness. Willow, for her part, had sensed where she wasn't wanted and screamed her lungs out whenever her dad grudgingly held her. It had been Tamara who'd done the midnight feeds, given the baths, changed the nappies – not that Andy had ever done much of those things, but with Willow it seemed so much more... deliberate.

And then he'd gone. Andy had been left alone with Willow while the twins were visiting their great-grandmother, and when his wife came home from work, she found him with a packed suitcase and a penitent but relieved expression on his face. Dazedly she'd listened as he'd flung words like 'space' and 'coping' in her face while Willow screamed. He'd walked out and after fifteen years, Tamara's marriage had expired not so much with a bang as with a whimper.

In the months that followed she'd been plunged into a state of depression that, if it had just been her and Willow, Tamara didn't know if she'd have come through. If it hadn't been for fourteen-year-old Marcie – her rock – Tamara would probably have crawled into bed and never got out again.

Years later, she still felt the guilt of those few months. Guilt that Willow alone hadn't been enough to snap her out of it. Guilt that she'd made her oldest daughter into a crutch and a confidante when she was just a child, forcing her to grow up too fast.

She gave a harsh laugh. Yes, *she* felt guilt, while Andy had been off enjoying the bachelor life. As if he could make the past fourteen years of his life just disappear, because he was a man and yeah, he basically could do that, couldn't he? Bastard. Bastard!

Tamara grabbed the laundry basket from the top of the washer and threw it down, feeling a catharsis that was all too fleeting as she watched the dirty clothes spill out.

How could Andy have been so cold, so distant with their baby, and yet now be ready to do it all again with a new child? He'd been 'too old' to cope with a baby at forty-one, but at forty-six he was apparently desperate to be a father again. The hypocrisy of the man!

Tamara tried to compose herself, then pulled up her brother's number.

'Milo, can I talk to you?' she mumbled.

'Tam? Are you OK? You sound awful.'

'I rang Andy. It… wasn't good.'

'Where are you?' Milo asked, his voice laden with concern. 'It's all echoey.'

'Hiding in the basement, smoking and listening to Judy Garland.'

'Fags and Judy? Wow, it must've been bad. What happened?'

She sniffed. 'Andy's having a baby.'

'Fuck!'

'Right? And now he wants to start seeing Willow. He wants her and the twins to get to know their new brother, and honestly, Mile, I don't know what to do.'

'Tell him to bog off. He never gave a shit about Willow before, did he?'

'I know.' She rested her forehead on her palm. 'And that was exactly what I said to him, before he told me about the baby. God, letting him back into our lives is the last thing I want, but… I'd have to be a total bitch, wouldn't I, to take that out on the baby? It's not his fault his dad's a feckless wanker any more than it's Willow's or the twins'.'

'That is true,' Milo conceded.

'That *prick*! He knew I'd never be able to say no once he'd chucked a new baby at me, and he's using the poor wee thing as a Trojan Horse to sneak back into our lives. And there's precisely bugger all I can do about it.'

'What are you going to tell the kids?'

'No fucking clue.' She stubbed out the remains of her cigarette and stuffed a couple of pieces of chewing gum into her mouth. 'But they'll be down here hunting for me any minute. Can you come over? I could really use some moral support.'

'Yeah, me too. I'm just heading to the Duck to meet Saf.' It was only then Tamara noticed that her brother sounded pretty upset himself.

'You're OK, aren't you?'

'Been better.' He sighed. 'West broke up with me.'

'Oh, Milo. I am sorry.'

'Can't you come to the pub? Then we can all wallow together.'

'No babysitter. Marcie and Dale have both got plans.' Tamara groaned at the sound of a car purring into the driveway. 'That's all I bloody need. Fran's here, I just heard her Merc pull in. I should've known she'd be round to grill me on deadline day.'

'You'll be in for it if she catches you smoking,' Milo said.

'I'm forty-five, I can do what I want.' She grimaced. 'I will though, won't I? Bollocks bollocks bollocks.'

'At least you can put off talking to the kids about Andy until tomorrow. And maybe she'll babysit for a few hours so you can come out.'

'That's a thought.' Tamara looked up as light flooded the basement and Marcie's silhouette appeared at the top of the stairs. 'Ugh, I've been rumbled. Got to go. I really am sorry about West, Mile. I never thought he was right for you, but I hate to think of you getting hurt.'

'Thanks, Tam. Try to meet us, eh?' He hung up.

'Mum?' Marcie said from the top of the stairs. 'Dale's gone for his driving lesson and Fran just turned up with Uncle Russell. Are you smoking down here?'

'No,' Tamara said, frantically wafting at the air. 'A fuse short-circuited. I've just been fixing it.'

Marcie smiled. 'Yeah, all right, I won't tell on you.'

Tamara went up the stairs and pulled her daughter into a hug.

'I love you, OK?' she whispered. 'Don't ever forget that, Marce.'

'Mum, I can't breathe,' Marcie said in a muffled voice. 'No offence but you stink. Of smoke, I mean.'

'Sorry.' Tamara loosened her grip and kissed the top of her daughter's black curls. 'I just want you to know I'm proud of you, and that I love you and your brother and sister very much. No matter what happens, that'll always be true. No matter what, Marce.'

'Yeah, I know,' Marcie murmured, managing to sound both pleased and mortified at the same time. 'Now can you stop being weird and embarrassing? Pretty please?'

'Say it back first or I won't let you go. You'll die of hugs before you ever get to your digs in Leicester.'

'All right, all right.' Marcie cast a cautious look over her shoulder, in case any of her friends should magically have materialised. 'I love you. There.'

'Damn straight.' Tamara gave her daughter a last squeeze before letting her go. 'Did you just say Uncle Russell was here?'

'Yeah, he came with Fran.' Marcie squinted at her mum's face. 'You've been crying, haven't you? What did the sperm donor have to say?'

Tamara grimaced. 'Do you have to call him that?'

'Why not? It's all he amounts to.'

'It's just so… graphic.'

'Did he upset you, Mum?' Her daughter looked so fierce, Tamara couldn't help smiling.

'Not really. Just... old memories.'

'What did he want?'

'He wants to see you. You and Dale, and Willow too. He's got a new young fiancée and it's resulted in some sort of epiphany.'

Marcie snorted. 'Epiphany, OK. What did you tell him?'

'I said that you and your brother were adults and it was up to you. And Willow...' She stopped, feeling a lump rise in her throat again. 'I... I'm not sure yet. Do you mind if we talk about it tomorrow, as a family? I don't want to do this while Fran and Russ are here. I know they're family too, but this is Horan business.'

Marcie still had her fixed in a worried gaze. 'Whatever you want, Mum.'

Tamara squeezed her arm. 'I honestly don't know what I'll do without you. And you know I'm sorry for... well, I'm just generally sorry.'

'You don't need to be,' Marcie said in the quiet, firm way that was going to serve her well when she had kids of her own. 'You've been great, Mum. Dad's been a douche. Let him be sorry if it's on his conscience. Anyway, I don't want to see him, and I know Dale doesn't.'

God, this kid was amazing. Calm, compassionate, confident... where did she get it from? Certainly not from her train wreck of a mother. Tamara felt a stab of guilt when she thought about the baby, knowing that that little revelation was going to change everything.

'We'd better deal with Fran so I can get you fed and take you to Ashley's,' she said. 'Where are they?'

'Kitchen. Fran's checking the cupboards to make sure we've been eating properly.'

Tamara groaned. 'Of course she is. All right, you hide in your room and I'll scare her away.'

When she reached the kitchen, Tamara found her grandmother at her glamorous best. Fran was in a flowing silk scarf, draped over an elegant white blouse and pastel-peach chinos, with her short, feathery silver hair freshly salon-styled as always. She was curling her lip at a tin of hot dog sausages. Her other grandson, Milo and Tamara's cousin Russell, was at the dining table feigning some very convincing interest as Willow talked him through the new edition of *The Willow*.

'You don't *eat* these, surely?' Fran asked Tamara, waving the sausages.

'Well I sure as hell don't do anything else with them.' Tamara pecked her cheek. 'Hi, Fran.' She nodded a greeting to her cousin. 'Russ. Always good to see you.'

'Hey Tam.' He stood up to clap her on the shoulder. 'How's business?'

'Oh, same old *Throstler*. Nothing ever changes.' She put the oven on to preheat. 'How about you? Things seem to be going well at *Lifestyle North*.'

'Well, I thought things were pretty good until I saw the quality of the competition.' He nodded to the pages of Willow's magazine and the little girl giggled.

'Uncle Russell, do you want to see my new slide bed?' she asked.

'Willow, I came over because I'd heard so much about your new slide bed that I just had to see it for myself,' Russell said earnestly. Willow clapped her hands and grabbed his arm to take him up to her bedroom.

Fran adopted the simpering expression she used only for Russell. 'He is good with her. What a shame he and Nikki never had children.'

'Mmm,' Tamara muttered. 'He's just generally excellent at everything. Wonderful, wonderful Russell.'

'Oh, don't be jealous. Make me a cup of tea, will you? I want to have a chat about the magazine.'

'It's not a magazine.' Tamara went to flick the kettle on. 'It's a periodical. Your rules.'

'Yes, all right, for official purposes it's a periodical. I can't go around calling it a periodical in the privacy of my own granddaughter's home, can I? It makes me sound a total arse.'

Tamara smiled. 'I'm glad you said that and not me. To what do I owe the pleasure then, Grandmother?'

Fran winced. 'Please try not to use the G word, Tamara. I feel a fresh wrinkle pop out every time it falls from your lips.'

Tamara made her grandmother a cup of green tea, plus a coffee for herself, then she popped her pasta bake in the oven and took a seat at the dining table.

'Did you come for an editor's report?' she asked. 'Milo's designed a draft layout for the new "On The Farm" column. The July issue went without a hitch. We've got some great articles, thanks partly to me but mainly to Saffie. I was thinking of promoting her to features editor actually.'

Fran raised an eyebrow. 'Can we afford that?'

'We can't afford much of a pay rise,' Tamara admitted. 'It's more so she's got it on her CV for when she decides to move on. She's more than earned it.' She took a sip of her coffee. 'But I would like to offer a small salary increase.'

'She certainly works hard. I think we could stretch to another thousand a year, don't you?'

'Definitely,' Tamara said, smiling warmly. It wasn't always this easy to get her grandmother to agree with management decisions. 'Thanks, Fran.'

'Well, I think you've proved by now that you know what you're doing.' Fran examined her keenly. 'But there's something wrong. What's happened, Tamara?'

'Nothing.' Tamara flushed. 'It's deadline day, isn't it? I've let myself get run down putting the mag to bed while the kids are off school, that's all.'

'That's a big porky pie.' Fran looked her up and down. 'No make-up. Dressed like you've been for a run and stayed in the same clothes without showering. Stinking of tobacco, eyes red...'

'Yes, all right, Holmes.'

'Well, what is it? Are the children all right?'

'I'm just... worried about Milo,' Tamara said, trying not to flinch. 'That lad he was seeing broke it off tonight. He's really upset.'

Tamara felt guilty about using her brother's personal life to deflect awkward questions about her own, but she was sure Milo would understand. Fran was bound to find out about his latest break-up one way or another; she always did.

'Well, I'm sorry to hear that,' Fran said. 'Still, it's no great loss, is it?'

How did her grandmother do that? How did she just *know* stuff? Tamara had given West only the briefest of mentions, and she was certain Milo hadn't talked to Fran about him. Yet she seemed to just know, somehow, everything that had been wrong with the relationship.

'No,' Tamara said. 'I mean, they didn't have much in common, but Milo really wanted to make it work. He'll be upset for a little while.'

'He ought to be used to it by now,' Fran remarked wryly, sipping her tea. 'What is that, four break-ups since Christmas?'

OK. Tamara was certain that neither she nor Milo had told Fran about his love life in that much detail.

'Yes, but this was the only relationship longer than a few weeks,' she said.

'And that's all? There's nothing else?'

Tamara turned her face slightly to avoid Fran's probing gaze. 'That's all.'

'Tamara, I'm your grandmother. I know when that's all, and this is not a "that's all" situation.'

'Fran, I... look, I don't want to talk about it at the moment, OK? Everyone's fine – me, the kids. There's just an awkward situation I've got to deal with. It... concerns their father.'

'Hmm.' Fran examined her face. 'All right, if that's what you want.'

Tamara blinked. 'You're giving up that easily?'

'Well, yes, if it's going to upset you.'

'Right.' Tamara stared at her for a moment before finishing her coffee. 'OK, can we talk about the mag if that's why you're here? I need to feed Marcie before I drive her to her boyfriend's.'

'I'm glad you brought it up.' Fran took a notepad from her clutch bag. 'I've got some feedback here from my luncheon club.'

'Oh God.'

Fran ignored her. 'Milly Henderson says she likes the new column on unusual churches, but she doesn't approve of the foul language that's started creeping in.'

'Eh? There isn't any foul language.'

'There was an "arse" and a "bloody" in the last issue, she informs me, and on the jokes page we used the word "berk".'

'That's pretty mild, isn't it?'

'Not if you know your rhyming slang, which Milly apparently does. Oh, and Peter Saunders is complaining about the size of the typeface again.'

'Fran, if we make the fonts any bigger we'll be a billboard.'

'I'm just passing on constructive criticism,' Fran said. 'We have to listen to our readers – that's what my father drummed into me back in the Fifties. It's what's kept us going for eighty-three years.'

'I'm not sure the pensioners at your luncheon club are a representative sample.'

'They're readers, Tamara. They all matter: every one of them.'

'All right,' Tamara said with a sigh. 'I'll give it some consideration. Anything else?'

'Charlie Pratt says we've been going downhill since 1958 and he could photocopy it for less than the cover price, but I wouldn't pay any attention to him, miserable old coot. Oh, and I've got someone I'll be sending for work experience in a couple of weeks.'

Tamara groaned. 'Who this time?'

'Keith Doherty, your Great Uncle Ray's sponsor at AA. He always wanted to work in the media, and now he's knocked the booze on the head he's desperate to make up for lost time.'

'Fran, I really don't think you're supposed to tell people stuff like that. How old is this guy?'

'Forty-eight.'

'Oh, no.' Tamara shook her head. 'Grandmother, I do not want a blind date. Especially not one disguised as work experience.'

Fran held up her hands. 'It's bona fide, I promise you. Blind dates were the farthest thing from my mind.'

'No, Fran. He's too old for work experience anyway.'

'It's never too late to pursue your dreams. No matter how old you get, today is always the first day of the rest of your life.'

'Well he can pursue his dreams somewhere else. I don't need middle-aged men making sheep's eyes at me while I'm working.'

'It's your funeral,' Fran said with a shrug. 'Ray tells me he's rather a catch.'

'Ray can take him out to dinner then. Can we please stay off my love life and stick to the mag?'

'Ah, yes. There is one other thing. Rather important, in fact.'

Russell reappeared in the kitchen, minus Willow.

'She's in her room,' he said in answer to Tamara's

enquiring look. 'Late breaking news. She desperately needs to add a feature on her slide bed to *The Willow* before it's finished.' He looked at Fran. 'Did you tell her?'

'I was about to.'

'What?' Tamara said. 'Why are you two so conspiratorial?'

'No need to look so worried,' Fran said. 'This is going to bring new opportunities for you, Tamara: you, Milo, and young Saffie too. I'm eighty-four years old; it's been a long time since I was able to inject fresh ideas into *The Throstle's Nest*. But with Russell and Nikki behind you, you've got a real chance of taking her back to her glory days.'

'How do you mean, with them behind us?'

'I'll be just the right amount of hands-on, Tam, I promise,' Russell said. 'I'm still a journalist first and foremost, and what's more I'm a great-grandchild of the founder, same as you. The last thing I'd want to do would be to change the character of a publication that's been in my family for nearly a century. I've always loved how offbeat it is.'

'But... hands-on with what?'

'That's what we're trying to tell you,' Fran said, beaming. 'I've decided to sell the business to Russell and Nikki. From now on, *The Throstle's Nest* is going to be part of the *Lifestyle North* stable.'

5

The Black Swan – or the Mucky Duck to its regulars – was next door to the *Throstle's Nest* offices, which were in two rooms of a converted mill. Both pub and mill were situated in Saffie's home village of Goosecliffe, on the outskirts of their nearest town, Braybrook.

Saffie had just put an order in with Alan, the landlord, when Milo showed up, his dazzling peroxide hair covered by the beanie again. She pulled him into a hug.

'How're you doing, love?'

'Been better,' Milo said. 'Although Tam sounds like a close rival when it comes to which of us is having the most depressing day.'

Saffie slid a pint of Black Sheep to him. 'More Andy woes?'

'Yeah. I'll let her fill you in on the specifics. She's just recruiting a babysitter then she's going to join us, hopefully.' He pecked her cheek. 'Sorry for ruining your date, Saf.'

'Don't worry about it. It was crap even before you rang.'

'We never have any luck, do we?' He sighed. 'West was the first decent lad I'd met in ages. I finally managed to get someone to like me who wasn't a commitment-phobe, bore, weirdo or wanker and I had to go and screw it up.'

'Oh, look on the bright side.'

'What bright side?'

Saffie nodded to the rest of her order as Alan dumped it on the bar. 'This one.'

Milo's eyes saucered. 'For me?'

'Yep. Fill your boots.'

'Oh, you little beauties. Come to Daddy.' Milo drew the five packets of pork scratchings towards him and kissed them one by one.

'See?' Saffie said. 'No more rhubarb infusion. No more *Antigone*. And as many pork scratchings as you can eat. Now tell me single life is so bad.'

'I'm ready to admit it has its perks,' Milo said as he tore open a pack.

'If you come round mine I'll even help you dye your hair black again, how about that?'

'Oh God, please.'

'That's £15.85, Saffie,' Alan said. She took out her purse to pay.

'Hey, we've had some more spectral happenings,' the landlord told her, presenting her with the card machine. 'My missus has been hearing wails in the night. Chains rattling, ectoplasm dripping down the walls, rocking cradles... all that ghost shit. What do you reckon?'

'For the last time, Alan, if you want us to plug the pub then you can pay for an ad,' Milo said. 'You're not getting in the "Haunted Pubs" section and this place has not got a ghost.'

'How do you know? Lots of people have probably died in here.'

'Why, did they see the price of your beer and keel over?'

'Ha-titty-ha, I'm sure.'

'Look, you never mentioned a ghost until we started running "Haunted Pubs",' Saffie said. 'Buy an ad, you tight git. We'll do you a discount, since you're an old friend of the firm.'

'Huh. No thanks, I'm not made of money.' He picked up a flyer and handed it to Milo. 'If you're looking for fresh advertisers to fleece, you could try hitting up my mate's sister. I said I'd put these out but she's going to need all the help she can get.'

'What is it?' Milo said, squinting at the leaflet.

'She's set up a dating agency. Can you believe that, in this day and age? She'll be bankrupt within the year.'

'A *dating* agency?' Saffie said. 'Those can't still exist, surely.'

'Retro, eh? There must be at least fifty apps for this stuff.'

'Oh, far, far more. Me and Milo have had profiles on most of them.' She nudged Milo. 'Come on, let's grab a table. See you, Alan.'

Milo was staring at the flyer.

'Milo?' Saffie said. 'What's up?'

'Hmm?' He looked up. 'Oh. Just reading this. Sounds kind of interesting actually.'

He handed her the flyer. It showed a couple gazing into each other's eyes with the words *The 24-hour Dating Agency* underneath.

'What's interesting about it?' she asked. 'Looks like predictably nauseating crap to me.'

'It's a bit different. The woman who runs it is a psychotherapist.'

'So?'

'Flip it over. You'll see.'

Saffie took a seat at their usual table and turned the leaflet over to read the back. A woman in half-moon spectacles and a white lab coat was standing next to a few paragraphs of text.

Do you despair of the cold, impersonal feel of app-based dating? Are you tired of awkward dates with people who are the wrong fit for you? Have you given up on ever meeting The One?

'Sounds familiar, right?' Milo said.

'Mmm.' She read on.

The 24-hour Dating Agency is a unique approach to matchmaking created by psychotherapist Dr Alison Sheldrake. Based on her extensive research, Dr Sheldrake theorises that it's possible to discover a deeper bond with the right person in a single twenty-four-hour period than over months of casual dates. Using scientific methods she developed herself, she will find you your perfect match and send the two of you on one, life-changing date.

****SOULMATE GUARANTEE!****

Dr Sheldrake guarantees you'll find your perfect match through her agency – or your money back!

'She's literally selling love at first sight,' Milo said. 'That's a pretty bold offer.'

Saffie snorted. 'Load of pseudo-scientific bollocks. I bet she bought her doctorate online. Probably in a job lot with the lab coat and specs.'

'Don't you think there could be something in it? I thought researching all those "Stranger Than Fiction" pieces had opened your mind.'

'Not that bloody far.' She patted her friend's arm. 'Milo, sweety-pie, that's your break-up talking. Alan's right: she'll go bust within months.'

'I think it sounds a bit like *Blind Date*,' Milo said. 'You've got three questions and a quippy roundup from Our Graham to work out if someone's your soulmate, then you get packed off on holiday with them. It's intense but you'd be bound to know at the end of it whether you had a future together, right? That used to be my favourite bit, seeing how the couples had got on at the end of their date.'

'I remember.' Saffie took a sip of her lager. 'Most of the time they'd only gone on for a free holiday and came away hating each other.'

'You're an unromantic motherflipper, aren't you, Saffie Ackroyd? They didn't always hate each other. Some of them ended up together.'

'Oh, come on. *Blind Date* was a terrible way to meet a partner. How are you supposed to tell if you're made for someone just by asking what flavour of ice cream they'd be?'

'You'd rather try the *Naked Attraction* method, would you? Let him ogle your bits to decide if you're his one true love? Very Disney prince, that is.'

'I'm not actually obligated to do either, Milo.' Saffie curled her lip at the flyer. 'God, can you imagine getting stuck with some absolute arse for twenty-four hours? And what happens overnight? Is a compulsory shag part of the deal? The whole thing stinks.'

'What stinks?' Tamara asked, sitting down with a glass of wine.

'Hey, you made it,' Milo said. 'You got a babysitter then?'

'Yeah, Fran and Russell offered to stay with Willow until Marcie gets home. Fran could obviously tell I was desperate.' Tamara took a gulp of wine. 'She was being suspiciously nice. I think she's mellowing in old age.'

Milo raised an eyebrow. 'What, our grandmother? The woman nicknamed The Gorgon when she was *Throstler* editor?'

'Seriously. She knew I had major life stuff occurring and she didn't grill me or anything,' Tamara said. 'I hope she's not ill.'

'She is eighty-four, I suppose. It's easy to forget that when she's haranguing you with all the energy of an angry squirrel.'

'So what's this thing that stinks, Saf?' Tamara asked.

'Milo wants to sign up for *Blind Date*.'

She frowned. 'Eh? A blind date?'

'Not *a* blind date. *Blind Date*. You know, with Cilla Black.'

'Right.' Tamara looked bewildered. 'I hate to break it to you, Milo, but I'm afraid dear Cilla's no longer with us.'

'Not the actual programme. It's this thing. The 24-hour Dating Agency.' Saffie handed Tamara the flyer.

'Well, why not? I've tried everything else.' Milo looked from his best friend to his sister. 'Hey, we should all do it. What have we got to lose? You've tried every dating service

55

going since you broke up with Kieran, Saf, and Tam, it's years since your divorce. High time you put yourself back out there.'

Tamara laughed. 'You're as bad as Fran. After the last shitshow I can promise you I am well and truly off relationships. I'm fine with it being just me and my kids.'

'Your kids'll be leaving home soon – two of them anyway. Wouldn't you like to meet someone new? Not everyone's an Andy.'

'Between Willow and work, I've got no energy for anything like that. Anyway, I agree with Saffie. Sounds a daft idea.'

'Come on, sis. Worst-case scenario, you have a miserable day out with someone you don't fancy.'

'No, Milo, the worst-case scenario is my date turns out to be a serial killer and chops me into bits. Sorry but it's a no from me.'

'And me,' Saffie said.

'Fine.' Milo tucked the flyer sulkily into his pocket. 'Trust you two to piss on my bonfire.'

'What happened about Andy, Tamara?' Saffie asked, ignoring him.

'Ugh. Him.' Tamara massaged her temples. 'He's having another baby. After the way he gave up on my Willow, him and this child fiancée are having a baby boy.'

'Fuck!'

'That's the usual reaction,' Tamara muttered. 'God knows how I'm going to tell my kids. There's a whole generation between the twins and this new brother. And Willow… I've got no idea how she'll react. She got really distressed that she might be forced to see her dad.'

'Hardly surprising, when he's a total stranger,' Milo said.

'I wish I could tell him to stick his access. None of the kids has got any interest in seeing him.' She sighed. 'I just can't see a way out of it. If I want my kids to have a relationship with their brother, which I do, of course, then the price is that we have to let their deadbeat dad back into our lives. Not to mention the young fiancée. Lord knows what she's like.'

Saffie patted her arm. 'Kudos for being mature enough to do the right thing for your kids though, Tam. I know it can't be easy after the way Andy treated you.'

'I just hope they take it well.' She glanced up. 'So what have you guys got to contribute to tonight's meeting of The Miserable Bastard Club?'

'I'm definitely the least miserable of us bastards,' Saffie said. 'Just a dull date to complain of. You and Milo are the ones riding high in the misery stakes.'

Tamara watched her brother guzzling pork scratchings, washing them down with big mouthfuls of beer. 'He looks like he's getting over it.'

'I'm comfort eating,' Milo said through a mouthful of salt and pig. 'Dumped people are allowed to do that. Especially after two months of enforced teetotal veganism.'

'It's not so bad, is it?' Tamara said. 'I know you really wanted this one to work, Mile, but you were fighting a losing battle with West. You guys were just too different.'

'Maybe you've got a point.' He sighed. 'I know West was… challenging. But he was cool and interesting, at least some of the time, and he liked me enough to care about my health and how I looked, and he made me into the sort of person I'd always dreamed about being. Plus he was really fit. Let's not forget that important point.'

'That's the problem,' Saffie said. 'Beautiful People Syndrome. The thing about the smoulderingly hot, Mile, is that they rarely meet you halfway. They've grown up believing they don't have to, because they're pretty and other people have always done exactly what they wanted.'

'She's right, you know,' Tamara said. 'Andy was the same. Spoilt by good looks.'

'You changed so many things about yourself for West, but what did he ever change for you?' Saffie asked Milo. 'Nothing. Did he?'

'I suppose not,' Milo murmured.

'And it's no good making you into the person you always dreamed about being if it was making you miserable,' Tamara said.

'Look, can you two stop being so bloody wise and just call him a bastard and tell me I'm too good for him?'

Saffie shrugged. 'All right. He's a bastard and you're too good for him.'

'I think the worst thing is wondering if this is it. If I'll ever meet anyone else decent when my prime's slipping away.' Milo popped another pork scratching in his mouth. 'Guys, tell me honestly: am I sexy?'

Tamara snorted. 'Not a question for me to answer.'

'Saf?' Milo asked. 'Come on, you're not related to me.'

Saffie squinted at him. 'Yeah. You're kind of sexy.'

'You mean it?'

'In a scruffy, gangly, speccy sort of way. I'd definitely swipe right on you if I didn't have the misfortune of knowing you.'

'You're not just saying that?'

'Milo, you're my oldest friend. Trust me, if I thought you were a moose I'd come right out and tell you.'

'Huh. You would as well.' He patted her hand. 'Cheers, love.'

'No worries.'

'Should I have Botox? I feel like I might need some Botox.'

'Don't you dare,' Tamara said. 'Botox is a slippery slope that'll leave you with cold, dead eyes and an inability to move your mouth.'

'Yeah, but young cold, dead eyes though.'

Tamara's phone pinged, and she glanced at it.

'Andy again?' Milo said.

'Just Fran. Marcie's brought Ashley home and she's left them in charge of Willow.'

'What did Fran come round for?' Saffie asked. 'Did she want a deadline day report?'

Tamara grimaced. 'That was the second act in my absolute belter of an evening. She turned up with Russell to tell me she'd sold *The Throstle's Nest* to him and his wife Nikki.'

Milo's eyes widened. 'What! Fran sold our magazine?'

'Don't worry, Russ and Nikki aren't going to lay us off. We're going to become a sister publication to *Lifestyle North*, but we'll still operate independently from our current offices and Russ has promised to stay out of the editorial side of things.' She finished her wine. 'This ought to be good: bring us some new opportunities. Especially for you, Saf. *Lifestyle North*'s huge among the regional glossies. There might be an opening there for you as a feature writer.'

'You really think?' Saffie said.

'When they've seen the quality of your work? I can't see why not.'

Milo examined his sister's face. 'If it's all sugarplums and tummy tickles, why do you look so worried?'

'Ugh, I don't know.' Tamara helped herself to a pork scratching. 'It's Russell, I think. Talking about "efficiency" and "workflow"; scary businessy words like that. I'm glad it's staying in the family, but I can't help worrying.'

'What's he like, this cousin of yours?' Saffie said. 'I'm picturing "greasy yuppie twat". I bet he's got a receding hairline and a ponytail, has he?'

'I wish he was like that. Then I could manage to hate him in a nice, healthy, uncomplicated way for being effortlessly successful, popular, bright, good-looking, our gran's favourite, and all the other things that make Russell Foxton eminently hateable as that one relative you've been forced to compare yourself with all your life. But I can't, because he's actually a really nice bloke.'

'Yeah?' Saffie raised an enquiring eyebrow at Milo, who nodded.

'It's true,' he said. 'Even Tam's kids like him, and children have got built-in bullshit detectors. He's their favourite uncle. Which is a bit galling when you're their actual uncle and he's just an honorary one.'

'He isn't their favourite,' Tamara said, smiling. 'Russ is a novelty, that's all. He turns up every once in a while and spoils them with attention and presents. They still love Uncle Milo best.'

'You want some more pork scratchings?' Saffie said, nodding to the empty bags littering the table in front of Milo.

'Better not. I think that was about four thousand calories I just ingested.' He patted his tummy. 'I need to watch the waistline if I'm getting back out on the dating scene.'

'You ought to let the dust settle on West first, surely?' Tamara said.

'No time. I'm not getting any younger here.' Milo took the dating agency leaflet from his pocket and examined it thoughtfully. 'I think what I really need is to try a different approach.'

6

Saffie shook her head. 'No way, Milo.'

'Come on. You piddled all over that twenty-four-hour dating thing; this is the least you can do to make it up to me.'

'Yeah, but speed dating? It's so… Noughties.'

Saffie was in the office, trying to finish a feature on a local metal detectorist who claimed to have discovered the remnants of a Viking horde just outside Wetwang. However, she was finding it hard to see her screen from behind the poster Milo was flapping in her face.

'It's only one evening,' he said in his most wheedling tone. 'Please, Saf? I don't want to go on my own.'

'Mile, it's in a community centre. I guarantee there'll be no one there under sixty.'

'I'm sure there'll be younger people. They must be pretty right on if they're running LGBT events alongside the ones for you lot.' He batted his eyelids. 'Go on. I've just been dumped, remember? This could be my one chance to meet the future Mr Milo Cook.'

'Ugh. If I say yes, will you get out of my face?'

He saluted. 'Sea Cadet's honour.'

'You were never a Sea Cadet, Milo. We're fifty miles inland.'

'I always wanted to be though. I'd have looked adorable in the little hat.'

'You'd have looked like La Toya Jackson.' She batted his poster away. 'All right, I'll do it. But next time I ask for a favour, you'd better bloody jump.'

He gave her a kiss. 'Thanks, bezzie.'

'Mistress Bezzie to you. I outrank you now I've been promoted to features editor.'

'Thank God you're not letting it go to your head.'

Saffie nodded to his sister's office. 'What about Tam? Speed dating sounds ideal for the busy working mum.'

'We can ask. It'd do her good to have a night out.'

Milo barged into Tamara's office-slash-broom-cupboard, exercising the little brother's prerogative not to bother knocking.

'Tam, what do you reckon?' he said, waving the poster. 'Fancy joining me and Saf for a bit of speed dating tomorrow night?'

She glanced up from her computer screen with furrowed brow. 'Milo, I'm busy here. You know what that means: busy? I mean, do you ever do any actual work?'

'What're you on about? I've designed six ads today.'

'Well, go design something else then. It's not five o'clock yet.'

He frowned. 'All right, what's rattled your knickers?'

'Ugh, sorry. I've just had an email from Nikki. Honestly, her and Russell don't even own this place yet and already they're handing down orders.'

'What orders are they handing down?' Saffie called from her desk.

'Hang on.' Tamara pressed print on Nikki's email. She put it on Saffie's desk so Milo could read it over her shoulder.

'More lifestyle features?' Saffie said. 'But we're not a lifestyle magazine. Our readers don't want features on the top ten Yorkshire shopping outlets or celebrities plugging their latest thing.'

'Nikki thinks it'll help us sell more ads,' Tamara said. 'A shift in tone means we can bribe them with free advertorial, she says.'

'Yeah, if we don't mind alienating our readers.' Saffie shook her head. 'That stuff's fine for *Lifestyle North* but it's not *Throstle's Nest*.'

'They couldn't overrule your decision as editor, could they?' Milo asked his sister.

Tamara perched on the edge of his desk. 'I suppose once they own the place they can do whatever they want. I'm disappointed in Russell though. As a journo, I'd expect him to understand the importance of editorial control.'

'I'm not impressed he's getting Nikki to do his dirty work for him. He's family; he should at least have the guts to send this stuff directly.'

'This is exactly what I was afraid might happen. What if they force these things on us? Try to turn *The Throstler* into one of those characterless spam mags that's nearly all advertorial?'

'Do you think your gran knows they're pushing for this?' Saffie asked.

'Dunno. Fran seemed determined selling to them was the

right decision though. As far as she's concerned, Russell the publishing wunderkind can do no wrong.'

'How are we supposed to make room for these new features?' Milo asked. 'Because if we have to lose "Novelty Vegetable Corner", I'll resign on the spot.'

Tamara smiled. 'Don't worry, Milo. I promise I'll fight tooth and nail for every amusingly malformed carrot.'

Saffie picked up the email. 'This Nikki's even trying to dictate what we put on the covers. Why doesn't she just take over as editor if she's such a bloody expert?'

'She is a bit of an expert, Saf,' Milo said. 'When her and Russell met, she was working for *Vogue*. When it comes to selling ads, she knows her stuff.'

'Yeah, she knows stuff about *Vogue*. Do they have a section dedicated entirely to rude vegetables? Do they flip.'

'That is an impressive USP, I admit.'

'I'll give her a call, see if we can find a middle ground,' Tamara said wearily. 'One lifestyle-type feature an issue wouldn't be so bad, as long as it had a flavour of *Throstle's Nest*. But I'm not having any of those listicle things that could've been written by an AI bot.' She rubbed her temples. 'I could really have done without this today. Sorry, Milo. You came in to ask me something before.'

'Oh. Right.' He handed her the poster about the speed dating event. 'Just wondered if you fancied this. Me and Saf are both going.'

'Under duress in my case,' Saffie said. 'It might be good for you though, Tam. Night off from the kids; meet some new people. The chance to forget you're a mum for a few hours could be just what you need.'

'Couldn't if I wanted to,' Tamara muttered, still massaging her temples. 'I need to take Willow shopping for new clothes. Hardly any of her trousers fit since her last growth spurt.'

'You can delay that a day or two, surely,' Milo said. 'She isn't growing that fast.'

'I can't put it off; not when she knows about it. She's buzzing at the thought of new things. That means tears if I even dare to suggest postponing.'

'Did you talk to the kids about the baby yet?' Saffie asked.

'That's tonight's fun and games.' She pressed her eyes closed. 'Oh God, I hope they take it well.'

When Tamara got home, Willow was skipping in the garden while Dale sat on one of the patio chairs, watching a video on TikTok.

'…ninety-eight, ninety-nine, a hundred!' Willow slightly tripped over her last jump, but seemed to decide it still counted. 'Dale! I did a hundred without stopping. Told you I could.'

'Good stuff, Will,' Dale said, not looking up.

She frowned. 'You were the one who dared me and then you weren't even watching.'

'I was, promise.'

'You weren't, you were on your stupid phone. You only dared me so you could do phone stuff instead of playing. I bet if I was on your phone you'd watch me.'

'Hey, that's not a bad idea.' Dale looked up finally. 'You could be a TikTok star, Will.'

'Oh, no.' Tamara gave Willow a kiss, then planted one on

Dale's dreadlocks. He jerked his head impatiently away. 'No social media until she's thirteen.'

'Did you see, Mummy?' Willow asked breathlessly. 'I did a hundred skips in a row. Dale wasn't watching but I did.'

'I was,' Dale said. 'If I wasn't watching, then how would I know you tripped on the last one?'

'That still counts!' Willow told him heatedly. 'I only tripped a tiny bit.'

'Yeah, I guess it still counts.' Dale broke into a rare smile. 'You did really good, Will.'

Tamara smiled to see the bond between them on display. Dale was a typical lad of his age in many ways: sullen, shy and unable to express himself in much beyond grunts. He lacked his twin's emotional maturity but he had the same good heart underneath the layers of teenage boy, and Tamara knew he was shaping up to be a wonderful man. She was proud of all her children, especially given the things they'd already had to contend with in their young lives.

She often reflected on the age gap between the older ones and the younger, and how it had helped mould them all. Tamara had been an older big sister herself – there were nine years between her and Milo, which had always gone hand in hand with a feeling of protectiveness – but fourteen years was a hell of a lot, and the eighteen years between the twins and Andy's new baby was a whole generation. It was scary really; closer to an aunt and uncle relationship than a sibling one.

But it had been good for her three, in a lot of ways. The twins had grown up helping to care for Willow, and Tamara was sure it had made them more nurturing and considerate than they might otherwise have been at their age. She hoped that being exposed first-hand to the demanding task of raising a young child had also taught them the paramount importance of practising safe sex until you were ready to be a parent, and instilled valuable life skills in them for when that time did eventually come. It was an unusual relationship they had with Willow – part sibling, part parent substitute – but one the whole family had learnt to adjust to. The twins had grown up fast thanks to Willow – too fast in some ways – but they'd learnt a lot that was going to help them in life too.

And now a new baby was coming to change the dynamic again, just when the twins were about to leave home and start the next phase of their lives. What would it mean for them all? Tamara felt guilty that she had to unleash some news on her children which was going to come as a big shock, possibly an unwelcome one, but it couldn't be put off any longer.

'Where's your sister?' she asked Dale. 'There's something I need to talk to you all about.'

'She's on the phone to Ashley,' Dale said, gagging theatrically. 'We came out here so we wouldn't hear, since we didn't have any sick bags. Right, Will?'

Willow nodded, sticking out her tongue. 'Last night when we were watching TV, they kept kissing and bursting out laughing when no one even said anything funny. It's so silly. I'll never do that when I'm big.'

Tamara laughed. 'We'll see. Dale, can you get Marcie and meet us in the conservatory? Tell her I asked if she could ring Ashley back later. We need to have an urgent family conference.'

Dale, whose attention had drifted back to the

all-consuming phone, opened his mouth to protest, but when he caught sight of his mum's expression he thought better of it.

'Sure.' He tucked the phone away and went to fetch Marcie.

'Right,' Tamara said when they'd gathered in the conservatory. 'I think you know what I need to talk to you about, don't you?'

Willow was colouring in a unicorn on the floor, looking quite unconcerned about the unprecedented family conference. The older two, however, had faces filled with worry.

'Dad,' Dale muttered. 'I told you I didn't want to see him. We're eighteen and he can't make us.'

Marcie nodded. 'Same goes for me.'

'I haven't got a dad,' Willow said in a faraway voice.

'Yes you have, you've got the same dad as us,' Dale said. 'He's just so shit he's not worth having.'

Tamara frowned. 'Dale.'

'Sorry.' He put an arm around his little sister. 'Sorry, Will, I didn't mean to swear. Dad gets me mad.'

'Well, did you tell him to eff off?' Marcie asked her mum. 'I don't mind telling him if you don't want to. On behalf of me, Dale and Will.'

'I don't want to talk to him at all,' Dale said. 'Will's got the right idea. He's nothing to do with us any more.'

'It's not quite as simple as that,' Tamara said, flinching. 'There are... complications.'

'Christ, he's not dying, is he?' Marcie's eyes widened. 'He's not, right?'

'No, nothing like that,' Tamara hastened to reassure her. 'I mean, what you ultimately decide to do is up to you. But there's a bit more to it than him just wanting to see you.'

Marcie snorted. 'He doesn't want us to go to his wedding, does he? Get me in a frilly bridesmaid's dress to play the doting daughter for Daddy? Not a chance.'

'I don't know. Maybe. But, um…' Tamara felt the words of her carefully prepared breaking-it-to-them-gently speech floating out of her brain like dandelion seeds on the wind. 'Well, I told you your dad's with someone new. Natalie. And she's… a bit younger than he is.'

'How much younger?' Dale asked.

'Well, she's… she's twenty-five, Dale.'

Dale curled his lip. 'Eurgh. That's rancid.'

'That means he's old enough to be her dad,' Marcie said. 'Hey, can anyone here spell "midlife crisis" for my diary?'

Willow looked up from her colouring. 'How old is your dad, Marcie?'

'*Our* dad, Will. He's forty-five, same as Mum.'

'No, he's forty-six,' Tamara corrected her. 'We were in the same year at university but he's nine months older.'

'Yeah, well that's worse, isn't it?'

'What's all this got to do with us?' Dale asked.

'I'm coming to that,' Tamara said as she floundered about in her brain. 'So, what did I just say? Yes, Natalie. She's twenty-five, and at twenty-five, um… people are often thinking about the next stage of their lives. Marriage, and… and the things that go along with that.'

Marcie, with her usual quickness, took one look at her mum's face and slowly shook her head. 'Oh Jesus. No.'

'I'm sorry, Marce,' Tamara said quietly.

'What?' Dale looked from one of them to the other. 'I don't get it. We know Dad's getting married; you told us.'

'She's pregnant,' Marcie murmured. 'This Natalie. She's pregnant by Dad, isn't she, Mum?'

'Yes,' Tamara whispered. 'Six months pregnant. Kids, I'm so sorry.'

Willow looked up from her unicorn. 'What does pregnant mean?'

'It means she's going to have a baby,' Dale said in a monotone.

'Oh. OK.' She went back to her colouring.

Tamara could feel her cheeks burning, although she wasn't sure why. Why should her colour rise, as if she was confessing something shameful? This was Andy's shame, not hers. He was the one who'd rejected his child and walked out on his family. He was the one who'd impregnated this girl young enough to be his daughter. Nevertheless, as Tamara sat there in her children's gaze, seeing their horror-struck expressions, her face was on fire.

'I'm sorry,' she repeated in a whisper. Dale just stared blankly, then jumped up and marched out with his face twitching.

Willow looked frightened now. She turned to her sister. 'Marcie? Why is Dale mad?'

'Because… because we're going to have another brother or sister,' Marcie said, in a voice choked with emotion.

'A boy,' Tamara whispered. 'It's a boy, Marce.'

'Because the lady's going to have a baby?' Willow asked, turning to her mum with an expression full of bewilderment.

'Yes, Will. Your dad's baby.'

'I haven't got a—'

'Yes you HAVE!' Marcie jumped to her feet. 'Stop saying that, Will! You have got a dad. We've all got a dad. And he's the biggest loser who ever walked the earth, and he left us all here to rot, and I *hate* him. I'll hate him till the day I die. If you knew what he wanted Mum to... and now... now there's going to be another baby and I don't know what to... to do.' Suddenly, she burst into tears. 'Mum, I'm sorry. I have to... I'm sorry.'

She walked out. Willow, realising now that something was seriously wrong, immediately burst into tears too. Tamara drew her on to her knee, kissing her hair as she rocked Willow's little body against hers.

Perhaps it was a terrible thing to think, but the distressed sobs of her youngest daughter brought Tamara comfort. It took away some of the helplessness by giving her something to deal with; something immediate that was within the scope of her skills as a mum. Dale and Marcie were grown up, and she couldn't cuddle away the tears as she had when they were small. But with Willow, she could still give balm to her hurt baby soul.

'It's OK,' she whispered. 'Everything's going to be OK.'

'Will... the baby... live here?' Willow managed to gasp.

'No, sweetie. He'll live with his mummy and daddy.'

'Will... will I live there too?'

'No, you'll stay here with your mummy.'

'Why is the baby our brother, if you're not his mummy?'

'Because you've got the same daddy. That makes him your brother too.'

Willow let out a snotty sob. 'Dale's my brother.'

'But people can have more than one brother, you know. Dale will still be your brother, even after you get a new one.'

'Why are Dale and Marcie mad with the baby, Mummy?'

Tamara held her tightly. 'They're not mad with the baby, they're mad with their dad.'

'Why?'

'Well, for reasons that are a bit complicated. No one's mad with the baby. He's just a little baby.' Tamara held her back to look into her face. 'Wouldn't you like to know him? You can play with him just like Evie's little sister, but this time he'll be yours.'

Willow's gasping sobs slowed a little. 'Mine?'

'Yes, love. Your baby brother.'

Willow, who for all of her young life had been the baby of the family, looked like the idea of a younger sibling rather appealed.

'Will I go to his house?' she asked.

Tamara nodded. 'Or he can come to our house.'

'And the... the man.' Willow seemed unwilling to accept that Andy was, in fact, her father. 'Will he come too?'

'Yes. He'll come with the baby, and the baby's mummy. But I'd be there too.'

Willow wiped her nose noisily on her sleeve. 'You promise you wouldn't go away?'

Tamara smiled, although her eyes were wet too. 'Not even to do a wee.'

Willow let out a damp giggle. 'Or a poo.'

'Not a single bodily function till they've gone.' She crooked a little finger. 'Promise.'

Willow linked it to seal the pact, apparently satisfied. 'OK. Can I still have new clothes, or will there only be enough for the baby now?'

Tamara laughed. 'Well, I think between us all we can

manage to keep you both fed and clothed. Yes, you can still have new things.'

She heard the conservatory door open and looked up. Dale had appeared, pale and red-eyed, but with a penitent expression on his face.

'Sorry,' he mumbled.

'Why sorry, sweetheart?' Tamara asked gently.

'For storming off. I wasn't mad at you, I was mad at Dad.'

'That's OK. You were feeling a lot of emotions, I know that.'

'Yeah, but... I guess you felt a lot of things too. When Dad told you, right? I bet that hurt and stuff.'

Tamara blinked. Her son was a good lad, considerate and kind when he wasn't doing battle with his ever-raging hormones, but he wasn't what she'd call sensitive. She might have anticipated that sort of intuitive empathy from Marcie, but from Dale it was something of a surprise.

'Yes,' she said. 'But that's all right, I can handle it.'

'It's OK if you need to feel things, Mum. Dad walked out and he didn't care about any of us, especially not you or the baby, and now he's having another baby like the last one didn't even count. If you want to shout about it, you should.'

She smiled. 'Dale, you're amazing, you know that?'

He flushed. 'Give over.'

Willow rubbed her fists in her eyes. 'Where's the last baby? Is there two babies?'

Dale laughed. 'I meant you, daftie. When you were a baby.'

'That was ages and ages ago though.'

Tamara kissed her head. 'I'm sure it seems like it to you.' She looked up at Dale. 'So, have you decided anything? Whatever you want to do, it's completely your choice.'

He flushed. 'I think... I think I'd like to see the baby. But not Dad.'

'I don't think it's a case of one or the other. If you want to see your baby brother then you'll need to have some contact with your dad.'

'Brother?'

'Yes. Your dad told me it's another boy they're expecting.'

He took a deep breath. 'Well, then... OK. For the baby, because it's not his fault his dad's a twat just like it's not our fault. But Dad had just better stay out of my face, that's all, or I'll... I swear I'll...'

'What will you do, Dale?' Willow asked, blinking at him.

'I'll...' Dale met her gaze, and unclenched the hand that had balled into a fist. 'Nothing, Will. Never mind.'

7

Saffie rubbed colour-preserving mousse into her hair as she waited for her taxi: the stuff which looked enough like blueberry ice cream that she'd once succumbed to an impulse to taste some (NB: didn't taste like blueberry ice cream. Tasted like hair mousse).

She didn't have high hopes for tonight's speed dating and had been planning to wear comfy dungarees and her Docs. But after mulling over everything Milo had said about dating fatigue and ageing, she'd decided it couldn't do any harm to make an effort.

So instead she was wearing nice flats and a vintage-style blue handkerchief dress. Because you never knew, did you? As Saffie was aware from the interviews she'd conducted for *The Throstler*'s 'Golden Oldies' feature, which highlighted local couples celebrating their golden wedding anniversaries, love could bloom in the unlikeliest places.

She'd been thinking about the Golden Oldies a lot lately. Milo was right: it did wear you down, all this time dating yet meeting so few relationship prospects. Saffie had had a profile on nearly every app going: Tinder, Hinge, OKCupid, Bumble, Match.com and God knew how many others. She'd been at it for years and she'd met barely a handful of men worth seeing again. Even those that had gone the distance hadn't gone much of a distance – two, three months at most. Kieran and the wedding that never was had made her wary in the first instance, and the Golden Oldies interviews had made her even warier.

The regular feature was supposed to be a sweet bit of fluff: a decades-long love story to brighten everyone's day. Certainly Saffie always wrote them up that way, knowing it was what readers wanted. A lot of them actually were like that – it was plain to see how some couples adored each other. Some still held hands, almost unconsciously, as if it had never occurred to them that there was any need to let each other go.

But some of the couples Saffie interviewed weren't so blessed. Yes, they were still married, but they weren't... they weren't *friends*. At best they muddled along, relying on each other purely because after five decades in each other's company, it was impossible not to. At worst they merely tolerated each other. Saffie hadn't yet met a golden couple who actively despised one another, but she was sure they were out there.

After the mistake she'd so nearly made with Kieran, Saffie had sworn to herself that no matter how lonely she might feel, she wasn't going to become someone who tolerated her partner in life without loving them. She wanted to be that old lady whose husband's hand was in hers when, in fifty years' time, some young journalist turned up to ask them what the secret of a happy marriage was. And she'd tell them 'friendship' – because if you couldn't spend fifty years with someone who was your best mate, then what the hell was the point spending them with anyone at all?

Milo had a different view, of course. He didn't have a Kieran to make him cautious: just too many years of being alone. Saffie curled her lip when she thought of West, and all the changes he'd got Milo to make in his efforts to turn him into the man he wanted him to be.

It really shouldn't be hard for someone like Milo Cook to meet the right man. OK, socially he could be kind of awkward. He tended to get over-excited when something was working and spook his partner by moving too fast, and he was terrible at picking up on red flags. Oh, and he fell in love too quickly – far too quickly.

He was a lovely guy though: Saffie had known him since secondary school. Milo was funny, fun, and not at all bad-looking. It seemed absurd that he'd never managed to find himself in a relationship for longer than six months. Saffie hoped he'd meet some better prospects than West tonight, if only to remind him there were plenty of less twatty fish in the sea.

Her taxi beeped outside. Saffie gave her hair a last scrunch and headed downstairs.

Milo was lurking by the door of the community centre. His curls – black again after a dye session with Saffie – were carefully gelled, and he was dressed in his best jeans and shirt. He also wasn't wearing his glasses.

'Hiya.' She pecked his cheek. 'Got your contacts in?'

'No, I've run out. I wanted to look my best though, so I left the gigs at home.'

She frowned. 'Can you see all right?'

'Yeah,' he said, rubbing his eyes. 'I mean, everything's a

bit fuzzy. It's like the difference between watching *Star Wars* in HD on a 32 in flatscreen compared to watching it on a clapped-out Blockbuster VHS on the telly you had as a kid. But I'm not about to do a Mr Magoo pratfall down an elevator shaft or anything.'

'Right.' She looked into his eyes, which were glassy and unfocused. 'If you say so. Shall we go in then?'

He glanced longingly at the bright lights of the wine bar across the road. 'Unless you fancy nipping in there for a stiff one? Dutch courage?'

'We can't, we'll be late.' She squeezed his elbow. 'It's just another date, Mile – or at any rate, lots of little ones. We're both experts by now, right?'

'I guess.'

'I suppose they'll split us up and send us off to the appropriate gender preference group,' Saffie said, peering through the door. 'If I'm not out here after then wait for me in the wine bar, OK?'

He groaned. 'I hope this wasn't a terrible idea.'

'If nothing else, it'll be an experience. Something to tell the grandkids about.'

'If we ever have any. Our success rate in finding life partners to do that sort of thing with currently stands at 0%.'

'Oh God, you're not about to suggest one of those if-we're-not-married-by-forty pacts, are you?'

'Ha! You wish. You're not getting your hands on top-notch sperm like mine that easily.'

Saffie sighed. 'Just when I thought my luck might be about to change.' She offered him her arm. 'Come on then. Once more unto the breach.'

*

While her brother was having a panic attack outside Braybrook Community Centre, Tamara was enduring the traumatic experience of trailing around the White Rose Shopping Centre with Willow.

'Mummy, look!' Willow pressed her face against a shop window. '*Paw Patrol* stuff!'

'That's a toyshop, Will,' Tamara said. 'We're buying clothes today. Come on.'

Tamara tugged at her daughter's hand, but Willow didn't budge.

'You said I could have a little toy though,' she said, in her most pleading voice. 'You *said*, Mummy.'

'I said at the end we could look at toys. We've got more things to buy first.'

'They've got the Mighty Pups Tower,' Willow whispered in a reverent tone. 'The one I wrote to Father Christmas I wanted for my birthday.' Willow always sent her birthday list to Father Christmas, because, as she'd told her mum and siblings, it seemed like she ought to write to *someone* important about it.

'Well then I'm sure that like Chase, he's on the case,' Tamara said, trying to keep her tone bright. It was late-night shopping tonight but there was only an hour until closing, and she had a lot to tick off her list. 'Come on, sweetie. I've got a list of Marcie's uni textbooks here. I don't want to miss the bookshop.'

'Eeek!' Willow clapped her hands. 'Mummy, Elsa dresses!'

'You've got an Elsa dress, Will,' Tamara said wearily. It was nights like this that made her feel being mum to a five-year-old was a young woman's game. 'Uncle Milo bought you one for Christmas.'

'Yeah, I've got the blue dress from *Frozen* 1. Not the white dress from *Frozen* 2. It's totally, totally different. Mummy, can't we just look really quickly?'

Tamara sighed. 'Five minutes and that's it.'

'Yay!' Willow skipped ahead into the shop. Tamara followed, her arms laden with shopping bags.

She glanced around as Willow went to drool on the Disney merch. They had a decent range of proper clothing as well as costumes. Perhaps she could tick the *Paw Patrol* pyjamas Willow wanted off her list.

She wandered over to the nightwear section and started looking through the rails. A couple next to her were browsing the Babygros and she gave them a vague smile.

The man looked round. 'Oh my God!'

Tamara jumped, knocking several pairs of pyjamas to the floor. For a moment, she just stared uncomprehendingly at the man looking at her with her ex-husband's face.

It was the first time she'd seen Andy since their divorce. He was still handsome at forty-six, his hair grizzled now at the sides – which of course suited him, the son of a bitch – but otherwise he looked exactly as she remembered him on that day... the day he'd left them all.

'Here, let me get those.' The woman he was with, blooming in a becoming purple maternity dress, flashed Tamara a warm smile before crouching to pick up the pyjamas she'd dropped. Tamara had a vague feeling she ought to help, the woman's pregnant frame registering somewhere in her consciousness, but she couldn't tear her eyes from Andy.

'Are you... what're you...' was all she could stutter.

Andy looked a combination of awkward, embarrassed and ashamed.

'We're, um...' He flinched as he looked down at his fiancée picking up the dropped clothes. 'Shopping. For the baby. Nat wanted to get him some Mickey Mouse Babygros. You?'

Tamara cast a nervous look at her oblivious daughter, who'd wandered over to the puppy tower thing and was humming the *Paw Patrol* theme as she played with the display model.

'Just picking up some bits for the kids,' Tamara told Andy, as breezily as she could.

The woman, Natalie, stood up. 'Oh, I'm sorry. Do you two know each other?'

'Yes. Um.' Andy rubbed his neck, avoiding eye contact. 'Nat, this is Tamara.'

'Oooh. OK.' Natalie's eyes went as round as her tummy. 'Well, that's awkward.'

She gave Tamara a hesitant smile. Natalie had a very likeable face; sort of sweet, in a way that made Tamara feel maternal against her will. Of course it would be typical of Andy to find himself a partner who was impossible to hate. All Tamara wanted was to discover that this twenty-five-year-old fiancée was a Grade-A bitch who more than deserved this piece of shit she'd once been married to, but no. Natalie looked pleasant and friendly and... well, *nice*. Damn her to hell.

Oh, and she was beautiful; like, just-stepped-off-*Love-Island* gorgeous. Tamara had expected that though. It was Andy, wasn't it? She'd have to be beautiful.

'I might go take a look at the baby toys.' Natalie pecked her fiancé's cheek. 'Come find me when you're done, babe.'

'Thanks, Nat.'

'She seems nice,' Tamara said when they were alone.

'She is.' Andy rubbed his neck again. 'So, um… you look good.'

'No I don't. Just say whatever you've got to say that's to the point.'

'Look, Tam, I'm sorry about this. Are the kids at home?'

'Marcie's at her boyfriend's and Dale's revising.'

'Marcie's got a boyfriend already?'

'She's eighteen, Andy.' Tamara felt as though she was recovering her equilibrium, although she still had one eye fixed on Willow. 'Not to mention that she's bright and funny and beautiful. Of course she's got a boyfriend.'

'Yes. Of course. Is this her first one?'

'Relationship? No, before Ashley there was Hannah, and before her was Jacob. She's been dating since she was fifteen.'

Andy blinked. 'Hannah?'

Tamara gave him a tight smile. 'There's a lot you've missed out on.'

'I guess there is.' He hesitated. 'Did you, um…'

'Tell them about the baby? Yes.'

'What did they say?'

'In a nutshell: they still hate you, but they're keen to get to know their brother. To quote Dale, "it's not his fault his dad's a twat any more than it's ours".'

Andy sighed. 'They do hate me, don't they?'

'What did you expect?'

'I tried to call them. Marcie didn't answer so I left her a message. Dale's changed his number, I think.'

'He hasn't. He just blocked you.'

'Oh.' He hesitated again. 'Where do we go from here, Tam? I'm genuinely determined to do better.'

Tamara cast another look at Willow and lowered her voice. 'Look, Andy, I'm not happy about this. I'm not happy you're back in my life, I'm not happy you've got the twins upset in the middle of their exams, and I'm not happy that you're getting me to do your dirty work because you know full well I can't refuse to let the children have a relationship with their brother. So in terms of where this goes next, it goes there with me calling the shots, OK?'

Andy looked taken aback. 'OK. Whatever you want, as long as—'

They were interrupted by Willow skipping over, holding up a box. 'Mummy, look! It's Elsa's palace in Lego. You can make it in Lego!'

Andy stared at Tamara, and she winced.

'Is this…' he said.

'Yes.' Tamara drew the little girl to her. 'This is my daughter, Willow. Willow, this is… an old friend. Andy.'

'Hello,' Willow said, politely but with little interest in this new grown-up. She was too young to notice the dumbstruck look on her father's face, or how the almond eyes were an exact reflection of her own.

'Hello Willow,' Andy said quietly. He nodded to the box she was holding. 'What have you got there?'

'*Frozen* Lego!' She giggled. 'I mean, not frozen like it's ice. *Frozen* like the movie.'

'Is that your favourite?'

'Yeah! And *Encanto*. I can sing all the songs without hardly forgetting a word.' Willow regarded him with more animation, happy to have an interested audience. 'Look, see?' she said, showing him the box. 'It's the Ice Queen palace.'

'That's pretty cool.'

She giggled again. 'Because it's ice. Ice is cool. That means cold.'

Andy looked at Tamara. 'She's funny, isn't she?'

'I know she is.'

Willow turned to her mum, still blissfully unaware of any atmosphere. 'Mummy, can I have it? You said I could have one little toy if I came shopping.'

Tamara didn't answer. She was staring at Andy, who was staring at Willow: taking in every curve of her face, every expression, every trick of movement. Tamara had never noticed how like her father Willow was until right now. And it hurt. It hurt her deeply. Because it meant that no matter how Andy had acted, there was a part of her daughter that would always be his.

Willow had asked a question. What was it? Oh, Lego, yes. Tamara forced herself into mum mode.

'It's little but it's expensive,' she told Willow. 'Sorry, sweetie, but that's really a birthday toy, not a going-shopping toy. How about a new Hatchimal instead?'

Willow wasn't prone to petulance, but they'd been shopping for a while and Tamara had noticed her getting increasingly peevish during the last half an hour. Willow hugged the box close, her bottom lip starting to jut.

'You didn't say anything about 'spensive,' she muttered. 'You said little.'

'I meant little in price, not size. Sorry, Will, but I can't afford it right now.'

'Um, can I...' Andy met Tamara's eye. 'Will you let me? As her... a friend of her mother's.'

Willow's face lit up. 'Yay! Thank you thank you thank you!'

Tamara shook her head. 'I couldn't let you do that, Andy.'

Willow blinked at her, her lip wobbling again. 'Why not? I said thank you and everything.'

'Well, because... I don't feel comfortable with it, that's why. I can't explain now.'

'Please,' Andy said quietly. 'Let me do this one small thing for her. I owe it to her.'

'You owe her a damn sight more than that,' Tamara muttered in an undertone, so Willow couldn't hear.

'I've always paid my share.'

'Not what I meant and you know it.'

'I know. Let me give her this now though.'

Seeing that Willow was approaching the edge of a proper wobbly she really didn't have the strength to deal with, Tamara acquiesced with a brief nod. Andy and Willow beamed at each other with the same smile, and Tamara felt another kick in her gut.

Desperate now to get out of this whole excruciating situation, Tamara took Willow's hand and hurried her to the counter. Andy lingered behind as he waved Natalie over.

'Good evening,' the shop assistant said as Willow plonked her toy on the counter. She smiled warmly at Tamara and her bags, then at Willow. 'Are we getting spoiled by Granny on our shopping trip? It certainly looks like it.'

Tamara actually started to turn and look behind her,

momentarily expecting to find that her mum had magically beamed herself here from her retirement cottage in Devon, before realisation dawned. A flush spread from her cheeks down her neck. Andy and Natalie were right behind her with their own purchases, no doubt revelling in her humiliation.

'Actually I'm her mother,' she muttered. She jerked her head in Andy's direction. 'And he's paying for that so you can put it on his bill.'

She swept the stupid Lego toy into one of the bags she was carrying, grabbed Willow's hand and marched out.

8

Milo was now on the third of his eight speed dates, and was surprised to find this one was going great.

There'd been a queue for the event when he and Saffie had walked in, and although it wasn't easy to make out faces without his glasses, there were at least a few lads who looked like his type. He hoped they were here for the boys and not the girls, which would be his usual luck: the hotties off to join the straights while he was left with a selection of men who all looked like Ken Barlow.

Milo's first two matches hadn't gone well. There were two age group categories and Milo was in with the twenty-three to thirty-eight-year-olds. His first speed date was with a man at the bottom end of that range – or a boy really. Jayden didn't look much older than the twins.

He might as well have been talking to Marcie and Dale too, for all the sense Jayden's conversation made. The lad had chattered about his interests – which included a bunch of YouTubers Milo had never heard of, anime and K-Pop – until Milo had felt about four million years old. Jayden's slang was totally beyond him: it was all 'extra' and 'salty' and 'yeet', to the point Milo was tempted to sneak a look at Urban Dictionary under the table. When he'd had to ask what 'basic' meant in the context of a Gregg's vegan sausage roll, Jayden's eyes had almost rolled back into his head. Milo was sure he'd only been one step away from getting an 'OK boomer' thrown at him.

His next date was more age-appropriate, but also terminally monosyllabic. Milo tried every conversation starter on his list and failed to elicit more than a one-word answer.

But this third guy, Christian, seemed like a great prospect. He was a bit fuzzy thanks to Milo's current lack of corrective lens technology, but Milo was pretty sure Christian had a good face. He'd started chatting easily as soon as Milo had sat down, ignoring the proscribed conversation starters to talk about things that were actually interesting: films he liked (which happened to also be films Milo liked), work stuff (he was a web designer, so lots of crossover there), and the one subject Milo had plenty of material on: terrible dates. They were currently swapping stories from their many years at the dating coalface.

'You do Grindr, right?' Christian asked, taking a sip of his pint. 'That's the best place to pick up the really *Shining*-level horror stories.'

'Not these days. People mostly just want hook-ups, and I'm not looking for that any more. I mean, sometimes, as a treat, but it's a relationship I'm interested in.' Milo looked longingly at Christian's pint. He hadn't realised there was a bar. 'How about you?'

'Same. I still hop on now and again though.' He laughed. 'God, I've met some sorts on there. I hooked up with this one guy and his room was full of Barbies. Hundreds of the things, all facing the bed. I couldn't get out fast enough.'

Milo laughed too. 'I feel you. I couldn't perform for a huge audience of Barbies either.'

'It was Ken who really put me off.' He nodded to Milo. 'Your turn again.'

Milo scrolled through his memory banks for something that could rival Christian's Barbie guy.

'Well, there was the dog guy,' Milo said. 'He had eight chihuahuas. Eight! I mean, who can possibly need that many chihuahuas? I nearly stepped on four of them getting to his room, and the little buggers would not stop scratching at the door the whole time we were in there.' He shrugged. 'Still slept with him though.'

He laughed, but Christian didn't join in. It was then that Milo noticed his date's expression had changed.

'I knew I recognised you from somewhere,' he muttered. 'Milo. I should've remembered.'

'Eh?'

'That was me! I was your dog guy,' Christian snapped. 'And for your information, I rescued those chihuahuas. I volunteered at an animal shelter and offered to foster a litter of eight orphan pups. Then I ended up keeping them all because I couldn't bear to give them away after I'd raised them by hand.'

Milo ran a finger under his collar. 'Shit.'

'And you never called me after, did you? You know, Milo, I really liked you. That was a shitty thing to do.'

Milo flinched. 'Look, I'm sorry. I should've called, but the sheer level of chihuahuas... I can't be the only one it put off. I was just a kid.'

'Twenty-three is not a kid.'

'You won't say that after you've talked to Jayden.'

Christian snorted. 'And now I'm just fodder for your dating horror stories, am I? I can't believe you didn't even remember me.'

'You were going by Chris back then, weren't you? Plus I haven't got my contacts in. Anyway, you didn't remember me either.'

'Because I was traumatised. You've got no excuse.'

Milo almost whistled with relief when the beeper went.

'Christian, I really am sorry,' he said as he stood up. 'I liked you too, I was just young and stupid. Don't hold it against me, eh?'

Christian made a noise that was half 'huh' and half snort, turning his face away. Milo prepared to move on, but something held him back.

'I meant that,' he said. 'I am sorry, and I did like you. I could, um… buy you a pint after?'

'I don't think so, mate. I've still got five chihuahuas.'

Christian kept his face averted. Milo stared at him for a moment, then he noticed the organiser frowning at him and moved to the next table.

He looked at the man sitting opposite. Tasteful designer clothes, manscaped beard, air of reeking superiority…

'Bollocks,' he muttered. 'West.'

In the neighbouring room, Saffie was just as relieved as her best friend to hear the beeper signal the end of another speed date. Things, however, were about to get a lot worse for her.

'Hi,' she said as she sat down in front of her next date, closely followed by 'oh shit' as that familiar musclebound form registered.

'Oh my God.' Kieran reached for her hands. 'Saffie. What the hell are you doing here?'

She snatched her hands away. 'Snorkelling the Maldives. What does it look like I'm doing?'

'So you're still single?'

'No, I'm married with four kids. This just felt like a good way to recruit a lover who likes his liaisons speedy and satisfying.'

Kieran blinked. 'You're married?'

This was one part of their relationship she remembered well: watching even the most obvious sarcasm sail over Kieran's head.

But he looked so delighted to see her that Saffie softened slightly. Kieran wasn't a bad guy. He was just... Kieran. Sweet, solid, but operating on an entirely different wavelength than she was.

'No, Kieran. That was just a joke,' she said in a gentler tone. 'I'm still single.'

He beamed. 'Me too.'

'Well, I'm sorry to hear that.'

'I tried all the dating apps but I never get anywhere with them.' He met her eyes. 'No one can compare, really.'

This was what he was like. Sweet, yes, but a bit creepy when he insisted on saying this stuff six years after they'd broken up. There had been a period after they'd split when it had all gone a bit... low-level stalky. Nothing really hardcore: liking all her selfies on social media, PMing her late at night with 'how you doing, babe?'-type messages, sending her flowers on her birthday; that sort of thing. He'd never frightened her, but it had been tough. Saffie hadn't wanted to hurt him any more than she had already, and yet she'd needed him to understand that when she said it was over, that was the final word on the matter.

'I never see you on any of the apps,' Kieran said. 'Don't you use them?'

She didn't have the heart to tell him that the first thing she did whenever she signed up for a new service was find his profile and block it.

'Er, no. I just thought I'd give this a try for a laugh,' she said. 'So, um… meet anyone nice?'

'No. I mean, nice, but not…' He gazed at her, that stricken-puppy-in-a-disused-mineshaft look that sent her guilt impulse into overdrive. 'Your hair looks good, Saf. It was pink the last time I saw you. Went with your dress.'

'Yes.' She wasn't sure what else to say to that.

'Did you keep it?'

'The hair or the dress?'

He just smiled wistfully, and she lowered her gaze.

'No,' she said quietly. 'I sold it.'

'I always thought it was daft, all that stuff, but I guess it really is bad luck.'

The beeper went, and Saffie thanked God, her lucky stars, Glinda the Good and anyone else who might be looking out for her as she stood up.

'Well, it's been nice to catch up, Kieran.' She started to move on, then stopped. 'And… look after yourself. I hope you meet someone.'

'Not sure I can again.' He watched her sadly as she moved to the next table.

*

When Saffie got to the wine bar, Milo was hugging a large red, which told her all she needed to know about his night.

'Margarita for the lady,' he said to the barman. 'On the tab, please, mate. We may be here some time.'

'I look that bad, do I?' Saffie asked when the barman had disappeared.

'I've never seen a face that screams "margarita drip, stat!" so loudly.' He patted a barstool. 'Come tell Uncle Milo all about it.'

'You first.'

'If you insist.' He started counting on his fingers. 'So, eight dates. Number one: nauseatingly young Gen-Zedder called Jayden who looked like he was one step away from asking me what I did in the war. Number two: monosyllabic social incompetent. Numbers three, five and eight I'd already hooked up with during my exhaustive trawl of the dating apps. Number six I don't even remember, he was that dull. Number seven: Ken Barlow lookalike. And number four…' He sighed. 'Number four was West.'

'Shit! Are you all right?'

'Yeah. Just pissed off.'

'Ugh, we must've been mad to go speed dating in a town this size. We were bound to bump into at least one of our exes.' Saffie nodded to the barman as he put her margarita down. 'Four is pretty bad luck though.'

'I'm working with a smaller pool of eligible bachelors, aren't I? I bet I've been out with most of the gay men around my age in this town.'

'That's true.'

'West was the only one who counts as an actual ex anyway. The others were all one-offs.' Milo scowled. 'Can you actually believe that bastard? We just broke up and he's already out on the bloody pull.'

'Fairness forces me to point out that you were also out on the bloody pull, Milo.'

'That's different. I'm the dumpee, I'm entitled to do some rebound pulling.'

'I wouldn't have thought West would go in for speed dating.'

Milo snorted. 'Apparently he was being ironic. Ironically trying to get laid, more like. I bet he ends up sugar-daddying that Jayden kid.' He took a gulp of wine. 'And you know what? That wasn't even the most traumatic date of the night.'

'Seriously?'

'No. That was number three. You remember on a night out God knows how many aeons ago, we met a lad called Chris who invited me back to his place?'

'What, Chihuahua Chris?'

'Yeah. It was him. I didn't recognise him – he's got a lot less twinky in thirteen years, and he goes by Christian now. Plus I didn't have my glasses, so he looked a bit like he'd been scribbled.'

'Bugger! Did he recognise you?'

'Not at first. We were getting on famously, swapping dating stories, then I casually dropped in how I'd once shagged this lad with eight chihuahuas.' He laughed grimly. 'That brought it all flooding back. How he'd really liked me and I'd never called him. You know, up until that point it was the best date I'd had in years. And we were only at it for two minutes.'

Saffie rubbed his arm. 'Poor Milo. That sounds excruciating.'

Milo massaged his ear lobe. 'I should've called him. I was a shallow bastard at twenty-three. All I could think was "Eight chihuahuas. Eight chihuahuas! Who the hell has eight chihuahuas?" Even then, my track record on spotting weirdos was pretty poor. I felt I'd be a mug to ignore an obvious flag like eight chihuahuas.'

'But you shagged him anyway.'

'Well yeah, I was twenty-three and he was hot. Like I said, shallow bastard. Shallow, randy bastard.'

'Did he mention the chihuahuas?'

'They were rescues, apparently. He'd fostered a motherless litter and ended up keeping them.' Milo groaned faintly. 'Oh God, how the hell do you confuse red flags with green ones? He's an actual nice guy who just wants to do lovely things for orphaned puppies. And I ballsed it up.'

'Definitely?' Saffie said. 'It's been thirteen years. I'd have thought he could find it in his heart to forgive you by now.'

'It's still fresh to Christian. You should've seen his face when I asked if I could buy him a pint.' Milo rubbed his eyes. 'Go on then, what was your trauma?'

She grimaced. 'Small-town woes again. I bumped into an ex too.'

Milo took one look at her face and shook his head. 'Not Stalky Kieran. Did he follow you?'

'No, this was a genuine coincidence.' Saffie paused with her margarita halfway to her lips. 'I'm sure it was.'

'Did he creep you out?'

'No, he was sweet.' She sighed. 'I bit his head off and he was just... *nice* to me. All puppy-dog eyes and delighted smile. You know, I was half convinced I'd made a mistake. That's how desperate things have got.'

'You need to see the list again?'

'Yeah, go on.'

Milo pulled up something on his phone. She smiled at a photo of the list the two of them had scribbled the day she'd broken things off: the pros and cons of Kieran. The columns were pretty even, but there were a few things written in red in the cons column. Those were the dealbreaker items.

Doesn't get my jokes
Never makes jokes
Won't watch films made before 1985
Obsessive gym meathead
Hates cats and musicals and musicals about cats
NOT BEST MATES!!!

That one was underlined, just in case the red ink, capitals and three exclamation marks didn't hammer it home.

'See? It was the right decision,' Milo said gently.

'I know that really. I suppose it's all just getting me down, same as you. As well as Kieran, I also encountered one foot fetishist who wanted to know how many pairs of shoes I owned and if I had any photos of me wearing them, a classic pub bore, a guy who looked like my dad, a guy who didn't look like my dad but did ask if I'd be willing to call him Daddy, and another three so nondescript I couldn't pick them out of a police line-up.' She waved to the barman. 'Could we have another round here? Cheers.'

Milo finished his wine. 'We're best mates.'

'And?'

'Maybe we really should make one of those pacts. You know, if-we're-not-married-by-forty.'

Saffie snorted. 'There're only two slight stumbling blocks, Milo. I don't fancy you, and you sure as hell don't fancy me.'

'You said I was sexy in the pub.'

'No, what I said was that if I didn't know you, you'd be sexy.' She punched his arm. 'Aww, don't look like that. That might not sound like a compliment but it is one.'

'Well, what are we going to do then? Die alone?'

'Keep plugging away, I guess.'

'Saffie, out of eight dates tonight, four were men I'd already been out with. I'm running out of options.' Milo seized on the new wine that had materialised in front of him.

'Maybe cast the net a bit further afield?'

'How far? London? Paris? Canberra?' He looked up at her. 'Sorry it was shit tonight, Saf. I feel guilty for wasting your evening.'

She claimed her second margarita. 'Don't worry about it, love. It's all good material for that novel I'm determined to write one day.'

'Maybe you could pitch it as a feature. Speed dating undercover.'

'Might've worked when it was still a novelty. Speed dating events are as old as Methuselah's granny. Where's the story?' She crushed some ice between her teeth. 'I do need fresh ideas though. I got three more rejections today.'

Milo sipped his new wine. 'So once again our abysmal love lives drive us to drink.'

'Are you going to have another sift through your apps tonight?'

'No.' Milo looked determined as he took the leaflet for The 24-hour Dating Agency from his wallet. 'It's time for something drastic. I'm going to sign up for this.'

9

Saffie was early to work the next day, which was impressive given her margarita tally the night before. She and Milo had really gone to town on drowning their sorrows, their night culminating in a lock-in at a back-alley pub. And then the ultimate humiliation: karaoke.

Milo had crashed at hers, and Saffie had a vague memory of helping him to send an email to Dr Alison Sheldrake at The 24-hour Dating Agency before bed. The only reason they were early to work was that Milo's warthog-level snoring as he topped-and-tailed with her meant there was bugger all chance of any further sleep.

Saffie opened the Gmail app on her phone while Milo went to flick the kettle on.

'Any nice rejections this morning?' he asked.

'This editor says he likes my style of writing but they've got a similar feature lined up already,' she said in a voice hoarse with the morning after the night before. 'I'll make sure he's last against the wall when the revolution comes.'

She skimmed through some others, the usual form rejections, then switched on her computer and opened her work emails. Milo came over with a cup of coffee.

'Look,' Saffie said, nodding to her screen. 'Email from your cousin. Subject: Future features. That sounds ominous.'

'What does he say?'

Saffie opened the email. It was very direct, beginning simply 'Saffie' – no 'dear' or 'hi'. In Saffie's experience, people like that were either still trying to get their head around the etiquette of formal digital communication, or they felt they were too important to waste time on endearments. She suspected Russell Foxton fell into the latter camp.

'He wants me and Tam to come up with a list of feature ideas ahead of an editorial meeting next month.' She shook her head. 'That's never been the way we do things. And since when do we have editorial meetings?'

'This must be Russell's version of not interfering editorially,' Milo said. 'What the rest of us might call "interfering editorially".'

'I can't come up with feature ideas that far ahead. We have to respond to things as they happen.' Saffie's gaze flickered back to the rejection email on her phone. 'Hey, you don't think he's going to have a problem with me pitching features elsewhere, do you?'

'I don't see why. The stuff you write as a freelancer isn't in competition with *Throstler* material. Fran's never been bothered.'

'Yeah, but this cousin of yours seems so much more… businessy. What if he bollocks me for moonlighting?'

'I'm sure he'll understand you've got a career to build that doesn't begin and end with this place.'

'Hmm.'

'That's all we need on top of the hangovers: emails from

management.' Milo poked out his tongue. 'Here, can you taste that too?'

'What?'

'That taste, like something died in my mouth. I think it might've been my dignity.'

'Very likely. You finally Sambuca-ed what was left of it to death.' Saffie rubbed her arm, which had a blossoming purple bruise from someone or something she'd banged into last night. 'We're getting too old for this, Mile.'

'Never has my body been keener to remind me that I'm not twenty-five any more.'

'Heard back from the date doctor yet?'

Milo shook his head. 'She won't be picking up work emails until after nine, I guess.'

'What's the next step after this?'

'The website says we make an appointment to have a chat. Then I fill in a questionnaire, they match me up with my perfect man and hey presto, you'll be on Best Woman duty for me within the year.'

Saffie drank her coffee. 'Wasting your time, mate. I can tell you exactly why you're still single.'

She dropped her head to her shoulder, her tongue hanging out of one side of her mouth as she impersonated Milo's throaty snoring.

'Get lost. I do not sound like that.'

'You sound worse. Like a tuberculotic steamroller. You were drooling as well, I could hear you dripping.'

'Yeah, well your feet smell like stilton so there.' He glanced at the rejection email on her phone. 'Any more ideas you can pitch then?'

She stared thoughtfully into her coffee. 'One.'

'What is it?'

'It's what you said in the bar, about an undercover feature on speed dating.'

'I thought you said there was no story in that.'

'There isn't.'

They were interrupted by the arrival of Tamara, looking even rougher than she had the day she'd received Andy's text. She was in her smartest work suit, her hair pulled into a bun, but her eyes were swollen and red. And there was someone else with her: a woman Saffie didn't recognise.

'Oh great,' she heard Milo mutter. 'Just what we need.'

'Saffie, this is Nikki, my cousin Russell's wife,' Tamara said. 'And our soon-to-be boss, of course.'

Nikki smiled tightly. 'I felt I ought to come in and introduce myself, since we're going to be working so closely together.'

Saffie looked one half of her new employer over. Nikki was Mediterranean in her colouring, deeply tanned, with glossy chestnut hair flowing over her shoulders. Everything about her was glossy, from her perfectly glossed lips to her long Shellac nails. Even her boobs, which looked suspiciously perky, were probably glossy. Saffie glanced down at her own costume of patched denim dungarees and Doc Martens and cursed silently.

There was something in Nikki's face that worried Saffie. No amount of gloss could hide the pronounced jut of the jaw that suggested Nikki Foxton was a woman not accustomed to being crossed...

'Cup of something?' Tamara asked Nikki politely.

'No, I can't stay. We're on deadline over at *Lifestyle North*. I just wanted to drop in and meet the staff ahead of our first meeting next month.' She glanced at Saffie and Milo, then at Tamara. 'Is everyone OK?'

'How do you mean?' Milo asked, grimacing as he heard his own croaky hungover voice.

'The three of you look a little… tired.'

'Well, we've been working hard, you see,' Saffie said. 'That's us. Busy busy busy, all the time.'

Nikki stared at her, as if trying to work out if this was supposed to be a joke. Eventually she decided to ignore it and turned back to Tamara.

'Right, well, I'll be seeing you again soon. Fran officially hands over to us next week,' she said. 'Does anyone have any questions before I go?'

This seemed to be rhetorical, as Nikki was already turning to leave. However, Saffie raised her hand.

'I have a question,' she said. 'This email from Russell about producing the features list months in advance. I don't think that's going to be workable.'

Nikki stared at her. 'I'm sorry?'

'I mean, maybe at *Lifestyle North* you can do it that way, but here we respond to things as they happen.'

'Mmm. In the pub, by any chance?' Nikki asked coldly, scanning Saffie's slightly green face.

'I'm serious. Maybe *Lifestyle North* works that way but *The Throstler* is fluid, not static. Isn't it, Tam?'

Tamara nodded. 'She's got a point, Nikki. That's never been the way we've done things.'

'Yes.' Nikki's lips pressed together in a thin line. 'Well, perhaps the way you've always done things is part of the problem.'

'I really don't see how that—'

Nikki held up a hand. 'I don't have time to discuss this now. We'll talk about it in our editorial meeting. Goodbye, Tamara.'

'That was all we needed today,' Saffie said when she'd gone. 'I expect she's going straight back to your cousin to tell him what a bunch of workshy drunks we are.'

Milo turned to his sister and examined her face. 'What's up with you, Tam? You look rougher than we do.'

Tamara smiled. 'That obvious, is it? I'm sure that in my youth I could cry all night and after a quick mint and cucumber face mask, no one was any the wiser.'

'Is it Andy?' Saffie asked.

'Course it's Andy.' Tamara sighed. 'Actually, no, he was just a witness.'

'To what?'

'The ultimate humiliation.' She went to put the kettle on. 'Last night, when I took Willow shopping, we bumped into Andy and his fiancée buying baby stuff.'

'Shit!' Milo said. 'Were you upset?'

'Well I wasn't arranging fireworks and a marching band.'

'Did Will freak out?'

'No, I told her Andy was an old friend. I'm going to have to tell her the truth though. She'll see him again when the baby comes.' Tamara mixed a coffee and went to perch on Milo's desk. 'Jesus, she looks just like him. How did I never see it before? It gave me this horrible sort of visceral sickness in my stomach, like he might snatch her away and there'd be nothing I could do about it. Like... like she *belonged* to him.'

Milo scoffed. 'He never even wanted her.'

'Well, he wants her now.' She lowered her eyes. 'And

it hurts, Mile. I know Andy is my kids' father and there's nothing I can do to change that. I know they ought to have a relationship with their new brother, and yet… and yet it's like a kick to the stomach every time I think of their dad building a bond with them after what he did. I just want him, all this, to go away again.' She choked back a sob. 'But it can't, can it? It's happening and I have to deal with it like a grown-up for my kids' sake, even though I really just want to scream and kick like an overtired fucking toddler.'

Milo slipped an arm around her shoulders. 'Scream all you want, Tam. There's only us here. You don't have to be the mum: you can be just as pissed off as you're entitled to be, guilt-free.'

She smiled weakly at him. 'Thanks, kidder.'

'What was the fiancée like?' Saffie asked.

'Oh God, you've never seen anything like her. She's got a voice like warm honey and a complexion like peaches and cream.' Tamara sighed. 'Beautiful.'

'Well, and so are you,' Saffie said stoutly. 'I don't know who decided twenty-five was inherently more beautiful than forty-five – although it goes without saying that it must've been a man – but it's utter bollocks.'

Tamara unconsciously ran her fingers through her hair. 'I'm not beautiful. I'm a tired, harassed-looking, prematurely grey old bag who looks like her own daughter's grandmother.'

'You don't look at all like Willow's grandmother,' Milo said. 'No one's going to think that, Tam.'

'Milo, they literally did. The shop assistant made a throwaway comment about Willow being spoilt rotten by her granny.'

Saffie shook her head. 'She didn't! What a thoughtless thing to say.'

'And Andy and Natalie witnessed the whole thing.' Tamara's face reddened. 'They were probably cackling about it together all the way home. I've never felt so utterly brought down in my life.'

Saffie wheeled her swivel chair over so she could squeeze her friend's arm. 'I'm sorry, Tam,' she said softly. 'Please don't let it get you down.'

Tamara sighed. 'I can't help it getting me down. I felt bad enough about how I looked before, but now...'

Milo's phone buzzed and he took it from his pocket.

'Reply from Dr Sheldrake,' he said. 'She's got an appointment free this Saturday.'

Tamara frowned. 'Sheldrake? From that "Blind Date" place?'

'Yeah. Saf and me had a bit of a traumatic time at the speed dating last night, and since nothing else seems to be working, I decided I'd give the twenty-four-hour date thing a go with or without you guys,' Milo said. 'I've got nothing to lose but my dignity, and I think most of that evaporated halfway through mine and Saf's duet of "Paradise by the Dashboard Light" last night when we started singing along with the sex noises.'

'Forward me her email, will you, Mile?' Saffie said. 'I'm signing up too.'

Milo frowned. 'Eh? I thought you said it was daft.'

'It's unique though, isn't it? I'm sort of curious as to how it all works. What's more, I reckon other people might be too.'

'What, you're going to write a feature about it?'

'Why not? A brand-new approach to dating; an insider's perspective. I doubt this Dr Sheldrake will object to the free publicity.'

'All right, brilliant,' Milo said, beaming. 'I can have a buddy to swap notes with then. And of course, after our dates we'll both be happily paired off at last.'

'This is strictly business, Milo. I'm not going to give my real name or job either. I don't want Dr Sheldrake to realise I'm investigating the place until I've written the piece or she might not agree to arrange me a date.'

'Saffie, there's a *soulmate guarantee*. That means you're bound to meet your perfect someone.'

Saffie laughed. 'You actually think that place is going to be the magic feather your love life needs, don't you?'

'I don't want to fly, Saf. I just want a decent chance at companionship and regular sex for the remainder of my time on earth.'

Milo noticed Tamara staring at him.

'What?' he said. 'You're not going to give me a "TMI", are you? I know I'm your little brother, Tam, but I am thirty-six. I'm assuming you didn't think I was still a virgin.'

'Forward me her email address too,' Tamara said.

Saffie blinked. 'But I thought you were dead set against dating again.'

'I certainly don't want a relationship, but after what happened last night, I could use an ego boost. Just one person who might actually find me interesting and attractive and, God forbid, sexy. I'm sick of sitting at home feeling like a sexless crone while Andy's making babies with some apple-cheeked young beauty.' Tamara caught sight of her haggard reflection in Milo's monitor and smiled sadly. 'One more moment in the sun: is that too much to ask?'

'There are many more waiting for you, Tam. For all of us.' Milo looked from one woman to the other. 'Honestly, you guys, this is a brilliant idea. I'm one hundred per cent sure of it.'

10

'Hey Russ,' Tamara said when she arrived home from the hairdresser's one Saturday afternoon two weeks later. Her cousin was in the kitchen, sipping a cup of tea as he flicked through the latest issue of *The Throstler*. 'Where's Will?'

'Fast asleep,' he said. 'I think I wore her out on our trip to the park. Oh, and Marcie's home. She's revising in her room with her boyfriend – at least, that's the official story. Dale ran in, grabbed a bag of crisps and went out skating with some friend.'

'That'll be Olivia. The girlfriend that isn't a girlfriend.' Tamara sat down. 'Thanks for babysitting. You didn't need to hang around once Marcie was back. She can keep an eye on her sister.'

'I didn't want to dash off without saying bye.' He pushed his dark curls out of his eyes and nodded to the mag he was reading. 'You've got some good stuff in this month.'

She smiled. 'Thanks, boss.'

'I mean it. Saffie, that feature writer – she's pretty good, isn't she?'

'I know. I wish we could hang on to her forever, but...'

'But?'

Tamara shrugged. 'Saffie's got career ambitions, same as we all had when we were rookie journos, and I know she never meant to get stuck at *The Throstler* for ten years. Let's face it, it's a dead-end job for her.'

'How did she get stuck there?'

'She was an old friend of Milo's from school. When she finished her NCTJ Diploma, he asked if we'd consider creating an internship for her. Just for six months, while she built up some bylines to add to her portfolio. She's been with us ever since.'

'It's not necessarily a dead-end job now, is it? Not now *The Throstler*'s part of a bigger enterprise.'

'Huh.' Tamara glanced at the mag. 'Did Nikki tell you she came to see us?'

'She mentioned it.' He smiled. 'She said you looked like you'd all been out on the razz all night. Wanted to know if that was par for the course in my family.'

Tamara smiled too. 'Listen, I had no part in that. Saffie and Milo had been to a traumatic speed dating night.'

'Was Nik OK with you? I know she can be brisk when it comes to business matters.'

'She was a bit overbearing,' Tamara admitted. 'I don't think Saffie took to her much. Or vice versa.'

'Well, it's all new to us still. We'll soon be well-oiled cogs in the same machine, I'm sure.' Russell nodded to her new hair. 'Looking good, by the way. What did you say the occasion was?'

She flushed. 'Oh. I've got a date coming up. That's top secret, OK? Don't tell Fran.'

'Wouldn't dream of it.' He stood up. 'I'd better get home. I'm glad you're dating again, Tam. It was long overdue.'

Tamara forced a smile.

She tried not to be jealous of her cousin. It was daft, really. They were grown adults. She was the elder by seven years and should have grown out of comparing herself to Russell long ago. But it was difficult, when he was so bloody perfect. Dating would be no struggle for Russ if he decided to sign up to an app. He'd be deluged with applicants for his company within minutes, because the lucky star he'd been born under had felt it was only right he be blessed with looks and charm as well as brains. Of course he hadn't meant anything untoward when he'd said Tamara's return to dating was long overdue. He hadn't been implying she was getting old and running out of time. But that's what she heard, all the same.

When Russell was gone, she called up the stairs for Marcie. Tamara heard the distinct sucking sound of her daughter's lips detaching from Ashley's, and a moment later she appeared.

'Hi Mum,' she said. 'I asked Ashley over. We're just revising for English on Thursday.'

'Right,' Tamara said, smiling.

Ashley poked his head out from Marcie's room, his cheeks flushed from whatever they'd just been up to. 'Hey, Ms Horan.'

'Just Tamara's fine, Ashley,' she told the lad for the umpteenth time, and he grinned nervously.

'You look, um, nice,' he said. 'I like your hair.'

'Oh.' She patted her freshly dyed curls. 'Thank you.'

There was a pause. Ashley rubbed his cheek, his store of girlfriend's mum small talk all used up. 'Er, Marce, I'll just…

wait for you in here. See you, Ms Horan.' He scampered back into the safety of Marcie's room.

Marcie examined her mum. 'He's right, you do look nice. Why the new look, Mum? I thought you were just getting a trim.'

'I asked the hairdresser to cover up the grey, and then I thought I might as well have a fresh style while I was at it. Does it look OK?'

'Yeah, you look younger.' Marcie narrowed one eye. 'You haven't got a date, have you? I thought you were meeting Uncle Milo for coffee this afternoon.'

Tamara flushed. 'I haven't got a date. Not exactly.'

Marcie continued to stare, and Tamara beckoned her down.

'Ash, I'll be back in a minute!' Marcie called before joining her mum at the foot of the stairs.

'All right, don't tell the others but yes, there is a date,' Tamara said in a low voice, guiding her daughter to the conservatory. 'Not today, but soon. Milo convinced me to sign up for this agency.'

Marcie snorted. 'A dating agency, seriously? I know you're from the Sixties or whatever, but you've got a phone. Why don't you just get on Tinder like normal people?'

'God, I don't want to start dating again,' Tamara said, pulling a face. 'It was a pain in the arse the last time, and then I ended up married to your father and we all know how that turned out. I just feel like I could do with... I don't know. The chance to feel attractive again. Flirt a bit, have some fun. My confidence took a real knock that night I bumped into your dad.'

'Typical,' Marcie muttered. 'Now I've got two parents having simultaneous midlife crises.'

Tamara looked into her face. 'You returned his call then?'

'Yeah,' Marcie said, colouring. 'An hour ago.'

'How was it?' Tamara examined her daughter's eyes. It looked like there might have been some tears.

'It was… painful,' Marcie murmured. 'It made me remember a lot of things I'd forgotten. Stuff I didn't really want to remember, but when I did, I was sort of… not glad, but it felt like I needed to remember.' Marcie's voice started to tremble. 'Then Dad was crying, so I started crying, and he… he said he loved me.'

'Oh, my love.' Tamara pulled her into a hug. 'I ought to have been here with you. I thought you were going to wait for me.'

'It's OK. I thought about it and it felt like I needed to do it by myself.' Marcie smiled tremulously. 'I thought I might be upset though, so I asked Ash if I could do it at his so he'd be there to give me a hug afterwards. He was great, Mum. Really supportive.'

Tamara felt a pang she tried to suppress. Of course Marcie would think of Ashley when she needed emotional support. She was eighteen and in love. The days when her mum was her first port of call for a hand to hold through the darker parts of life were long gone. Still, it couldn't help but hurt as Tamara was reminded once again that her daughter was moving away from her and towards independent adulthood.

'Did your dad ask you to forgive him?' Tamara asked softly.

'No. He didn't ask me for anything. I was glad of that. That he didn't make it all about him, or ask me to say things only to make him feel better. He just wanted to know about me. About Ashley and exams and… life.' Marcie held back from the hug to look into her mum's face. 'It was true, you know. When he said he was working in Vienna, he really was. I always thought he made it up.'

True or not, that was a pretty shit excuse for barely speaking to your kids in four years. They had phones in Vienna, didn't they? Tamara almost said so, but she bit her tongue. Marcie was old enough to make her own decisions about her relationship with her father. As her mum, Tamara needed to be supportive without letting her own feelings about Andy get in the way.

'What will you do now?' she asked.

'He wants to see me,' Marcie said in a low voice. 'Meet up somewhere, and introduce me to Natalie.'

'Did you agree?'

'I said I'd meet him, but I'm not ready to meet Natalie. Not yet.' She curled her lip. 'I can't believe he's marrying someone so much younger. I can't believe she's having his baby! Makes me want to vom. Why do you think he's with her, Mum?'

Because he's a shallow, selfish bastard who can't think beyond the death-throe twitchings of his pathetic middle-aged penis…

'I suppose because he fell in love with her,' Tamara said, keeping her face fixed.

'I bet she's a gold-digger,' Marcie said, anger creeping into her tone. 'She'd have to be to want to have a baby with someone as ancient as Dad. He's rich, right?'

'Well, he's… comfortable, I suppose. But I'm sure that's not it.'

That definitely was it.

'Anyway, I'm sure you'll like her,' Tamara said. 'Even I couldn't help liking her.' She gave her daughter a last squeeze. 'Well done, sweetie. I'm very proud of you. And if you need me to come with you when you see him—'

'Nah, that's OK. I asked Ashley to come.'

'Oh. Good.' Tamara tried not to feel deflated. 'Your brother's mind is still made up, I suppose?'

'Yeah. Dale says he can't forgive Dad in ten million years, no matter what he says. That's how I felt too at first, but…' Marcie trailed off. 'It's all right, isn't it, Mum? I mean, I do miss him, kind of. Or, not him personally but having a dad, and all the stuff we used to do together. I thought he was the coolest person till he walked out on us and you told me what he wanted to do about Will. I mean, him wanting you to get an abortion.'

Tamara flinched. 'I never should've told you that. I was depressed and in pain… but that was no excuse. It was between me and your father, and you were too young to understand. I've let myself forget that too many times.'

'No. I'm glad I know,' Marcie said in the firm, quiet way that made her sound older than her eighteen years. 'I can't ever see him the way I used to, but… I do want to give him a chance to be in my life again. I feel like I need to, for me as much as him. Closure or whatever.'

'Just be careful, sweetheart. I don't want you to get hurt again.'

'Are you hurt, Mum?' Marcie asked, making eye contact.

She blinked. 'Me?'

'Yeah. That I want to see him. I guess you think I ought

to hate him. And I do – I did. But it feels… kind of more complicated than that.'

Tamara grimaced. 'Honestly? I am a little hurt. Not that you want to see him; that's perfectly natural. I suppose that he's back in my life, and he's got a claim on my kids I can't help feeling uncomfortable about. I know that in your mind, he's your dad first and foremost.' She was quiet for a moment. 'But to me, he's someone I once fell deeply in love with. Someone I believed I'd be sharing the rest of my life with. When your dad left me, it felt like a betrayal of so many feelings – so many promises. And now he's getting ready to share his life with someone else, someone young and beautiful, as if he's getting an upgrade on a clapped-out old car…' She sighed. 'But I shouldn't be talking about this to you. As usual.'

'It's OK, Mum. I'm not a little kid any more: you don't have to feel guilty about telling me this stuff. I get it.'

'I'm sure you do, Marce, but that side of things is between me and your dad. I don't want to poison your relationship with him any more than it has been already.' She kissed the top of her daughter's hair. 'Go on, go back to Ashley. I'm just going to check in on Will, then I'm off to meet Milo and Saffie to sign up for this agency.'

Marcie blinked. 'What, are all three of you doing it?'

'Yes. It's our work summer outing.'

She headed upstairs and peeped around the door of Willow's room. The little girl was awake now, sitting on the floor fitting red and white Lego blocks together.

'Hello, my love.' Tamara went in to give her a kiss. 'Did you have a nice time at the park with Uncle Russell?'

'Yes. We had McFlurries, Malteser ones, and he let me go on the big kid slide.'

'Are you building your fire station again?'

Willow nodded. 'I'm making it different this time. I'm going to put the bridge on the roof.'

'That's a good idea.' Tamara glanced at the *Frozen* Lego kit Andy had bought her, still in its shrink-wrap. 'Why don't you make something new though? You've still got Elsa's palace to build.'

'No thank you,' Willow said in a faraway little voice. 'I want to make my fire station now.'

Willow had refused to touch the Lego kit since Tamara had had a little talk with her about who the man they'd seen in the shop really was. There'd been tears when Willow had discovered the truth, and further denials of any relationship between her and her dad. Then when she'd calmed down, she'd become oddly quiet – and remained that way for the past couple of weeks. Tamara suspected Willow was being troubled by thoughts and emotions too deep for her five-year-old brain to process.

God, why did Andy have to come back into their lives? Marcie was sobbing in her boyfriend's arms when she was supposed to be revising for A-level English, Dale was repressing his emotions about Andy entirely, and Willow was in denial about the fact she even had a dad. And Tamara had no idea how to help them all through it.

She bent over Willow and kissed her hair. 'Let's have a fun day tomorrow, shall we? Just us two,' she said softly. 'We can go to the big park where the ducks are, and to the swimming pool with the waterslide, then we'll get a sundae at the ice cream place. All the toppings you want.'

'OK.' Willow's focus was still on her Lego.

Tamara smiled. 'I thought you might be a bit more excited at the thought of sprinkles.'

Willow looked up. 'Sprinkles?'

'That's what I said.'

'And a flake?'

'And strawberry sauce. Anything you want, Will.'

Willow grinned and threw her arms around Tamara's neck, because at five there were few matters so weighty that the promise of an ice cream sundae with sprinkles couldn't break through. Tamara held her daughter's little body tight against her.

'I'm going back out for a little while, OK?' she said. 'If I'm not home in time for tea, ask your sister to heat it up for you. Ashley's here, so be sure to knock before going into Marcie's room.'

Willow stuck her tongue out. 'Are they kissing?'

'I'm afraid they might be,' Tamara said, smiling. 'I won't be too long, all right?'

'OK.' Willow's attention drifted back to her fire station, and now the excitement of the promised sundae had worn off, her face resumed its preoccupied look. Tamara cast a last worried look back at her as she left the room.

Saffie had arrived early at the address Dr Alison Sheldrake had emailed. She, Milo and Tamara had arranged it so they all had their appointments that afternoon, and she'd discovered a convenient cafe on the same road where they could hole up until it was their turn.

She peeped through the cafe's blinds to get another look at the place.

The 24-hour Dating Agency was situated in a typical Braybrook crumbling terraced house. It looked like it had been a shop in a former life, with a big glass window for displaying whatever wares had been on offer, but the glass was whitewashed over now and there was no sign to mark the place out as a dating agency. It looked like it was being refurbished; either that or Dr Sheldrake felt that extreme minimalism was likely to appeal to her clients.

If she had any. Saffie had been here nearly an hour and she hadn't seen anyone go either in or out. What if there weren't any matches for her? She was paying £500 for this, plus the £50 deposit.

Saffie glanced at her notes, familiarising herself with the cover story she'd cooked up. It was exciting really: a bit like being a secret agent. And since she was only likely to be doing this once, Saffie had gone to town on making herself sound both interesting and glamorous.

She was now Philomena Lightfoot, professional adventuress – well, all right, not adventuress, but she felt archaeologist was pretty close. Some real Lara Croft vibes.

She did feel guilty about pulling the wool over Dr Sheldrake's eyes, but it was bound to be against some sort of ethics code for psychotherapists to set someone up on a date for purely research purposes. Not very fair on her match. Still, it was only twenty-four hours; the bloke was hardly going to fall for her. He'd get a nice day out and his money back, and besides, he probably wouldn't even like her. Whatever algorithm the agency used to work out soulmate potential would be skewed by the fact she'd concocted an entirely fake life for herself. And Dr Sheldrake would be happy enough, Saffie was sure, when the feature sold and she got all that lovely free publicity. No, Saffie's conscience was clear.

True, there was a nagging voice in her head that sounded like Milo, asking 'but what if you like the guy?' Saffie ignored it. She'd been dating for years and managed to like very few guys, and that was when she was really trying. The odds of her liking this one were about a million to one. The only occasions when million-to-one shots worked out were in *The Throstler*'s 'Stranger Than Fiction' section, and Saffie was pretty sceptical about most of those.

She waved as Milo and Tamara came in.

'I found Tam lurking in the car park, wondering if it was too late to back out,' Milo told Saffie.

'I wasn't trying to back out. I was just battling some last-minute nerves.' Tamara took a seat and glanced at Saffie's notebook. 'Who's Philomena Lightfoot?'

'I am,' Saffie said, flushing. Now other people were here to scrutinise it, the oh-so-glamorous name sounded a bit daft. 'It's my cover story.'

The waitress approached, and Milo and Tamara ordered a coffee each.

'Just give them your real name,' Milo said to Saffie when they were alone again. 'This Dr Sheldrake's not going to google you, is she?'

'I fancy being Philomena though,' Saffie said. 'I can't be a femme fatale while I'm boring old Saffie Ackroyd. I need sex appeal.'

'Philomena Lightfoot,' Tamara said thoughtfully. 'Sounds like a treatment for ovine foot rot.'

'No, Philomena Lightfoot is a purple gel you put on verrucas,' Milo told her. 'Seen it in Boots.'

'Fine.' Saffie scribbled it out and wrote down a new name. 'There. I'll use my middle name and my mum's maiden name. Nice, plain Michelle Williams.'

'Michelle Williams?' Milo said.

'Yep. You happy with that?'

'Yeah, fab. Loved your work in Destiny's Child.'

'I thought Michelle Williams was the blonde one in *Dawson's Creek*,' Tamara said.

'That was the other Michelle Williams. Heath Ledger's missus.'

'Ugh, there's Michelle Williamses all over the bloody shop.' Saffie scrubbed that secret identity out as well. 'You two pick me a name then.'

'All right,' Milo said. 'Saffie Ackroyd. That's a good name.'

'I can't be her, she's boring as flip. Pick me an interesting name.'

'Use that formula for finding your porn star name,' Tamara said. 'Name of your first pet plus the first street you lived on.'

'I thought it was name of your granny and the last thing you ate,' Milo said.

'That's for your drag queen name. I guess either could work though.'

'OK, that gives me… either Bonnie St James or Clara Granola,' Saffie said. 'Which sounds more femme fatale?'

'The first one, definitely.'

'Right.' Saffie wrote it down. 'Bonnie St James, archaeologist, at your service.'

Milo frowned. 'Archaeologist? What the hell do you know about archaeology?'

'Enough to make polite conversation. I did a recce on Wikipedia last night.'

'I can't help feeling you're making this unnecessarily complicated, Saf. Why do you need to be a femme fatale anyway? Just be yourself.'

'Look, Mile, it's my mission. I know what I'm doing, OK?'

'All right, Mr Bond.' Milo turned to his sister. 'Your hair looks good, Tam. When did you have that done?'

'This morning. I thought we'd probably have to have our photos taken. I didn't want to look like the Bride of Frankenstein for whoever I'm matched with.'

'It takes years off you,' Saffie said with an approving nod.

'Thanks,' Tamara said, smiling. 'Even my elder daughter doesn't hate it so it can't be too bad. How do you think this agency works then? Do they just make notes on our hobbies, family, career et cetera then feed us through some sort of matchmaking machine?'

'I guess it's something like that.'

Milo glanced at his watch. 'Well, I'm about to find out. My appointment's in five minutes. Wish me luck.'

The two women held up their crossed fingers to him as he went to meet his fate.

11

It was around an hour later when Milo returned.

'Well?' Saffie said, trying – unsuccessfully – to keep the breathless urgency out of her voice. 'What happened?'

He drew a zip across his lips. 'I'm sworn to secrecy.'

'Milo, come on,' Tamara said.

'Honestly, I can't.' He took a seat. 'I had to sign a document stating I wouldn't share their methods with non-clients. Obviously once you two are officially clients, we can have a good jaw about it.'

'Don't be daft. We're practically clients, aren't we?'

'Tam, I can't. I *signed* something.'

Saffie shook her head. 'You are such a swot.'

'A legal document's a legal document, isn't it?' Milo said. 'When your mum's a lawyer, you grow up thinking a formal signature might as well be written in your own blood.'

'He's right, unfortunately,' Tamara told Saffie. 'I think we've both got a mental block about it.'

'You mean I have to go in blind?' Saffie said. 'I was relying on you to brief me, Milo.'

'Oh, relax. It's nothing scary.' He slapped her on the back. 'Anyway, all will shortly be revealed. It's your turn. Off you go, Ms St James.'

'Eh?'

'You're Bonnie St James now, aren't you? Archaeologist adventurer?'

'Oh. Right.' She stood up. 'All right, here I go. See you on the other side.'

Saffie headed to the whited-out shop that was apparently home to The 24-hour Dating Agency. Inside was a long hallway, the plaster walls unpainted and unadorned, with one door on her left and another at the end. The end door had a Post-It stuck to it with 'Dr Alison Sheldrake' scribbled on in biro.

She knocked, and was summoned with a brisk 'come in!'

The room Saffie entered was as bare as the hallway. It contained just a handful of things: two swivel chairs, a large cardboard box with a laptop on it, a second, smaller cardboard box full of untidy papers and files, and Dr Sheldrake.

The date doctor didn't look at all like her photo on the flyer. There was no lab coat, no half-moon specs. Dr Sheldrake was dressed in jogging bottoms, trainers and a hoodie, her hair piled up in a messy bun. She looked young for a psychotherapist – certainly no older than Saffie herself. She smiled in a businesslike way and gestured to the spare swivel chair on the other side of her cardboard-box desk.

Saffie took a seat, wondering for the first time if this whole thing was actually legit. Anyone could get some leaflets printed and stick them on the bar of a pub, couldn't they? The agency was in a rundown shop with no signage; unpainted inside; barely any furniture. The so-called doctor whose venture this was looked like she'd just got back from the gym. And Saffie, Tamara and Milo had each parted with £550 to become clients of this supposed business...

God, that'd be the most obvious con in the book, wouldn't it? The lonely, the desperate, the romantically inept: they were easy prey for unscrupulous bastards. Nearly everyone wanted to meet The One, and the longer people stayed single, the keener they were to try anything that promised to make the elusive happily-ever-after happen for them. Just look at Milo.

Saffie regarded Dr Sheldrake with a new wariness.

'Good afternoon,' the doctor said. 'It's Philomena, isn't it?'

Saffie cursed silently. She'd forgotten she'd set up a burner email under that name. That meant she was stuck with it.

'Er, yes. Well, it's just Phil to my friends.' Her imaginary friends, of which she'd always had many.

She waited, expecting Dr Sheldrake to offer similar first-name terms, but no. Apparently she was very proud of her almost certainly fake doctorate and had no intention of letting anyone forget about it.

'I don't have a surname on file,' Dr Sheldrake said. 'You didn't give one when you contacted me. What is it?'

Shit. What had she gone for again? She'd tossed so many about with Milo and Tamara, she couldn't remember.

'Er... St James,' Saffie said. 'Philomena St James.'

God, that was so much worse than whatever she'd had before! That was a Pony Club name for tittering debutantes with more pashminas than chromosomes. Great, now she was probably going to be matched with some braying wanker called Guy whose dad owned an investment bank.

Was St James even pronounced St James as a surname?

Maybe it was like St John and the correct pronunciation was actually Sinjim or something. Dr Sheldrake was probably silently guffawing at her ignorance.

'So... how do we do this?' asked the artist formerly known as Saffie Ackroyd: now the Right Honourable Lady Philomena St James-pronounced-Sinjim. 'Do you need to take my photo?'

'That won't be necessary,' Dr Sheldrake said. 'Names, photos, jobs: we don't work with that kind of information. We like our couples to meet each other without any of the unfair prejudices that can be conjured from arbitrary factors such as appearance or career choice.'

Saffie frowned. 'But my job as a... an archaeologist is a big part of who I am. Seems odd not to talk about it with my date.'

'Oh, you can talk about it. We just feel it's better if your sharing is done on the date itself, rather than in impersonal fashion beforehand.' She smiled tightly. 'The last thing we want is for you to meet your match with your mind already made up.'

'And that would be the royal we, right? I mean, it's just you, this place, isn't it?'

Dr Sheldrake raised an eyebrow. 'Do I detect a hint of hostility, Ms St James?'

Saffie flushed. 'No. Just... I suppose a little cynicism about your methods.'

'Oh, well, if that's how you feel.' Dr Sheldrake stood up and presented her hand. 'Thanks for coming in. Of course you'll be given a full refund, less your deposit, and no hard feelings.'

'Hey! Wait,' Saffie said, feeling panicked. She needed to

write this feature! Assuming this place was, in fact, legit, it was the best lead she'd had in ages. 'I never said I didn't believe it worked, did I?'

'I'm sorry, but I'm afraid we – yes, the royal we – can't work with clients who aren't one hundred per cent committed to our way of doing things,' Dr Sheldrake said, maintaining her stance. 'I'm very picky about who I agree to take on as a client, Ms St James. The people I help have to be completely invested in the match I make for them or the whole principle behind a twenty-four-hour date is compromised.'

Fine words for someone with a box for a desk…

'I am committed, honestly,' Saffie said. 'I'm just intrigued as to how it works. It's unique, you have to admit that. Yes, that was what drew me to you – God knows I've tried everything else – but I would like some more details. I don't think that's unreasonable.'

Slightly mollified, Dr Sheldrake took her seat again. 'I suppose that's fair.'

'So if you don't pass on my date's name or photo, what do I get to know about him? Anything?'

'You'll be asked to fill in a questionnaire about yourself, which will end with a section for a 200-word personal statement. The questions are for our benefit in the first instance, to help us find your match: they will be shared with your date, but not until the day itself. But the personal statement is written directly from you to him and sent in advance. You can say whatever you like, and we encourage you to write from the heart – the only rule is there's to be no mention of names, appearance, job or anything else of that nature.'

'To avoid prejudicing each other, right?'

'Exactly. The questionnaire is designed to strip off the protective outer layers and get right to the heart of a person. Capture their essence, if you like. Your match will be selected on the basis of that.'

That sounded a bit... witchy. Saffie wasn't sure she was any too keen on having her essence captured, whatever that meant. It reminded her of the old superstition about getting caught between two mirrors.

'What questions will I have to answer?' she asked.

'You'll find out,' Dr Sheldrake said.

'So that's the mysterious "method" your leaflet was talking about? A questionnaire?'

'There's a little more to it than that. The questionnaire is common to all, but the method of matching and the dates themselves are bespoke to each individual. Just let me know when you're ready and I'll send you to the other room to fill it out. And mind, once you've done so there can be no going back.'

'Right.' That sounded ominous. Saffie tried to ignore the unsettled churning of her stomach. 'Well, now's as good a time as any. I'm not getting any less single here.'

'Just go out of here and take the door on the right. You'll find the questionnaire and a pen on the table in there.'

'Thanks.' Saffie stood to go, then paused. 'You really believe this works, do you?'

'I know it does.'

'So you've had a lot of successes?'

Dr Sheldrake smiled. 'Let's just say I don't offer a soulmate guarantee lightly. I'm not a fan of returning money, Ms St James.'

'And this essence-capturing questionnaire: you just feed it through some sort of algorithm and it finds my perfect match, right?'

Dr Sheldrake shook her head. 'All matches are done by hand. There's really no substitute for the human touch. If we already have a suitable match on file then I'll email you within twelve hours with your partner's personal statement. If not, I'll let you know you've been filed and added to our waiting list.'

Saffie discovered that the second room was as bare as the rest of the place, containing just a single chair and a table with a biro, a few sheets of A4 and a dead bluebottle on it. There was a meaty man in a suit standing by the window, his hands clasped behind his back. Who was he, Saffie wondered: some sort of exam invigilator? Security guard, protecting the precious questionnaire so she couldn't leak any of these mysterious 'methods'?

Saffie nodded a greeting, but the man continued to stare straight ahead. She wondered if he was forbidden to move, like a Tower of London beefeater.

Saffie took a seat at the table. She brushed off the dead bluebottle, turned over the paper and skimmed through the questionnaire, expecting to find questions about her hobbies, preferences in men; that sort of thing.

But there was nothing like that. Honestly, the thing had to be a gimmick. It read like one of those tests for establishing whether or not you were a psychopath. Questions included the following:

You come home to discover your house is on fire. There is only time to save one item. What do you choose?
Tell me about the time you laughed the loudest you ever have in your life.
Is there a song that makes you cry?
Favourite pudding and why?
What's the one skill you never learned but wish you had?
Tell me a joke.
If you had a boat, what would you name it?
What is your greatest regret?

And a dozen more, all equally irrelevant and offbeat. Finally there was a space for Saffie to write the personal statement that would go direct to her match, and last of all, the small print disclaimer Milo had mentioned. Saffie swore under her breath. She'd been hoping it would be multiple choice so she could get it over with quickly.

OK. Question one: what would she save in a fire? Well, she was assuming 'item' meant something inanimate; presumably her cat Nigel was already safe in this scenario. So the answer was…

Nothing. There was nothing not alive that she'd run into a burning building for. Yes, she had things with sentimental value – her grandfather's watch; all her family photos that she'd been meaning to scan for years. She even had a few things that were valuable, like her collection of rare pulp fiction novels. But they were just things. The photos were the most valuable because they contained a lot of memories, but she wasn't going to risk her life for them.

Could she put that? It probably made her sound selfish,

choosing her own worthless life over precious memories. Maybe she should say she'd save the photos. But then Dr Sheldrake might know she was lying. She seemed a bit keen to oust clients she didn't think were giving it their all. Saffie scribbled down her answer: *nothing, if I've got myself*.

Next up was the question about the time she'd laughed loudest. Ah, now that one went with an embarrassing story that Milo wasn't going to thank her for telling...

Three questions later, Saffie looked at her watch. It had taken her quarter of an hour just to answer those few, and she had fifteen to go yet, plus the personal statement.

She glanced at the invigilator, but he might as well be stone for all the moving he'd done. Saffie would swear he'd never even blinked.

She needed to stop overthinking every question and get it done. It was obviously a gimmick anyway: no doubt the questionnaire would remain unread and Dr Sheldrake would match her to the first heterosexual bloke of a suitable age whose name she pulled out of a hat. There was no way this could actually work.

There was definitely no way this could work. Was there?

I2

By the time both Saffie and Tamara had finished their sessions, it was well past teatime. The cafe had long closed and Milo and Saffie had repaired to a nearby pub to wait for Tamara, where they were currently sharing a basket of chips.

'Help yourself,' Milo said when his sister joined them.

'Thanks.' Tamara took a chip. 'God, that took ages.'

'Well? How was your sesh?' Saffie asked.

'Hang on. Let me go to the bar before we start comparing notes.'

When Tamara had got herself a drink, she sat down at their table.

'So. Definitely not what I was expecting,' she said. 'What did you two put for that "item you'd save from a burning building" question?'

'My diary,' Milo said. 'I had this image of a bunch of hunky firemen finding it and tittering over the rude parts while I'm groaning on a stretcher.'

Saffie raised an eyebrow. 'What, you keep a diary?'

'What's so surprising about that? Sign of greatness, keeping a diary. They'll probably publish it in years to come.'

'What's in this diary then? What was yesterday's entry?'

'Er… Aunty Carol's birthday.' He turned to Tamara. 'What about you, Tam? What did you put?'

'The kids' baby boxes where I saved all their milestone stuff. First tooth, lock of hair and all that. I know that's technically three things.' She smiled. 'I know, classic boring mum answer.'

'What about you, Saf?' Milo asked.

'Oh. Nothing.'

'Go on, you can tell us.'

'No, I mean literally nothing: that's what I put,' Saffie said. 'Assuming Nigel was all right, there was nothing inanimate I wanted to risk my life to save.'

'Oh.' Milo blinked. 'That's kind of sad.'

'I guess it is.' She shrugged. 'And now I'll get an equally sad match. Good thing I'm not in it for real. Hey, what did you put for the song that makes you cry, Tam?'

She laughed. 'Peter Andre. "Mysterious Girl".'

'I think that makes most people cry,' Milo said. 'Why that?'

'It was playing on hospital radio while I was giving birth to the twins. Obviously I've got some traumatic memories associated with it.' She shook her head. 'I don't think I answered a single question without referencing my kids. I so need a life beyond mumming.'

'That's why you're here, isn't it?' Milo said. 'What did you put, Saf?'

'"When She Loved Me" from *Toy Story 2*. I can't hear it without thinking about poor Jessie the doll stuck under the bed for a decade. You?'

'"It's Raining Men".' He swallowed the last of his pint. 'That's depressed me for years. Foul lies.'

'I wonder how long it'll be till we get our matches,' Tamara said.

'I got my mine already,' Milo told her. 'The email popped up on my phone an hour ago. We were waiting until you got here to read it.'

'Bloody hell, that was quick.' She nodded to his phone. 'Go on, open it.'

He did so, frowning as he read through the personal statement from his match.

'Read it out then,' Saffie said. 'Does he sound like a good one?'

'He sounds… you'd better hear it for yourself,' Milo said, and read it aloud.

OK, not really sure what to write here. Genuine guy looking for a genuine guy, I guess? Sort of feels like that's not for me to say, but I suppose it's OK to blow your own trumpet in these things. Like to have a laugh, animal lover, movie fan but not in a hardcore goes-to-conventions-in-cosplay sort of a way; more in a slobbing-with-a-beer-at-home sort of a way. I like the Great Outdoors in palatable doses, oh, and the sea. And Aeros; big, big fan of Aeros, especially the minty ones. So if you love the sea and minty Aeros… God, this is a nightmare. Did I write enough words yet? This is why my mum used to describe me as 'not test-motivated' (see also, my exam results). Anyway, can't wait to meet you if you still want to after reading this. See you soon, maybe, whoever you are. Bye.

'Wow,' Saffie said, blinking. 'Well, he does sound genuine.'

'And you do like Aeros,' Tamara said.

'Everyone likes Aeros, Tam.' Milo frowned at the email. 'I can't decide if he sounds awesome or a bit mad.'

Saffie shrugged. 'He was on the spot, wasn't he? Mine wasn't much better. It read like a job application.'

'And he likes animals and films,' Tamara said. 'That puts him head and shoulders above West. You like that stuff too, Mile.'

'Well yeah, but there's a difference between liking Labradors and Marvel and liking pythons and David Lynch,' Milo said. 'West liked films, as long as they had subtitles and were at least three hours long.' He glanced again at the email. 'Alison's suggesting the weekend after next for our date.'

'Did Dr Sheldrake say you could call her Alison?' Saffie asked.

'Yeah. Didn't she say that to you?'

'Er, no.'

Tamara's phone lit up with an incoming email. 'Oh! My match just came through too.'

Saffie glanced at her own phone, which remained dark and silent. 'How come you got yours before me? You only just finished your questionnaire.'

'Perhaps my essence was easier to match than your essence.'

'Thanks very much.' She nodded to Tamara's phone. 'Open it then.'

Tamara did so. Like Milo, her brow had soon knit into a frown.

'What?' Milo said. 'Does yours read like he's writing it while having a panic attack as well?'

'No. It reads… well, listen.'

Hey there, lady trivia hounds! I've got a bucket list to tick off, and top of the list is going on *Pointless*. There's the option of a celebratory snog if we win, but only if it's with me and not Alexander Armstrong. If it works out, I think me and you could go all the way (i.e., *Eggheads*). If you think you've got what it takes to be my perfect *Pointless* teammate, then I can't wait to meet you. There will be a test though, because I do expect to take home that trophy. Just FYI.

Saffie frowned. 'Is he joking?'

'No idea,' Tamara said. 'Do you think he is?'

'Well if he is, that's a pretty bold statement,' Milo said. 'He must be a funny guy.'

'And if he isn't…'

'Then he's completely socially dysfunctional,' Saffie said. 'And it sounds like you're going on *Pointless*.'

'Oh God.' Tamara dropped her chin on to her fist. 'It's the second one, isn't it? He's going to test me for trivia ability and chop me up if I'm found wanting.'

'I think it's a joke.' Milo paused. 'It's almost certainly a joke.'

'It's my own fault,' Tamara said gloomily. 'Why the hell did I make that questionnaire all about my kids? All I wanted was a moderately sexy man who could show me a good time. Now I've managed to make myself so unappealing and charisma-less that I've been allocated someone from the dregs of the oddball pile.'

'I reckon you should give the man a chance,' Milo said. 'He's probably just got a deadpan sense of humour. Also, there's a money-back guarantee, don't forget. Complete refund if you don't meet your soulmate.'

'What happens next then?' Saffie asked. 'Does it say in your emails?'

'Yeah,' Milo said. 'I have to email back with my availability, then once Alison's confirmed the date with my match I'll be given a map reference and a time to turn up. We've each got to wear a yellow carnation in our buttonhole.'

'You've got to be kidding me.'

'Nope.' He glanced at the email again. 'All details of the date itself are top secret until I get there. We'll both be sent a set of sealed envelopes with the itinerary but we're forbidden from opening them until the day. Apparently we get half an itinerary each, written as cryptic clues.'

Saffie shook her head. 'It's like something from some old film.'

'Anything seems worth a shot at this point. Even yellow carnations.'

'It's a red rose for me,' Tamara said. 'I'm supposed to stick it in my hair.'

'I wonder what flower I'll have to wear.' Saffie looked again at her phone. 'And why haven't I got a match?'

1. *The Nojito*

Cool, crisp and crazy refreshing, this not-so-naughty-

but-definitely-nice summer ~~belter banger~~ *zinger is every bit as good as its alcoholic cousin. By swapping the rum for a shot of lime syrup, you can enjoy a summer classic with none of the guilt* ~~of a standard of a normal~~ *of a regular…*

Saffie gave up and closed her laptop, which had been resting against a dozing Nigel for the last half an hour. She was trying to write a commission piece for a food and drink website, but she wasn't feeling it. The title was 'Born-again Virgins: Ten Summer Classics with a Mocktail Twist'.

All it was doing was making her thirsty for something with all of the guilt and all of the rum. But it was a school night, and she, Milo and Tamara had been doing post-work drinks at the Duck too often recently. She shifted Nigel's floppy, unresponsive form to the sofa cushion and went to make a cup of tea instead.

This wasn't the sort of thing she wanted to be writing. Saffie didn't mind working for lifestyle sites – the money was piss-poor but it was still money, and any writing credit that wasn't for *The Throstler* had to help her career long-term. But these listicle pieces were just like homework assignments where the teacher had specified 'give an account in your own words' to stop you copying verbatim from the textbook. All Saffie was doing was recycling stuff from elsewhere, changing a few details and adding a bit of introductory fluff to create something new, because at the end of the day a mojito was always a mojito. Good writers borrowed, great writers stole, and hack writers borrowed, stole, padded, fudged and fluffed until someone was willing to pay out.

There was no meat to these sorts of features: just waffle and shoeshine. She was far prouder of the stuff she wrote for *The Throstle's Nest*, as offbeat as it was. There was something satisfying about conducting an interview and writing it up into an engaging feature, even if the interview was with the wife of an alien from Kepler-62.

While she was waiting for her tea to brew, Saffie took out her phone and checked her emails.

Nothing. Still. It was well over the twelve-hour period within which Alison Sheldrake had told her she could expect to receive details of her match. Had Saffie been banished from the agency for failing to conceal her snark? Did they not have a suitable match for her yet? Shouldn't she have been told one way or the other?

Saffie wondered whether to email, but decided to wait just a little longer. Dr Sheldrake hadn't liked her, she could sense it. Saffie was still anxious to write this feature and she didn't want to rock the boat by being a bother.

She carried her tea into the living room and snuggled up against Nigel. He flickered his eyelids at her before going back to sleep. Her elderly tom spent a limited amount of time awake, but in the cuddle department Saffie couldn't ask for a better companion.

She glanced again at her laptop, wondering whether to have another go at her mocktails feature, but decided against it. She'd do it tomorrow, when hopefully she'd be in a better frame of mind for writing fluff.

Now the feature on the dating agency: that was the sort of thing Saffie had always dreamed of writing. Going undercover, sniffing out her story, getting the 'straight dope', like a reporter in the golden age of newspapers. Even when she'd been a kid, that had been a world long gone. Now they were at the tail end of the print era it was even further away, but a girl could dream.

Saffie had had a lot of dreams once. She'd wanted to write for a living – that one, at least, had come true, although *The Throstler* wasn't what she'd pictured. She'd wanted to be an ace reporter, like Hildy Johnson in one of her favourite old films, *His Girl Friday*: straight-talking, strong and fierce in a man's world. And she'd wanted to meet someone she could share it with: a partner who was both soulmate and best friend. Now she was heading for thirty-six, and... well, she supposed one out of three wasn't bad. She had a writing job. She had a very cuddly cat. She had two brilliant best mates who she got to work with every day.

But there was one thing Saffie tried not to admit to anyone – not even herself. She was lonely. That was something it was OK for Milo to confess, but as a feminist, she couldn't help feeling she was letting the side down a bit. She should be happy without a man, shouldn't she? Content in and of herself. Still, when she was alone in bed with only the perpetually snoozing Nigel for company, she couldn't help thinking that it must be nice to fall in love.

Saffie jumped, disturbing the cat, when her phone buzzed.

This was it! Her email from the agency. Saffie almost knocked the phone to the floor as she fumbled to snatch it up.

It was the same format as the ones her friends had got: a list of potential dates, instructions about what would happen, and then what she was really looking for – the personal statement from her match. Saffie devoured it eagerly.

Can I just take a moment to apologise? I don't know what you did to piss off Alison Sheldrake, but greetings from the bottom of the dating slush pile. I've been single since my marriage ended two years ago. Tried the apps but I find that whole scene a bit stressful. At least this way, I can leave finding matches to someone who might actually know what they're doing.

So, about me. I like to learn things and I've usually got a new hobby on the go. At the moment I'm teaching myself crochet. Yes, seriously. Seriously! Come on, stop laughing. I've made a huge hat and a tiny scarf so far (scale is a skill that still eludes me). I have been known to make people laugh, though I couldn't say if they're laughing at me or with me. Always wanted to travel but never seem to find the time to go too far from my own doorstep.

And now, about you. I hope you're smart and you like to read and talk and laugh, and that you'll say kind things about my crochet efforts. I hope you might like to travel with me one day. I hope you're reading this and smiling at the adorable goofball rather than backing away from the rambling madman. I hope you're The One. I guess we'll find out, eh?

Saffie realised she actually was smiling and forced her lips straight. She was in this for the story, that was all. Just the facts, Jack.

This guy did sound nice though. Likeable, quirky, a bit charming. Saffie wondered what he was making of her statement. She only had a vague memory of what she'd scribbled down. Dedicated, enthusiastic, twenty years' previous dating experience… half dating profile, half job application.

She started typing a reply to Dr Sheldrake to confirm that yes, she was available the Saturday after next and would be waiting for her date with white roses in her hair.

13

The day of the dates came. Tamara was ironing in the conservatory when her son appeared.

She liked ironing. Running the hot metal over each crease, watching it disappear. All right, this probably wasn't how most people would prepare for a date – no doubt Milo and Saffie were tweezing, gelling and shaving madly as they got ready to meet their matches – but it was doing wonders for her blood pressure.

'Mum, I'm going to the skate park.' Dale frowned. 'What's up with you?'

'Oh, nothing.' Tamara wiped her eyes. 'It's just the steam.'

'Right. I'm going to Olivia's so don't make me any tea, 'K?'

'I'm going out, Dale. I told you three times. I won't be back till tomorrow.'

'Oh right, that. Who's looking after Will then?'

'Fran. She should be here any minute.' Tamara peered at him. 'All OK? You look tired.'

He rubbed his eyes. 'I'm all right.'

'Dale?'

'OK.' He thrust his hands into his pockets. 'I kind of… talked to Dad. Marce made me.'

Tamara blinked. 'You talked to your father?'

'Yeah, last night. Marce said if I didn't and Dad died or something then I'd regret it, even if I only told him I hate him.'

Tamara felt that familiar sensation of being punched in the stomach. So Andy had made another conquest, had he? As angry as Dale sounded, Tamara could tell he was starting to crack. And she had to pretend to be wise and unflappable, like mums were supposed to be, while inside her head she was screaming.

'So your sister convinced you to change your mind?'

'Kind of. And Olivia was telling me about her dad: how he'd gone off to have a baby with someone else when she was five, and now he's all about his new family and doesn't give a shit about her or her sister. It made me think that yeah, Dad's a prick, but he's not that level of prick, you know? Like, he still wants to know his old kids even though he's having a new one.'

And this was the low bar men had to live up to. You managed the occasional Christmas gift for the children you barely saw and you were dad of the fucking year apparently. Get that man a medal.

'What did you say when you spoke to him?' she asked.

'Well, I told him I hated him like Marcie said.' Dale scrunched up his face, trying to hide the emotion working there. 'After that I didn't say anything. Dad said a bunch of stuff, but I didn't say anything.'

'But you didn't hang up.'

'No. I just… listened.'

Tamara left her ironing and went to give him a squeeze. For once, he didn't cringe and wriggle away.

'Are you OK?' she asked quietly.

'No.' Dale made a choking noise. 'I do hate him. I'm sick of thinking about him and all the stupid things he said. I don't want to do this, Mum.'

'What can I do to help you?'

'Nothing.' He extricated himself from the arm around him. 'I'm a fucking adult, aren't I? It's up to me to sort my screwed-up life out.'

'Dale, you don't have to—'

'I don't want to talk about it, Mum, all right? I just...' A sob forced its way out. 'I just want the whole thing out of my head. Dad, all the... the feelings and stuff.'

'Feelings don't work that way, sweetie,' Tamara said softly.

'I'll make them. I will. Look, I've got to go.' With a goodbye grunt, he strode out.

Tamara was returning to her ironing, feeling about as helpless as she ever had, when Dale reappeared.

'Sorry, Mum,' he said in a softer voice. 'Here.'

He kissed the top of her head – an easy feat now he towered over her – before disappearing again. Tamara smiled as she folded Marcie's favourite plaid pinafore dress and started ironing one of Dale's sweatshirts.

A few minutes later, Fran appeared: well-groomed, vigorous and reassuringly matriarchal as ever.

'Dale told me I'd find you in here.' She shook her head. 'Housework before a date? And you're not even ready. Oh, Tamara.'

'What? I am ready.'

'Oh.' Fran scanned her outfit of skinny jeans and vest top. 'You're wearing that, are you? Well, I'm sure you know best.' She gestured to Tamara's face. 'Your mascara's running.'

'Shit, is it?' Tamara rubbed under her eyes.

'Why the tears?'

'It's the steam.'

'It isn't.' Fran's gaze fell on the pile of ironed clothes. 'The twins' things?'

Tamara shook her head. 'How do you always know stuff?'

'Call it grandmotherly intuition.'

Tamara held up Marcie's plaid dress and smiled at it sadly. 'She loves this. It's been too tight in the bust for ages, but she won't let me adjust it. Says she can't risk me ruining it.' She sniffed. 'It feels so strange, Fran. Thinking that in a few months, there won't be any more of their things in the ironing basket.'

'Mmm. Until the holidays, when they bring a whole term's worth of washing and ironing back for you.'

'You know what I mean. For the first time in eighteen years, I won't have all the children here with me.'

'It's a big life change for you,' Fran said softly.

'The house is going to feel so empty,' Tamara murmured. 'It seems a blink ago they were babes in arms. I suppose one day I'll drop off for a nap, and when I wake up Willow will be grown up and packing her bags.' She looked up at Fran. 'Did you feel this way when Dad and Aunty Carol moved out?'

'Are you kidding? Your grandad and I booked ourselves a cruise the day our lives became child-free again.' She rubbed Tamara's back. 'Still, we missed them. That's the circle of life though, isn't it? Don't think of it as losing your children so much as a stepping stone towards gaining some grandchildren.'

Tamara laughed. 'We must've been a terrible disappointment to you. I mean, apart from wonderful Russell, obviously.'

'Oh, wonderful Russell nothing,' Fran said. 'I'm proud of all three of you. That's why I entrusted the magazine to you, Tamara. You were a natural successor to me as editor, and I was thrilled we were able to keep it in the family.'

'You sold it to Russell though.'

'Because it was time for me to retire and Russell was in a position to buy it. That was under the strict proviso that you and Milo would remain in your roles and you would retain complete editorial control.'

'Mmm. I might have a word with you about that sometime.' Tamara glanced at her watch. 'But right now, I've got to rush. I'm sorry to ask you to babysit for so long, Fran. I know Will must be a handful at your age, but the twins both had plans, Russ has got something on and obviously Milo's on his own date. Marce'll be home at four from her Saturday job.'

'I'm not decrepit yet, Tamara. We're going to have a wonderful time.'

Tamara smiled. 'Yes, she's been looking forward to a game of Magazines with the family expert. I'll just say goodbye, then I'll get off.'

Willow was in her room, colouring. The little girl was still being unusually quiet. She'd show moments of brightness, but whenever she wasn't occupied she'd lapse into silence. Any attempts to get her to share what was wrong just resulted in a puzzled 'I don't know, Mummy'. Tamara knew that was true: Willow really didn't know what was wrong. She just knew that something in her life had become… unbalanced. More and more frequently, Tamara had woken to find a little body had crept into her bed in the night.

She was actually really worried. If it hadn't been for Marcie arguing the case for her date today, she would've cancelled.

'Hello sweetie,' she said to Willow. 'Fran's here now, come to look after you until Marcie and Dale get home. I'll be back as early as I can tomorrow, OK?'

Willow blinked at her. 'You're going away?'

Tamara crouched down. 'You know I am, Will. I'm going on a… to meet someone.'

'But not to sleep though.' Willow's eyes widened with fear. 'You never said to sleep!'

'Will, I did. We talked about it last night. Don't you remember?'

Tamara couldn't understand it. Yesterday Willow had seemed quite sanguine about a day without her parent, excited to play at Magazines with Fran. The little girl had been without her mum for the odd night before so it was hardly a novelty. And yet now, Willow looked scared stiff at the thought of her mother leaving her.

'Mummy, no!' she yelled. 'You can't go. You can't! I don't want to be on my own at bedtime. What if bad dreams come?'

Tamara sat Willow on her knee, rocking her and making soothing sounds. 'Marcie will be here, and Dale. They can chase the bad dreams away, can't they?'

'Not as good as you can,' Willow said in a voice that

was half whisper, half whimper. 'Mummy, you won't go, will you?'

'Well...' Tamara thought on her feet. This guy had probably already set off for Scarborough, which was where her email that morning had told her she was going, and it was too late now to let him know she wanted to call it off. She didn't have his contact details: she only had Alison Sheldrake's email address, and by the time the message had been relayed, he'd likely have arrived. What could she do? The guy didn't deserve to be stood up, even if he did turn out to be a socially dysfunctional weirdo.

'All right, how about you spend a lovely day with Fran playing Magazines and I'll be back to put you to bed?' she said to Willow. Tamara would just have to tell the guy that their twenty-four-hour date needed to be chopped down to a six-hour date. It was better than standing him up and she couldn't think of another way round it. She couldn't bear the thought of Willow's distress if she wasn't here for her at bedtime; not after the way she'd been lately.

Willow sniffed. 'I want you to play Magazines too though, Mummy. I don't want you to go see the man.'

The man... that was what she always called Andy. Was that it? Did she think...

'Will... you know I'm not going out today to see your dad, don't you?' Tamara said softly.

Willow's body stiffened. 'I haven't got a dad.'

'I'm not going to see the man we met in the shop. Is that what you're worried about? I'm going to see... someone else.'

'Who?'

'Someone nice. A friend.'

'What's his name?'

Tamara floundered. 'Er... Norbert.'

Willow sniffed. 'I don't believe you. That's a silly name for a real person. That means he must be a pretend person.'

'Will, honestly, it's the truth. If I can promise you one thing, it's that I want to see your da– the man at least as little as you do. Now does that satisfy you, or am I going to have to drive you to Scarborough so you can see for yourself?'

14

Saffie, meanwhile, was already in the car on the way to her date. Her email had instructed her to be outside the Corn Exchange in Leeds by 10.30 a.m., where she'd recognise her date from a white rose in his buttonhole. In her pocket were numbered gold envelopes containing clues that would guide her and her date to the places they'd be visiting today. It was all very Willy Wonka.

After wrestling with the distinct feeling that Dr Sheldrake was watching her, Saffie had peeped at the contents of envelope number one. The card inside made no sense to her though. All it said was this:

It's not all swings and roundabouts when Dr Jekyll's in the frame.

What the hell did that mean? She could never solve cryptic crossword clues: her brain just didn't seem to function that way. Hopefully her date would have more advanced riddle-solving skills.

Dr Sheldrake had said Saffie would be shown her date's questionnaire answers today too, but they hadn't been included in the email. Was there a photocopy in one of the envelopes, maybe? Did her date have her answers already? What would he make of her refusal to run into burning buildings, or the terrible dad-like joke she'd told (*Why can't dinosaurs clap their hands? Because they're dead*), or the fact that her favourite pudding was the very boring, very school-dinnery jam roly-poly?

Jam roly-poly was definitely one of the least erotic puddings: probably just ahead of spotted dick in the sexiness stakes. If her date were to judge her by pudding, he'd already have her marked down as stodgy, predictable and with a tendency to lie heavily on the stomach. She ought to have put sticky toffee or Death by Chocolate; something luscious and irresistible, the femme fatale of the dessert world.

Saffie slammed her foot on the brakes as the traffic lights up ahead changed from amber to red.

What was wrong with her this morning? Distracted, overthinking every little thing, physically shaking with nervous energy. It was only another date, and a fake one at that. Still, she couldn't help dwelling on the man she was going to meet. Her thoughts kept returning to the agency's soulmate guarantee, the one Milo set such store by. It all felt a bit… well, magical.

She really needed to hand the 'Stranger Than Fiction' research over to Tam for a bit. It was doing some funny things to her normally sensible, cynical brain.

There was another question that hadn't been answered too. This was a twenty-four-hour date. It started today at half past ten, and Saffie guessed it ended tomorrow at the same time. What happened overnight? Presumably they'd be provided with rooms at a hotel, but… one each? It would be creepy as hell if Sheldrake expected two virtual strangers to bunk up, whatever her theories on discovering soulmate potential through ultra-intensive dating.

She was here now, at the NCP nearest their meeting point. No backing out. Saffie parked, tucked her white rose behind her ear and got out of the car.

At the Corn Exchange, she scanned the shoppers for fellow white-rose-wearers. She couldn't see any men who—

'Hello?'

Saffie spun round to see who'd touched her shoulder. She seemed to be in fight or flight mode, and for a second she almost legged it out of sheer animal instinct.

'Sorry,' the man said with a warm smile. 'I didn't mean to make you jump. I thought I could see a stalk poking out of your hair, but I needed you to turn around to see if it had a white rose on the other end.'

Saffie pulled out the rose, feeling flustered. 'Are you, um…'

'From the agency?' He gestured to his buttonhole.

Saffie relaxed and let herself laugh. 'You crocheted your rose?'

'Yeah. Good, isn't it?' He detached it from his blazer and handed it to her. 'For you.'

She smiled as she pinned it to her Fifties rockabilly-style dress. 'Thank you.'

'Richard,' the man said.

'S– Phil.'

'That's not a girl's name I hear every day. Is it short for Phyllis?'

'No.' She flushed. 'It's short for… for Philomena. It's, um, an old family name.'

'Is it? My commiserations to your family.'

They stood in silence, taking each other in.

Richard was around six feet tall: a good height for kissing – not that Saffie was thinking about kissing. He was probably in his late thirties, with thick black curls and tawny-gold skin. Some crinkles around the dark brown eyes suggested he did a lot of laughing, and he had a dusting of stubble. What Saffie mainly noticed, though, was his smile, which was wide and warm and illuminated his whole face. Unsmiling, he was a decent-looking man of his age. Smiling, he was beautiful.

She hoped he wouldn't be doing too much smiling today. She had a job to do.

'Well?' she said as he examined her. 'Am I what you were expecting?'

'You're a bit more... blue than I'd imagined,' he said. 'Blue's good though. Everyone likes blue. How about me?'

'I don't think I'd formed a picture of you. All I could see were two legs sticking out from under a pile of yarn.'

He laughed. 'I'm worried you're a bit cool for me actually. I mean, I crochet flowers whereas you've got this whole punk vibe going on.'

'Trust me, once you've got to know me you'll find I couldn't be further from cool,' Saffie said. 'I collect 1950s pulp fiction.'

'See, that's the type of thing that sounds pretty sad if you're someone like me but inherently cool for someone like you. Classic coolness double-standard. You could probably even pull off alternative trainspotting.'

A throat cleared. An elderly man and his wife were standing behind them, looking irritated.

'Are you two going to be breaking up the mutual admiration society any time today, or are my wife and

I supposed to walk out into the oncoming traffic?' he demanded.

'Sorry. Blind date.' Richard took Saffie's arm and guided her towards the glorious sandstone Corn Exchange. 'Come on, Phil. Let's finish this meetcute inside.'

'Is that what we're having?'

'Course we are. We're adorable.'

Inside, Richard guided Saffie to a bench. He still had his arm linked with hers, and Saffie was surprised at how natural it felt to have it there. She took out her envelopes.

'Snap,' Richard said, producing an identical set of his own.

'I guess we should open one and find out where we're going,' Saffie said. 'I hope we're not getting sent on a guided tour of a fish-gutting factory or something.'

But before they could open the first envelope, their mobiles emitted simultaneous pings.

Saffie took hers out and glanced at the screen. 'It's from Dr Sheldrake.'

'Mine too.' Richard swiped to open it and raised an eyebrow. 'Seriously? There's nothing you'd save from a burning building?'

'Nothing not alive.' Saffie opened hers too. It contained questions one and two from Richard's questionnaire. 'Is this how it's going to work? Is she going to drip feed us our questionnaires throughout the day?'

'Seems so. You know, I was sceptical about that place when I signed up, but I have to admit they give a very thorough service.'

Saffie wasn't listening. She was reading the answer

Richard had given to the first question: the item he'd save from a burning building.

'A notebook?' she said. 'Out of everything you own, the thing you'd save is a notebook?'

'Yeah,' Richard said, looking embarrassed. 'It's not just any notebook. It's my first notebook; the one I used to jot stuff down in when I was at school.'

'What's in it?'

He shrugged. 'All sorts. I went through a phase of creating sci-fi comic strips when I was about fifteen. And I used to do caricatures of teachers and classmates, and the occasional diary entry. There's a lot of me in that old jotter – of the boy I was. If it burnt, I'd feel like a little part of myself had burnt with it. I've filled hundreds of notebooks since then, but if I could only save one it'd be that one. The beginning of everything.'

Saffie stared at him, and he smiled awkwardly.

'Probably sounds daft to the person who can't think of a thing she'd risk her life to save,' he said.

'No, I think it's pretty amazing actually. I guess I just don't have anything that means as much to me as your notebook does to you.'

'Really? Not a thing?'

She shrugged. 'I've got lots I'd hate to lose. Old family photos; my pulp fiction collection. But there's nothing that feels like part of me. I'd rather have myself, even if I lost everything else.'

'That makes sense. It feels kind of sad though.'

'A friend of mine said that as well.' She summoned a smile. 'Getting a bit maudlin for this early in a date, aren't we? Normally it takes at least two margaritas to get this sort of philosophical musing out of me.'

He smiled too. 'Well, I'm sure there'll be time for that later. Shall we find out where we're going?'

'OK. I've got the first envelope.'

'Me too,' he said, showing her a gold envelope with a number one on it. 'I guess that means they're in pairs.'

She grimaced. 'I kind of cheated. I had a little look in advance. The message makes no sense though.'

He shook his head. 'I specifically said "no rebels or rule-breakers", and they've sent me a tattooed blue-haired punk who cheats at dates.'

She smiled and handed him her envelope. 'You take a look. I hope you're better at these than I am.'

It's not all swings and roundabouts when Dr Jekyll's in the frame.

'Oh right,' Richard said. 'Easy one to start us off, eh?'

Saffie raised an eyebrow. 'You reckon that's easy?'

'Well, yeah. It's pointing us to where in the city we have to go.'

'Go on then, explain it to me. I have never in my life cracked a cryptic crossword clue.'

'OK, swings and roundabouts – you'd find those in a park, right? And Dr Jekyll's alter ego was…'

'Mr Hyde. Hyde Park?'

'You're forgetting about "in the frame". It's Hyde Park Picture House, isn't it?'

'Oh God, that's so easy!' She laughed. 'Every time I hear the answer, it makes me feel thick for not working it out.'

'Let's see what's in my envelope.' Richard opened it up.

11.45am. Tickets on front desk. Walk to Eastgate and catch 56 bus.

'Well, there's nothing cryptic about that.' He stood up. 'Seems like we're going to see a film.'

While Saffie's pretend date was becoming pretty real over in Leeds, Milo was preparing to meet his match in York.

His spirits were high as he found a side street where he could leave his car. Despite his best friend's cynicism, the soulmate guarantee that had first caught his attention was still buoying him up. The questionnaire had teased out a different side of him than the one he'd been projecting via the dating apps; captured more of the real him. Dr Sheldrake, too, had impressed him with her quiet confidence.

Confidence. Yeah, as in confidence trick. He could hear Saffie's scoffed comment as they'd compared notes. But it had to be on the level, didn't it? No one operating an elaborate con would have business premises that looked like Alison Sheldrake's. Milo had seen enough episodes of *Hustle* to believe that a genuine con artist would at least have the place painted.

He checked his watch. 10.43 a.m. He was meeting his date at eleven outside the Minster, by the statue of Constantine the Great. Tam, who had to drive all the way to the coast, might still be in the car, but Saffie should have met her match by now. Milo wondered how it was going; if she was giving it a proper shot despite all that undercover bollocks.

He patted his pocket to check he had his envelopes,

straightened the yellow carnation in his buttonhole and set off towards York Minster.

Milo must have read through his date's personal statement a dozen times, and he still couldn't decide if the guy's obvious nervousness was a bit weird or a bit adorable. Quite possibly it was both. 'Nervous, weird and adorable' probably was his type, although for years he'd believed his type was 'confident, cool and buff'. The exact opposite of him, in other words. But that was the sort of thinking that ended in West, and look how that had turned out.

He was nearing the Minster now, the courtyard bustling with tourists. He squinted, trying to pick out any flash of yellow that might be his date's flower, but the weekend crowd was too thick. There was a guided tour being shown around by the statue of Constantine and he practically had to fight his way through.

Sure enough, there was a man leaning on the railings – a man with a yellow carnation pinned to his T-shirt. He was about Milo's age, messy blond hair, nice smile, kind of cute. He was also, unfortunately, rather familiar. The smile disappeared as soon as he registered Milo.

'Oh, bloody brilliant,' Christian said. 'Milo the dog-hater. It had to be you.'

15

On the east coast, Tamara was quarter of an hour late and getting later by the second.

'Mummeeeee!' Willow wailed. 'I need a weeee!'

'You just had a wee, Will. I'm not stopping again.'

'But I'm going to do a sick.'

'You just said you needed a wee. Which is it, a wee or a sick?'

Willow hesitated.

'I need a wee and then a sick,' she announced.

'Well, cross your legs and keep your mouth shut. We'll be there in five minutes. You were the one who begged to come.'

'But it's so faaaar!' Willow's eyes lit up as she caught sight of the sea. 'Ooh! Can we paddle?'

'Later. First we need to find the man – I mean, Norbert and take him for coffee so he knows me ditching him is nothing personal.'

'What's ditching?'

Tamara sought for a child-friendly explanation.

'It's like when your friends ask you to play but then run off to play with someone else,' she said.

'Oh.' Willow looked thoughtful. 'Maybe your friend could come paddling too. If he'll be sad.'

Tamara laughed. 'Well, we can ask.' She turned into the car park. 'Let me grab a ticket, then we'll walk to the beach.'

Tamara parked and paid at the meter. She was about to set off when she remembered her red rose. She tucked it behind one ear, making Willow giggle.

'That looks silly,' Willow said.

'I thought it might make me look princessy. Like Belle. You remember, the enchanted rose?'

'Oh yeah!' Willow cocked her head. 'You're prettier than Belle though, Mummy.'

Tamara laughed. 'OK, what are you after?'

Willow just blinked at her, and she smiled and held out her hand. 'Let's go then, junior princess.'

Tamara recognised her date at once from the fresh-cut red rose in his buttonhole. He was sitting on a bench, reading a newspaper. She was relieved to discover he didn't look like a serial killer – although then again, did they ever? Not looking like serial killers was probably why serial killers had such successful runs. The fact that Norbert looked relatively harmless didn't prove anything.

'Mummy, why are we stopping?' Willow asked as they ducked behind an ice cream van.

'Shh,' Tamara whispered. 'I just… want to get a look at something.'

She peered around the van at her date.

He wasn't bad-looking. He wasn't exactly what you'd call good-looking either – he had thick, grizzled red hair and his Superdry polo shirt and stonewashed jeans could have come straight from the middle-aged dad's starter kit – but there was something in his face that interested Tamara. He looked good-natured, but there was a certain wryness in his smile as he read his paper that seemed to match the offbeat sense of humour he'd shown in his dating statement. His age, she guessed, would be somewhere in the late forties. A battered leather case at his feet looked like it might contain a musical instrument.

God, he wasn't planning to serenade her, was he? Tamara hoped he'd take the news this was only going to be a flying visit graciously.

She squinted at what he was reading. It wasn't a newspaper, now she looked properly. It was...

'A comic?' she murmured.

Willow looked up at her. 'Where's a comic?'

'Never mind.' She gave her daughter's hand a squeeze. 'Come on. There's my friend over there.'

She led Willow to the bench.

'Hi,' she said. 'Um, are you... Dr Sheldrake sent you?'

'Oh. Hello.' The man stood up. 'I thought you must've spotted me and run the other way. I was about to go home.'

'I'm so sorry.' She nodded to Willow, who was staring at the man with wide eyes. 'My daughter. Unfortunately there was a childcare emergency. This isn't going to be the date you hoped for, I'm afraid.'

'These things happen. As a grandad, I know all about being the emergency childcare.' He bent to Willow's level and smiled. 'All right, short stuff? What's your name then?'

Willow looked at her mum, who nodded to let her know it was OK.

'Willow,' she said in a hushed voice.

'Just Willow?'

She shook her head. 'Willow Francesca Horan.'

The man held out a hand. 'Professor Harry Hamilton. Nice to meet you, Willow Francesca Horan.'

Willow looked at the hand but didn't shake it. 'My mummy said you were called Norbert.'

'Did she? That's funny, I was almost sure I was called Harry. But mums are usually right.'

Willow finally returned his grin. Tamara had to admit, it was pretty infectious.

'Are you really a professor? Like at Hogwarts?' Willow's only encounter with the word was via Harry Potter.

'Well, in my line of work it's more of an honorary title.'

Tamara wondered what Harry meant by that. Was he an academic? Surely not.

'Interesting reading material,' Tamara said, indicating his copy of the *Beano*.

Harry laughed. 'I like to get one every now and again, keep up with the changes in Beanotown since I was a boy. Mind you, it's not the same since they got rid of Lord Snooty.'

'Did they?'

'Yes, he was disgraced in the Cash for Honours scandal. Four years in Belmarsh and his career never recovered.'

Was that a joke? The man was so deadpan, it was hard to tell. Tamara smiled uncertainly.

'I should warn you now that I'm rubbish at *Pointless*,' she said.

'Hmm. How about *Only Connect*?'

She shook her head. '*The Chase* is the only one I ever get answers on.'

'That's something, I suppose. Tell you what, let's start

with a few games of Trivial Pursuit and work our way up from there.'

He beamed at her, and Tamara, feeling like she was starting to get the hang of this strange date of hers, smiled back.

Willow, puzzled by this grown-up nonsense talk, pointed to Harry's suitcase. 'What's in there please?'

'Ah, now, I'm afraid that's a professional secret I can only share with very good friends,' Harry said, bending down. 'And I never consider someone a very good friend until they've let me buy them a knickerbocker glory with a chocolate-covered banana.'

Willow's eyes went wide. 'Chocolate-covered banana!'

'Sounds good, right? My granddaughter Jenny would eat them until she was sick if I let her.' He straightened up and smiled at Tamara. 'Well, shall we? The cafe's less than ten minutes away.'

As they walked, Willow, who'd found her voice now, subjected Harry to a barrage of questions about his grandchildren – a girl and two boys, aged from four to seven. In quick succession, she wanted to know where they went to school, what their favourite foods were, whether they liked *Paw Patrol* and a million other things, all of which Harry answered with patience and humour. By the time they got to the ice cream place, Tamara felt like she knew him ten times better than she would ever have done without Willow present.

Harry was certainly great with kids. What was more he enjoyed their company, which wasn't always the same thing

– Andy had been popular with kids, but his patience with them had worn thin far too quickly. Tamara was even willing to admit that Harry was quite handsome, in an unobtrusive sort of way – at least, he was when he smiled, which he did warmly and frequently. It was funny how a single shift in expression could seem to alter someone's entire personality.

The cafe he'd brought them to, Banana Splits, was on the promenade overlooking the beach. They claimed a table outside.

Bananas were a major theme in the decor, with banana-shaped seats, banana-print parasols and banana-yellow tables. There was a little play area too, where a couple of children were hitting each other with inflatable bananas in an all-yellow ball pool. Willow took it all in with shining eyes.

Harry handed Willow a menu. 'Well, short stuff, what's it to be? I highly recommend the knickerbocker glory, but it's your choice.'

Willow sent a longing look towards the ball pool.

'You can play first if you'd rather,' Tamara said, seeing where her gaze was directed. 'There'll be plenty of ice cream left afterwards.'

'Yes please, Mummy.'

'All right, off you go. Don't forget to be gentle with the littler children if they want to play with you.'

Willow started to go, then turned back to Harry. 'You won't go home, will you?'

Harry looked pleased at this mark of regard. 'Not if you don't want me to.'

Willow shook her head. 'I want to see what's in your suitcase.'

'Ah, that'll be worth the wait, I promise.'

When she'd gone, Tamara smiled awkwardly. 'So what is in the case?'

Harry's green eyes sparkled. 'I told you, it's a trade secret. Not to be disclosed until after your knickerbocker glory.'

'What trade is that?'

'All will be revealed.'

There was a pause as Tamara cast about for further conversation-starters.

'You seem to know Scarborough pretty well,' she said.

'Yes, I used to work here as a younger man. These days I'm here pretty often with the grandkiddies.' He smiled. 'Anyway, thanks for coming. I'd all but given up hope.'

'I really am sorry. I did make childcare arrangements, but...' She cast a glance at Willow in the ball pool, where she'd befriended the two younger children and was proceeding to boss them about. 'Willow got into a panic about me leaving her and refused to stay with the babysitter.'

'First night without her mum?'

'That's the strange thing. She's been without me lots of times and she's been absolutely fine.'

A waitress approached and they ordered a couple of teas.

'What do you think was different about this time?' Harry asked when they'd both been brought a beverage. 'Or was it totally out of the blue?'

Tamara regarded him, wondering how much to share. She wasn't quite sure what to make of Harry. He certainly wasn't what she'd call her type – she'd have swiped left like a shot if she'd stumbled over him on a dating app. Odd, a bit dorky, and his good looks were so subtle you might miss them if you never saw him laugh – admittedly difficult, given how often he did so, but he wasn't the type to turn heads in the way her ex-husband had always had no trouble doing. When Tamara had made the decision to address her self-esteem problems with some no-strings-attached adult fun courtesy of The 24-hour Dating Agency, the man she'd pictured providing that had been a far cry from Professor Harry Hamilton.

But the hair-gelled toy boy she'd envisioned would be long gone by now, wouldn't he? Unlike Harry, with his wry smile and kind eyes. Tamara had turned up to a date with a kid in tow, expecting to encounter at least indifference, if not actual annoyance, but Harry had welcomed the pair of them as if this had been the plan all along. And here he was, looking at Tamara with warmth and understanding, like he had all the time in the world for this complete stranger and her problems. And God, she could really do with someone to share them with.

'No,' she said in a low voice. 'She's been behaving out of character for weeks now. Ever since she met her father for the first time – or rather, the first time in her memory. He hasn't seen her since she was a year old.'

'That sounds like it must've been difficult for both of you.'

Tamara nodded, feeling an involuntary lump rise in her throat. 'It's been… painful. When my divorce came through two years ago, Andy had already cut contact with our two older kids to a bare minimum, and Willow he wanted nothing to do with at all. And now he's engaged and having another child, he suddenly wants them all back in his life. I can't help raging inside at how unfair it is that he left me to do all the dirty work, just so he can pick his kids up when it's more convenient. And Willow's going through something I don't understand, that even she doesn't understand, and I feel so utterly... so completely helpless.' She choked on a sob. 'You know?'

'I think so,' Harry said, in a quiet, even voice. 'Let it all out if you want. I can be a pretty good listener.'

16

Tamara did let it all out. She'd been keeping so much bottled up, and this stranger with the understanding eyes felt like just what she needed. All her fears about Andy, Natalie, the new baby and her ex's relationship with his existing kids. The resentment she was only barely keeping a lid on as she tried to do the right thing for her children. The burgeoning feeling of emptiness as her two eldest prepared to fly the nest. How frumpy and unattractive she'd been feeling compared to her ex-husband's young bride. Her worries about how to help Willow. It all spilled out as Harry nodded sympathetically.

'Feel better?' he asked when she was done.

'Weirdly, yes.' She accepted the tissue he handed her. 'I didn't realise how much I needed that.'

'The kindness of strangers.' He examined her face. 'Can I offer some advice?'

'Go on. I could do with some.'

'Your little girl is… what, six?'

'Five.'

Harry nodded to Willow, giggling as she searched for the toddlers she'd befriended under a mass of plastic balls. 'She's having the time of her life right now, isn't she?'

'Yes.' Tamara smiled fondly. 'It's lovely to see her enjoying herself. She's taken so little interest in the world outside her head lately.'

'I'd say it's exactly what she needs. The best cure for a little girl weighed down by adult worries is to make time to just let her be a child. Find the fun.'

Tamara thought this over.

'You might be on to something,' she said. 'Perhaps it would've helped her more if I'd been making time for play instead of trying to get her to open up about what's wrong.'

'Like you said, she probably doesn't understand that herself. Seeing you worried might just have been another cause for distress.'

'True,' Tamara said slowly. 'Thanks, Harry.'

'So what will you do?'

'I suppose since we're here, I can turn it into a fun mini holiday. It's a long time since we've been to the seaside.' She grimaced apologetically. 'Sorry we'll have to cut our date short.'

'Do we have to?'

'Well, I presume you don't want to trail around with me while I entertain a hyperactive five-year-old. I'm sorry you're not getting the grown-up date you were anticipating.'

'Oh, grown-up dates are overrated,' Harry said, flicking a hand. 'Most grown-up things are. Honestly, I'd love to tag along. Some of the best days of my life have been spent here with the grandkids.'

Tamara hesitated. 'You really want to?'

'Absolutely. I'd like to get to know you better, and since your children are obviously a big part of your life, it follows that I'd like to get to know them better too.'

'But the date won't be kid-friendly. You can at least go enjoy whatever Dr Sheldrake's arranged on your own.'

He laughed. 'A date with myself? No thanks.' Harry took out one of his envelopes. 'Let's take a look. It might be something we can all do.'

He read the clue, frowned, then passed it to Tamara.

The world could be your oyster at the OK coral, if you wish upon a slippery star.

She blinked. 'OK corral? What is it, a rifle range?'

Harry took the card back. 'Wish upon a slippery star. Hmm. Some sort of planetarium, do you think?'

'But why's it slippery instead of shooting? And what's it got to do with oysters?'

They were both silent, pondering.

'Hang on,' Tamara said slowly. 'Pass me that.'

Harry handed her the clue. She read it again, then slapped her forehead with her palm.

'Well that's embarrassing,' she said. 'And me a professional editor.'

'Eh?'

'It doesn't say corral, does it? It says coral. Coral, oyster, slippery star – as in, a starfish. It's the Sea Life Centre.'

He groaned. 'Of course it is. I should've got that, I do the cryptic crossword every week.'

'Wow. The *Beano*'s gone upmarket since my day.'

He laughed.

Willow came running up, for once looking as happy and free from care as a little girl of five ought to do.

'Mummy, I'm hot from playing,' she said breathlessly. 'Can we have ice cream?'

'We certainly can,' Harry said. He glanced at Tamara. 'And after that, how would you like to go see some fish?'

Willow pulled a face. 'Fish?'

'I mean big, exciting fish, like sharks. And there are penguins and seals too.'

'Ooh!' Willow's face lit up. Seals were her current favourite animal in the whole world. 'Yes please!'

'Are you sure about this, Harry?' Tamara asked.

'Completely. I'll gladly stretch to the price of a child's ticket to retain the pleasure of your company.'

The waitress came over to collect their teacups and Harry ordered more drinks plus three knickerbocker glories. Willow scoffed her ice cream like she hadn't eaten in days, the sea air giving an edge to her appetite. Her mouth was covered in chocolate and she was beaming like her face might split. As soon as the last mouthful had been gulped away, she pointed to Harry's case.

'Now can I see?'

He smiled. 'All right. I think now we're knickerbocker glory buddies, you're ready.'

He opened the battered case. Tamara peered over, trying to see what was in it. The case was just the size for a saxophone. But she stared when instead of an instrument, Harry took out a bear puppet in a top hat and bow tie and sat it on his knee.

'Ladies and ladies-in-waiting, may I introduce The Magnificent Geoffrey?' he said solemnly. His left hand had disappeared inside the puppet, but with his other he picked up his cup of tea and put it to his lips.

Geoffrey waved at Willow. 'All right, short stuff?'

Willow let out a screech and clamped her hands to her mouth.

'Mummy, how does it talk?' she whispered.

'Cheek!' Geoffrey turned to Harry, who was still drinking his tea. 'You know, Hamilton, I didn't come here to be insulted.'

'Really?' Harry said. 'Well, I'm here so you'd better get used to it.'

'Listen, pal, I don't have to put up with this. I was this close to getting a gig with Nina Conti.'

'You mean you got thrown *out* of a gig with Nina Conti.'

'Close enough.' Geoffrey turned back to Willow. 'I don't ask how you talk, do I?' He cocked his head. 'You're pretty ugly for a bear.'

Willow giggled. 'I'm not a bear. I'm a human.'

'In that case you're even uglier.'

Tamara couldn't help laughing along with Willow. It was kind of embarrassing: she was well aware that all eyes in the cafe had now turned to look at her date. But he'd made her laugh until her tummy hurt, and she couldn't remember the last time she'd been able to do that.

'You're very good,' she said.

'Of course he's good,' Geoffrey said, drawing himself up. 'We're not amateurs, madam. We've played some of the biggest dumps – I mean, some of the finest establishments in Barnsley.'

Harry nodded. 'And Doncaster. None of your rubbish.'

Tamara wasn't sure whether to address the bear or Harry. She decided that for the sake of her dignity, she'd carry on the conversation with the human half of the double act.

'Why The Magnificent Geoffrey?' she asked Harry.

'Because of my magical prowess, naturally,' Geoffrey said. 'Harold, the cards.'

Harry rolled his eyes at Tamara. 'You had to ask.'

He took a pack of cards from his suitcase and fanned them out in front of Willow.

'OK, short stuff, prepare to be amazed!' Geoffrey said with a theatrical flourish. 'Go on, pick a card. Don't let me see it.'

Willow took a card from the pack. A crowd of kids had gathered now, watching the show. Willow preened slightly, proud that it was her new friend getting all this attention.

'Now put it back in the pack,' Geoffrey instructed. Willow did so, and the bear put one hand on his forehead as he assumed an expression of intense concentration.

'I see it. I see it clearly through the magical mystical ethereal ether. Your card is...' he paused for effect – 'the Eight of Clubs!'

Willow shook her head.

'Right. Sorry, I wasn't concentrating properly. I was thinking about last night's football result.' Geoffrey put a palm to his forehead again. 'Then it's... the Three of Diamonds!'

Willow giggled and once again shook her head.

'OK, best of three. King of Spades.'

She shook her head again. Harry put the cards down and prodded Geoffrey in the back.

'Geoffrey, you're embarrassing me,' he muttered. 'You can never do this one. It's humiliating.'

Geoffrey turned to face him. 'That's The Magnificent Geoffrey to you, Hamilton.'

'Fine. I can see it's up to me to bail you out.' Harry

rummaged in his jacket pocket and passed a card to Willow. 'There you go. Your card.'

Willow's eyes went wide. She nodded mutely.

'All right, what was it?' Geoffrey asked Harry. 'Jack of Hearts, right?'

'Close. Mr Bun the Baker.'

'I knew it all along.' Geoffrey took a bow for the assembled kids and parents. 'Ladies, gentlemen and assorted riffraff, I have been The Magnificent Geoffrey, and he has been The Unremarkable Professor Harry Hamilton. Future performance dates can be found on our website. Thank you for your appreciation.'

One of the parents started a round of applause, which was enthusiastically taken up by the others. A few even threw coins into Harry's case.

When they'd gone, Harry glanced into the case. 'Well, I've earned enough to cover our tea and ice cream. Never say I don't know how to treat a lady.'

'That was *brilliant.*' Willow beamed at Geoffrey, her new best friend, while Harry tucked his cards away.

'Despite my lifelong fear of ventriloquists' dummies, I'm forced to agree,' Tamara said. 'So this is your actual job?'

'I'm afraid so.'

'Don't you ever feel embarrassed?'

Harry glanced at Willow, who was stroking Geoffrey's fur. 'Not as long as the little ones are smiling. To be honest, it's been a long time since I stopped caring what people thought of me. Much to the chagrin of my kids when they were teenagers.'

Tamara wished it was as easy for her to just stop caring what people thought of her. How liberating would it be to just do whatever you felt like, whenever and wherever you felt like it? No hang-ups, no inhibitions... although in her case it would probably manifest as an offbeat fashion choice rather than public conversations with a bear in a dicky bow.

'And this is what you've always done? Ventriloquism?' she asked Harry.

'Kind of,' Harry said. 'I actually started out more humbly, putting on Punch and Judy shows on the beach here.'

'Then I gave him his big break so he could hang up his swazzle,' Geoffrey said. 'Hamilton owes everything he's got to me.'

Harry nodded. 'About £3.20 in loose change and a banging case of sciatica from lugging him around the variety clubs.'

Tamara laughed. 'What on earth made you bring Geoffrey today?'

Harry shrugged. 'He's usually able to make people smile when I can't. I woke up with the feeling he'd be needed.'

Willow was still regarding Geoffrey with a sense of overjoyed wonder while the bear pretended to sniff behind her ears.

'Well, you weren't wrong,' Tamara said, smiling at her daughter. 'Thank you. Er, both of you.'

17

In Leeds, Saffie and Richard were emerging from Hyde Park Picture House.

'Perfect atmosphere for enjoying the classics,' Richard said, turning to look at the glazed terracotta façade of the 108-year-old cinema.

Saffie nodded. 'That's how films that age ought to be seen. By gaslight.'

'They used to call those modesty lights. So the usherettes could spot courting couples getting frisky on the back seats.' Richard smiled at her. 'We were pretty well behaved though.'

Saffie felt her cheeks heating.

'There's a park around the corner. Shall we have a walk?' Richard asked.

'That sounds nice.'

He tucked her arm through his, and Saffie, still riding a wave of 1940s-style chivalry from the old film they'd seen, didn't object.

'I can't believe they were showing *His Girl Friday*,' Saffie said. 'That's my favourite classic film.'

'I could tell by the way your eyes were shining,' Richard said, smiling. 'Why?'

'I loved Hildy when I first saw it as a kid. She was a real role model for me: the way she forged her place in a man's world. She made me want to become a journalist.'

Richard raised an eyebrow. 'Is that what you do?'

Saffie mentally kicked herself. 'No, I'm an archaeologist. But that was what I wanted to do when I was eight.' She looked up at him. 'How about you?'

'Oh, that's easy. When I was eight I wanted to be a Thundercat. That or Wolf from *Gladiators*.'

She laughed. 'I can see you as a Thundercat. A spandex posing pouch would suit you.'

He grinned. 'Ah, then have I got a surprise for you later.'

There was a comfortable silence as they strolled through the park in the summer sunshine, inhaling the scent of blooming roses.

'Do you think Walter wants Hildy back because he loves her, or because she's his best reporter and he wants to stop her quitting the paper?' Saffie asked.

Richard shrugged. 'It probably amounts to the same thing for him. His life is his job. Same for Hildy.'

'Was that the first time you'd seen the film?'

'Actually, it's a bit of a favourite, although I didn't see it for the first time until my ex-wife went through this "discovering the classics" phase.' He laughed. 'I can empathise with Hildy these days. It's a tough gig, working alongside your former spouse.'

'You know that from experience, do you?'

He guided her to a bench near a statue of Queen Victoria and they sat.

'Sadly,' he said. 'It's not so bad. The split was amicable, as far as these things can be. I think Carla just has a tendency to forget she's not my wife any more.'

'In what way?'

'She makes decisions without consulting me, as if I'm automatically obligated to go along with what she wants.' He shrugged. 'I shouldn't complain. She's a good businesswoman. I just wish she'd treat me less like a husband and more like a business partner.'

'Can't you talk to her?'

'It's hard to without rocking the boat. I want to keep things as friendly as possible so we can continue working together. And Carla's... let's call her a forceful personality. She doesn't like to be crossed.' He paused. 'Maybe I am a bit like Walter. I don't want to lose Carla when she's an asset to the business so I let her have things too much her own way. That's the problem with marriage: it's habit-forming.'

'What business is it?'

'It's a nursery. For plants, I mean. I've probably made it sound a bit more cut-throat than it actually is.' He shuffled to face her. 'How about you? Ever been married?'

'Oh. No. Well, nearly.'

'Nearly?'

Saffie shuffled her feet. Did she want to tell him this? She hardly ever talked about this. But there was something in Richard's face that seemed to let her know it was OK.

'As in, I was literally hours from the aisle,' Saffie said quietly. 'It was... a bit of a runaway bride situation.'

'You're kidding!'

She shook her head. 'I was in my wedding dress and everything. My fiancé had gone to pick up the hire car, and my best mate came over to help me with my hair. It was pink then. When my friend got to my flat, he found me in the cupboard wailing about having made the wrong choice.'

'Cold feet?'

'That's just it. It wasn't cold feet. It was more like… a moment of clarity.' She sighed. 'I've felt awful about it for years. The guy I was with was attentive, affectionate, kind; everything most people would want in a partner. I'd talked myself into thinking he was The One, because I felt like time was running out and he had to be. Then it was as if a switch flipped and I realised I was about to commit myself for life to someone I had nothing in common with, just because he sometimes brought me flowers.'

'So this friend of yours…'

'Mi– Max,' Saffie said, remembering at the last minute that having given herself a fake name, she should probably do the same for all of her nearest and dearest. You never knew who you might have in common. 'He was great. He made me tea, then between us we made a list. Everything I liked about my fiancé, and everything I didn't. And I realised that it really wasn't cold feet. I didn't love him. We weren't best friends, the way I've always thought couples needed to be. So I just… ran.'

'Where to?'

'Scotland, with Max. My mum's got a caravan in Fort William I had a key to. I rang my fiancé from Max's car and sobbed a load of incoherent nonsense at him, trying to explain. The worst thing was that he was utterly lovely about it, although it took him a long time to accept that I didn't want to be with him. Still, I felt like such a failure. Like I'd let everyone down – let myself down.'

'Here.' Richard handed her a tissue.

'Thanks.' She mopped her eyes. 'God, I'm sorry. I don't know what made me tell you that. I never tell anyone that.'

'Too painful?' he said gently.

'No. It just makes me sound like a total flake. Excellent way to send my dates running for the hills.'

He shrugged. 'Not me.'

She laughed wetly. 'Richard, you're too good to be true.'

'Honestly. I think it took a lot of guts, facing up to something you knew was wrong for you at the eleventh hour.'

'The guy was so hurt though. And the pair of us are still paying for it.' She pressed her eyes closed. 'Six years later, I've still got a cupboard full of unopened bottles of Prosecco that'd been destined for the reception. They're either vintage or way past their sell-by date by now. Bit like me really.'

'I know what might make you feel better.' He nodded to her handbag. 'Take a look at your phone.'

'My phone?'

'Yeah. There's another email from the good doctor: it popped up on my smartwatch while we were watching the film. I want you to read my answer to that question about the song that makes you cry.'

She blinked. 'OK.'

Saffie took out her phone and opened the email.

'"Beautiful Boy". John Lennon,' she read. 'Why?'

Richard smiled, looking down at his shoes. 'My dad used to play me that when I was a kid. Lennon wrote it for his younger son, Sean. My dad wasn't much good at expressing his feelings, so he'd play me the song as a way of telling me he loved me. I thought that when I had a kid of my own, I'd play it for them.'

'But you didn't,' Saffie said softly.

He shook his head. 'Carla never wanted kids. I did, but I was in love and I thought being with her was more important. That was just one of a number of things I tried to repress because I didn't want to face the fact that on a fundamental level, we weren't right for each other.' He looked at her. 'The thing is, I really knew it the whole time. I knew it when I proposed and I knew it the day I made my wedding vows. And now I'm thirty-eight, I'm newly divorced, I may never be a dad – all because I didn't have the strength of character to do what you did and walk away.'

'I walked away on my wedding day, Richard. That's a pretty shitty thing to do.'

'It's better than walking away the day after.' He took out his envelopes. 'Well, shall we find out where we're going for lunch?'

'OK. I guess you've got the clue this time.'

Richard opened Envelope Two, which contained the following:

It's tea for mew and mew for tea, to leave you feline purrfect.

'Ooh!' Saffie clapped her hands. 'I can get this one!'

'OK, go on,' Richard said, smiling.

'Don't you know it?'

'Haven't a clue.'

She narrowed one eye. 'You're just saying that because I'm excited about finally getting one, aren't you?'

'I swear, I've got no idea.'

'Liar.'

'Honestly. You'll have to explain it to me.'

'It's a cat cafe, isn't it? There's not much else it could be with that level of cat-based punnery.'

Richard raised an eyebrow. 'We're having lunch at a cat cafe?'

'Apparently.'

'Well, all right. But I'm not sure I'm going to be able to eat a whole one.'

Christian folded his arms. 'No.'

'Come on, mate, don't be like that,' Milo said, putting a hand on his shoulder. 'We might as well go on this date while we're here. I said I was sorry about insulting your chihuahuas, both past and present. I'm sure Mitzi, Loki, Luna and Chip are a great bunch of pups.'

'You forgot about Bailey.'

'Yeah, that was deliberate. Bailey sounds like a right twat.' Milo grimaced as Christian glared at him. 'Sorry. Joke. Didn't come out as funny as it sounded in my head.'

'Give me one good reason why I should waste my brainpower solving shitty cryptic clues to go on some shitty date with some shitty guy who ruined his chance with me once already.'

'Because the shitty guy is sorry for being a shitty guy and is now a much older, less shitty guy who really wants to make things up to you.' Milo paused. 'And because if you don't, we won't get our money refunded.'

'Huh.'

'"Huh" as in "yes, I'll grudgingly go on a date with you" or "huh" as in "sod this, I'm going home"?'

'"Huh" as in… I'm still thinking about it.' Christian turned to face him, scowling. 'Well then? What's the answer to this stupid clue?'

'I don't know, do I? We have to work it out together, that's half the fun.'

'Whoopee.' Christian glanced listlessly at their clue card. '"By 275, Nurse Florence would be high as a kite." I have no jeffing idea what that means.'

'Let's puzzle it out.' Milo took the card. 'OK, so, there's only one Nurse Florence anyone knows.'

'Nightingale. And?'

'Well, what do we know about her?'

'Known as the Lady with the Lamp, served in Crimea...' Christian paused as he thought it over, and Milo noticed his grumpy expression fade a bit. 'Or, something to do with birds. Nightingale and kite... could be a bird sanctuary?'

'What about 275 though?'

'Maybe it's a pun. Crimea – cry me a river. Boat trip down the Ouse? 275 could be the boat number.'

'That doesn't account for "high as a kite" though.'

They both fell silent again.

'You got anything?' Milo asked after a while.

'No. You?'

'What you said about the nickname rang a bell – the Lady with the Lamp. I just can't think where I...' He trailed off as a lightbulb dinged over his head. 'Lamp – lantern!'

Christian stared at him. 'Eh?'

'Come on.' Milo dragged him towards one of the information boards dotted around the Minster.

'There,' he said, pointing. 'That tower. It's called the Lantern Tower. That's why I had lamps on the brain: I overheard the tour guide talking about it when I met you by the statue.'

'"At 233 feet tall, the Lantern Tower is the highest spot in

York",' Christian read from the board. '"Once you've made your way up the 275 steps to the top –" 275!'

'High as a kite, 275, lanterns – it all fits. I guess we're supposed to go to the top.'

'You're disappointed they hadn't arranged something involving kicking dachshunds or mutilating schnauzers, I suppose,' Christian muttered.

Milo nudged him. 'Come on, don't start sulking again. Admit it, you were enjoying that bit of puzzle-solving.'

'Huh.'

'Again with the "huhs". Look, regardless of what my actions in the past might've led you to believe, I am very much a dog person. Just give me a chance.'

'Huh.' Christian looked at him. 'Fine, let's go. But that doesn't mean you're forgiven.'

Milo beamed. 'Great.'

Christian was sulky all the way up the huge octagonal tower, but when they reached the top, even he had to admit it was a view to take your breath away. A reluctant whistle escaped his lips as they looked out over the glorious pinnacles and carvings of York Minster.

'They've had some cowboys in here,' Milo murmured. 'That gargoyle's picking its nose, look.'

Christian let out a reluctant laugh, and Milo smiled. 'That's better.'

'We came here on a school trip once,' Christian said. 'A lad in my class found a mooning gargoyle. I used up a whole roll of film on it. Never laughed so much in my life.'

'Is that what you gave as your questionnaire answer?'

'No, I'd forgotten about it. There's nothing funnier than a bare bum to a ten-year-old, is there?' He took out his phone. 'Speaking of which, Dr Sheldrake's emailed some of our answers.'

Milo straightened up. 'Has she? Did you read mine?'

'No. I was busy being aloof.'

'Sulking, you mean.' Milo smiled as charmingly as he was capable of. 'Come on, am I forgiven? I've grovelled and snivelled until I couldn't snivel and grovel any more. I've apologised to each and every one of your chihuahuas, even that knobhead Bailey. I've made you laugh with comedy gargoyles. After all that, I must've earned another chance.'

'I'd better read your questionnaire answers first,' Christian said. But he was smiling.

Milo got his phone out to take a look at the email.

'You keep a diary?' Christian asked, raising one eyebrow.

'Yeah.' Milo shook his head. 'Why is that so surprising to everyone?'

'Am I in it?'

'I didn't keep one when I was twenty-three.' Milo hesitated, then decided that if he was investing everything in today he might as well go for broke. 'But... you were in it last week. After we met at the speed dating.'

'What did you write about me?'

'Well... you might want to see my answer to the question about my greatest regret.'

Christian stared at him. Milo, suddenly embarrassed, looked down at his phone. His eyes skimmed to the song that made Christian cry.

'"It's Raining Men",' he read.

Christian smiled. 'Yeah, I went for the gag answer. Nothing more depressing than that song coming on in a club when you've been single for aeons.'

Milo looked up. 'That's what I put too.'

Christian scrolled down his email and laughed. 'So you did. And there was me thinking we had nothing in common.'

Their eyes met. Christian looked away first, turning to gaze out over the Minster turrets. Milo, feeling flustered, turned to look too, and they stood in silence.

'So... we should open another envelope, I guess,' Christian said. 'I hope we're going to eat. I'm starving.'

'You had the first clue, so I must have this one.' Milo opened his second envelope. '"When houses of straw and sticks were blown down, then there was uno." Oh God, that sounds harder than the last one.'

'They always sound hard until you get them.' Christian took it from him, his brow creasing. 'Well, we know it's something to do with the three little pigs. Two houses blown down leaves the one made of bricks.'

'House of bricks. I guess that could be a pub.'

'It'd be a pretty strange name. I mean, all non-pig-constructed buildings are made of bricks, aren't they?' Christian was silent. 'Maybe it doesn't mean the house. Maybe it means the pig. Are there any pubs with "pig" in the name in York?'

'Dozens, but none I can think of that fit the clue.' Milo read it again. 'Uno. Why uno? Why not one?'

'That's Italian, isn't it? What's Italian for pig, Milo?'

'Er... porcini? No, hang on, that's mushrooms.'

'It's something like that though.'

'Oh!' Milo said. 'There is a restaurant called Il Porcellino. That can't be the answer though.'

'No, that has to be right. The Little Pig, that must mean. Why do you think it can't be that?'

'That place is really fancy. There's no way it can be included in what we paid for our dates. It's got Michelin stars and everything.'

'It must be. Nothing else fits.' Christian opened his second envelope. '"Clifford Street, 12.30 p.m. Reservation under Froman." Does that sound right?'

'Well, it is on Clifford Street. Who the hell is Froman though?'

Christian shrugged. 'A contact of Alison Sheldrake's maybe. Shall we then?'

Milo smiled. 'Let's.'

18

Tamara swiped the key-card to unlock her room in one of the seafront B&Bs, then held the door for Harry. Willow was on his back with her head lolling, fast asleep. Harry laid her gently on the double bed.

'Sorry,' he said to Tamara. 'I didn't mean to break your daughter. It was that final donkey ride did it, I think.'

Willow curled up into a ball, her favourite sleeping position. Tamara went to tuck her in.

'And I'm sorry we're back at the hotel before it's even six o'clock,' she said while she manoeuvred an unresponsive Willow under the covers. 'Some hot date, eh?'

'Well, speaking for myself I've had a lovely day.' He hesitated. 'I'd better leave you to it. I won't bother staying overnight.'

The dating agency had booked Harry a room further down the corridor, Tamara had been relieved to find, although the fact both rooms were doubles suggested it was up to the individual couple if they'd prefer to let one room go to waste.

'Don't rush off on our account,' she said. 'You don't want to miss the all-you-can-eat breakfast buffet, do you?'

Harry looked awkward. 'I just don't want you to feel like I'm crowding you.'

'Of course you aren't. You're surprisingly good company.'

He smiled. 'Surprisingly?'

'Well, you know. For someone whose best friend is a talking bear.' Tamara nodded to a small fridge. 'Look, there's a minibar. Stay for a nightcap, at least.'

'Actually, a cuppa would be nice. If you're sure that's OK.'

'That sounds lovely.' She went to flick on the kettle.

'Let's go in the en suite,' Tamara said when they both had a drink. 'I don't want to wake Willow.'

Harry smiled at the lightly snoring lump. 'She looks dead to the world.'

'I know. Soundest I've seen her sleep for weeks.'

Harry followed her into the bathroom. He perched on the bathtub while Tamara sat on the closed loo seat, and they sipped their teas in comfortable silence.

This certainly hadn't been the day Tamara had anticipated when she'd signed up for the agency. She'd been hoping for one day off from her kid-focused routine to recapture a little of her youth, when she'd been bright-eyed, fresh-faced and desirable – at least to some people. Nothing serious, but a day of very grown-up fun to help restore the self-esteem that had been shattered by Andy's unwelcome return to her life. And what had she got? A family day out with her five-year-old daughter, an odd but weirdly likeable former Punch and Judy man and a dicky-bow-wearing bear who sucked at card tricks.

And yet it had all been... rather nice. Really nice, in fact, in a wholesome seaside sort of way.

After the Sea Life Centre, the three of them had eaten candy floss and rowed around the boating lake, cuddled some truly tiny baby goats at a petting zoo, and got happily wet through at the water park. They'd finished with a visit to the beach for paddles, donkey rides and a tea of fish and chips off their laps. Today, Willow had been the happiest her mum had seen her in ages. Harry had been absolutely right when he'd said that what she needed was to enjoy being a kid.

Their last cryptic clue had seemed to point to drinks at a cabaret club, but they'd skipped that in favour of the beach trip. To be honest, Tamara would have been happy to give that a miss even without a kid. When it came to adult thrills, her eyes were probably bigger than her belly these days. She was about half an hour from zonking out next to Willow and sleeping until the breakfast bell went.

Anyway, if Willow hadn't tagged along then Tamara wouldn't have been able to enjoy the date as much as she had. She knew she'd have spent the whole time worrying about whether her daughter was OK at home. She wouldn't have got to know Harry as well as she had either. His questionnaire answers had been enlightening, but it was the way he'd interacted with Willow and Geoffrey that had really helped Tamara understand him. She wasn't about to fall madly in love with him, but she was glad she'd met him. Very glad.

'Penny for them?' Harry said.

'Hmm?' She looked up from her tea. 'Oh. Sorry. Just musing on some family stuff.'

Harry looked a bit awkward. When he was performing with Geoffrey he oozed confidence, but when the only voice he had to rely on was his own he sometimes came over all shy.

'I had fun today,' he said.

Tamara smiled. 'Me too.'

'What made you want to come? I mean, why did you sign up?'

'Oh, just… a moment of madness. I told you Willow met her dad recently. Well, his fiancée Natalie was with him and it sparked a bit of a confidence crisis. Her so young and beautiful, and me so… me.'

Harry rested a hand on her arm. 'Don't do that, Tamara. Put yourself down like that.'

She laughed bleakly. 'I didn't need to the night I bumped into Andy. Someone else did it for me.'

He frowned. 'Your ex? What did he say?'

'Not him.' She grimaced, closing her eyes. 'Oh God, I can't tell you. It's too humiliating.'

'Course you can. We're friends, aren't we?' He looked bashful. 'At least, I hoped we might be.'

'We are, but… it's hard to talk about.'

'Want me to get Geoffrey out?'

Tamara laughed. 'He wouldn't understand.' She swirled her tea. 'The shop assistant mistook me for Willow's granny. Right in front of Andy and Natalie. I could've died.'

'Rude,' Harry said, looking satisfyingly offended on her behalf. 'She must've been pretty short-sighted, that's all I can say. Why did that make you want to sign up?'

Tamara sighed. 'Oh, I don't know. My brother and our friend were doing it, and I felt so miserable that I just thought "what the hell". I needed something to cheer me up.'

'Did it work?'

She smiled. 'Not the way I thought, but… yeah.'

'Then amen to that.' Harry held up his teacup and Tamara chinked it with hers.

'How about you?' she asked.

'My kids did it. It's six years since their mum and me divorced. My son and daughter took it upon themselves to decide I was lonely and paid for me to register. Early birthday present to mark my fiftieth in three months.'

'What made you write all that about *Pointless*?'

'I hoped my perfect person would be on my wavelength. Find it funny.' He looked at her. 'Did it work?'

'I couldn't decide if you had a wicked sense of humour or you were a raging sociopath,' Tamara said, laughing.

'Hopefully the former. Mind you, I would be up for it.'

'You'd lose. I've never, ever got a pointless answer.'

'But I'd have the pleasure of your company for a while. That's as good as a trophy.'

She smiled. 'Top flirting, well done.'

'Thanks. I was practising on Geoffrey before we came out.'

'So were your kids right? Are you lonely?'

Harry shrugged. 'I suppose I must be. I mean, the person I spend most of my time talking to lives in a suitcase. Ventriloquism's the type of job that can send you strange after a bit.'

'Given you just admitted to flirting with your dummy, I'd be inclined to agree. You've got an amazing talent though, Harry. What made you want to do that for a job?'

'Sure you want to talk about this? I thought you had a phobia about dummies.'

'Only the wooden ones.' She shuddered. 'With their staring eyes and flappy jaws. Ugh.'

'You've not seen *Dead of Night*, have you?'

'No, why?'

'Just take my word for it and don't.' Harry finished his tea. 'It was a guy called Ray Alan who inspired me to get into it. His dummy was this drunk aristocrat, Lord Charles. Remember them?'

'On TV a lot in the Eighties?'

'That's right. I used to watch Alan's face: see which muscles twitched when Charles was talking and how he made the sounds. Ventriloquists used to get away with that "gottle of geer" stuff when they were on stage or radio, but to survive in the television era they had to up their game. Alan spent a lot of time minimising any lip movement. Some say he's the best there ever was.'

Tamara laughed. 'Radio ventriloquism? Really?'

'It seems unbelievable now. Yet there was a time when Peter Brough and his dummy Archie Andrews were the biggest radio stars in the country.' He smiled. 'But I'm boring you, sorry. I know I tend to "geek out" over this stuff, as my kids might say.'

'No, it's interesting,' Tamara said, and was surprised to find she meant it. 'How did you find Geoffrey's voice? He's got bags of personality.'

'Oh, there's a little bit of everyone in Geoffrey. My dad; an old boss. And me, I suppose. Geoffrey's the voice in my head that says the things I'd never dare. It's amazing what you can get away with when you're a bear in a top hat.' Harry shuffled closer to her. 'Anyway, tell me about you.

I've been talking about me and Geoffrey all day, and all I know about you is that your ex-husband needs a thump.'

Tamara trawled her brain for something that he didn't already know. 'Well, the twins are—'

Harry held up a hand. 'Not about your kids. Something about you. Tell me… tell me what you wanted to be when you grew up, and if it came true like it did for me.'

Tamara smiled. 'I think I basically wanted to be my grandmother. My brother, our cousin and me spent a lot of time with her as kids and she scared the bejesus out of us – well, she still does. But she was an amazing role model.'

'In what way?'

'She was very glamorous, very confident – or formidable might be a better word. When she strode into a room, she commanded it instantly. Her dad – my great-grandad – started this magazine. *The Throstle's Nest*: do you know it?'

'Yes, my dad's a subscriber.' He raised his eyebrows. 'Your family own that?'

She laughed. 'I know, the shame of it.'

'Not at all. My dad loves that little mag. So your grandmother worked in the family business?'

'Eventually. Her dad offered her a job on the mag when she left school, but Fran wanted to make her own way and turned it down to take a secretarial job with one of the regional newspapers. Through talent and graft she became one of the first female reporters on staff, and she managed to get married and have twins while she was rising up through the ranks. Then when she felt she'd earned her stripes, she applied for a job back with her dad. Twenty years later, she took over from him as editor.'

'I think I might want to be your grandmother when I grow up as well,' Harry said. 'Did you get what you wanted?'

Tamara shrugged. 'Well, I'm *Throstler* editor, but it's not the place it was in its glory days. I haven't got a staff of fifteen at my disposal. I've got a staff of three, and one of them's me. Anyway, I'm certainly no Fran.'

'Why do you say that?'

She lowered her gaze. 'I'm not tough. I can't even cope with what's happening with my ex. Fran would just...' Tamara sighed. 'I don't know. Make Andy disappear somehow with the sheer force of her personality. Nothing fazes her, even now she's in her mid-eighties. Whereas any sign of trouble and I'm down in the basement, smoking the secret fags I keep there and running through worst-case scenarios to a soundtrack of Judy Garland.'

'I don't know why you think so little of yourself, Tamara,' Harry said earnestly. 'You've brought up three kids practically single-handedly; you manage your own business. Most people would say that's pretty damn impressive.'

'Perhaps I'm ashamed that I didn't do what Fran did and earn my stripes somewhere other than the family business. I studied English at university and walked straight into a job at *The Throstler*, knowing I was being trained up to take the editor's chair. That feels more like nepotism than achievement.'

'You really think that? Because the woman you were just describing doesn't sound like she'd give a handout to anyone unless they'd earned it.'

'I just wish... I wish she was prouder of me.'

'She has to be.'

'Not as proud as she is of my cousin Russell. I might

be the editor but he's the one she sold the business to. The one who can do no wrong.' Tamara wrapped her hands around the now empty teacup. 'I try to talk tough around her but deep down I've always had this need to impress her. Ridiculous, isn't it? Still craving my grandmother's approval at forty-five years old.'

'You've got my approval, if that's any good to you.' Harry reached out to brush his fingers over her cheek. 'I think what you've achieved in your life is amazing, Tamara. I think your kids are amazing – I know one of them is from experience, and the other two can't be otherwise with the mum they've got. And I think you're amazing.' He was leaning closer now. 'What's more, I think you're beautiful. You barely look old enough to have teenage kids, let alone be anyone's grandmother. And I'd like to kiss you, if that's all right.'

Tamara found herself fascinated by Harry's eyes. You couldn't help it when they were this close up. They were a quite compelling shade of green: warm and full of humour.

'Could I?' Harry said. Whether it was old-fashioned chivalry or shyness, he clearly wasn't the type to kiss without permission. Tamara felt half disappointed that he was leaving the decision up to her rather than seizing the bull by the horns, so to speak. That meant she had to do what she ought to do instead of what she wanted to do.

'It's... not a good idea,' she said with a sigh. 'I've had a lovely time, Harry, but I don't think I need to tell you that emotionally I'm a bit of a state. My life's not ready for a relationship yet. It's got too many other things going on in it. The kids, the Andy thing, work...'

'You wouldn't say you might be overthinking this a bit?' Harry's hand was still on her cheek.

'Absolutely.' She smiled a little shakily. 'I'm a mum. Overthinking's what I do.'

'Tamara, you are so much more than just a mum.' Harry withdrew his hand. 'But if that's your decision.' He took out his mobile phone. 'Here. Take my number.'

'Harry, I can't—'

'Just friends, that's all.' He looked up to meet her eyes. 'We are friends, right?'

She smiled. 'Yes. We're friends.'

'Take it then. After that it's in your hands, and if I never hear from you again… well, I'll be pretty disappointed. Still, I'll cross my fingers and hope for better things.'

19

'Oktoberfest in June,' Milo said as he and Christian watched an oompah band in lederhosen march past. 'It'll never catch on.'

'Still, it has its perks.' Christian raised the stein of German beer Milo had bought him from one of the chalet-style huts. '*Prost*, Milo.'

'*Prost*.' Milo took a sip of his beer, which was refreshingly cool, if hugely overpriced.

A woman was browsing one of the market stalls, clutching a lead attached to a tiny pug. It started sniffing a discarded hot dog by Milo's feet and he bent to tickle its ears. The little chap wagged his stubby tail, showing off his multitasking skills by simultaneously scoffing the sausage.

'See that?' Milo said to Christian, nodding to the pug's wagging tail. 'He likes me.'

Christian smiled. 'All right, point made. You don't need to pet every dog we meet.'

'So do you believe me now? I do not, and have never, disliked dogs. Eight just seemed like a lot, that's all. I don't think it was unnatural to worry I might find myself tied to the sort of man who commissions oil paintings of his pets and refers to them as his "fur babies".'

'Eight probably did seem excessive if you didn't know how they came to be there.' Christian met Milo's eyes. 'You could've asked me about it instead of walking out on me though.'

'I know. I'm sorry. That makes about the 383rd time I've apologised, but I genuinely am sorry that in my early twenties I wasn't the well-rounded, communicative lad I eventually evolved to be.'

'Well, since you got the beers in at house-mortgaging cost then you're forgiven,' Christian said. 'Just promise me you'll be better behaved when you meet the next generation.'

Milo smiled. 'Am I invited over then?'

'You might be.'

'Five chihuahuas is still a lot. Not that that bothers me in the slightest, at all, but aren't they a handful?'

Christian shrugged. 'They can be, but after I adopted my first litter I kind of got used to being the chihuahua guy. And they're very small, so they really only count as one and three-quarter dogs if you think of them in terms of, say, collies.'

Milo thought about West: the way he'd shudder at the thought of having anything living expelling oxygen and CO_2 all over his pristine flat. He smiled fondly at Christian.

'It's been a good day,' he said softly. 'Are you glad you didn't flounce when you saw it was me?'

'Let's say I'm coming round to the idea.'

'You came round to the idea when I ordered you profiteroles at Il Porcellino. Now you're just playing hard to get.'

Christian tossed his head. 'It preserves my mystique.'

'So, shall we see what the last clue is? We should try

puzzling it out before we dull our deductive powers with beer. A stein's what – two pints?'

'Yeah. Those Bavarians know how to drink.' Christian took out his final envelope and opened it.

He read the clue then handed it to Milo. It just said this: *What's the connection?*

'Between what?' Milo asked. 'Us? Sheldrake can't know we already had a history, can she?'

'I don't see how. Open your envelope, see if it helps.'

It felt like cheating, opening the second envelope without solving the clue, but Milo's brain was going fuzzy and he felt like he wasn't on top riddling form. He opened his envelope.

Open your maps app and find the nearest hotspot before your bubbles burst. Everything you need is waiting.

'That just reads like another clue.' Milo shook his head. 'Bloody Sheldrake. She knew we'd try to cheat.'

'Hotspot, hmm. Could be a sauna?'

'What about the bubbles?'

'Champagne bar then.'

'It's the other card that's the clue though. What's the connection?' Milo frowned. 'What *is* the connection? I don't get what that means.'

'Could it mean… is there a connection between the things we've done today?' Christian said. 'You know like how sometimes in a pub quiz, all the answers link together to give you the last one? Like they begin with consecutive letters of the alphabet or spell out a word; something like that.'

'You might be right,' Milo said. 'So first, what did we do? Went to the fancy restaurant.'

'No, we went up the Lantern Tower first. Then the restaurant.'

'Right. And then... then we went to watch the footie, didn't we?'

Christian nodded. 'Then the art gallery, then here.'

'I don't see what connects those things. They seem totally random.'

'I don't know,' Christian said slowly. 'There's a bell jingling somewhere; I just can't quite...'

Silence fell. Then Christian's eyes widened and he pulled out his phone.

'What?' Milo said. 'Did you get it?'

'In one of your questionnaire answers you mentioned you like cheesy Eighties films, right?'

'Yeah, and?'

'And I said something similar. I reckon Sheldrake's picked up on that and she's...' Christian tapped at the screen and laughed. 'Of course! Bubbles. Hotspot. Hot *tub*. There's a spa less than a mile away.'

'All right, how the hell did you get that?'

'It's that name, Froman. We had to give it at the restaurant to claim our table. It's been nagging at me all day.'

Milo blinked at him. 'Am I being incredibly dim here or did you swallow something hallucinogenic with your beer?'

'Come on. What classic Eighties film features a day out where the characters take a trip up the city's highest skyscraper, blag their way into a posh restaurant, go to a sporting game, visit an art gallery and watch a marching band in lederhosen?'

Milo laughed as the penny dropped. 'Oh my God. Was our date *Ferris Bueller's Day Off*?'

'Right down to namechecking Abe Froman, the sausage king of Chicago.' Christian showed him the location of the spa on Google Maps. 'And what was the last item on Ferris and co's agenda? A pool party, right? This place is a spa-hotel with pools and hot tubs. I bet that's where Sheldrake's booked us in for tonight.'

Milo squinted one eye at him. 'How'd you get so smart?'

'Misspent youth. And they said all that TV would rot my brain.' He slapped Milo's shoulder. 'Well, drink up. I'm assuming when it says everything we need is waiting, there'll be a pair of trunks each. I never thought it'd be this easy to get your clothes off again.'

An hour later, Milo and Christian were each sipping a glass of champagne as they shared a hot tub.

'So we got both kinds of bubbles,' Christian said as he toasted Milo with his flute. 'I don't think I've ever been on such a high-class date. Shame about the oik they set me up with.'

'Cheeky sod.' Milo flicked water at him and Christian, laughing, held his glass up above his head.

'I'm starting to understand why Alison Sheldrake's office is so bare though,' Milo said. 'If all the dates she organises are like ours, she must be barely breaking even. The restaurant alone must've cost a big chunk of what we paid for this.'

'I wonder why she does it. It must be a lot of hard work.'

'Who knows?' Milo murmured as his eyes drifted down. 'Maybe she's got a Fairy Godmother complex.'

Christian smiled. 'Ahem. My face is up here, mate.'

'I know where it is. I've seen that already though.'

'I suppose I should be flattered you still think I'm worth checking out,' Christian said, dipping his head to catch Milo's wandering eyes. 'I'm not in the same shape I was at twenty-four.'

'You look the same to me.' Milo ran an appreciative gaze over Christian's firm, shining body. 'Although I do need to conduct a bit more research before I can deliver a verdict with one hundred per cent accuracy.'

'Oh?'

'I mean, I'd need to see you fully naked. Otherwise it's not a fair comparison, is it?'

'Mmm. You know what really gets me going in a man? Scientific rigour.'

Milo smiled. 'Come here.'

He shuffle-paddled to Christian so they could kiss.

'I've wanted to do that all day,' Milo whispered when they broke apart.

'I've been waiting for you to do that all day. You were too busy pointedly stroking dogs.'

'Chris?'

'Yeah?'

'You believe in love at first sight?'

'I didn't yesterday.' Christian reached up to smooth the damp hair away from Milo's face. 'But I'm coming round to the idea.'

'I mean, technically this is love at second chance, isn't it? Technically we've known each other thirteen years.'

'Right. And if you were to come back to my hotel room now...'

'...then it'd be nothing we hadn't done before,' Milo finished for him.

'Might as well.'

'Since we're here.'

'In the interests of scientific rigour.'

'Exactly.' Milo stood up and grabbed his towel. 'So what are we waiting for?'

Saffie looked down over the twinkling lights of Leeds as she sipped her margarita on the balcony of the hotel bar.

She and Richard were the only people out here. They were sharing a bench under a canopy dotted with fairy lights, drinking in the view, the atmosphere and the warm night air.

'Tired?' Richard asked softly when he heard her sigh.

'No. Content.'

'Me too.'

He slipped an arm around her and Saffie snuggled into it. It had been the most perfect day, and this, here, with soft jazz playing, Richard's arm around her and the lights of the city below, felt like the perfect end to it.

After the cinema, they'd made friends with some quite adorable kittens at one of the city's cat cafes (Richard, she was pleased to discover, was a fellow cat person). After that they'd visited a real hidden treasure of a bookshop – seriously, why didn't more dates happen in bookshops? – where Richard had bought her a pulp fiction novel to add to her collection. It was called *No Mortgage on a Coffin*, with a suitably lurid cover illustration of a scantily clad woman standing over a corpse: a real collector's piece. Then, after dinner at a burlesque club, they'd finished up here in the Sky Lounge of their hotel for cocktails. Their bookings included a double room each, Saffie had been relieved to discover. Or had she? Three margaritas down, she was starting to wonder.

'Thanks again for my book,' she said to Richard, sliding it out of its paper bag. 'I feel bad for not getting you a present.'

'You could get me your phone number.' She could feel Richard's hot breath on her cheek. 'I've always wanted one of those.'

She smiled and took out her phone. 'All right. Make sure you use it though. I hate giving people presents that end up just sitting in a drawer.'

'Regularly, I promise,' he said, taking out his own phone to copy it. Saffie went back to examining her book, running one finger over the cover.

'You know, you're not at all my type,' she said dreamily. 'All clean-cut and pretty.'

'Likewise. I've never been into inked, grungy girls. Should we call it a day now, do you think?'

'It's probably for the best.'

Richard handed back her phone, taking the opportunity to plant a kiss on her cheek as he did so.

Saffie felt... happy. Content. With the soft jazz playing, she seemed to be half in a dream – the kind you never wanted to wake up from.

'Sign it for me,' she said to Richard, holding out the book.

He smiled. 'You know I didn't write it, right?'

'Go on. Something to help me remember today. I want to remember every bit of today.'

'Won't that devalue it though?'

'It'll make it more valuable to me.'

'Well, if you're going to put it like that. Have you got a pen?'

She passed him one from her handbag. He opened the book and scribbled something, then passed it back to her.

To Phil,

I hope you won't need this book to remember the day we met. I hope I'll always be there to remind you. Don't forget me.

R x

It gave Saffie a jolt to see the fake name. She kept forgetting she was still Philomena. Numerous times today, she'd been on the verge of coming clean to Richard about her original intention in signing up to the agency.

Of course that was all done with. She wasn't going to write a feature about this. It was too... too sacred. She'd never believed in love at first sight, and Dr Sheldrake's theory about getting to know each other better in an intensive twenty-four-hour period than through months of dates had sounded like so much guff, but Saffie was forced to admit that today had been one of the most wonderful experiences of her life. An instant click, such as she'd never had with a date before. Then with every new conversation, every shared experience, they'd discovered something else they had in common. It felt fated, although Saffie didn't believe in fate. It felt like magic, although Saffie had never believed in magic. It felt... right.

Was that what Richard was feeling too? She looked again at the message he'd written. *Always.* On his personal statement, he'd said he hoped she'd be The One...

'You've finished your drink,' he said. 'Another?'

'Oh. No, thank you. Three's my limit if I don't want to

end the night dancing on the tables.' She looked up to meet his eyes, which seemed almost black in the dim glow of the fairy lights. 'Richard, do you think... what I mean is, do you believe in...'

He shook his head. 'No.'

'You didn't let me finish.'

'Love at first sight, right? That's what you were going to say.'

'Well... OK, yes.' Something was making her bold, and it wasn't the tequila. 'So you don't believe in it?'

'I thought I did, when I was younger. When I met my wife, I was convinced that was what I was experiencing. We just had this instant spark, you know? Bam, like lightning. We spent so long staring at each other before either of us remembered it was good manners to actually speak.'

OK. This felt a bit painful, actually. Saffie knew there was no need to be jealous of Richard's ex-wife – ex being the operative prefix – but she couldn't help feeling a pang.

'But you weren't in love with her,' she said, making it a statement rather than a question. She didn't want to sound needy.

'Well, no. I didn't know anything about her, so how could I have been?' Richard finished his wine. 'We had chemistry, but it was lust really. I romanticised it because I was at a point in my life where I was craving something more meaningful. Love came later, when we'd learned who the other person was out of bed as well as in it. So no, I don't believe it's possible to fall for someone the moment you see them.'

'Oh.'

Richard brushed his fingers over Saffie's cheek. 'But I

believe that when you know someone, you know,' he said quietly.

'You know what?'

'If you're right for each other. If you've got a future. I think you can figure that out pretty quickly, if you just open yourself up.'

'And have we...'

'You still need to ask?' Gently he drew her to him and planted a soft kiss on her lips. Saffie let out the tiniest sigh as he drew back.

'That was good,' she whispered.

'Thanks, that's reassuring. I'm a bit out of practice.'

'So am I.' She looked up at him, his features slightly fuzzy after three cocktails. 'It's strange, isn't it?'

'What?'

'Today. This. Us. It all feels a bit... a bit like...'

'Like magic,' he finished softly.

'Yeah. Like magic.' She smiled dreamily at him. 'You know, I think I am a little tired. Shall we go to one of our rooms? We can have a nightcap from the minibar before bed.'

'Nightcap as in nightcap or nightcap as in *nightcap*?'

Saffie laughed. 'Don't push your luck. It's nice talking, that's all. I'd like to do it a bit more, somewhere private and... spongy.' She shuffled her bum on the uncomfortable wicker bench.

'Whatever you want, Phil.' Richard stood up and offered her his arm. 'Come on. I'll walk you home.'

Saffie grunted as she drifted back into consciousness. A sliver of saliva had escaped while she slept, and she instinctively wiped it away.

She was in a semi-recumbent position on her bed – or not her bed. This bed was bigger and squishier. Flocked wallpaper, silk sheets... where was she? This wasn't her room. This place was all posh and plush – well, apart from the pillow behind her, which was lumpy as hell. She wriggled against it as she tried to smooth it out.

'All right, no need to give me bruises,' a deep voice said. 'I was starting to think you'd never wake up.'

The date! That's where she was: in her room at the hotel in Leeds.

Saffie shuffled into a sitting position. She was still in her date dress, although someone had pulled the duvet over her legs. Richard was sitting next to her on the bed, one arm around her.

'Did we fall asleep?' she murmured.

'Eventually.' He bent to kiss the top of her head. 'We finally talked ourselves to sleep about 2.00 a.m., I think.'

'Oh God, I'm sorry.'

'Don't be.' He gave her a squeeze. 'I can honestly say it was the most fun I've had in a girl's bedroom with all my clothes on.'

She yawned. 'I can't believe we talked all night. Hey, do you think room service would bring us up a couple of full Englishes?'

'Not for me. I need to rush off, I've got to work. I can ask them to send your breakfast up on my way out if you like.'

'Why, what time is it?'

'Nearly eleven. You really zonked out on me.'

'God, really? I don't think I've slept until eleven since

university.' Saffie looked up at him. 'So our date's over. We're past the twenty-four-hour cut-off.'

'And here I am running straight out on you. I'm sorry, I wish I could stay to share breakfast.' He searched her face. 'Until next time?'

'Until next time.'

Richard kissed her before standing up.

'Don't forget me,' he said quietly.

'Don't let me. You've got my number.'

'Yes.' Richard was quiet for a moment. 'I'll see you soon, OK? This has been...'

'Unforgettable.'

'That's the word,' he said, smiling. 'Goodbye, Phil.'

20

It was Monday before the three friends were able to compare notes on their dates. When Saffie arrived at work, Milo was at his desk, humming dreamily.

'Where's Tam?' she asked.

'She texted to say she was picking us up takeout coffees.'

'She must be in a good mood.' Saffie picked up a *Lifestyle North* that had appeared on her desk. 'Did you put this here?'

'Yeah. There was a boxful of back issues in the porch. I think Russell and Nikki want us to wade through them before next week's editorial meeting.'

'Jesus.' Saffie sat down, then swivelled to examine him. 'You look like you're in a good mood yourself.'

He smiled. 'I might be.'

Tamara came in with three takeout coffees.

'Here you go,' she said, handing them round. 'You're welcome.' She perched on Milo's desk. 'Well, who's going first?'

Saffie nodded to Milo. 'Someone was just about to share why he's humming soppy songs.'

'It may have gone rather well,' Milo said. 'Really well actually.'

'Go on, tell us.'

'Well, it started off pretty unpromisingly. My date nearly walked out when I turned up.'

'Harsh,' Tamara said. 'You're not that ugly.'

Saffie was watching his face. 'Not another lad you'd been out with before?'

'Spot on,' Milo said. 'It was Chihuahua Chris again. What are the chances, right? But I managed to turn it around with my trademark charm, and after that it was all lederhosen and sexy fun in a hot tub.'

'That sounds a bit niche,' Tamara said. 'I didn't get any tight leather on my date.'

'It wasn't our idea. You'd have to take it up with John Hughes.'

Saffie and Tamara stared blankly at him.

'It was all based on *Ferris Bueller's Day Off*, we discovered.' Milo looked at them. 'Do I take it your dates weren't inspired by cheesy Eighties films?'

'No, funnily enough.' Saffie lifted an eyebrow. 'So did you get a refund on the double room you didn't use?'

Milo shook his head. 'How do you always know?'

'I'd recognise that smug recently-got-lucky simper anywhere.'

'Well, is it true love like the soulmate guarantee promised?' Tamara asked him.

Milo flushed. 'I don't want to run away with myself. I've done that too many times before. But yeah, I think it's definitely, one hundred per cent the real thing.'

'That's some nice not running away with yourself,' Saffie said.

'I'm justified this time. We practically exchanged I-love-yous on the date. Not quite, but close.'

Saffie smiled. 'I'm glad it went well. I liked that guy.'

'Go on, your turn,' Milo said. 'How was your foray into dating espionage? Did you get everything for your feature?'

'The feature's not happening. Not now.'

'Don't tell me that after heaping scorn on the idea, you actually met someone you liked?'

'You know I hate admitting when I was wrong, Milo.'

'So you're not going to.'

'No. But this guy, Richard… you know, I'd given up on the idea that there might be men in the world who could be simultaneously warm, charming, single and heterosexual. But honestly, after one day I felt like I'd known him all my life. I told him things I've only ever shared with you guys before. Even what happened with Kieran.'

'So it was true love for you too,' Tamara said.

'I'm not going to start talking about love. That's bad luck. But… let's just say I think there's a good chance that could be where we're heading.'

'You only used one of the rooms yourself, I take it?' Milo said, lifting an eyebrow.

'We did, but not like you think.' Saffie smiled at the memory. 'We just stayed up all night and talked. Early in the morning we dropped off, then woke up cuddling fully clothed. It was pretty adorable.' She sighed. 'I feel really guilty for lying to him. How do I explain the fake name and job when he calls me? I wanted to come clean on the date, but we were having such a good time, I couldn't bear to ruin it.'

'I'm sure he'll understand. Once you explain that you're not going to write a feature about it after all.'

'I hope so.'

Milo nodded to his sister. 'You next, Tam. Was *Pointless* guy a weirdo or was he just funny?'

Tamara hesitated. 'Kind of both. He's a professional ventriloquist.'

Saffie snorted. 'You're kidding. Are there still ventriloquists?'

'At least one, yeah.' Tamara smiled. 'He was a real buff on the subject, bending my ear about the glory days of variety. He brought his dummy with him too.'

'Christ on a bike,' Milo muttered. 'The guy took a *ventriloquist's dummy* with him on a date? Even I can't top that, and I've been on some real stinkers.'

'I call serial killer,' Saffie said. 'That's the most serial-killery thing I've ever heard. Your instinct was right, Tam.'

'If he'd wanted to murder me he had plenty of opportunities. No, I think he was just a slightly odd nice guy. Anyway, I couldn't really complain about the dummy after I'd turned up with a kid.' Tamara smiled in answer to their enquiring looks. 'Yeah, there was a Willow crisis. She had a meltdown and refused to stay with Fran. So much for putting being a mum to one side and recapturing my youth.'

'Oh, Tam. I'm so sorry it didn't work out,' Saffie said, reaching over to squeeze her arm. 'I suppose one of us was bound to be unlucky, but I know how much you needed this. Will you ask for your money back?'

'No.' Tamara fell silent. 'No, it sort of worked out. Not as a date, but Harry was fun to hang out with. Plus he was great with Willow, and she just loved Geoffrey, his dummy.

It wasn't the creepy kind; more like a cute little muppet. After the hard time she's been having, I was grateful to see her having fun.'

'But you didn't fancy this weird ventriloquist, surely?'

'Oh God, no.' Tamara laughed. 'No, not at all. I was so embarrassed when he got the dummy out in public and started performing with it. But he was sweet, and he was very kind to Willow.'

'You need to tell him you don't want to see him again though,' Milo said. 'I know you, Tam; you're too nice.'

'I tried to let him down gently by telling him I wasn't ready for a relationship and just wanted to be friends. It wasn't a lie either; I really don't want a relationship right now.'

Saffie shook her head. 'Seriously, do not go down the "just friends" route. I tried that with Kieran. He'll turn into one of those friendzoney guys who spend all their time heart-reacting your selfies and making puppy-dog eyes at you because they think a certain period of being your mate ought to be rewarded with a shag.'

'Harry's not like that,' Tamara said – slightly warmly, Saffie felt. 'He is a genuinely nice guy. Not my type, but... nice. I would like to stay friends.'

'Just be careful, that's all. Friendships are painful when one side wants more than the other can give.'

A week later, Tamara was drinking her pre-work coffee and smiling at a funny meme Harry had sent her on WhatsApp.

'Who's Harry?'

She jumped as Marcie appeared behind her.

'God, don't do that,' Tamara said, patting her heart. She stuffed her phone back into her pocket.

'He's that date guy, right?' Marcie said, unceremoniously pushing her mum's feet off the sofa so she could sit down. 'I thought you said he was a weirdo.'

'I'm sure I said something much politer than that.'

'Yeah, but after three years of dating I know all the codes for weirdo.'

Tamara smiled. 'You're a real veteran.'

'More than you. You haven't dated since Princess Diana was still alive.'

'That is a gross exagger…' Tamara trailed off. 'Christ, no it's not. I haven't been out with anyone since I met your dad in 1996. Well now I'm depressed.'

'So why are you WhatsApping this weirdo with the creepy puppet then?' Marcie asked, helping herself to the remnants of her mum's breakfast croissant. 'You said one date and that was it.'

'We're just texting, that's all,' Tamara said, as carelessly as she could manage. 'As friends.'

'Are you going to see him again? "As friends"?' She did the air quotes to make sure her mum didn't miss the unsubtle irony in her tone.

'We might do at some point. Not a date but a coffee or something.'

'Why?'

'I was thinking of your sister. She keeps asking when we can see Geoffrey again. Plus I did tell the guy we could be friends so it seems mean to just ghost him.'

Marcie rested a hand on her mum's arm.

'Don't do it just because you're lonely, Mum. You'll only regret it later.'

'Oh, don't start being all wise. That's my job.' Tamara patted the hand on her arm. 'I told you, Marce: just friends. Admittedly I've been out of the dating game for a long time, but even without the ventriloquism, Harry Hamilton is nothing like my type.'

That was true. Harry wasn't at all the sort of man Tamara used to go for. When she had been dating, way back before the millennium when dinosaurs still walked the earth and a voddy and Coke was less than a quid a pop down the student union, Tamara's type had been the cocky, swaggering, charm-on-legs Andy Horans of the world. Marriage had taught her some sharp lessons in that department – mostly that the sort of lad who can show you a good time in the clubs and in bed isn't necessarily going to be optimum husband and father material. Still, when Tamara pictured her perfect man, it was nevertheless someone typically handsome, broad of chest and shoulder, with a cheeky wink and a lopsided grin. Someone in the Chris Hemsworth mould; a far cry from Harry Hamilton. And yet...

Tamara had lied to her best friend, her brother and her kids, but she couldn't lie to herself. The truth was, she hadn't thought Harry was a weirdo at all. She'd found him interesting in all his geekery, and his kindness to Willow, his offbeat sense of humour and his refusal to give a damn what anyone thought of him had imbued him with a unique charm all of his own. Tamara had been embarrassed when he'd attracted so much attention in the cafe with Geoffrey, that was true, but he'd made her laugh at the same time. And there was something that still haunted her about his smile… his eyes…

Marcie was watching her with one eye narrowed. 'Mum, are you sure you're not crushing on this weird old guy?'

'Don't be daft.'

'Positive? Because you've been acting really funny since you got back.'

'Oh, I'm just worried about—' Tamara bit her tongue. About Andy and the new baby, she'd been going to say, but she didn't want to push her anxieties about that on to Marcie. 'About Willow,' she finished instead. 'She's still so quiet.'

'I know,' Marcie said soberly. 'She seems sort of… stuck in her head. It's not good for a little kid to be like that.'

'Hence why I was thinking of calling Harry, to see if him and Geoffrey can bring her out of herself. They did a great job of it the day we all went out.'

Tamara's phone pinged. She took it out of her pocket, expecting it to be another cheesy meme from Harry, but no such luck.

Hey. Listen, Nat and me are having a barbecue in a month and I've invited the twins. I wondered if you'd like to bring Willow? I'd like her to meet Natalie. She's due soon and it'd be good for them to meet before the baby arrives. Bring Milo or someone if you want. Andy x

Tamara scowled as she read it. The kiss at the end was particularly irksome.

'You never said your dad had invited you to a barbecue,' she said to Marcie, trying not to sound accusing.

'Oh. Yeah,' Marcie said, her attention fixed on her own phone as she scrolled through her messages. 'That's OK, right? Me and Dale said we'd go meet Natalie.'

'You don't need my permission.'

There must have been a note of bitterness in Tamara's voice, as Marcie looked up from her phone with a concerned expression. 'Are you pissed off with us?'

'No.' Tamara forced a smile. 'No, of course not. I'm surprised you didn't mention it, that's all.'

'Sorry, I forgot. Did Dad text you about it?'

'Yes. He wants me to bring Willow.'

Marcie was still watching her face. 'You don't need to go. We can take her.'

'No, that's OK. I promised her I'd be with her when she saw her dad again. I don't think she'll go unless I do.'

'You sure you'll be OK with that? I mean, with Dad and Natalie and everything?'

'I'm an adult. I'll cope.' She stood up. 'I need to get to work. Have a good day, love.'

When Tamara arrived at the office, Milo was already there, working on some page layouts.

'Bloody hell,' she said, blinking. 'What's this in aid of? It's not even nine o'clock.'

He shrugged. 'I felt like making an early start.'

'Is this because we've got our first official meeting with the new management today? Are you trying to score Brownie points by pretending you're not the lazy, workshy swine you really are?'

'It's Russ, Tam. He already knows,' Milo said. 'No, I got up early to go for a jog, then I thought I might as well come in and get a head start on some odds and sods.'

'*You* went for a jog?'

'Yep, with Chris and his dogs. They slept over at mine last night.'

Tamara picked up the post and chucked it on Saffie's desk. 'I hope he's not going all West on your ass with this fitness stuff.'

'Actually, it was my idea. And you know, without West reminding me what a slob I am every time I needed to get my breath, it was quite fun.'

She smiled. 'I'm glad it's going well. Any sign of the L-word yet?'

'I'm biding my time.'

'Why? You said you were most of the way there on your date.'

'There's no rush,' Milo said. 'I've got previous in the "dropping the L-bomb too soon" department. I'm not going to scare this one off, Tam. Chris is the best thing that's ever happened to me, which is why I have to not tell him he's the best thing that's ever happened to me until we hit at least the two-month mark.'

'Probably wise.' Tamara started flicking through the new issue of *Lifestyle North* that had dropped through the letterbox with the post. 'This must be hot off the press. It's not due in shops for two weeks.'

'I guess they wanted us to have a copy of the latest before the big meeting.'

'Mmm.' She idly turned the pages. 'Has Saffie heard from that guy Richard yet?'

'Not the last I heard.' Milo shook his head. 'I don't get it. He sounded mad keen on her. He even bought her a rare book for her pulp fiction collection. Who goes out of their way to act like you're the woman of their dreams then ghosts you right afterwards?'

'You don't think he could've found out she lied to him?'

'I can't see how.'

'Well, it's only been a week, I guess,' Tamara said, still turning the pages of their sister magazine. 'Maybe he had to... to...' She trailed off.

Milo looked round from his computer screen. 'What?'

'Oh my God,' Tamara whispered, still staring at the magazine.

'Tamara, what is it?'

'This feature, in their new issue. It's... Russell wrote it.'

'Well?'

'It's... it's a feature on the agency.'

'What, our agency?'

'Yes, our agency. The 24-hour Dating Agency.' She pushed the magazine under his nose. 'Milo, Russ is Richard.'

21

Milo snatched up the magazine. 'No! He can't be.'

'He's Richard, Mile – Saffie's Richard. He joined the agency using a fake name to get material for a feature.'

'But that was Saffie's idea!'

'What was my idea?' Saffie asked as she walked in. Milo hastily shut the magazine.

He glanced at Tamara, who shook her head slightly.

'Er, nothing. I mean, this page layout.' Milo nodded to his monitor. 'You suggested making this feature a DPS. Good call.'

'Did I?'

'Still no word from Richard?' Tamara asked.

Saffie sighed. 'Not a dicky bird. I can't understand it. I know eight days isn't all that long but I'd have expected something.'

'I'll make coffee,' Milo said, standing up.

'Yeah, cheers.' Saffie glanced at the mag on his desk. 'Oh God, it's today, isn't it? Our big meeting with The Devil Wears Prada and spouse. I suppose I'd better look through this before they get here.'

'No!' Milo and Tamara made simultaneous dives for the magazine, but it was too late. Saffie had already opened

left an important file at home and they'll have to go with you to get it.'

'Why would they have to do that?'

'No.' Saffie squared her shoulders. 'No. I'm going to have to face him. I work here and if I want to stay working here, I need to do this.'

Tamara looked at her. 'You're sure?'

'What choice do I have?' She sucked in a deep breath and let it out slowly. 'OK, Tam. Let them in.'

Saffie didn't have time to process everything she was feeling before Tamara opened the door. It still hadn't sunk in that Richard, the man she'd bared her soul to over the course of one life-changing day, was a different person entirely to the one she'd thought he was.

She'd been wondering why he hadn't got in touch. Now she knew. It was because he was a liar. He'd never cared for her. He had a wife. He'd just been using her for his feature – the way, as her conscience would remind her, she'd been planning to use him. Except she hadn't, had she? It would have felt like a betrayal after... after she'd half-fallen for him.

Or for Richard. Not Russell Foxton, whoever he was. All she knew about that guy was that he wrote a bloody rude email and he took a very creative approach to his marriage vows.

She could hear Tamara making polite-sounding chitchat at the front door and sank deeper into her chair.

'Don't say anything, Mile, OK?' she whispered. 'Just... act like you don't know.'

'What for? He'll recognise you straight away.'

'It's less humiliating this way. Please.'

'Whatever you need, Saf.' He fixed on a smile as a nervous-looking Tam led in their visitors.

Saffie's desk was partly shielded from view by the printer behind her. By peeking through the small gap between the printer and the wall, she could see the door without whoever was at the door seeing her. For a few moments, at least, she could stay hidden.

Yes, there was Richard – or Russell, as she'd have to get used to calling him. The same tawny-gold skin and unruly black hair; the same deep brown eyes that had looked so earnestly into hers. A sob threatened to escape and she pressed her eyes closed.

He didn't look as he had on their date. He was sterner; smarter. Yes, he was smiling, but not with the warmth he'd so convincingly faked that day. This wasn't the irresistible smile that had first caused her to lower her guard; it was all business.

Nikki was with him, resting her fingers lightly on his forearm. As before, she oozed style, confidence and subtle yet compelling sex appeal. Saffie sank down further into her chair.

'Well, guys, here they are,' Tamara said with false brightness. 'New bosses, same as the old boss.'

Russell laughed. 'I hope we won't be as terrifying as all that.'

Milo flashed Saffie a worried look before standing to greet the new arrivals.

'Russ,' he said, shaking hands. 'Good to have you on board.'

'Glad to be here. I never thought I'd find myself heading up the family business, but it feels sort of like my destiny.'

Why hadn't he thought he'd be heading up the family business? Too good for it, was he? Also – 'heading up'? Tam was the editor. So much for not interfering.

'We're certainly looking forward to the challenge of helping you become bigger and better,' Nikki said in her smooth, assured tones.

'Well, shall we get started?' Russell said. 'Nik and I are going to see a potential new printing firm this afternoon so we don't want to hang about.'

'A printer for us?' Tamara said.

'That's right.'

'But we've got a printer. We've been using them for decades.'

'And they've been overcharging you for decades,' Nikki said. 'You can get a far better deal.'

Russell nodded. 'Never let loyalty stand in the way of competition, Tam. It's the little guy who takes the hit.'

'But they're the little guy too. They're a small family-owned business just like we are. I'd really rather—'

'It does no harm getting some rival quotes,' Nikki said, in a tone that tried to soothe without compromise. 'But we're missing someone. Where's the writer – Sally, isn't it?'

Saffie grimaced. OK, this was it. Fixing her face into a careless smile, she stood up.

'Actually,' she said, 'it's Saffie.'

22

Saffie had to give Russell his due. For a few seconds, he looked shocked. He even opened his mouth to speak. Then it snapped shut, he assumed an expression of studied blankness, and he... nodded to her. The bastard went and *nodded*!

His wife – wife! Married, nodding bastard! – didn't seem to register that anything was wrong. She just smiled in a vague, businesslike way.

'Ah, good,' she said. 'Well, then we're all here. Let's go into the meeting room, shall we?'

'We haven't got a meeting room,' Tamara said. 'There's just this room and my office, and that's half the size of a shoebox.'

'Oh.' Nikki cast an underwhelmed look around. 'I suppose we'll have to make do in here then. Saffie, could you make some drinks? Russ and I both take our tea well brewed, with milk and no sugar.'

Right. So despite her recent promotion, she was the sodding tea lady now.

'Sure thing,' Saffie said through teeth that were cringing in her gums.

Russell's gaze followed her to the kitchen area, and Nikki tapped his arm to bring his focus back to her.

'Russ.'

'Yes. Right.' He grabbed a spare chair and wheeled it to Milo's desk, where he spun it round and straddled it. Saffie should've guessed he'd be a straddler. He probably knotted cardigans around his neck and played golf. Really, she'd had a lucky escape.

'So, um, did you take a look at the mags we sent over?' he asked. Saffie was satisfied to note that despite the straddling manoeuvre, his unflappable confidence seemed to have evaporated slightly.

Tamara nodded. 'But I'm not sure what you're expecting us to learn from them. *Lifestyle North* isn't *The Throstler*.'

'There's plenty you can learn,' Nikki said. 'If you look at the businesses that promote themselves with us, you can see the standard of advertiser we're luring in. There's no reason you shouldn't aim higher too, with us behind you.'

'And how would we entice those sorts of businesses? With features exactly like the ones every lifestyle mag on the shelves is offering?' Tamara demanded. 'I don't want to be difficult, Nikki. I can see you're trying to help us grow, but we won't keep our readers if we start fiddling with our USP.'

'We know,' Russell said. He made a studied attempt to ignore Saffie as she brought the drinks over, although she saw him flinch when she leaned over him to put his down. 'It's your baby, Tam – Fran was insistent on that when she signed the place over. But we do need to think about how to futureproof ourselves if we still want there to be a *Throstler* for the next generation. The average age of our subscribers is over sixty, and their numbers are dwindling every year.'

Tamara was silent. Saffie had seen the subscription figures too, and she knew there was no arguing with the facts.

'We have some younger subscribers,' Saffie said as she pulled up a chair. 'Our international subscribers tend to be under forty-five. That shows we can appeal to that demographic: it's just a case of getting to the people who are going to want what we've got to offer.'

Nikki gave her a sharp look, as if she resented the contribution. Saffie wondered if she knew, about her and Rich– Russell. Well, if she did she'd have to take that up with her husband.

'That may be true,' Nikki said. 'But it's also true that you're less invested in the magazine's future than the rest of us in this room, Saffie – please don't take offence. All I mean is, you're not one of the family so you can walk away more easily. Fran told us you were looking for a new position.'

Tamara leapt to her defence. 'Saffie's been with us for nearly a decade, Nikki. She's known Milo for over twenty years. That makes her practically family.'

Saffie smiled at her before turning back to Nikki. 'And I'm not looking for another position. I might be, one day – I've got career ambitions the same as everyone, and there's only a limited amount I can achieve at *The Throstler*. But at the moment, I pitch the odd freelance feature and that's all.'

She was aware that Russell, who'd been gazing anywhere but at her, finally turned his eyes in her direction when she mentioned her freelancing. He had the expression of a man who'd just put two and two together.

'Personally, Nik, I think we could use an outside perspective,' he said, turning finally to his wife. 'Ph– Saffie's the only person in this room who hasn't been either born into this business or married into it. She's probably got insights we're too close to things to see.' He made eye contact with her and nodded encouragingly. 'Please, Saffie, go on.'

Heat was creeping down her cheeks to her neck. Saffie tried to pretend she was talking to someone else. He was just her boss, that was all. Nothing else.

'Well, we've always been sort of... viral, haven't we?' she said. 'As a cult phenomenon, I mean. The younger readers like us for a different reason than the older local subscribers. They like us because we're... well, weird. More lifestyle stuff isn't going to appeal to that sort of young person.'

'So what would you recommend?' Nikki asked coolly, with an almost imperceptible undercurrent of sarcasm.

'I think we ought to capitalise on that. Not changing the content necessarily, although a reader survey to get some feedback couldn't hurt. But perhaps more bespoke promotion to the outlier groups that we know enjoy the mag, rather than relying solely on word of mouth.'

'Such as what?' Russell asked.

'That's your area. I'm just the features editor. But I guess targeted ads on social media, that sort of thing?'

There was silence. Nikki looked unimpressed by what she probably thought was a pretty basic idea, but Russell seemed thoughtful.

'You might be on to something,' he said at last. 'Tam, what do you think?'

Tamara nodded. 'It's a good idea. I've put forward the

idea of a reader survey before, but Fran was reluctant to budget for it. But if you two are committed to investing in our future, then it's better to go down that route than to fiddle blindly with our content.'

'Nik?' he said.

'We can look into it, perhaps,' Nikki said, somewhat grudgingly. 'Russ, we ought to go. I think we've got enough food for thought until our next meeting.'

'Next meeting?' Milo said. 'Are we a meeting sort of business now?'

'We thought it would be good to touch base once a week while Nikki and me are getting to grips with everything,' Russell said. 'Don't worry, I'll keep them short. And next time, I'll bring biscuits.'

'Make sure they're good ones. Jammie Dodgers at a bare minimum.'

'For you, Milo, I could probably even stretch to chocolate Hobnobs.' Russell unstraddled himself and stood up. 'Er, Saffie. Before we head off, can I have a quick word in Tam's office?'

Saffie shot a look at Milo, who gave a slight shrug, as if to say 'what can I do about it?'

'Er, yeah,' she said when no excuse for escape presented itself. 'Very quick, because… I've got work to do.'

She followed him into Tamara's office, where he shut the door and pulled down the blind.

'All right, *Richard*, what the hell?' she demanded in an angry whisper.

'I believe that's my "what the hell", *Phil*. The archaeology business going well, is it?'

'Oh, no. You do not get to guilt trip me about this.' She

jabbed a finger. 'You told me you ran a nursery. With your *ex*-wife. You lying cheating toerag scumbag bloody—'

'All right, I get the idea.' He threw himself into Tamara's chair, not bothering to straddle this time. 'Look, calm down. They'll hear if you keep calling me names at that volume.'

'Doesn't matter.' Saffie sat down opposite him. 'They know all about it.'

He frowned. 'They don't, do they?'

'It was Tam who spotted your sodding feature. It's only out of respect for me that they're keeping schtum. I assume you broke it to the missus, did you?'

'When would I have done that?' He brushed his palm over his forehead. 'She knows there was a date. She doesn't know it was you.'

'Right. So she's just looking daggers at me because she doesn't like me.'

'That's just her manner.' He leaned forward, his expression softening. 'Saffie, I didn't lie to you. Not about anything important.'

She laughed. 'Anything important! Your name? Your job? Your fucking *marriage vows*?'

'All right, that sounds bad. But you lied too.' He looked at her keenly. 'I suppose there's a feature about to pop up about me somewhere, is there? If it hasn't already.'

'No, Russell, because unlike you I scrapped that plan. I ditched it as soon as I got to know you, because I—' She stopped, biting her lip.

'I know. Me too,' he said quietly, displaying that uncanny knack for knowing what she was going to say before she said it. 'Saffie, I didn't lie to you about being married.'

She laughed. 'You what? I was literally just talking to your wife.'

'All right, I only half lied about being married. Nikki and me are separated. We've got three months until our separation period is up and we can file for divorce, then I'll legally be a free agent. Morally, I'm one now.'

'You honestly expect me to believe that? She was practically nibbling your ear lobe out there.'

'Believe it or don't, it's still the truth.'

A choking feeling rose in Saffie's throat and she struggled to fight it back.

'If it really meant something to you, then how come you wrote the feature?' she demanded. 'I didn't because I couldn't bear to betray the connection I thought we'd experienced. That you wrote it when I couldn't tells me everything I need to know about Russell Foxton.'

For the first time, he looked ashamed.

'I didn't have any choice,' he muttered. 'I'd arranged it with Alison. She paid for an ad on the back of the free publicity. I couldn't back out with only days until deadline.'

Saffie stared at him. 'What did you just say?'

'I said it was right before deadline. You know how it works.'

'Not that. Are you saying... Alison Sheldrake *commissioned* you to write this?'

'No. I suggested it and she agreed, then Nik sold her an ad on the back of it. That's how we do things.'

'You were in it together? She used me to promote her dating agency by sending me on a fake date with a married man? That... that's against every code of ethics going, Russell!'

'Except it wasn't fake. I was genuinely a client – or at least, I was open to the idea of meeting someone new.'

'I can't believe this!'

'You know, Philomena, you take some impressively towering moral high ground for someone who spent as much of our date as I did lying through her teeth.'

'But I didn't exploit you for a feature, did I?' Saffie said, trying to keep her voice low. 'I mean, what was your best outcome from this? Lie to me, sell out the connection we'd built while totally ghosting me, then apologise and we'd skip off into the sunset?'

He flushed. 'I guess... kind of? I didn't use your real name in the feature – or what I thought was your real name. I didn't mention any of the personal stuff you told me. I just wanted to write about my experience of twenty-four-hour dating for other people who might be interested. If you read it, you'll see I gave you a glowing review.'

'How fucking delightful of you. I'm thrilled you managed to sell a single ad on the back of my abject humiliation, Russell, really I am. Full page, was it?'

He grimaced. 'Half.'

'Right. Good to know what I'm worth.'

'Russell!' Nikki's voice called. 'Are you coming?'

'Just finishing up!' Russell called back. He lowered his voice again. 'OK, you're right. I shouldn't have written the piece. I'm sorry. But other than the fake name, the fake job and a slightly creative interpretation of what consti- tutes an ex-wife, everything I told you that day was true,

Saffie. I had an amazing time with you, and I'd really like it if—'

'Oh, no.' She stood up, laughing. 'There is not a chance in hell that I would ever, ever go out with you again. I'm going to get my money back from Alison Sheldrake, then I am drawing a line under this. From now on, Russell, we work together and that's it.'

23

Saffie's best hope now was that Russell and Nikki would leave the team at *The Throstler* to get on with things, and other than the weekly editorial meetings, she'd have minimal contact with her new bosses.

But despite having made her views on ever wanting to see him again quite clear, Russell Foxton was apparently as obtuse as he was annoying. It felt like every few days he was dropping in – sometimes with Nikki, sometimes without – to 'see how they were getting on'. The office was starting to smell permanently of his rancid aftershave.

'He's here again, isn't he?' Saffie asked Milo when she walked into work one morning.

'Yeah, him and Nikki are in with Tam,' Milo said. 'How did you know?'

'I can smell him.' Saffie sat down and switched on her computer. 'What is it this time?'

'God knows. I think he's just mediating between Nikki and Tam, hoping to prevent a punch-up.' Milo gestured to a steaming cardboard cup and a muffin that were sitting on her desk. 'He did bring us coffees and buns though.'

'I don't want him bringing me stuff. You have it.'

'I've had mine.' Milo went to stand by her. 'Go on, Saf. It's just coffee from the boss.'

'No way. They'd turn to ashes in my mouth.' She pushed the bun away so she didn't have to look at it.

He squeezed her shoulder. 'Back on the apps yet?'

'No. I'm still… processing.' She looked up at him. 'You're in early again. The dog-and-a-jog routine with Chris still going strong?'

'Yeah,' he said, smiling soppily. 'Everything's going strong. Things are… I'm really happy, Saf.'

'I'm glad one of us made it.' She patted the hand on her shoulder. 'And despite my personal wretchedness, I'm glad it was you.'

'Thanks, bestie.' He ruffled her hair. 'Oh, I had a Chris-related favour to ask actually. Next Saturday, would you be available to dog-sit?'

'Me? What for?'

'Chris has got a meeting arranged with a client so I said I'd mind the hounds for the afternoon. I totally forgot I've got plans that day.'

'What plans?'

'I told Tam I'd go with her to this horrific barbecue of Andy's. Can you, Saf? It'd only be for a few hours.'

'I don't know, Mile. Five's a lot of dogs for one person to handle.'

'Nah, they're tiny. I've had hamsters bigger than those guys.'

Saffie still hesitated. 'I've got an interview to do at six: a Golden Oldies couple. I can't turn up with a shoebox full of chihuahuas.'

'I'll be back well before then.' Milo fluttered his eyelashes. 'Please, for me?'

She sighed. 'Oh, all right.'

Tamara's office door opened and Russell emerged, looking flustered. Saffie nodded to him.

'Morning, Dick.'

'Please stop calling me that.' He lowered his voice. 'Nik's here. She's in there talking to Tam.'

'In that case, good morning *Sir*.' Saffie whipped off a salute and turned back to her computer so she could start pointedly ignoring him.

'I got you a muffin,' he said.

'And I'm sure I don't need to tell you where you can stick it.'

'Come on, Saffie, it's only a muffin.' He flashed her a winning smile. 'Chocolate fudge. That's your favourite, right?'

'That was information you acquired from me under false pretences and you ought to be ashamed to refer to it.' She picked up the muffin and made a show of throwing it in her wastepaper bin.

'Hey!' Milo said. 'I'd have eaten that.'

'I'd also have eaten that,' Russell said.

Tamara's office door opened again and Nikki emerged, closely followed by Tamara.

'I don't see that we need the results of the reader survey before pushing ahead with changes,' Nikki was saying. 'It's obvious your content is alienating younger people, and that puts off potential advertisers.'

Tamara shook her head. 'I won't put advertisers ahead of loyal readers, Nikki. Selling ads is important because it allows us to produce a quality mag at a price people can afford. The mag isn't a vehicle for the ads.'

'Then in a decade you'll have no magazine,' Nikki said coldly. 'Adapt and survive, Tamara. I can't see why you're being so stubborn about this. Sales is my area.'

'And editorial content is mine.'

Russell frowned at his wife. 'Nik, we had this conversation. If Tamara wants to wait for the reader survey, that's what we'll do. It's her magazine.'

'It's *our* magazine,' Nikki said. 'You said you supported me on this.'

'No, I said I agreed we had to adapt to secure the magazine's future. I also said I wouldn't overrule Tamara's decisions. She's the editor and her say is final.'

'You journalists with your editors and your ethics,' Nikki said, flicking a hand. 'Today's reality is that advertisements are all that are keeping print media viable. I wish you'd stop harping on about these old-fashioned things and let me do my job. It's all our futures I'm working to protect.'

'Futures, or profits?' Tamara snapped.

Nikki shrugged. 'What's the difference?'

Saffie, who'd held her tongue for as long as she could, spun in her swivel chair.

'Nikki, you can't dictate the content of the mag to sell more ads,' she said.

Nikki turned a look of dislike on her. 'I'm sorry? *Can't*, did you just say to me?'

'Nothing wrong with your hearing. That's good,' Saffie said, ignoring the alarmed waggling of Milo's eyebrows. 'Tamara's the editor and she's responsible for the magazine's content. That's not some old-fashioned idea from the golden age of newspapers; it's literally her bloody job description.'

Nikki tried to look superior. 'No offence, Saffie, but this is a management conversation. It's a bit outside your pay grade.'

Oh. Outside her pay grade, was it? Saffie mentally rolled up her sleeves. Milo's eyebrows were dancing the lambada over his glasses, but there was no way she was backing down now.

'So what you're saying, Nikki – again – is that I'm not one of the family so my views don't count.'

'That's exactly what I'm saying,' Nikki said coldly.

'At least I care about the mag and its readers more than arse-kissing potential advertisers. Besides, you're not one of the family either, are you?'

'Of course I am. By marriage.'

'And soon you'll be divorcing right back out again. Maybe then you can make the teas, eh?'

'Saffie, that's enough,' Russell said sternly.

Nikki nodded. 'Thank you, Russ. About time you spoke up.'

He turned to face his wife. 'You're no better. Saffie's worked here for ten years and she's entitled to a voice. Pay grades don't enter into it.'

Milo raised his hand. 'We don't actually have pay grades. Just permanently low pay. Actually, I was wondering if you might like to review…' He clocked Nikki's black expression and lowered his hand again. 'Right. Not the time. Sorry.'

'You're just going to allow her to speak to me like that, are you?' Nikki demanded of Russell.

Russell laughed. 'What do you want me to do, challenge her to a duel?'

'I want you to fire her!'

'Well I'm not going to, and since you can't without my agreement, it isn't happening.'

'We'll see about that.' Nikki glared at Saffie before turning to the door. 'Russ, I'll wait for you in the car. We'll be having words.'

She swept out.

'Nice job standing up to her,' Saffie said to Russell.

'Thanks.'

She shook her head. 'I was being sarcastic. Seriously, is that the best you can do?'

'What more do you want me to do? It's her business just as much as mine. And she's right: sales is her area. She knows more about it than any of us.'

'Russ, you told me you'd speak to her about trying to interfere with the content,' Tamara said. 'Why is she still pressing me on it?'

'She's advising you, that's all. Obviously the ultimate decision is yours.'

'Is it? Because it feels a lot like the ultimate decision is do what she wants or she'll be looking for a more cooperative editor.'

'I wouldn't let that happen.'

'How would you not let that happen?' Tamara demanded. 'It's not like she listens to you.'

'That's not true. Nik and me built a successful business through mutual respect for the skills each of us could bring to it.'

'It's a shame she can't treat the rest of us with respect then,' Saffie said. 'Or is having an opinion on that outside my pay grade?'

He flushed. 'Look, I'm sorry about that. She really doesn't like you.'

'No shit,' she said drily. 'Why not? Did you tell her it was me who... from the feature?'

'No, and I wasn't planning to. The last thing we need in here is more tension. Just stay out of her way, all right?'

'I would if we could count on you to stand up to her. But you don't, do you, Russell?' Saffie nodded to the door. 'Go on. She's in the car, waiting to "have words". Time to bend over and take your paddling.'

'I'm going to ignore that comment. But I do have to go.' He went to the door, then paused. 'Saffie?'

'What?'

'Check your emails. There's one from me. Bye, team.'

When he'd gone, Saffie dropped her head on to the desk.

'"Bye team", ugh,' she muttered. 'Next he'll be forcing us to do group high-fives.'

'I am one Nikki-team-talk away from stashing an emergency bottle of Gordon's in the bottom drawer of my desk,' Tamara said. 'Russ says he's on my side, then he sits there in silence while she tries to bully me into submission. I get that it's difficult keeping things on an even keel when you run a business with your nearly-ex-wife, but what they've got isn't a partnership; it's a dictatorship.'

'What's the email about, Saf?' Milo asked. 'Business or pleasure?'

'Subject: feature idea.' Saffie skimmed the text and laughed in disbelief. 'Oh my God. This is a new low.'

'What?' Tamara said.

'Russell's suggesting a feature called Narrow Escapes.

About people who've called off weddings at the last minute and been all the happier for it.'

'OK.' Tamara was silent while she mulled this over. 'Well, that's one of his better suggestions. At least it's people-focused. It's not thinly disguised advertorial.'

'But don't you get it? He's suggested it because… because he wants me to write it! Because I've got the necessary experience.'

'After ditching Kieran,' Milo said. 'Does Russ know about that?'

'Yes he does! I told you, I opened up to him about it on our date.' Saffie hid her face in her hands. 'This has to be humiliation rock bottom. As if being tricked into falling for someone for a magazine feature wasn't pretty far down in the depths, the man who orchestrated it is now casually using deeply personal information as the basis for light, humorous copy. That he's going to make *me* write for him.'

'It's probably coincidence,' Tamara said soothingly. 'I'm sure he wouldn't want to humiliate you.'

'There's no way it can be coincidence.' Saffie's brow knit. 'He's mocking me. Well, he can stick it up his arse.'

She tapped out a reply, as fast as she could before the others tried to talk her out of it.

No, no, a thousand times no. And don't you dare use personal information I gave you on the day that shall not be mentioned to exploit me at work again. Screw you, Russell.

Saffie could see Tamara opening her mouth to protest,

but she hit Send before either she or Milo had time to engage their vocal cords.

'Saf, you really should try not to let your anger get the better of you,' Milo said gently. 'We know you're hurt – rightly so – but Nikki's already gunning for you. You don't want to give her more ammo.'

'Right at this moment, she could sack me and welcome. I am so sick of Russell and Nikki and this whole fucked-up situation.' Saffie stood up. 'Right. I'm taking an early lunch. There's someone I have to see.'

Saffie banged on the door of The 24-hour Dating Agency, which was locked – again. This was the third time she'd come down here to confront Alison Sheldrake, and each time it had been shut up.

Well, she wasn't giving up this time. She needed to have some serious words with the matchmaker from hell, and she wasn't leaving until she'd had them – no, not if she had to chain herself to the bloody door.

Saffie had just raised her fist to pound the door for a third time when it opened. She only just managed to arrest her movement before she ended up giving Dr Sheldrake a black eye.

'You know, you could have just come in,' Dr Sheldrake said.

'The door was locked.'

'It always swells after damp weather. Next time, give it a kick.'

'There won't be a next time,' Saffie snapped as she

followed Dr Sheldrake down the bare corridor to her office. 'If I ever see you again, it'll be in court.'

'Let's keep this civil, shall we?' Dr Sheldrake ushered Saffie into her office and gestured for her to take a chair.

'Civil!' Saffie ignored the chair and remained standing. 'Just what the fuck did you think you were doing, knowingly setting me up with an undercover journalist? A married one at that!'

Dr Sheldrake took a seat, looking as calm and unruffled as Saffie was white-knuckled and seething. 'I found the best match for you based on the information you gave in your questionnaire. That's all there was to it.'

'Do you know how many ethics codes you've broken?'

'No. How many?'

Saffie faltered. 'I don't actually know, but I'm sure it's loads. I bet you could be struck off.'

'Because I arranged you a date with a man who didn't tell you the whole truth about himself?' Dr Sheldrake met her eye. 'Perhaps that was part of the reason I thought you'd be well matched, Ms... Ackroyd, isn't it?'

Saffie scowled. 'Russell told you.'

'I have my own resources for discovering these things.'

'No, Russell told you, like the snake in the grass he is,' Saffie snapped. 'You know Russell Foxton is my new boss? I might have to leave my job because of this.'

'Well, I'm sorry for that. It's a dangerous game, going undercover.'

'You know, I was half buying it, all this a-bit-of-magic-but-just-the-right-amount-of-science mumbo jumbo. But it's smoke and mirrors, isn't it? Out of the four people I know who've used this agency, only one's ended up in a decent relationship, and that was more thanks to luck than you.'

'Oh?'

'Yeah, Milo and Christian had a connection from years before they rocked up on your doorstep. It was pure fluke that they were matched with each other. Whereas Tamara's guy was weird, I got someone who was just using me for a mag feature, and Russell only signed up to sell you a bloody ad.' Saffie could feel her cheeks burning. 'You're a fraud, *Dr Sheldrake*. I should've trusted my gut.'

Dr Sheldrake shuffled some papers. 'Look, did you enjoy your date?'

'Well yes, but—'

'And did you feel you had a genuine connection with the match I arranged?'

'At the time, yes, but that doesn't mean—'

'Then I did what I promised. That's all I can offer people: the rest they have to do for themselves.'

'And what about your soulmate guarantee?' Saffie demanded. 'I suppose you're going to tell me that's not legally enforceable, are you?'

Dr Sheldrake shrugged. 'You're welcome to claim your money back. It's a simple matter of filling in a form.'

'All right, give it to me. I'll fill it in now, then I can put all this behind me.'

'I can email it, but I'm afraid you can't submit a refund request until three months after your date.'

'Ah, so there is a catch.'

'That's what you agreed to.' Dr Sheldrake rummaged

in her cardboard box filing cabinet and handed Saffie the last page from her questionnaire, the one that included the agency's small print.

Dr Sheldrake was telling the truth. The small print did specify that no refund request could be submitted until three months following the date. And…

'Oh Christ,' Saffie muttered. 'I signed my real name.'

Dr Sheldrake smiled. 'As I said, I have my resources.'

'I can't believe you set me up.'

'And I'm not impressed that you lied to me,' Dr Sheldrake said, sharpness breaking through the icy calm. 'Under the circumstances, I think I'd be quite justified in rejecting any claim for a refund. I won't, however. You can submit your form subject to the original terms and conditions, as you agreed.'

'By which time you'll have disappeared without trace, right? If this wasn't one big con, why would you make people wait three months?'

Dr Sheldrake smiled. 'Because sometimes, it takes people a little while to realise what it is they really want.'

24

Tamara was working late. Marcie and Dale, perhaps realising that family time was dwindling as university drew closer, had offered to take Willow to the cinema to see the latest Pixar film. With the prospect of an evening to herself, Tamara had decided to stay on at the office for a bit while she collated the results of the early reader surveys.

Except she wasn't actually working. She was watching her phone. Whenever she tried to focus on the questions, she found her gaze drifting back to it. Eventually it lit up with a WhatsApp message, and she snatched it up eagerly.

She opened it and laughed. As usual, Harry had sent her a meme as a conversation-opener.

Me: I'm in my prime
My knees: the f**k you are

The message with it said *Today's meme theme is the joys of middle age. Your turn.*

Tamara tapped a message back.

I thought you'd forgotten meme o'clock today. You're late!

She attached a suitable meme and pressed Send.

Sorry, came the reply. *Surprise visit from my son and his wife. How's life, Tam?*

Tamara replied with a GIF of Kermit the Frog typing frantically. *Working late :-(*

Tamara, you work too hard. Come out for a drink with me instead. I can meet you at your local.

Tamara's fingers hovered over the keypad.

She was tempted. For the past month, she and Harry had been exchanging memes, chatting about life and generally getting to know each other. He'd become Tamara's little island of calm in her crazy mixed-up world. Whenever she'd had another showdown with Nikki, or she was worrying about Andy and the kids, she always found herself reaching for her phone for a bit of Harry time.

But when he suggested meeting up, or even talking on the phone, she always found an excuse. The kids needed her. She had to work. She was tired after a long day. As much as she liked Harry, something always held her back from taking the next step in their friendship.

She'd told herself at first that it was the kids, but she knew that was bullshit. Willow would be thrilled she was seeing 'the Geoffrey man', and the twins were adult enough to be happy for her. Dale might be a little resentful, perhaps, but he'd soon get over that, and besides, the twins would be moving out in a few months. No, it wasn't them.

It was Andy. Bloody Andy, who'd hurt her so much when he'd walked out on his family that Tamara didn't know if she was even capable of falling in love again. Her heart had closed itself off that day, and as much as Tamara wanted to get to know Harry better, she didn't know if she could ever offer him more than friendship. He'd said he was fine with that, but she knew he wanted more. Saffie had been absolutely right when she'd said that friendships were painful when one side wanted more than the other could give.

But they couldn't just be meme buddies forever. And after all, a drink was just a drink, wasn't it? It wasn't a date. She went out for platonic drinks with friends all the time.

Tamara was still hovering, wondering what reply to give, when another message popped up.

Hey. Are you still coming to the BBQ on Saturday? Just to let you know Nat's decided the dress code should be smart-casual. Hope that's OK for you and Willow. Andy x

Tamara scowled as she read it. Not that there was anything particularly offensive in it. She found that just being reminded of her ex-husband's existence was enough to provoke a state of rage these days.

That man! She'd once suffered a mini breakdown because he'd walked out of her life, and now, when all she wanted was to be rid of him, he couldn't leave her alone.

She flicked back to WhatsApp.

Not tonight, she told Harry. *Andy worries. I'll text tomorrow.*

A reply popped up seconds later. Tamara smiled at the photo of Harry and Geoffrey sitting next to each other on the sofa with deadpan expressions and a can of beer each.

Boys' night in it is then, Harry's message read. *Sleep tight, Tam x*

Tamara sent a laughing emoji back and put the phone in her desk drawer, where it couldn't distract her any further.

It was amazing how differently a message from the two men in her life could make her feel. The excited anticipation whenever Harry texted her, and the stomach-plummeting dread when she saw she had a message from Andy. And yet that man had been her world, once, just as he was now presumably Natalie's. The poor cow. She had no idea what she was letting herself in for.

Tamara was making a second attempt to absorb the findings of the reader survey when she heard someone unlock the front door.

She glanced at her phone. Six o'clock. Who was coming in at this time? Had Milo or Saffie forgotten something?

'Hello?' she called out.

A second later, her office door opened and Russell popped his head in.

'Hey, Tam,' he said. 'Sorry to barge in on you.'

She shrugged. 'It's your business. Nikki's not with you, is she?'

He smiled. 'No, you're safe.'

Tamara brushed her hair back from her forehead, feeling the beginnings of a headache. 'What did you come in for? Dropping off more *Lifestyle North*s?'

'I came to talk to you,' he said, helping himself to a chair.

'How did you know I was here?'

'You told me. You said in your email this morning you were planning to stay late and go through the readers' surveys.'

'Oh. Right.' She massaged her temples. 'Sorry, Russ, I'm not with it tonight. I might have to leave the readers' surveys for another evening.'

He frowned. 'What's up, Tam?'

'Oh, nothing. I mean, my ex-husband, but when isn't he a pain in the rear?' She flicked through the sheaf of surveys. 'Anyway, I added a few of these to the feedback spreadsheet so it wasn't a totally wasted night.'

'How's it looking?'

Tamara waggled her mouse to wake up her computer. 'It's interesting reading. We've got a small but significant number of international subscribers with an average age twenty years younger than our local subscribers. While the locals like the features on regional news and characters, the international subscribers tend to list the quirkier stuff like "Stranger than Fiction". I think Saffie's right: that could be a bigger market for us if we can look at ways to tap into it.'

'Nik isn't going to like that. International subscribers don't bring in local advertisers. She wants us to be tapping into a younger demographic in this area.'

'Well I don't mean to be rude, Russ, but that's kind of tough. The only way we could do that is to change the whole nature of the magazine. Sorry, but that's not going to happen on my watch.'

He sighed. 'I know. Nikki's not family; she doesn't really get *The Throstler*.'

'But you do. You're not going to let her turn us into a mini *Lifestyle North*, are you?'

'Of course not. I just think there must be a compromise.' He cast a listless glance at the pile of reader surveys. 'You're right: *The Throstler*'s unique and it ought to stay unique. But at the same time, Nikki's right: if we don't adapt, we won't survive. We're losing subscribers at a worrying rate. There has to be a middle ground.'

'Well, what is it?'

'I don't know, do I? I was sort of hoping the surveys would give us a clue, but all they seem to be telling us is that we've got two wildly varying groups of readers.'

Tamara looked again at the spreadsheet where she was collating feedback. 'You know what you should do?'

'What?'

'Talk to Saffie.'

He frowned. 'Saffie?'

'Yeah. She knows *The Throstler* better than anyone outside this family, but she's detached enough to inject a healthy dose of perspective into how we do things. She's smart, she's savvy and she's got great ideas when Nikki shuts up and lets her get a word in. The reader survey was her idea, and while it might not have produced much insight in terms of selling ads, it's been brilliant for helping me get fresh content ideas. Saffie Ackroyd is the best thing that ever happened to this mag, Russ.'

'You think a lot of her, don't you?'

'Why wouldn't I? She's proved herself and then some over the past decade. I just wish we could keep her.'

Russell smiled sadly. 'The problem is, Saffie doesn't want to talk to me.'

He sounded wistful, which wasn't an emotion Tamara was used to seeing in her eternally confident, cocksure cousin.

'Is that any surprise?' she asked.

'I never meant… it was a mistake.' He sighed. 'Cards on the table, Tam. I didn't come looking for you to talk about *The Throstler*. I wanted to talk about Saffie. Saffie and me, I mean.'

'To me? Why?'

'Well, she's your friend. I thought you might be willing to

help a cousin out with a bit of love life advice.'

Tamara raised an eyebrow. 'You're asking me for advice on your love life? Am I really your best option?'

'Sadly, yes.'

'And why should I give you advice? You really hurt her, you know. You could easily have scrapped that article the same way she scrapped hers.'

He pressed his eyes closed. 'I know. It was stupid. We'd sold an ad on the back of it, and I didn't think I could let Alison Sheldrake down when we'd committed to it.'

'And then you rub salt in the wound by suggesting a feature about runaway brides when you know what she went through with Kieran. What was that about?'

'It never occurred to me she'd make that connection. I was just thinking about the interviews with the Golden Wedding couples, trying to come up with something to kind of bookend it. Something we could use to sell a few ads within the wedding industry.'

Tamara shook her head. 'Always it's ads with you.'

'I've screwed up utterly, Tam.' He looked up to meet her eyes. 'Will you help me out? Please.'

She couldn't help smiling at his earnest expression. He looked so helpless, it was quite refreshing. Russell had never been helpless in his life.

'Convince me first,' she said. 'What is it you actually want me to help you with?'

'I just want Saffie to trust me again. To believe me when I say I'm sorry for writing the article.'

'To what end? To get her into bed?'

'Come on, I'm not a horny teenager. No, because…'

'Because?'

'Because I really felt something that day,' he said quietly. 'I know she doesn't believe me, and you're right, that's hardly surprising. But it's true.'

'What did you feel?'

'The beginning of something.' He laughed bleakly. 'Then I buggered it up and it ended up being the end of something instead.'

'And you want to reset things? Go back to beginnings instead of endings?'

'That's exactly it. To explore what could've been if I hadn't made such an almighty mess of everything.' He sighed. 'I made so many mistakes with Nikki. Our marriage should have ended long before it did – should never have happened in the first place, probably. It'd be easy to blame her – the way she can be – but it was my fault. I could see the relationship wasn't healthy but I was so desperate to make things work that I wouldn't face up to it. I couldn't bear to think of us repeating that car crash my mum and dad went through when they divorced. And now I've met someone who might actually be The One in a way Nikki never really was, I've gone and cocked it up in a totally different way. What the fuck is wrong with me, Tam?'

He looked serious and sad: more vulnerable than Tamara had seen him since childhood.

'It is a shame how it panned out with Saffie,' she said in a softer voice. 'Tell me how it happened.'

Russell pushed his fingers into his hair. 'It was daft really. Nikki took a call from a potential advertiser asking what our rates were—'

'Alison Sheldrake.'

'Right. Sheldrake said we were out of her price range,

but I thought the business could make an interesting feature and we offered that as a sweetener. So she booked a half page and we said we'd send someone over to scope it out.'

'And that someone was you.'

Russell laughed bitterly. 'Yeah. I thought it'd be a laugh.'

'Did you even want a date or was it strictly business?'

'I told Saffie I was open to meeting someone but that was a fib, to be honest. I wasn't thinking about relationships at that point. But that changed pretty soon after meeting Saffie.'

'Why? She's nothing like your usual girlfriends.'

He laughed. 'Tell me about it. I don't know, there was just… something. She was so different from anyone I'd met before. It felt like even though on the surface we were these completely different people, there was something inside us that was… the same. Does that make sense?'

Tamara thought about Harry, a faint smile on her lips. 'Yeah, I get that.'

Russell struck his forehead with the flat of his palm. 'God, why did I write that stupid feature? So we'd have lost an advertiser and had to find some last-minute content for a few pages, so what? I suppose I thought it was unlikely she'd see it.'

'So you did it because you didn't expect to get caught?' Tamara shook her head. 'Not good, Russ.'

'No, I mean I knew she probably would eventually. I just thought that by the time it came to her attention, we'd know each other well enough for her to find it funny. The mag wasn't due on shelves for three weeks after our date.'

'And then you delivered it straight into her hands two weeks in advance of the on-sale date. That's pretty bad luck.'

'I didn't know she worked here, did I?' He peeled Post-it notes idly from a pad on her desk. 'What do you think I should do? I can't just walk away, never knowing if this could have been... you know, it.'

'You need to earn back her trust,' Tamara said.

'I know that, don't I? How though?'

'Put yourself in her shoes. She goes on a date for an undercover feature and ends up forming a genuine bond with someone who might be her actual soulmate.'

Russell blinked. 'She said that?'

'Not in so many words, but it's kind of obvious. Then she discovers he was also undercover, and unlike her he went ahead and used their bond for a magazine feature. Everything he told her was a lie: from his name to his feelings for her.'

'But it wasn't a lie!' Russell protested. 'I mean, OK, the name and job, but not the feelings.'

Tamara shrugged. 'How does she know that? All she knows is you've told her a catalogue of lies and used her for your feature. There's no reason for her to trust one thing more than another.'

'So how do I fix it?'

'You can stop lying to her, for a start. You told me not five minutes ago that you lied to her even after the date about having been open to a relationship when you signed up for the agency.'

'Well yes, but only because I didn't want her to think—'

Tamara held up a hand. 'No more lies, Russ. Come clean, about all of it.'

'But that'll just get her even more pissed off with me.'

'Maybe, but it's a clean slate from then on. And...' She

pondered for a moment. 'I think you need to make a gesture of some kind. Open up to her about something personal.'

'Like what?'

'I don't know, but something. What she told you on the date, about Kieran – that's really tough for her to talk about. And then she felt you betrayed that when you suggested she write a feature about it.'

'I told you, I never meant—'

'I know,' she said soothingly. 'I'm just saying, that's how it must feel to her. She made herself vulnerable and you exploited it. If you could find a way to make yourself equally vulnerable, show her the real you, that might go some way to showing her there's more to Russell Foxton than deceit.'

'How though?' Russell rested his chin despondently on one fist. 'She hates me, Tam. I don't think she's going to be in the mood for a heart-to-heart.'

'Yes. That is a problem.' Tamara considered things. 'OK, because I really think you mean it and because Saf deserves to be happy… leave it with me. If I can get Milo on board, between us we might be able to cook something up to help you out.'

25

'And you're sure your friend is going to be OK looking after them?' Christian asked again.

'Chris, she'll be fine,' Milo said, putting his hands on Christian's shoulders. 'Saffie grew up with dogs. She knows the drill.'

OK, Saffie's St Bernard had died when she was seven, but it still counted. Anyway, Nigel was essentially a floppy, meowy dog, wasn't he? Saffie had all the transferrable skills she needed to mind Chris's canine brood for a few hours.

'Not five at a time though. You know what a handful they can be.' Christian cast a worried look at his dogs. Three were asleep on Milo's sofa, one was burrowing underneath it for the chew she'd stashed there, and six-month-old Bailey, the baby of the bunch, was about to cock his leg against a yucca plant. He stopped when he noticed his dad's eye on him, assuming the dog equivalent of a 'who, me?' expression.

'I never like to leave them alone,' Christian said. 'Chip has to have his tablets at four and Luna gets separation anxiety, and Bailey… well, he just eats everything.'

'They'll be with her for three hours tops,' Milo said. 'I can't leave Tamara to go to her ex's horrific barbecue on her own.' He gave Christian a kiss. 'Go on, get going. You don't want to be late.'

'Right.' Christian still looked anxious. 'If you're sure she'll be fine.'

'You want to vet her yourself? She can't be more than a few minutes away.'

'No, you're right, I ought to go. I don't want to get stuck in weekend traffic.' He returned Milo's kiss. 'See you later, Mile. I hope your family thing goes well.'

'Thanks, Chris. We'll miss you.' He nodded to the dogs. 'These guys and me, I mean.'

Christian smiled. 'Likewise.' He waved to his dogs. 'Be good for Uncle Milo, chaps.'

When he'd gone, Milo squeezed himself on to the sofa between Loki and Mitzi, who took up a surprising amount of space when they spread out. He reached out to stroke Loki's ears.

That was the second time he'd dropped an 'I'll miss you' without Christian reciprocating. 'Likewise' wasn't quite the same as saying it back. As for 'I love you', they seemed further away now, six weeks after the event, than they had been on their twenty-four-hour date.

Chris had been very quick to run away when Milo had suggested he stay to meet Saffie too. Did he think things were moving too fast?

In a lot of ways, things were going great. They hung out nearly every day. There was lots of good sex, and lots of good cuddling afterwards. Milo knew this was the best relationship he'd ever had. And yet...

Things had just gone wrong so many times before.

West had dumped him when Milo had suggested he meet Saffie and Tamara, and West was just one in a long line of boyfriends who'd bolted once they had Milo Cook marked down as Mr Too Much, Too Soon. He'd been trying so hard not to make that mistake with Christian, but as happy as they were, it felt like they were moving away from where Milo wanted to get to rather than towards it.

And if Chris did think things were going too quickly, then what would happen? One day it'd be 'we need to talk', followed by 'it's not you, it's me', and a heartbroken Milo would be thrown back on to the scrapheap of thirtysomething singledom. Except this time there'd be no climbing back off, because after experiencing what he'd had with Chris, Milo was certain he was ruined for other men.

There was a knock on the door, and he pulled himself out of his reverie to let Saffie in.

'Here I am for these ruddy dogs then.' She frowned at his expression. 'You OK, Mile? You're giving off vibes of glumness.'

'Oh, just worrying Chris is going off me. Same old same old.'

'He's not allowed to go off you. You're the only one of the three of us who's managed to find happiness and it'll destroy my faith in both love and humanity if it doesn't work out.' Saffie followed him into the living room. 'You don't really think that, do you?'

'Dunno. Maybe.' He gestured to Luna spreadeagled on the sofa. 'Pull up a chihuahua.'

Saffie sat down and gave Luna's tummy a rub. The little dog twitched her leg appreciatively.

'Cute, aren't they? I didn't know dogs came in these sizes.'

'It's a liberty describing them as dogs, if you ask me. Sizewise, there really ought to be a cut-off point at which dogs end and rodents begin.' Milo sat down on the other side of Mitzi, who rolled over and laid one paw on his thigh. 'You're right though, they are ridiculously cute.'

'Surely Chris wouldn't entrust his precious rodent dogs to you if he was planning to dump you.'

Milo sighed. 'Maybe I'm just being paranoid. After West and the others, I've developed a bit of Tam's Worst-case Scenario Syndrome.'

'What makes you think he's going off you?'

'Well in some ways things are going great. But it felt like we were so close to exchanging I Love Yous that day, and now...'

'He still hasn't said it?'

Milo shook his head gloomily. 'I can't even get an "I'll miss you". And he practically threw himself out of the window when I suggested he stick around to meet you.'

'Well, it's only been six weeks,' Saffie said. 'You've got the rest of your lives for soppy love declarations and meeting each other's mates.'

'Yeah. I hope so.' He tickled Loki absently under the chin. 'I hope so.'

'What time do you have to be at Tam's barbecue?'

'Not for an hour. I wanted to brief you on looking after the Bark Brigade.'

'Bark Brigade sounds like a knock-off version of that cartoon Willow likes.'

'Heh. It does.' He pointed to Bailey, who'd edged up to a houseplant and was sniffing it with interest. 'That's the one to watch: the rebellious teenager. The other four mostly just snooze when they're not out on their walk, but he's solid mischief.'

'What do I need to do then?'

Milo handed her a Post-it where he'd scribbled down the dogs' itinerary. 'They have their tea at five o'clock. I ought to be back by then, but if not, their food's in the kitchen – I've written down how much they get each. Bailey's on special puppy stuff so his is separate.'

Saffie looked at the dogs, who were all a sandy yellow colour, large of ear and small of body. 'How will I remember which one's Bailey?'

'Because he'll be the one causing trouble,' Milo said. 'They can have a beef chew each at four o'clock, which is when Chip has his arthritis medicine, and they usually have a half-hour walk now and a longer one after tea.'

'It's the walking that worries me,' Saffie said. 'There's so many of them! What if I lose one and don't notice?'

'That's why I told you to come round early. Then you only need to manage a couple. Me and Chris can take them for their longer walk later this evening.' Milo stood up. 'Come on. We'll go to the woods.'

Once the Bark Brigade were on leads, humans and dogs left Milo's little brick terrace and took the dirt track up to the woods.

'You're right, this isn't so bad,' Saffie said as she watched her charges, Chip and Bailey, sniffing in the undergrowth. 'It's even making me a bit pup-broody.'

'Oh, Bailey'll have cured you of that by the time I get back from Andy's barbecue.' Milo handed her a roll of poo bags. 'Here. These'll help.'

'Dogs this big can't produce much poo, surely.'

'Don't you believe it. These guys are poo machines.'

They walked through a tree-lined picnic area and headed towards a rocky clearing.

'At least you've finally convinced Christian you are a dog person,' Saffie said. 'That must be the basis for true love.'

'If it is, he's not letting on,' Milo said, watching Luna scoffing someone's leftover sandwich.

'Be patient.'

'What about your blind date? Have you stopped wanting to slap him yet?'

'Huh. Yes, but only because I'd get more satisfaction from slapping his wife.'

'Russ is OK,' Milo said, recalling the conversation he'd had with Tamara about his cousin's love life woes. 'I know he cocked up, but he's not a bad guy. He knows he made a mistake.'

'Or I made the mistake when I thought there could be something between me and him.'

'Couldn't you talk to him?'

'About what? His allergy to the truth? Or his attitude that women exist to be emotionally exploited for magazine features?'

Milo considered challenging this, but he knew there was no point when Saffie's scowl reached that level of glower. Russell might be family, but Milo's first loyalty would always be to his best friend.

Still, it was a shame. They could make each other happy, those two. Unfortunately, them making each other happy relied on Saffie learning to trust Russ again, which wasn't looking likely any time this millennium.

'No, Russell showed his true colours when he went ahead

with that stupid feature.' Saffie stooped to pick up a banana peel and put it in a nearby bin. 'I'm thinking of looking for a new job actually.'

'Well, why don't you?'

'Oh, right. I'd miss you too, mate.'

'Go on, you know I would,' Milo said, nudging her. 'But you have always said you don't want to stick around *The Throstler* forever. Maybe it is time to think about the next step. We're all getting older.'

'Yes, it's really started to feel like the clock's ticking this year. Plus there's a strong chance that one day soon I'm going to beat Nikki to death with the microwave spatula.' Saffie picked her way over a rocky patch of ground, trying to keep her balance as the dogs strained to get to the next exciting smell. 'I've even had a look on some job sites. There's a few things that might suit me. I just can't bring myself to go for them.'

'Why not?'

'I just... don't want to leave it like this. With the future all wobbly and Nikki doing everything she can to make *The Throstler* into something it isn't. I love that bloody mag, as daft as it is.'

'I know. Me too.'

'I don't want to leave you guys alone to cope with Nikki either,' Saffie said. 'She can sack me if she wants, but at least I'll know I did what I could to back up Tam.'

Milo smiled at her. 'Aww. That's sweet, Saf.'

She smiled too. 'And me not even family.'

'Nikki can sod off with that. You're more family than she – shit!'

It happened so quickly. One minute there was Saffie, picking her way over the rocks with Bailey and Chip. Then there was Saffie, Bailey, Chip... and the squirrel. After that the scene became a mass of leads, sandy-coloured shapes and a vague sense of flailing limbs to the frantic accompaniment of barks and squirrel squawks. When the dust settled, the squirrel was gone, Bailey and Chip were sitting erect with their best 'aren't I a good boy?' faces on, and Saffie was on the ground clutching her ankle.

'Oh my God!' Milo fell to his knees at her side. 'What did you do, Saf?'

'Rolled my ankle when they made a dash for that squirrel,' she said through clenched teeth. 'Fuck *me*, that hurts!'

'Did it crack?'

'There was a definite crunch, yeah.'

'Then it could be a fracture. Can you walk?'

'I... think so.'

Milo helped her to her feet. Her face turned even more ghastly from the pain of putting weight on the damaged ankle, but she forced herself to stay upright, leaning heavily on Milo's shoulder.

'We need to get you to A&E,' Milo said.

'I can't. I've got to—' Saffie sucked in a pained breath. 'There's the Golden Oldies interview later. And you promised Tam you'd be at Andy's barbecue. There's no time for A&E.'

'Saffie, your ankle might be broken. That takes precedence over everything else.'

'But what about this lot?' She nodded to the dogs.

Milo paused. He couldn't, could he? But he'd told Tam

he'd do what he could to give Cupid a helping hand, and for it to happen, just like this... that had to be fate, surely.

'Just let me send a couple of texts,' he said to Saffie. 'Then I'll see if I can shepherd five dogs and one damsel in distress back to my place while we wait for the cavalry.'

26

'Marcie, did you put Willow's rucksack in the car?' Tamara asked as she bustled around the kitchen, throwing random foodstuffs into a carrier bag.

'Yes, Mum. I packed everything you asked me to, as I've mentioned several million times already.'

Dale poked his head through the door. 'Are we going or what?' He frowned. 'Mum, what're you packing all that food for?'

'We can't turn up empty-handed, can we? I forgot to tell your dad that Marcie was vegan now, and Natalie might not have had time… time to…' Tamara trailed off, her eyes widening. 'Oh God, I forgot to check dates! We'll poison everyone!' She tipped the bag out on the kitchen table.

Dale shook his head. 'She's cracked up.'

'September 2022,' Tamara muttered as she checked the date on the first tin. 'That's OK. And this one's December—'

Marcie put a gentle hand on her shoulder.

'Mum, you can't put it off forever,' she said quietly. 'I already told Dad I was vegan. It's time to go.'

'We can't go until Uncle Milo gets here,' Tamara said absently, her gaze fixed on a tin of beans.

'I thought he was meeting us there.'

'No, I told him to come to the house so we can go in together.' She looked up. 'He ought to be here by now. Where's my phone?'

'Oh yeah, that's what I came in for.' Dale handed it to her. 'It just boomer pinged so I guess you got a text.'

Tamara read the message from her brother.

'Oh shit,' she whispered.

'What?' Marcie said. 'Is he going to be late?'

'No, he... he can't come. Saffie's hurt. Not dangerously, but a sprained ankle – maybe a fracture. He's got to find someone to take her to A&E while he minds Christian's dogs.'

'All right, if we're not waiting for him then let's go,' Dale said.

'Dale, you don't understand. I... I can't do this alone. I have to have Milo.'

Dale exchanged a look with his twin.

'Why don't you let us go on our own, Mum?' Marcie said in a voice that sounded like she was dealing with someone on the verge of meltdown, which probably wasn't far from the truth. 'I told you there was no need for you to come.'

'I have to. I promised Willow.' Tamara closed her eyes. 'Right. You two, get your sister in the car. I just... need to pay a quick visit to the basement.'

'How's the pain now?' Milo asked as Saffie sat with her ankle elevated on a footstool.

'Worse than when I did it.' She removed the pack of frozen peas to examine the damaged ankle. 'Oh God, it's the size of a cantaloupe! And you cannot tell me blue's a healthy colour for a body part. When's the taxi coming?'

Her phone buzzed, and she took it out.

'I didn't call a taxi,' Milo said.

Saffie didn't hear him. She was too focused on reading her text message.

'This is turning into a real cracker of a day,' she muttered.

'Who's it from?'

'My mum. She picked up the latest issue of *Lifestyle North* this morning. Apparently she was fascinated to read all about this flaky tattooed chick with blue hair and a predilection for pulp fiction novels who signed up for some avant-garde new dating agency.'

Milo frowned. 'I thought Russ said he left out your personal details.'

'He left out what he thinks were my personal details, but he left in plenty that the people who know me can identify me from. Hair, hobbies, dress sense, tattoos, age – I mean, who else can it be?'

'Is your mum upset?'

'Oh no, she's all in favour. She's probably hoping she can finally shift the party favours that've been taking up space in her garage since my last wedding got called off. And guess what? She's ringing her ever-so-lucky daughter later for the inside scoop on the new man in her life.' Saffie groaned. 'I need to stop using the term "rock bottom" every time something humiliating happens to me. It's like waving a lightning rod around in a thunderstorm and shouting "Thor's a big fanny!" at the top of your voice.'

The doorbell rang.

'I guess that's my taxi,' Saffie said, lowering her foot. 'Help me to the door, can you?'

'I told you, it's not a taxi. I arranged a lift.'

'Who from? Everyone we know's doing stuff.' Saffie clocked the guilty expression on Milo's face and frowned. 'Milo, who from?'

Milo rubbed behind his ear. 'Well, like you said, everyone's busy, and I've got the pups to mind, and, um, I didn't think you should be on your own, so... I texted a mutual friend.'

'Oh my *God*. Milo, you absolute...' She nodded to the door. 'If that's who I think it is, you can tell him to sod right off again.'

'Saffie, you have to have someone. You can hardly walk.' Milo went to answer the door.

Saffie groaned when Milo ushered Russell inside. 'I knew it.'

He looked so bloody smug, that was the worst thing. As if she personally had begged him to rescue her, like a poor, helpless damsel in distress.

'I'm told a taxi service and supportive shoulder are needed,' he said, smiling with a quite infuriating expression of self-assurance.

'Then you were misinformed,' Saffie said coldly. 'Sorry you've wasted your precious time.'

'Really? Because your ankle looks like a post-transformation Veruca Salt.'

'Minor sprain, that's all. Bye, Dick.'

'Don't listen to her,' Milo said, swooping to scoop up Bailey, who was gnawing on the leg of the coffee table. 'She can barely put weight on it, let alone walk. Could be a fracture.'

Saffie folded her arms. 'I'm not going with him.'

Milo deposited Bailey on the other side of the room, where there was less opportunity for mischief. 'What's your alternative plan then? Stay here until it turns gangrenous and your foot drops off?'

'Rather that than go anywhere with him.'

'Oh, don't be like that,' Russell said. 'I'll take good care of you. I won't even speak to you if you don't want me to.'

Saffie turned a look of dislike on him. 'Where's the missus?'

'At her house, I should think, spending time with her boyfriend. Did you think we still lived together?'

'I never gave your living arrangements a moment's thought.'

He dropped to a crouching position. 'Come on, let's get you to the car. It's against company policy for staff to have gangrenous limbs dropping off all over the place. I'd hate to have to give you a written warning.'

Saffie winced as she tried to flex her ankle. It really did hurt, and it was so swollen now that she had hardly any movement in it. Mortifying though it was, she was going to have to go with Russell.

'Fine,' she said through gritted teeth. 'But don't speak to me.'

'Whatever you want, Saffie. Mile, you take the other side.'

Milo crouched by her too. Saffie stretched her arms around their necks and they helped her to her feet.

She grimaced as she put weight on the ankle. Through a combination of instinct and need, she leaned into Russell as the two men helped her to the car.

Ugh. That stupid aftershave. What did it smell like? Some sort of stinky tree, cedar or whatever. Why did he always wear the same stuff? It reminded her too much of a day she was now desperate to forget.

'Look after her, Russ,' Milo said when they'd deposited her in the passenger seat of Russell's BMW. 'Saf, I'll call you later.'

'Can I really not talk to you?' Russell said when they were on their way to the hospital.

Saffie glared at him. 'So you drive a BMW, do you? How very predictable.'

He shrugged. 'It was mine and Nikki's. She got the house, I've got the car.'

'Sounds like a fair swap.'

'We'll get everything divvied up properly when divorce wheels are in motion.' He glanced at her in the mirror. 'Anything else you want to know about my marriage? Feel free to ask away.'

'Yeah, one thing.' Saffie shuffled to face him, pain making her fearless. 'Why the fuck don't you tell your bloody wife to stop interfering with Tam's job? You've had a long career as a journalist, and you know you'd never stand for some new manager telling you what you could and couldn't put in your own mag. On top of that, it's your great-grandad's legacy – Fran's legacy, and you and Nikki seem intent on pissing that legacy right up the wall. So go on, Russell Foxton, riddle me that.'

He blinked. 'Whoa. Is that the ankle talking?'

'Partly, and the fact that I've stopped caring whether

you sack me or not.' Saffie met his eyes in the mirror. 'Do you really care more about keeping in your ex-wife's good books than you do about your family?'

'Saffie...' He sighed. 'I wish I could get you to understand. You've never been married.'

'Thanks for reminding me about that. Did you have another new feature idea that can only be tackled by your resident ageing spinster? "Giving up on life: a single woman's guide" maybe?'

'I swear I never had a thought in my mind about your relationship history when I suggested that feature. It just came to me.'

'Huh. I bet it did.'

'Look, I didn't mean to offend you. All I mean is, you've never been married so you don't realise what a... an investment it is. All those years, sharing everything – money, homes, possessions. Each other. When it ends there's so much baggage, physical and emotional.'

'Can you really not see how toxic your relationship with Nikki is? I don't mean when you were married, I mean now. A relationship, whether business or romantic, involves give and take. Compromise, communication. It doesn't involve manipulation and gaslighting.'

'That isn't what's happening. You see the worst of Nikki. She's not always that way.'

'The fact she's sometimes that way ought to be enough to ring alarm bells.' Saffie looked at him. 'Can you deny she calls all the shots in your relationship?'

'She... likes her own way. Perhaps I do let her have it more often than she should – not always, I hasten to add. There are reasons, Saffie.'

'Yeah? What reasons?'

He glanced at her. 'Your parents, are they still married?'

'Yes. Why?'

'Mine aren't – I mean, they weren't. They were long divorced when I lost my dad twenty years ago.'

'I'm sorry,' Saffie said automatically.

'Thanks. Anyway, him and my mum divorced when I was ten. It turned nasty – it doesn't take much to turn these things nasty, even when they involve nice people. It was rough on all of us, but worse for my dad. He had a complete mental breakdown. It's not just a separation: it's your whole way of life, falling down around your ears, and sometimes it's someone who once loved you with all their heart acting like they hate your guts.'

Saffie watched his face, flickering with emotion.

'You think that could happen to you?' she said, her voice slightly softer.

'I think it could happen to anybody. Nikki and me shared a lot of our lives and I don't want us to become enemies now that's over. That's why I go out of my way to be cooperative at work. I suppose it looks to you like I let her have her own way too much, but I'm really just trying to keep everything working.'

'But when you take that attitude, it's your cousin who suffers. You know, Russell, Tam really looked up to you. All the time I've known her, she's talked about this talented cousin who's her gran's favourite and had this incredible high-flying career. You've really dropped in her estimation lately.'

He frowned. 'She thinks I'm Fran's favourite?'

'Well, yeah.'

'But Tam's her favourite; everyone in the family knows that. Why do you think she got offered a job at *The Throstler* straight from uni while I had to work my balls off doing tea rounds on the local paper? Fran had her pegged as the next editor from about five years old.'

'That's not how she sees it.'

'It's how it is. I thought she knew that.' He turned into the hospital car park. 'Here we are. I'll get as close to the door as I can.'

27

'Well, here we are,' Tamara said with false brightness as she parked up next to someone's Jag. There were so many fancy cars here, her ancient Polo ought to be quite safe from any marauding car thieves.

Andy and Natalie's drive was more like a car park, surrounded by acres of trim green lawn. Behind it sat their humble abode: a huge, white, angular building with a lot of windows. Andy had obviously been doing well for himself since he'd thrown off the shackles of his wife and kids.

'Is this where the baby's going to live?' Willow asked.

She'd been quiet all day as they'd prepared to see her dad again, but she hadn't let out a peep of either enthusiasm or objection. She'd submitted to being dressed in her best party frock, scrubbed and brushed, before climbing into the car without a murmur.

'That's right,' Tamara said.

'His house is loads bigger than ours.'

'That's because his mummy and daddy have got more money than us.'

'But you said we had the same daddy.'

'Yes.' Tamara dug her nails into her palm. 'Yes. You do.'

Marcie rested a hand on her arm. 'Mum.'

'Sorry. I'll be OK.' Tamara spotted a familiar figure leaning against a battered Ford Escort and broke into a smile. 'Oh, thank God. He made it.'

Willow squeaked. 'Mummy, look! It's Harry! Harry and Geoffrey are here!'

It was certainly Harry, although Geoffrey wasn't actually in evidence – Willow obviously assumed that wherever one was, the other was sure to be around.

Harry looked rather good – handsomer than Tamara remembered. He'd obviously made an effort in what she guessed were his best shirt and trousers. Tamara was surprised to feel her tummy jump when he waved, smiling his face-transforming smile.

That was the thing about Harry Hamilton: he crept up on you. You tried to laugh him off, convince yourself he wasn't the falling-in-love-with type, then weeks later you'd be asking yourself why you were unable to stop thinking about the man. Already she felt stronger, knowing he was here.

'Who the hell is that?' Dale demanded as Harry approached.

'It's Mum's date from that agency.' Marcie turned to scrutinise her mum's pink cheeks. 'It is, right?'

'Yes,' Tamara said, feeling herself blush. 'I didn't know who else to ask. Be nice, kids, please.'

Willow had already run to fling herself at Harry's legs. He laughed as she hugged him.

'All right, short stuff, I missed you too.' He glanced at Tamara. 'Well, here I am.'

Tamara beamed at him. 'Thanks for coming at such short notice.'

'Where's Geoffrey?' Willow asked breathlessly.

'He wasn't included in the party invitation.' Harry clocked her look of dismay. 'But don't worry, I told him he could wait in the car. He'll be here to say hello.'

Willow bounced on her heels.

'You guys have *got* to meet Geoffrey,' she told her older siblings with the smug air of someone in on a very exciting secret. 'He's so *funny*! Wait till you see, Dale.'

'Yeah. Great, Will.' Dale examined Harry, radiating hostility. Tamara flushed with embarrassment.

'Um, this is Dale, my son,' she said. 'And his twin sister, Marcie. Kids, this is Harry Hamilton. He's my… friend.'

'Lovely to meet you both.' Harry held out his hand to Dale. 'The man of the family, eh? Your mum talks about little else but you and your sisters.'

Dale glared at the hand. 'All right?' he muttered.

Marcie shot her brother a look and gave Harry's hand a shake. 'Hi. Er, Mum and Will told us about you.'

'All good, I hope?'

'No, she said you were weird and you hang out with a talking bear,' Dale said, looking up defiantly.

Harry laughed. 'Well, that's as accurate a description of me as I've ever heard. I suppose we should show our faces at this party, shouldn't we?'

Tamara nodded, relieved to be able to get Dale and his glares out of Harry's sight. 'Yes, let's go.'

'You told this guy all our private family business?' Dale muttered to her as they walked towards the house.

'Dale, please, not now,' Tamara murmured back. 'I've got enough on my plate without you going into a sulk.'

'What did you have to ask him along for?'

'Because Uncle Milo couldn't come and I... I needed someone.'

'What for? You've got us.'

'That's not the same,' Marcie whispered. 'We're here for the baby, and Dad. Harry's just here for Mum. I get it.'

Tamara smiled at her. 'Thanks, Marce.'

They followed the sound of revelry to the back of the house, where a marquee had been erected. Andy never had been one to do things by halves, whether it was hosting a barbecue or walking out on his family. There was a bouncy castle for the kids, and a sound system filled the air with music. Young, beautiful people were milling around, eating burgers and drinking Prosecco. There wasn't a single person Tamara recognised. Obviously when Andy had had his so-called epiphany, he'd decided to get himself a whole new set of friends.

Tamara spotted Andy behind the barbecue, talking to an attractive woman she assumed must be a friend of Natalie's. Natalie herself was chatting to a group a little distance away, beautiful as always with one hand resting proudly on her swollen belly. Tamara couldn't help noticing she looked a little pale, however, and although she smiled and laughed as she played the good hostess, her gaze would keep drifting over to Andy and the woman he was with.

Andy caught sight of them first. He nodded to Tamara, looking embarrassed. She looked embarrassed right back. Then he frowned as he noticed Harry, holding Willow's hand.

Natalie spotted the family group through the crowd and came hurrying towards them.

'At last! The guests of honour,' she said, beaming.

'Everyone, this is Tamara, Andy's first wife, and her children – I mean, Andy's children.'

The partygoers looked a bit taken aback. Clearly none of them had been briefed about their host's complicated family structure.

Andy put down his tongs and came over.

'Nat, don't make a fuss,' he said in a low voice. 'They must feel awkward enough already.'

Natalie's face fell. 'Sorry. Was I making a fuss? I was just trying to make them feel welcome.'

'You weren't making a fuss at all,' Tamara said, giving her a swift hug. 'Thanks for inviting us. I'm sorry—'

She stopped. What was she sorry for? That for Willow's sake, she'd had to turn up to a party the hosts would evidently rather she hadn't been invited to? She quickly changed tack.

'Not long left now,' she said. 'You're glowing, Natalie.'

Natalie laughed. 'Thank you. I think "glowing" is the only socially acceptable compliment you can pay a pregnant woman, isn't it? I'm sure it must be a euphemism for "huge".'

Tamara laughed too. 'You call that huge? I'll have to show you a photo of me when the twins were nearly due.'

Natalie fixed her with a grateful smile, evidently pleased the ex-wife hadn't turned up just to scratch her eyes out.

Andy, for some reason, looked irritated to see them getting along so well. Perhaps he'd been looking forward to watching the women in his life scrap over him. Or maybe he just didn't fancy the idea of his wives past and future being in a position to gang up on him. He didn't say anything, however, but turned his attention to the twins.

'Hi, you guys.'

Dale just glared at him. Marcie, after a moment's hesitation, stepped forward to give him a hug. However, at the last minute she seemed to think better of it and shook his hand instead.

He smiled. 'Come on, Marce, is that it?'

'What did you expect?' Dale demanded.

The other partygoers, picking up on the fact there was an atmosphere – and not a very jolly one – subtly started drifting off, leaving them in their own little space.

'OK. I suppose that's fair.' Andy faltered. 'So… Marcie told me you passed your driving test. First time as well. Well done, son.'

Dale shrugged.

Andy turned to Willow. 'Hi again, kiddo.'

Willow just stared, clinging tightly to Harry's hand.

Andy tried again. 'Did you make your Lego palace?'

Willow continued to stare, and if a five-year-old's looks could wither, this was as withering a one as had ever graced the face of a primary-schooler. Then she turned to Natalie.

'Is that where the baby is?' she asked, pointing to Natalie's tummy.

'That's right, sweetie. But it won't be long before he's ready to come out and meet us.'

'What's he called?'

Natalie glanced at Andy. 'Shall we tell them?'

'If they promise to keep it top secret,' Andy said, smiling.

Natalie bent to address Willow. 'We've decided his name's going to be Cody. I mean, if that's all right with you. He's your brother.'

'Is he really properly my brother?'

'He really properly is.' Natalie winced as Cody took a well-aimed kick at her insides. 'And he's shaping up to be a real little monkey.'

Willow giggled. 'My mummy says I'm a little monkey.'

'Do you want to feel him?'

Willow looked at her mum, then gave a cautious nod. Natalie took the little girl's hand and guided it to her stomach.

Willow squealed as she felt the baby move. 'Mummy, he kicked me!'

Tamara smiled. 'I'm sure that must mean he likes you.'

'Babe, why don't you get everyone drinks?' Natalie asked Andy.

'Right.' He looked at the twins. 'J2os OK for you kids?'

'I'll have a beer,' Dale said.

Andy frowned. 'Beer?'

'He's eighteen, Andy,' Tamara reminded him once again.

'Right. Of course. I'll be back in a minute.'

Tamara couldn't help noticing how Natalie's worried gaze followed him to the house.

'Will, do you want to go on the bouncy castle?' Dale asked his sister. 'I can go on with you if you're scared.'

'OK!' Willow put her hand in her brother's and they headed for the bouncy castle. Natalie, meanwhile, fell into conversation with Marcie, asking her how her exams had been going.

'He's a good lad, your lad,' Harry said softly to Tamara.

'At heart. Although in this case he just wants an excuse to go on the bouncy castle like the big kid he is.' She looked up at him. 'I'm sorry he was rude to you. It's tough being eighteen, especially without your dad around.'

'What lad isn't protective of his mum? He doesn't want to see you get hurt.'

'Thanks again for coming, Harry. I really didn't want to do this on my own.'

He smiled. 'I thought you'd never give me another chance to see you.'

'I nearly didn't,' she said, grimacing. 'Sorry. I've been… trying to come to terms with a few things.'

He nodded to the house, where Andy was heading back with an ice bucket filled with assorted bottles. 'I don't think your ex likes me very much.'

'Believe me, that's a point in your favour.'

Natalie had finished her conversation with Marcie and turned her friendly smile on them.

'So I guess this is your boyfriend,' she said.

Tamara flushed. 'Oh. No, just a friend. This is Harry.'

Andy reached them and put the beer bucket on the ground.

'Who's this guy, Tam?' he demanded, with considerably less charm than his future wife.

Natalie glared at him. 'We were just covering that, Andy. This is Tamara's friend Harry.'

Harry put out his hand. 'Harry Hamilton.' He was showing quite admirable restraint, Tamara thought, given the views he'd expressed on their date about Andy's eminent need for a thump.

Andy shook Harry's hand firmly and briefly. Men seemed to have made a whole language out of handshakes. Tamara identified this one as the classic 'just watch it, mate'.

'What do you do then, Harry?' Andy asked in an offhand tone.

Oh great, they were going to have a man-off. Why? Surely Andy didn't care who his ex-wife knocked about with now he'd moved on to younger, beautifuller things? Some blokes didn't seem to be able to help themselves. It was their way of saying 'once mine, always mine'. He might as well whip his knob out and piss a territory circle around her.

Tamara had been dreading this. As grateful as she was to Harry for coming, she'd been picturing Andy's sneer when he discovered what he did for a living the whole drive over. It was the same look she'd imagined on his face the night the shop assistant had mistaken her for Willow's granny.

'I'm in the entertainment industry,' Harry said.

'What sort of thing?'

'I'm a comedian. My partner's the brains of the operation though. I just do as I'm told.'

'A comedian!' Natalie said, sounding impressed. 'We'll have to get you boys together for a chat. Andy's an event planner. That's how we met: I was working as a model and he hired me to be one of the demo girls at this vintage car show.'

Ah. A model. Of course she was...

'Anyway, he's always looking to add new acts to his books,' Natalie continued.

'Providing they're of sufficient quality.' Andy cast an unimpressed look at what Harry was wearing, which, while smart enough, evidently wasn't the sort of expensive stuff Andy always chose to clothe himself in. 'Good money in comedy, is there?'

'God, no. I haven't got a bean,' Harry said cheerfully. 'Still, you have to laugh, as I said to a particularly sour-faced audience last week. Seriously, you have to. Otherwise we'll lock the doors.'

'Was that a joke?'

'Oh, absolutely not. I never do unpaid labour.'

Andy continued to stare at him. Natalie shot Tamara a nervous glance.

'So. Harry. You and my daughter look pretty close,' Andy said at last.

'We're good friends, yes.'

'Hmm.' Andy turned to Tamara. 'No offence, Tam, but you have had this guy DBS-checked, right?'

Tamara raised her eyebrows. 'I'm sorry?'

'Andy, Christ!' Natalie elbowed him sharply. 'Come on. I need you to help me in the house.'

'I'm good here, thanks, babe.'

'Come in the *fucking* house, Andy.' She summoned a smile for Harry and Tamara. 'Sorry, we just… need to check on the jacket potatoes. We'll be back soon.'

28

'God, Harry, I am so sorry,' Tamara said when they'd gone. 'I don't know what's up with him, pulling this alpha male crap.'

'I suppose he's finally realised he should never have let you go.'

She shook her head, smiling. 'Does nothing upset you?'

'Not a lot. At some point I decided to stop caring what other people thought of me – I mean, you have to when you spend your working life with your hand up a bear's arse – and since then I've bounced through life pretty happily.' He turned to look at her. 'Although I'll confess to being a bit upset when I thought you weren't going to let me see you again.'

'Sorry about that. Like I said, I had some thinking I needed to do.' She squinted at him. 'You look good.'

'Thanks. I would say "you too", but of course that's a given.'

She smiled. 'Have you been practising your flirting?'

'Why, am I getting better at it?'

'Maybe.'

'So how are you feeling? This must be tough for you.'

Tamara glanced around the garden, with its throng of

beautiful people and the beautiful home in the centre of it. She thought about the beautiful mother and the successful father who'd sworn to give their baby everything. This was to be the beautiful world, the charmed life of Cody Horan. Why him and not Willow? Why had Tamara's baby grown up without a father – why had Andy chosen Cody when he'd rejected his daughter?

'I suppose I feel... resentful,' she told Harry. 'Not of the baby. He's just a baby. But... I guess that Andy chose him and not our kids.'

'That's understandable. What will you do when he arrives?'

'Suck it up, I suppose. Be the mum. Smile while my kids repair their relationship with a father who doesn't deserve it. Same thing I always do.'

'It's OK to let it all out sometimes, Tamara. You're not just their mum, you're a person too. It's not good to bottle things up.'

'I have to, don't I? This is important to them, getting to know their new brother. I can't let my feelings about Andy bugger it up.' She smiled wistfully. 'Did you see Willow's face when she felt him kick?'

Harry smiled too. 'She's going to love him.'

Andy and Natalie were approaching from the house, Andy looking suitably chastened. He was carrying a pile of gift-wrapped presents.

'Beer, mate?' Andy said to Harry, nodding to the bucket he'd brought out earlier. Natalie nodded approvingly at him, and Tamara felt a twinge of fellow-feeling for the woman. She well remembered what hard work it was, parenting a fully grown man-baby alongside your actual babies.

'No thanks,' Harry said. 'I'm not much of a drinker.'

'You don't drink?'

'I'll have a wine or beer occasionally, but mostly I prefer a soft drink. Besides, I'm driving.'

Andy shot a look at Tamara that clearly said 'Figures'. Andy had always found things like teetotalism and veganism highly suspicious, especially in men.

Harry must've read the thought in his face.

'Yeah, I know,' he said. 'But trust me, nothing takes more guts than strolling into a working men's club full of beered-up, burly blokes with your hand up a bear's backside and nothing inside you but a lime and soda.'

Andy blinked. 'Your hand up a bare what?'

'B-E-A-R,' Harry said. 'Geoffrey, my business partner. He's always accusing me of being too controlling; I can't think why.'

Andy looked confused, and Tamara sighed. 'Harry's a ventriloquist,' she explained.

'Right. God, I had no idea you still got those.'

Andy stared at Harry like he was some great curiosity. Then, catching Natalie's disapproving look, he pulled his gaze away.

'Um, we've got some things for the children,' Natalie said, nodding to the gifts. 'That is, Andy has. I hope that's all right, Tamara.'

Actually, Tamara felt that it wasn't really all right. But there was no way to say so without sounding appallingly rude.

'Of course.' She called to Marcie, who was watching Dale and Willow on the bouncy castle. 'Marce, can you fetch your brother and sister? Your dad wants you.'

Harry tapped her elbow. 'I'll disappear for a bit. This sounds like it might be a personal moment. Don't worry, I'll be around if you need me.'

The twins rejoined them, swinging Willow between them.

'What is it?' Dale asked. 'Am I allowed a lager now or what?'

'You can have one when you've finished bouncing,' Tamara said. 'Fizzy stuff'll only make you belch.' These were the sorts of dilemmas that occupied a mum of teens.

'Guys, your father's got some things to give to you,' Natalie told them.

Dale frowned. 'What things?'

'Well, they're really from Cody,' Andy said. 'To remind you, um... that we're a family. A weird one maybe, and God knows there's no one to blame for that but me, but in the interests of starting to make things up to you...'

'You can't buy us back, Dad,' Marcie said. 'If you want us to accept you again, you have to put the effort in.'

Dale nodded. 'Marce is right. There's no shortcut.'

Tamara felt a glimmer of pride in the two of them.

'I know that,' Andy said. 'There's no obligation. But take these, please, for Cody's sake.'

He handed Marcie an envelope, a larger parcel to Dale, then held out something squishy-looking to Willow. She didn't take it, so he put it down in front of her.

Tamara plucked Andy's elbow and drew him aside.

'You got them presents without consulting me?' she murmured as Marcie, after a moment's hesitation, started opening her gift.

'Nat thought it was a good idea,' Andy whispered back.

'She wanted today to be about putting our family back together.'

'Families can't be made in an afternoon, Andy. Besides, I'm their mother, not Natalie. You check this stuff with me, OK?'

'You don't have to be so touchy about every little thing. I didn't get them guns or anything.'

Tamara glanced at Natalie. 'I hope you're looking after that girl. She looks tired and worried. Well, are you?'

'Of course I'm looking after her. What's it to you anyway? You're not her mum, Tam.'

'No. I'm just old enough to be.'

He turned to face her. 'So, the ventriloquist guy. You can't honestly be sleeping with him?'

'What business is it of yours?'

'Hey, it's your life. I just thought you had better taste. Or is it scraping the bottom of the barrel time? I suppose every woman gets to that age.'

God, couldn't she just slap him! 'Trust me, Andy, Harry Hamilton is ten times the man you—'

She was interrupted by a shriek from Marcie.

'What is it, Marce?' Tamara said.

'Two tickets to *La Belle Sauvage* down in London!' Marcie squeaked. 'You know, the *His Dark Materials* prequel?'

Andy smiled. 'Good choice, right?'

'I've been dying to see it, but there's no way I could afford it.'

'You remember me buying those books for you when you were small?' Andy said softly. 'I felt like you were getting so grown up when you started wanting to read your own bedtime stories instead of begging for Daddy to do it.'

Marcie looked down, smiling sadly. 'I remember.'

Tamara flinched as she remembered too. Yes, Andy had always read the bedtime story. He'd done the playtimes, made the dens, pushed the swings; the fun stuff. Dealing with bodily functions, feeding, illnesses, the mundane business of keeping their children alive: that, of course, had been her job.

'So, will you keep them?' Andy asked Marcie. 'I told you, they're from Cody as much as me.'

'I… yes.' Marcie hesitated, then went to give him a hug. 'Thanks. Thanks, Dad.'

Andy hugged her tightly, and Tamara found she was forced to look away. She couldn't bear it.

Dale had unwrapped his present too and was staring at it.

'I can't believe this,' he whispered.

'The Tony Hawk SS 540,' Andy said as Marcie let him go. 'God, I wished I could've afforded something in that class when I was skating.'

Dale looked up at him. 'You used to skate?'

'Sure I did. I was pretty good back in the day.'

Dale looked at his mum, who nodded. 'It's true. He had the ego to prove it.'

Dale's attention drifted back to the skateboard. He trailed his fingers lovingly over it.

'Olivia's going to totally flake when I show her this.' He closed his eyes, as if fighting a battle within himself, then looked at Andy. 'Thanks.'

'Thanks…?'

'Thanks… Dad.'

Andy smiled and held out a hand. After a second, Dale reached out to shake it.

Willow hadn't touched her parcel. Andy dropped to his knees to talk to her.

'Aren't you going to open yours?'

She stared at him in silence.

'Come on, I know you can talk,' he said, smiling. 'It's OK, sweetheart. Dale and Marcie opened theirs.'

'Are you really my dad?' Willow asked.

'I really am.' He lowered his head. 'I haven't been a very good one. But from now on, Willow, I'm going to be the best dad I can be – to you and Cody, and Marcie and Dale too. If you'll let me.'

'How come I never knew I had a dad before?'

'I suppose you forgot. Because you hadn't seen me in a long time.'

Willow put her head on one side. 'I think I remember you. A bit.'

'Will you open your present? It's from me and Cody, to say thanks for being his new big sister.'

Willow hesitated. 'From Cody too?'

'That's right.'

'Well… if Cody wants me to.'

She tore off the paper, then clamped her hands to her mouth.

'Mummy, it's the Elsa dress!' she squealed. 'The *Frozen* 2 Elsa dress!'

Tamara forced a smile, willing her lips not to wobble. 'That's great, sweetie.'

'So, any chance of a thank-you hug?' Andy asked Willow.

Willow paused for a moment, then put her arms around his neck. Tamara watched her last ally fall, and the tear she'd been holding back slipped down her cheek.

'I'm going to find a glass of wine,' she announced.

29

Two hours later, the party was still going strong. The sunlight was growing mellow, and strings of Chinese lanterns illuminated the beautiful garden. A water feature chattered; people laughed.

Tamara was sitting on a bench in an arbour, sipping her third Prosecco. She hadn't had enough to make her feel drunk, but enough to make the whole experience more bearable. Still, she should probably call it a day after this one in case she ended up saying something to her ex she was really going to regret. Not that he didn't deserve it, but she'd hate to upset Natalie.

She was over the limit though, which meant she was going to have to call a taxi to get them all home – unless Dale felt confident enough to drive, since he'd decided not to have a beer after all. He'd only passed his test a week ago. They'd gone out for a meal to celebrate… another milestone… another step towards adulthood, and away from her.

If she listened, Tamara could make out the sounds of her children. Marcie and Dale had discovered a couple of kids from their school among the party-goers. Marcie was chatting animatedly to one of the girls, telling her about the modules she'd be taking when she took up her place at

Leicester to study drama. Dale was talking about skating with another lad, showing off the new board Andy had got him. And... Geoffrey. She could hear Geoffrey. Harry was putting on a show for Willow and some other littles. God knew what Andy was making of that, but Tamara was past caring now. She wished she could go home and curl up in bed with the duvet over her head, but the kids were having such a nice time, it didn't seem fair to make them leave early.

'Hey,' a gentle voice said. 'Mind if I join you?'

Tamara looked up. 'Natalie. Of course, go ahead.'

Natalie manoeuvred herself with some difficulty on to the bench. 'Oof. I'll be glad when I get this rhinoceros-sized baby out of me.' She cast a jealous look at Tamara's Prosecco. 'God, that looks good.'

'Ah well, not long to go. Keep a bottle on ice, eh?'

She nodded to the kids gathered around Harry. 'That chap you brought's a big hit. My six-year-old niece laughed so much at his bear's magic act that she snorted lemonade out of her nostrils.'

Tamara smiled fondly. 'Him and his bloody embarrassing bear.'

Natalie looked at her. 'Are you embarrassed? I'd be proud as anything.'

'Would you?'

'Yeah, I mean, if my boyfriend was unselfish enough to give up his time at a party to keep the kids entertained. I'm sure he'd far rather be here talking to you.' She grimaced. 'Sorry, he's not your boyfriend, is he? I forgot.'

Tamara gazed thoughtfully at Harry. 'Don't worry about it.'

Natalie met Tamara's eyes. 'So… today can't have been easy for you.'

'Or for you.'

'No, but I'm glad we did it. I feel like it's cleared the air between us.'

'Was there air to clear?'

'Isn't there always in situations like this?'

Tamara smiled. 'You sound like you've done this before.'

'Thankfully not – and never will again, I hope.' Natalie took a deep breath. 'Look, Tamara, I know you probably think it's fake as hell. I mean, I would, if I were in your position. Young slapper entraps older man then plays nicey-nicey for the abandoned wife and kids just so she can feel superior.'

'I never thought any such thing.'

'Yes you did.'

'Well, maybe before I knew you,' Tamara admitted, discovering a store of *in vino veritas* at the bottom of her Prosecco. 'Twenty-five-year-old models don't tie themselves to men old enough to be their dads for love very often, do they?'

'No.' Natalie was silent for a long moment. 'No. They don't.'

'But you do love him.'

Natalie nodded. 'Very much.'

'What do you see in him?'

'What did you?'

Tamara considered this. 'I suppose… he had that cocky, cheeky quality that's good for charming silly young things. He was cool and popular and fun. He made me laugh. But…'

'...but you can't build a future on charm,' Natalie said. 'I know.'

Tamara examined her face. 'Is everything OK between you two? I don't want to cross a line, but things have seemed a bit tense all night.'

Natalie sighed. 'You noticed that, did you? Yes, we had a row right before the party.'

'What about?'

'Andy keeps going on about getting a nanny for the baby. I told him I don't want a nanny – I want me and him to do everything, like other parents do. But he says we can afford it so why not cut ourselves some slack? I can't help feeling like...'

'Like what?'

Natalie closed her eyes. 'Like it's happening again,' she said quietly. 'Not quite the same as it did with you, but already he's finding ways to be less of a dad to his new baby. I wanted him to rebuild his relationship with his kids because I needed him to prove he could do this, and perhaps... perhaps because I needed to convince myself he really could be a better man. And now...' She trailed off.

Tamara's gaze drifted to Andy, who was tête-à-tête with the same young woman he'd been talking to when they arrived. She was laughing at something he'd said, no doubt with far more hilarity than the joke deserved.

'Who is that?' she asked Natalie.

'His step-cousin, Eloise.'

'You keep looking at them.'

'I can't help it. She's one of those women stuck in permanent flirt mode, and Andy just laps up the attention.

And here I am the size of a house – how am I supposed to feel about it?'

'You don't think he's cheating?'

'No. It's an ego boost for him, that's all. But given I'm weeks from giving birth to his child and my self-esteem isn't exactly at an all-time peak, I don't think it's too much to expect him to reserve his dubious charms for me, do you?'

'I agree completely,' Tamara said, shooting Andy a dirty look. 'Have you talked to him about it?'

'I tried to. He just laughs at me and says Eloise is family and I shouldn't be so daft.' Natalie let out a small sob. 'She's not family. Her dad married Andy's aunt when they were both adults. They're not related at all.'

Tamara felt only mildly tipsy, but nevertheless, the wine was making her bold. Perhaps it was a bit weird, given Natalie was about to have her ex-husband's baby, but there was something in the woman's youth and vulnerable position that brought out Tamara's maternal side. She put an arm around her shoulders.

'You poor thing,' she said softly.

'Oh God, please don't pity me. I can't bear it.'

'This isn't pity, it's empathy – trust me, I've got plenty reserved for any woman forced to put up with my ex. And while honesty forces me to confess that I briefly entertained the thought you might be a bit of a gold-digger, I can honestly say that when it comes to Andy Horan, you're too good for him.'

Natalie smiled. 'Thanks, Tamara. What should I do, do you think?'

'Lay down the law,' Tamara said firmly. 'I was married to that man for fifteen years and if I know one thing, it's that if you give him an inch he'll take a light year. If you don't want a nanny, tell him you're not having one. And you can tell him from me that if he even thinks about cheating on you, I personally will remove his testicles while he sleeps.'

Natalie gave a wet laugh. 'That's surprisingly comforting.' She glanced at Harry, who was coming over. 'Here's your friend. I'm going to duck into the house and get my eyes sorted out. I don't want anyone to know the hostess has been bawling at her own party. Thanks for listening, Tamara.'

'Any time, sweetie.'

Natalie disappeared before Harry noticed her streaky mascara.

'Just came to check up on you,' Harry said as he took Natalie's place on the bench. 'Willow's with Marcie and Dale.'

'Where's Geoffrey?'

Harry laughed. 'Taking a breather in my car boot. It's exhausting, being magnificent. What have you been up to?'

'Chatting to Natalie. Comparing notes on my evil ex.'

'You two are getting on then?'

'Very well.' Tamara shook her head. 'Seriously, how does Andy do it? He's a self-absorbed, arrogant wanker and he's always been a self-absorbed, arrogant wanker. The sort of man who walks out on his kids is only capable of so much in the way of personality-transforming epiphanies. And now he's managed to convince someone to marry him who's not only a gorgeous model half his age: she's also a bloody delight. And he's already neglecting the poor wee mite.'

'That man doesn't deserve good things. All he does is take them for granted.'

'Tell me about it.'

He shuffled on the seat to face her. 'How are you doing? It's been an emotional afternoon for you.'

'Well, I've spent most of it feeling like I wanted to burst into tears.' She sighed. 'But it's done the kids good. It'll be easier now, when they come to see the baby. Especially for Willow. I think it's helped her deal with her demons.'

'I think you're right.'

Tamara smiled at him. 'You and her are still getting on like a house on fire, I take it?'

'Yeah, she seems to trust me. Well, probably more Geoffrey than me. She was telling him all her secrets.'

'What was she telling him – I mean, you?'

He shrugged. 'All sorts. I know she's worrying about what it's going to be like when her brother and sister leave home. That she's anxious about what this new relationship with her father means, and if she's going to have to stay here for overnight sleeps. That she's excited about being a big sister, and afraid that if you and her dad fall out then she won't be allowed to see the baby – she's picked up on the tension between you two. Oh, and she's planning to wear her new Elsa dress to Evie Chambers' party next week.'

Tamara blinked. 'She told you all that?'

'More or less.'

'She never told me all that,' Tamara said absently. 'I had no idea the twins leaving home had been on her mind.'

'Because she senses it's on your mind,' Harry said. 'She doesn't want it to worry you, so she keeps it to herself. Anyway, I tried my best to help via Geoffrey.'

'I'm amazed you stuck around after Andy went out of his way to make you feel small.'

'I couldn't leave you to face it alone, could I?'

'You've been a gentleman through and through, which is more than I can say for the host.' Tamara smiled at him. 'You know, I'm glad I didn't talk myself out of going on our date. It was a close-run thing for a while.'

He rubbed his neck. 'Tamara...'

'What?'

'Will you answer honestly if I ask you something?'

'I suppose so.'

'I embarrass you. Don't I? I mean, my job, with Geoffrey and everything. You were embarrassed to ask me here today. To be your... friend here, and meet your ex-husband.'

'Don't be ridiculous.'

'Come on, I'm not an idiot. When I get Geoffrey out, you pull the same cringey face as my kids when they were teenagers.' He sighed. 'I know I'm nobody's dream man, Tamara, but I sort of hoped—'

Tamara reached out to put a finger on his lips.

'All right, you're embarrassing as hell,' she said quietly. 'You trail that bloody bear everywhere, just to see if you can make someone smile. You don't give a damn what people think of you, and when you talk about ventriloquism you sound like the dorkiest dork I've ever met in my life.' She leant forward to plant a soft kiss on his lips. 'But you know what? It turns out that actually is my dream man.'

He blinked. 'OK. I'm not sure about the words, but I liked the actions.'

'What I'm trying to say is, I like you, Harry. Not just because you make my daughter laugh, or because I've reached a certain age like Andy said, or for any reason than... I like you. And I'd like, um...' She was losing the thread a bit now. 'I suppose, to see you again. An official date, not just friends.'

He smiled. 'Even though I'm the dorkiest dork of all the dorks?'

'Ah, but therein lies your charm.'

'Can I kiss you properly now?'

'I really wish you'd stop asking and just get on with it.'

Harry wrapped his arms around her as he pressed his lips to hers. As a kisser he was surprisingly confident; just the right mix of firmness and tenderness. Tamara was vaguely aware of someone approaching but she ignored it, carried away on a wave of soft, cushiony lips.

'Oh my God,' a voice she recognised muttered, while someone else let out a peal of laughter. She let Harry go and looked around.

Andy had appeared, and he was laughing at her. What was worse was that Marcie and Dale were right behind him.

'Evening,' Harry said to the new arrivals. He sounded entirely unfazed at being caught snogging by her ex-husband and adult kids, which was more than Tamara could say for herself. 'Now your line is "I hope we aren't interrupting anything". You were, by the way.'

'Where's Will?' Tamara managed.

'On the bouncy castle,' Marcie said. 'Mum, what's going on? Are you… drunk?'

'Oh my *God*,' Dale said again, groaning.

'I'm not drunk. I had three glasses of Prosecco, that's all.'

'It's OK, Mum,' Marcie said gently. 'There's no need to lie. We understand.'

'Well I don't understand!' Dale exploded. 'You've been

over here getting hammered and having a quickie with the weird ventriloquist guy? Seriously, Mum, what the fuck?'

'I'm not drunk, OK?' Tamara got to her feet. 'I am actually capable of kissing men I like when stone-cold sober, as upsetting as that might be for you, Dale. And what, I'd like to know, is wrong with that? I'm a grown-up.'

'Dale's right, Tam,' Andy said, in what Tamara felt was a pretty pathetic attempt to curry favour with his son. 'Suppose I'd brought Willow over? You want her to see you like this: pissed as a fart with this guy feeling you up?'

'Are you kidding me?' Tamara laughed. 'Are you seriously fucking *kidding* me?' She pointed at Andy. 'Don't you *dare* start on me about parental responsibility. The number of times you rolled in hammered after I'd worked all day and then come home to feed the kids, help them with their homework, put them to bed. The number of nights you spent in the pub while I raised our children – your children.' She shook her head. 'You'll never change, Andy. Natalie could do so much better, just like I could have.' She seized Harry's hand. 'Like I have.'

Dale groaned. 'Oh God, no.'

Tamara swivelled to face him. 'And you! You come over here to tell me I've failed you as a mother because, what, you don't like my boyfriend? Because I've had a couple of drinks on what has to be one of the most painful, emotional afternoons of my life?' She swallowed a sob. 'When I've had to watch you... let him... after four years. Four years! What would it take for you to forgive me for walking out on you like that? I'll tell you, Dale: nothing. There's nothing I could do to make that up to you, because when you're the mum, abandoning your kids is unforgivable. Oh, but when you're the dad you can walk out on your responsibilities, your wife, your kids, and society just shrugs and says "well, boys will be boys". All he has to do after four fucking years is shove a few expensive presents your way and all is forgiven. When he walked out on us. Barely spoke to you in years. Tried to get me to abort your sister against my wishes, for Christ's sake!'

Dale blinked. 'What?'

'Mum, please. Stop,' Marcie said in a low voice. 'You shouldn't be saying these things. Not here.'

But it was too late. The dam had been opened, and all the emotions Tamara had been struggling to keep pent up came pouring out.

'Do you two really think he's changed?' she demanded, pointing at Andy. 'The only reason he got in touch is because his young, beautiful fiancée demanded he prove he could be a good dad before they had a baby together. It was nothing to do with you, or any of us. Nothing to do with regret or… or… love.'

'Tamara, that's not true,' Andy said in a low voice.

'It bloody is. Natalie told me.'

Dale turned to his dad. 'So you're saying she didn't make you do it?'

Andy hesitated.

'Well, did she?' Marcie demanded. 'Did Natalie make you get in touch with us?'

'She… it was more complicated than that,' Andy said, flushing. 'That wasn't the reason I wanted to be back in your lives.'

Marcie shook her head. 'I cannot believe we fell for your bullshit again,' she said in a low voice.

'Marcie, please.' He put a hand on her arm, but she shook it away.

He turned to Dale. 'Dale. Son. Just hear me out.'

He grasped Dale's shoulders, but the boy pushed him away with enough force that Andy stumbled back against the arbour. He remained leaning against it, looking dazed.

'Do not fucking touch me, Andy,' Dale growled. He went to put an arm around the uncontrollably sobbing Tamara. 'Mum, come on. I'll drive us home.'

'Will... she can't see...' Tamara turned to Harry, who was a ginger blur now through the tears. 'Can you, um...'

Harry nodded. 'I'll take Willow back, if Dale can look after you.'

'Harry, I'll come with you. I can give you directions,' Marcie said. 'Dale, get Mum in the car. Take her round the long way so Will won't see.'

Dale nodded and guided Tamara out, shooting his dad a look of pure disgust as he went by.

30

Russell got to his feet as Saffie reappeared in the A&E waiting area, leaning heavily on a crutch.

'Well, what's the verdict?'

She glared at him. 'I said you could go. I'm quite capable of calling a taxi.'

'And I said I wasn't going anywhere until I'd deposited you safely at home.' He bent so she could lean on him. Saffie hesitated, but was forced to acknowledge that she needed more support than the crutch was affording her. Reluctantly she put an arm around his shoulders.

'See? I can be useful,' he panted as he supported her to the door.

'Yeah. You make a great stick.'

'So? Is it broken?'

'Just badly sprained. The doc told me to keep it iced and rest it as much as possible.'

'How long will it take to recover? I'm sure we can arrange for you to work from home.'

'I should be able to put my weight on it within a week, but it'll be a lot longer until it's back to normal.' She caught a whiff of Russell's aftershave and instinctively recoiled.

'Look, no offence, but can you manage to smell like something else?'

Russell turned his neck to try and sniff himself. 'Why, what do I smell of now?'

'Aftershave.'

'OK,' he said, blinking. 'And what would you like me to smell of?'

'I really couldn't care less.' She winced. 'Just... different aftershave.'

'I love those subtle feminine ways you have to convey when you're pissed off with me, like begging me to sod off and telling me I stink.' With an effort, he unloaded her into his car. 'Let's get you home so you can be free of my irksome, odoriferous company.'

'Yes. Home.' She leaned back and closed her eyes. Then they shot open. 'No! What time is it?'

'Quarter past five. Why?'

'Shit! The Golden Oldies. They're expecting me at six.'

'Who are The Golden Oldies? Sounds like a Sixties covers band.'

'For the mag.' She turned to glare at him. 'You do actually read *The Throstler*, don't you?'

'Well I didn't buy it to wrap my chips in. Do you mean the elderly couple interviews?'

'Yeah. There's a pair living in a static caravan near Skipton. I'm supposed to be interviewing them.'

'Can you rearrange?'

'I don't want to mess them about. I mean, they're in their mid-seventies. There's probably only so much planning ahead they're prepared to do at this stage.'

Russell sighed and started the engine. 'Give me the address.'

They arrived at the caravan just over forty minutes later.

'Wow,' Russell said, blinking. 'That's a lot of gnomes.'

'It's the sign that worries me.' Saffie nodded to a plaque set among the colourful garden gnomes, which bore the legend *Sheila and David's Love Shack II*.

'What do you think happened to the Love Shack I?' Russell asked.

'I dread to think.'

Russell supported her to the door. 'You ever interviewed a pair of Septuagenarian swingers before?'

'Just another day in the life of intrepid reporter Saffie Ackroyd.' She used her crutch to knock, and an elderly lady with an expression of mischief lurking in her eyes opened the door.

'Oh,' she said when she saw Saffie clinging to Russell's shoulder. 'Has there been an accident?'

'Sprained ankle,' Saffie said with a grimace. 'But it's OK. Is it Mrs Mills?'

'That's right.'

'Saffie Ackroyd from *The Throstle's Nest*.' She nodded to Russell. 'This is my boss, Russell Foxton.'

'Here in my unofficial capacity as a beast of burden and stick substitute,' Russell panted. 'Do you mind if I dump my heavy employee in the umbrella stand?'

'Oh. Yes. Come in.'

They followed Sheila Mills to an open-plan living room and kitchenette, where her husband was boiling the kettle.

'David, there's been an accident,' his wife told him. 'This young lady's sprained her ankle.'

'Oh dear,' David said, radiating concern. 'Was it one of the gnomes?'

Saffie laughed as Russell lowered her on to the sofa. 'No, it was a chihuahua-related incident. I'm honestly fine.'

'Now, you must have something on it,' Sheila said. 'Have we got any peas, David?'

David bent to look in the fridge's freezer compartment. 'Afraid not, light of my life. There's a spaghetti bolognese.'

'Well, that'll have to do.'

'I'm fine, honestly,' Saffie repeated. But Sheila ignored her, and a minute later she found herself with her foot elevated while she held a ready meal against her ankle.

'Don't you dare laugh,' she muttered to Russell.

'Nothing could be further from my mind.'

'Then why is your mouth twitching?'

'It's a spasm I always get in the presence of frozen food. Have you got your Dictaphone?'

She grimaced. 'Balls. No, it's at home.'

'Never mind. I can take notes for you.' He took out a notebook and opened it at a page half covered with Teeline shorthand.

'Would you like a biscuit with your tea?' David called from the kitchenette.

'We're OK, thank you,' Saffie said.

'Now, you must have a biscuit after coming all this way,' Sheila said. 'David, put the Jaffa cakes out.'

'You know, my treasure, Jaffa cakes aren't actually a biscuit,' David told her.

'Oh, don't start, Mr Know-it-all.' Sheila gave his bottom an affectionate pat. 'Honestly, who'd get married?'

When they were sitting down, Saffie started the interview. They always followed the same format: how did the couple meet, what's the secret of a strong marriage, et cetera. After a few prompts, the couples would generally gabble on for themselves.

'So how did you first meet Sheila?' Saffie asked David, nibbling on a Jaffa cake.

David grinned at his wife. 'Oh, Sheila was the town floozy. All the lads had their heads turned daft over her, but she was determined she wasn't going to settle. I had to be very patient, admiring her from afar. Once she'd ticked all the other boys off her list, it was my go at last. I swore to myself I'd keep hold of her, no matter how long I had to wait to make an honest woman of her.'

Sheila shrugged. 'Well, it was the Sixties. Us girls had just started to realise it was all right for us to enjoy ourselves too. Do you know I was the first at my school to get a bikini? It scandalised my parents, but I was having too much fun to care.'

David's eyes hazed. 'I've got many happy memories of that bikini.'

Russell smiled as he scribbled in shorthand. 'You must've been quite a looker, Sheila. Why did you decide to stick with David?' He caught Saffie's look. 'Oh. Sorry, your interview.'

'Yes. Thank you, Russell.' She turned back to Sheila. 'Er, yeah. Why did you decide to stick with him?'

'I was getting to that age. Life can't be all boyfriends and bikinis, can it?' She nudged her husband. 'And I suppose he made me laugh.'

David smiled. 'She knew when she was on to a good thing. You know, she was the one who proposed to me.'

'How did she do that?' Saffie asked.

'At the top of the Big Dipper in Blackpool. I'd never been on a roller coaster before and I was just about to lose my lunch over the side. I said yes out of surprise as much as anything.' He took his wife's hand. 'And here we are, three kiddies, seven grandkids and two great-grandkids later. Lucky for them I'd just eaten, eh?'

Saffie laughed. 'So what's your secret? How did you make it last?'

David cast a fond look at his wife. 'What do you think, my life's delight and all my joy?'

'Well I didn't hang around for your daft jokes.' Sheila smiled at him. 'I suppose… teamwork. It's always been the two of us against the world.'

'I think in the end, we both decided there wasn't anyone else we liked being with as much as each other,' David said. 'I don't know about all that soulmate business. Me and the wife are hardly Cathy and Heathcliff. But I don't think, if I could live a thousand years, I'd find a better wife than Sheila. Or a better friend.'

'Sweet couple,' Russell said when they were driving back to Saffie's.

Saffie was flicking through the notes he'd made. 'Yeah. Pragmatic and romantic in equal measures. I suppose you have to be after fifty years.'

'They were right though.' Russell turned the car into Goosecliffe. 'There can be flowers and fireworks – I had that with Nikki, in the early days. But you need to be mates too or you'll never be truly happy.'

'I've always thought so,' Saffie said absently. She looked up. 'But let's keep the conversation work-related, eh?'

'Right. Sorry. I thought we were.' He nodded to the notebook. 'I'll take a pic of those and email them to you to transcribe.'

'Thanks.' Saffie stopped at a caricature on one of the pages. It was Nikki, dressed in a St Trinian's-style headmistress outfit and waving a riding crop.

Saffie laughed. 'Did you draw this?'

'Oh. Yeah. I'd better tear that out before she sees it and personally wrings my neck. It'd just been one of those days, you know?'

'You're not bad, are you? I mean as an artist.'

'Thanks,' he said, smiling. 'I told you I did a bit of journaling – well, more doodling. I've always got a notebook on the go full of feature notes, diary pieces, sketches and other rubbish. It helps keep my brain clean, dumping it all on paper.'

'So that was true.'

'I told you, Saffie. Everything I told you that wasn't about my name, my job or my marriage was true.'

'Even the crochet?'

'Especially the crochet. You should see my flat. Wall to wall in doilies.' He pulled up outside her place. 'Come on, let's get you in.'

'It's fine. I've got my crutch.'

'You know you can barely support yourself with that thing. Let me get you inside, then I can go home knowing I kept my promise to Milo.'

He helped her inside and on to the sofa, where she propped her leg on the footstool.

'Anything frozen to put on it?' he said.

She pointed to the kitchen door. 'There's a bag of ice cubes in the freezer.'

'Right.' He fetched it for her.

Saffie assumed he'd go then, but Russell showed no sign of wanting to leave, sauntering around examining her pictures and bookshelves.

'This must be the famous pulp fiction collection.' He smiled, taking out the book he'd bought her. '*No Mortgage on a Coffin.* I'm glad you kept it.'

Saffie shrugged. 'Course I did, it's rare. Shame I let you lower the value by writing in it.'

Russell opened it at his message. *Don't forget me. R x* Saffie could see the words in her head.

'I meant it,' he said quietly.

'Russell, please. It's really not the time. Can you go?'

'I want to tell you something first, Philomena.' He smiled, his eyes still fixed on the book. 'How ever did you come up with that daft name? It made you sound like a cheese spread.'

Saffie couldn't help smiling too. 'Thanks. That's actually what I was going for.'

He put the book down. 'Saffie, I need to make a confession.'

'What is it?'

'I said that nearly everything I told you on our date was true. I changed a few names and my job, but everything else... my relationship with my dad, how I felt about fatherhood: those aren't things I talk about with just anybody. I talked about them with you because somehow I knew you'd understand.'

'OK,' Saffie said cautiously. 'Why are you telling me now?'

'I need to come clean about something I told you afterwards.' He closed his eyes. 'When I said I signed up to the agency because I was genuinely in the market for a relationship, that wasn't strictly true.'

Saffie frowned. 'What?'

'I hadn't planned to start dating again while I was still married. Not because I'm not over my ex or anything,' he added hastily. 'It just felt like, paperwork-wise, I should wait until my divorce was in progress before I thought about meeting someone new.'

'So you signed—'

'—for the feature, yes. I know that wasn't very fair on my date, but I thought there wasn't much chance of her falling for me in a day, and, well, it was too good a feature to miss out on.'

Saffie remained silent, remembering how she'd entertained very similar thoughts herself.

'Then why did you act like it was real?' she demanded when she'd processed this new information. 'All that touchy-feely business, taking my arm, flirting and being charming. That stuff in your statement about hoping you'd meet The One. For someone who wasn't open to a relationship, you gave a pretty convincing impression of someone who was.'

'I'm sorry. That was wrong. But it started being real quite quickly, after I got to know you.'

THE 24-HOUR DATING AGENCY

Saffie snorted. 'Did it? I have a distinct memory of you telling me I wasn't at all your type.'

Russell smiled. 'And I have a distinct memory of you saying the same. Types seemed not to matter very much after a bit, didn't they?'

'No,' Saffie said quietly, speaking half to herself. 'No, they didn't.'

'I'm not going to ask for forgiveness. What I did was utterly wrong and stupid. I hate myself for writing that damn feature and betraying your trust. But I am genuinely sorry, Saffie. And if there was ever any way for me to make it up to you...'

'Russ, please. Go now, can you?' She closed her eyes for a long moment. 'I mean, thanks for helping me today, but... I need you to go.'

'Yes. I should.' He fell silent, but he didn't leave. 'So... truce then? At work, I mean.'

'Maybe. But you need to be a better boss. To all of us, and especially Tamara. It isn't fair the way Nikki treats her.'

'You're right. I've let Tam down trying to keep the peace when I ought to be fighting her corner. I'll do better.' He started to leave, then paused. 'Um, I actually brought you something. I was about to wimp out of giving it to you, but I remembered Sheila and David...' He trailed off, then took something from his jacket and put it on her bookshelf.

'Your notebook?' Saffie said. 'I thought you were going to photograph the Golden Oldies notes.'

'It's not the one I was using earlier. This is... an older notebook. Actually, it's my oldest notebook. I wanted you to see it.'

Saffie squinted at it. It was true: this one was larger and more battered, faded... old.

'You mean the one you'd save from a fire?' she asked. 'That was true too?'

'It was all true, Saffie. Everything I said or did or felt that day was real. Please, just take a look.'

'Why?'

'I don't know. Something Tam said made me think it might help.' He met her eyes briefly, then he was gone.

With the aid of her crutch, Saffie hobbled over to the bookshelf then sat back down with Russell's notebook.

'He couldn't just have bloody given it to me,' she muttered to Nigel, wincing as pain surged through her ankle.

She examined the notebook. It was a tatty old thing with a sticker on the front announcing in spidery schoolboy joined-up that it was the property of Russell Sidney Foxton, class 10BW.

Why had he wanted her to see this? Standing up to his wife would be a far better way to get into her good books. Not that confronting Nikki was going to compensate for the feature he'd written about her, but it'd be a start.

She opened the notebook at a hand-drawn comic strip in which a young space explorer called, coincidentally, Russell was having an adventure. Against her will, Saffie found herself smiling.

She quickly learnt that Russell had been a pretty geeky fifteen-year-old: good at art and English, a natural storyteller, but shy, socially awkward and something of a loner.

As she turned the pages, Saffie soon became invested in the quiet boy who noticed everything and everyone, but went out of his way not to be noticed himself. The occasional musing, a sort of irregular diary, documented Russell's unrequited crushes, his hopes and dreams, the bullies who tormented him and his delight in escaping to the world of imagination. She learnt of his grief over the death of a family pet, Buddy the dog, and the painful memories of his parents' divorce five years earlier. He wrote of how he wished he could see his dad more, and his mum's hard expression whenever he raised the subject. There were caricatures of relatives, teachers and fellow students – even one of Fran.

In the latter part of the book, there was a change. Russell's mum relented, and suddenly he was seeing his dad nearly every weekend. Saffie could feel the boy's delight glowing from the page – and she could feel the deep, deep well of his grief when he finally found out why.

Russell had told her his dad died twenty years ago, when he was eighteen. Eighteen was no age to lose a parent… and fifteen was no age to find out that your father was dying. To see him growing weaker, knowing there could be just a few years or even months, was devastating to think about.

'Oh God, you poor kid,' Saffie whispered.

She remembered something Russell had shared with her – the John Lennon song, 'Beautiful Boy', that reminded him of his dad – and blinked back tears.

Of course Russell would run into a burning building to save this particular notebook. Because it wasn't just scribblings and teenage angst. It was the private thoughts of a boy spending his last precious time with his father. It was all that Russell had left of his dad.

31

When Tamara arrived home from the barbecue, she let Dale and Harry guide her to her bedroom like an invalid. She actually did feel drunk now, although it wasn't from the wine. She was drunk on emotion: all those feelings she'd tried so hard to keep down, which had finally spilled out in her meltdown at the barbecue. Now the tears had come, she didn't seem able to make them stop.

'Willow,' she gasped to Harry as he held open the door to her bedroom. 'Can you... just distract her or something. I don't want her to realise there's anything wrong. Tell her I'm lying down with a headache. I'll be myself again soon, I promise.'

He nodded. 'I'll get Geoffrey on the case. Take as long as you need.'

Dale shot him a suspicious look.

'We don't need him,' he said to his mum. 'Me and Marce can look after Will.'

'Dale, please, I don't have the energy for this. Let Harry deal with it. She loves that bear.'

Wearily Tamara went into her bedroom and lay face down so the pillow could absorb her tears.

She knew everything she'd said to Andy had been fair.

And yet... she was ashamed of herself. Not for Andy's sake, but she should never have said what she said in front of the twins. Dale had had no idea his dad had suggested terminating when Tamara had unexpectedly found herself pregnant six years ago, and he was far from mature enough to cope with that information. And Harry, the way she'd introduced him to them as her boyfriend... oh God, it made her cringe to think about it.

And... Andy. What Tamara had told the twins about Andy. It was true that it was only Natalie's persuasion which had brought him back into their lives, but not every truth needed to be told. The pair of them, Marcie especially, had looked so hurt. And God knew what the knock-on effect would be on their relationship with their baby brother when he arrived. Perhaps Andy wouldn't let them see him now Tamara had let her big mouth run away with her – perhaps even Natalie would close ranks against her. She hoped she hadn't ruined everything.

After about an hour, the sobs finally subsided and Tamara felt able to get up and wash in the en suite. Her face in the mirror was pale and pinched.

Her watch told her it was well past Willow's usual bedtime, but it wouldn't do the little girl any harm to stay up late for once. Still, Tamara needed to show her face in the living room before her youngest child started to worry. She applied a bit of make-up to hide her pallor, then headed downstairs.

When she peeped in the living room, she found a funny little scene. Marcie and Willow were giggling their heads off as Harry sat on the sofa between them with Geoffrey on his lap. They were watching *Moana*, one of Willow's favourites, and Geoffrey was making them laugh by doing exaggerated impressions of the characters. Apparently, impressionism was another of Harry's talents.

'Do the chicken now,' Willow said in the bossy voice she only used within the family: a sure sign she liked someone. Geoffrey obediently squawked like Moana's chicken sidekick, and the girls laughed. Dale was sitting in the armchair trying to look sulky, but Tamara could see his lips were twitching.

'Hey, guys,' she said, smiling a little sheepishly.

'Mummy!' Willow ran to hug her. 'Are you still poorly?'

'No, sweetheart. I just had a headache from the noisy party, that's all.' She swung the little girl into her arms and gave her a tight hug.

'I wanted to bring you orange squash but Harry said you needed to have a sleep,' Willow said.

Tamara smiled at him over her daughter's shoulder. 'Harry's very kind. I was tired.' He smiled back.

'Mummy, Geoffrey's being so silly. He can do impressions of everyone! And he knows all the words to "You're Welcome" and he sings it just like Maui.'

'He's a bear of many talents.' Tamara put her down again. 'Thanks, Harry. And thanks, Geoffrey. You guys must want to get home to your beds now.'

'Don't mind me,' Geoffrey said, crossing his legs comfortably. 'Nice gaff you've got here, Mrs H. Crack us a beer, will you?'

She laughed. 'I thought you weren't a beer lover,' she said to Harry.

'I'm not. The bear drinks like a fish though.' Harry stood up, hoisting Geoffrey into his arms. 'But you're right, we've intruded on you long enough.'

'You haven't intruded at all.'

There was a knock at the door.

'Expecting somebody?' Harry asked.

Tamara shook her head. 'Not at this time of night. Hang on and I'll see who it is.'

She answered the door, and stared when she discovered Natalie on the doorstep. Her eyes were even more swollen than Tamara's. It had started raining too, which, coupled with the pregnant belly, gave the poor girl a bedraggled, waif-like appearance.

'Sorry to turn up like this,' Natalie said with a damp smile. 'Only you were so nice to me before, and I... I didn't know where else to go.'

'Oh my God! Natalie, what on earth is wrong? You look like death.'

'It's Andy.' Her face contorted with a sob. 'I've left him.'

'Morning,' Tamara said when Natalie joined her at the breakfast table, about a week after her unexpected guest had turned up.

With difficulty Natalie manoeuvred her huge tummy into a seat at the dining table. 'Good morning.' She nodded to a cup of tea. 'Is this for me?'

Tamara laughed. 'You know it is. You don't have to be polite, Nat. This is your home for the time being so feel free to treat it that way, OK?'

'I feel awful for intruding. If I had anyone else I could go to...'

'Nonsense. We've loved having you – me and the kids.'

As if to prove her point, there was the sound of little feet thundering down the stairs and a second later Willow joined them.

'Hi, Natalie!' she said, beaming at her.

'Hello trouble.' Natalie presented her cheek for a kiss. 'You're up early.'

'I wanted to see if Cody was awake.'

'He's been awake all night, the little terror. Bruising his poor mummy's insides.'

'Can I feel?'

Natalie nodded, and Willow rested a hand on her tummy. Her face shone with delight when she felt the baby kick.

'He'll be coming soon, won't he?' she asked.

'I hope so. If I get any bigger I won't be able to fit through the door.'

Willow giggled.

'Will, do you want to go get your uniform on while I make your breakfast?' Tamara asked. The little girl hesitated, and she smiled. 'Don't worry. I promise Natalie and Cody will still be here when you come back down.'

'Well, OK.' Willow disappeared upstairs again.

It was funny how their bizarre situation had quickly started to feel normal. Tamara didn't know how many women would be willing to give shelter and succour to their scumbag ex-husband's heavily pregnant new squeeze, but, well, what was she going to do? Natalie had needed someone, and the sight of her tear-stained face and swollen belly the night she'd appeared on the doorstep had easily burrowed into Tamara's protective instincts. She knew how it felt to be left up shit creek without the proverbial paddle by that man only too well. And if Andy wasn't going to man up and be the dad his new baby needed, then Tamara would just do what she'd been doing for four years now and do the job herself.

Actually, Natalie had proved a delight as a house guest. Willow had warmed to her immediately, and even the older two had welcomed her. Tamara had been worried about Dale, who could be territorial about his home and family in a way his siblings weren't, but he and Marcie both seemed to recognise that here was yet another victim of their dad's incurable fecklessness. After some initial wariness, Marcie had accepted Natalie in a way she might have struggled to do under their previous circumstances. Dale, meanwhile, had shown a level of consideration for her condition that Tamara found rather touching, often asking if there was anything Natalie needed to make her more comfortable. Natalie, laughing, would usually answer that what she needed was their brother to make an appearance before she popped. And so it was a bonding experience between the kids and their unborn sibling as well as their future stepmother – or not, as the case may be. Natalie still hadn't made up her mind what to do about Andy.

'Have you heard from him today?' Tamara asked as she stood to make Willow's breakfast.

'No but I'm sure I will,' Natalie said with a wry smile. 'I usually get a text around ten asking if I'm ready to talk yet, then a drunk-sounding voicemail in the evening trying to explain himself.'

'About Eloise?'

'Naturally.' Natalie sighed. 'And that's the problem, isn't it? That he thinks this is all about him flirting with Eloise, when it goes so much deeper than that.'

'Did he tell you there was nothing going on?'

'Course he did. Just a bit of harmless social flirting, he said, and he swears it'll never happen again. But that's not the point.'

She let out a small sob, and Tamara went to sit by her.

'What exactly did happen that night at the barbecue?' she asked gently.

'Nothing. That's just it: nothing happened. We had another little row over the nanny, but we'd been rowing over that regularly for weeks so it was nothing new.' She sloshed tea around her mug. 'It was watching him with Eloise that triggered the revelation. Not because I thought they might be sleeping together. It just hit me that the man I was having a baby with... that even though he was so much older than me, he had about as much maturity as a teenage boy. I was with someone so vain he needed the constant admiration of younger women to feel like a man, and so selfish he didn't care who he hurt while he was pursuing it. What sort of father could he be when he'd never learnt to put anyone ahead of himself?'

She pressed her eyes closed, fighting back tears, and Tamara stretched an arm around her.

'I had to find that out the hard way too,' she said softly.

'I just wish I knew what to do,' Natalie whispered. 'He says if I give him another chance it'll all be different. But I really thought he'd changed before, when we decided to try for a baby, and I was wrong. I don't want to be a single mum, but I don't want to take a chance on a man who's going to leave me and my baby high and dry just like he did to you guys.'

'You wouldn't be alone, Nat.' Tamara nodded to her pregnant belly. 'You're part of the family now – both of you. And in this house we always look after our own.'

Natalie smiled. 'Thank you, but you've already been more than kind. I can't stay here forever. I need to make a decision.'

'You stay for as long as you need to.' Tamara looked earnestly into her face. 'Don't go back to him just because you feel like you've got no choice.'

Natalie shook her head. 'Why are you so nice? A normal ex-wife would've crowed over me getting my well-deserved comeuppance and merrily sent me packing.'

'Oh, don't be daft. Any half-decent person would've done the same.'

Dale came in with Willow and, yawning, threw himself down at the table. Natalie hastily wiped her eyes before either of them noticed she'd been crying.

'All right?' he muttered, which was as much greeting as you ever got from him.

'Morning, grumpychops.' Tamara stood up and ruffled his hair. He jerked his head away, and she went to put a couple of slices of bread in the toaster for him before giving Willow her bowl of cereal.

'Mummy, when are Harry and Geoffrey coming again?' Willow asked as she tucked in.

'Tomorrow, I think,' Tamara said, getting the margarine out of the fridge. 'I invited them to come and watch TV with us again.'

Natalie shot what appeared to be a significant look at Dale, who flushed, rubbing his neck.

'Um, Mum?' he said.

'What?'

'Me, Nat and Marce were talking, and we thought... it's Thursday tomorrow.'

'What bright children I spawned,' Tamara muttered as she hunted for the marmalade. 'Eighteen and already knows the days of the week! The boy's a genius.'

'Give up,' he mumbled. 'I was going to say that it's Thursday, when neither of us have got stuff on, and we thought, um... well, we can look after Will for you. If you want.'

'If I want what?'

'If you want to go out. You and the bear guy.'

She blinked. 'Dale, are you giving me your blessing to go on a date with Harry?'

'Yeah. Nat said you hadn't really had a proper one, because there's always Will or us lot around, and it'd be a nice thing for us to do for you.'

'I thought you didn't like me seeing him.'

'Well yeah, I mean, he's a total geek, but...' He rubbed his neck again as he drifted still further from his comfort zone. 'It's good that he's not a dick though. I mean like Dad. And it's good that you're happy when he comes. I like that.'

'Awww.' Tamara left the fridge and went to give him a hug from behind. 'You're a good boy, aren't you?'

'Mum, get off,' he mumbled, flushing bright red.

'All right. Just a couple of seconds longer.' She held on to him for a moment before letting go. 'Thanks, Dale.' She looked at Natalie. 'And thanks, Nat. That was a very kind thought.'

Natalie smiled. 'I'd say a bit of babysitting is the least I can do after the way you've all looked after me.'

'And I can't wait to return the favour when Cody joins us,' Tamara said. 'I'm dying for some baby cuddles. Is it OK with you if Natalie and the twins babysit you tomorrow, Willow?'

Willow nodded, her mouth stuffed with cereal. She swallowed hard.

'Natalie says we can play Magazines,' she said breathlessly. 'And she never played so I can show her everything to do.'

Tamara laughed. 'I hope she's prepared to be bossed about then.'

Natalie finished her tea and eased herself to her feet. 'I'd better prepare myself to face the day. Not that I've got anywhere to go, but you never know when His Lordship might decide to put in an appearance. I don't want to arrive at the maternity ward in my pyjamas.'

Tamara followed her out.

'Thank you,' she said when they were out of earshot of the kids. 'That was a really nice thing you did.'

'Oh, it's nothing,' Natalie said. 'An evening's babysitting isn't much to pay you back for putting me up.'

'I don't mean that. I mean the way you seem to have got through to Dale. I was worried he was really going to struggle to accept me with someone new.'

'He just needed a nudge. He's got a kind heart, and he's growing up every day.'

Tamara sighed. 'I know. It's terrifying the rate they do that.'

Natalie smiled. 'I forgot to mention, there is a rule we've set for this date tomorrow. Marcie insisted on it.'

'What is it?'

'You're not allowed to mention your kids. Not a word, Tamara, OK? It's got to be all about you and Harry enjoying yourself like love's young dream, as you are.'

Tamara laughed. 'I'm not sure we can pull off being love's young dream without one of us putting our backs out. But you can tell Marce, rule accepted.'

32

That the date conspiracy went beyond her immediate family became obvious to Tamara when she received a WhatsApp from Harry the following morning. It just said *Wear a cocktail dress. I'll pick you up at half six. Can't wait x*

Tamara tried to go about her day as usual, going to work, doing her jobs around the house, but she found it hard to focus. Her insides had gone all giddy and fluttery. She felt like a teenager again, waiting for her big hot date. It was daft really, but she couldn't help it.

She was about to deal with some washing up when Marcie appeared in the kitchen.

'I'll do that, Mum,' she said. 'You ought to be getting ready.'

'Thanks, Marce.' Tamara glanced at her watch. 'You're right, I ought to hop in the shower.'

'Excited?'

Tamara smiled. 'Can you tell?'

'You were humming to yourself like a Disney princess doing the housework.' Marcie nodded to the open dishwasher, where a full bottle of mayonnaise was nestled among the crockery. 'And I don't think you meant to put that in there, did you?'

Tamara grimaced. 'Well spotted. That should've gone in the fridge. I must be away with the fairies.'

Marcie gave her a squeeze. 'I'm glad you're looking forward to it. And don't forget the rule, OK? You're not allowed to say one word about us.'

'It's hard when I'm so proud of you but I'll do my best.' She kissed her daughter's curls. 'I am excited. Is that weird?'

Marcie shrugged. 'A bit. I mean, you're both dead old, and Harry's not exactly Henry Cavill, is he? But it's good though.'

'You like him, don't you?'

'Yeah, he's nice. A hundred times nicer than Dad – not that that's hard. I did think he sounded like a total dork when you first told me about him and the bear, but...'

'But what?'

'I get it now: why you like him. He's weird but totally in a good way, and he's funny and you laugh a lot when he's here like you hardly ever did with Dad. I think he's the best thing that's happened to you since—'

'—since your dad left. Yes, I think you're right. Harry's... special.' She paused thoughtfully. 'And yet I'd never have picked him. If I'd stumbled over Harry Hamilton on an app, I wouldn't have given him a second look. And now...'

'Now you're falling in love with him,' Marcie said simply.

Tamara blinked. 'What?'

'Mum, I know you. It's no good trying to deny it. There's too much of you in me.'

Tamara looked at her daughter as if she was seeing her for the first time: this clever, confident adult, so self-assured and perceptive. The realisation that, at some point when she hadn't been looking, her daughter had made the leap from child to woman made Tamara well up for a moment.

'Whatever happened to my little girl?' she said quietly.

Marcie smiled. 'She's still here, don't worry.'

'You're so grown up now, Marce. You kids seem to grow up in big chunks whenever I close my eyes.'

'I suppose this business with Dad and the baby made us all grow up a bit. Even Will. Even you, Mum, I think.' Marcie gave her a hug. 'Now go make yourself pretty. Harry'll be here in an hour.'

Harry arrived at half six on the dot, as promised. His appearance when he showed up took Tamara's breath away for a moment.

'Wow,' she said, scanning his dinner suit.

He took in her blue cocktail dress with an awed gaze. 'Wow yourself.'

'I'm going to make Marcie retract that comment about Henry Cavill,' she murmured as Harry offered her his arm to escort her to the taxi.

'What?'

'Nothing. I just had no idea you could scrub up so well.'

Harry cast an anxious look down his body. 'Does it look OK? I let my kids dress me. I think they might've overestimated my ability to pull off the James Bond look.'

'You look so handsome I'm a bit worried you're out of my league.' She gave him a kiss. 'Where are we going then, Mr Bond?'

'First we're going to eat at eye-watering expense that I'm not going to allow you to pay a penny of, and then… you'll have to wait and see.'

Tamara felt a thrill as she joined him in the taxi. When

she'd signed up for The 24-hour Dating Agency all those months ago, she'd wanted a night of no-strings-attached fun to give her self-esteem a boost. Her romantic feelings had moved on since then – Marcie was right, they'd all changed over the past few months. When it came to Harry Hamilton, she now knew she wanted the strings to remain very much attached. But it did feel like she was finally getting the sexy, grown-up fun she'd longed for back when all this had started.

When they arrived at their destination, Harry opened the door of the taxi for her.

This wasn't just any restaurant. This was the sort of restaurant with waiters in evening dress and bouncers on the door. Tamara didn't think she'd ever been anywhere so swanky.

'Wow!' she said.

'My second wow of the night,' Harry said. 'I hope that means I'm doing something right.'

'Harry, are you sure you can afford this place?' Tamara whispered as he guided her to the door.

'Don't worry, Geoffrey's paying. We've been getting a lot of big jobs lately. And to think they told me ventriloquism was a dummy's game.'

Harry gave the maître d' his name and they were shown to a table, illuminated by flickering candlelight. A bottle of champagne was waiting for them in an ice bucket.

'How big were these gigs you've been getting?' Tamara asked as Harry poured them each a drink. 'Are you opening at the Palladium?'

'Well, I might've had to dip into my savings a bit too.'

'Why are you doing this, Harry? You know I'd be just

as happy with a bag of chips on a park bench. If you were with me.'

He reached for her hand. 'Tamara, I know I'm not what you had in mind when you signed up to the agency. You told me what you wanted – some beefcake with more muscles than brains to take you out on the town and help you feel young again. Well, I'm never going to be The Rock no matter how many weights I lift, but when I'm with you, when you kiss me, I feel like I could move a mountain. I wanted to do something to make you feel the same – to show you how much you mean to me.'

He sounded so earnest, and for once there was no trace of humour in his tone. Tamara pressed his hand against her cheek.

'That is how I feel,' she said quietly. 'I've been in a daydream all day, giddy like a teen, just waiting to see you tonight.'

Harry looked pleased. 'Have you?'

She nodded. 'You didn't need to do all this just for me. That would've been the same whether we were in a swanky restaurant or the local Pizza Hut. An adult date with no kids—'

'Ah-ah!' He zipped his lips. 'Marcie's rule, remember?'

She smiled. 'Sorry. Last mention, I promise.'

'I know I didn't need to do it.' He caressed her cheek. 'I wanted to. You spent too much of your life with a man who took you for granted, Tamara. Tonight I wanted to take you out and treat you the way you deserve. Like a… superhero.'

She laughed. 'A superhero?'

'Well I was going to say like a queen, then it struck me

it sounded a bit twee and old-fashioned. You're definitely more Wonder Woman.'

'I bet you say that to all the girls.'

He beckoned to her. 'Come here.'

'Why?'

'Why do you think? So I can give you a kiss.'

She glanced around at the other diners. Harry instantly knew what she was thinking.

'Don't worry about them,' he said. 'They've got their own love affairs to absorb them.'

Tamara smiled. 'You know, when I met you I couldn't understand how anyone could have the nerve to just start performing with a talking bear in public. I was so embarrassed when everyone was looking at us in that cafe. And now...'

'Now?'

'It's one of the things I like best about you. About being with you. Kissing in restaurants, not caring who's watching – I'd never have dreamed of doing something like that before we met. Life's exciting with you.'

'I'm glad,' he said softly. 'So any chance of that kiss?'

'Wait. I want to get this out first.' Tamara took a deep breath. 'I wanted to say that you make me laugh, and you make me realise it's OK to think about who I am and what I want instead of being completely occupied with what's expected of me as a mum, and... you're not the man I would've picked.' She grimaced. 'Sorry, that sounds brutal. I mean I wouldn't have picked you if we'd met through the usual singleton channels, because... because I didn't understand then. I thought dating was just a simple matter of chemicals and matching someone's characteristics against your idea of a type. I know better now.'

'What are you telling me, Tamara?'

'I'm telling you that you're not the man I would've picked, back when we first met, but… you're the one I need. You're good for me, and you… sort of fit me. Like a jigsaw piece, or… no, that's not a good analogy. Like the little yin and yang teardrops, you know: different from each other but fitting together to make a circle. Making me the best me I can be. And I… Marcie made me realise that I—' She stopped suddenly. 'Ugh, sorry. I'm blathering.'

'Oh well, we can soon fix that.' He leaned over the table to stop her lips with a kiss. Tamara soon forgot about the other diners as she let herself surrender.

'I certainly wouldn't have marked you down for someone who could kiss like that when we met,' she said breathlessly when he drew back.

'It's nice to know you weren't just after me for my famed foreplay prowess.' He pushed a menu to her. 'We'd better order, before you start tearing my clothes off on the table. I'll be honest, it's happened before.'

Tamara felt herself blush. God, she really was all the schoolgirl stereotypes today! Nearly forty-six and blushing because a boy was flirting with her, like a virgin on her first date. She'd be embarrassed if it didn't feel so wonderful. How had she ever thought Harry wasn't the type to sweep a woman off her feet? When he'd kissed her just now, it had sent blood rushing to parts of her body she'd thought had long since thrown the towel in and gone into early retirement.

'So what are we going to do after this?' she asked, still a

little breathless. If he said he'd booked them a hotel, she'd be quite happy to skip the pudding course.

'That's my big surprise,' he said, smiling. 'I had a little help with it from the people you keep at home who we aren't to mention.'

The waiter, who'd presumably been waiting at a discreet distance while they finished snogging, came over to take their food order. None of the dishes had prices on them, Tamara noticed: that's just how classy the place was.

'Go on, give me a hint,' she said to Harry when the waiter had gone.

'I could, but it would involve me singing and I think I've embarrassed you enough for one night. Let's just say I had one shot at getting this right and I wasn't going to throw it away.'

She narrowed one eye. 'That sounds like one of Alison Sheldrake's cryptic clues.'

'Maybe it is. Any guesses?'

She thought for a moment. Then her eyes went wide. 'No. Way!'

He laughed. 'By George, I think she's got it.'

'*Hamilton*? Are we going to see *Hamilton*?'

'That's right, the touring production. Marcie and Dale reliably informed me it was your favourite thing in all the world.'

Tamara practically squealed. 'Oh my God, it is! I've wanted to see it live on stage for so long.'

'Then tonight, Cinderella, you shall go to the ball.' He reached for the champagne bottle to top up their glasses.

'Um, Harry?' Tamara felt bashful suddenly.

'Yes?'

'What happens tonight?'

'Well, I'm glad you asked. Usually I'd expect the sun to go down and the stars to come out. I've been observing for a while and I've started to spot a pattern.'

'I mean, what happens with us?'

'What, after the theatre?'

Tamara nodded shyly.

'We could have a nightcap in the theatre bar.'

'And then?'

'And then I'll give you a goodnight kiss and take you home.' He glanced at her. 'Unless that's not what you want?'

Tamara shook her head.

'You're sure?' he said quietly.

'I think we've waited long enough.'

'Will Willow…'

'She's fine with the twins and Natalie. Nat sort of hinted she wouldn't expect me home early. I can get back in the morning before Willow gets up for breakfast.'

'Unless I wear you out.'

She grinned. 'You can give it your best shot. Go on, I dare you.'

Harry took her hand and pressed it to his lips. 'Oh, Tamara. You really shouldn't have said that.'

'That was perfect,' Tamara said when they were enjoying a glass of wine in the lobby bar after the performance. The other theatregoers had drifted off, and they had the place almost to themselves. 'Thanks for this, Harry. It's been amazing.'

'Well, don't post your TripAdvisor review just yet. The best could be yet to come.'

She giggled. It sounded weird coming from her lips: sort of joyful and youthful. Tamara hadn't heard herself giggle since sometime in the early Nineties. She probably hadn't enjoyed herself this much since then either. Except that now she was an adult, and didn't have a curfew dictating what time she had to be home.

'Don't make promises you can't keep,' she said slyly.

He smiled. 'That sounds like a challenge.'

'You betcha.'

He leaned over to kiss her. 'I'll book us an Uber.'

'Wait.' She put her hand on his.

'What's up?' he said softly.

'I just wanted to tell you, before we do this...' She took a deep breath. 'I had a wonderful time tonight.'

'I'm glad.'

'And I... that is, Marcie made me realise...'

Harry nuzzled into her neck. 'You don't have to say anything.'

'I want to. Marcie thinks... I'm falling for you.'

'And what do you think?'

'I think... that ship's already sailed. Do you know what I'm trying to say?'

'I know,' he whispered. 'Why don't you say it?'

'I'm... scared.' She tilted her neck to give him easier access to the shoulder he was kissing, paying no attention to the disapproving elderly couple who were the bar's only other occupants. 'I've shut myself off from it for so long. I tried to tell myself I wasn't capable of it any more, that Andy had—'

'Don't talk about Andy. Will it help if I go first?'

'Yes,' she breathed. 'If you want to. If you mean it.'

'Mean it?' He gave a breathless laugh. 'Never have I meant anything more in my whole life. I love you, Tamara.'

She almost laughed aloud, it felt so good to hear the words.

'I love you too,' was the last thing she heard herself say before he once again claimed her lips.

33

The next day was a momentous one for *The Throstler*: deadline day for what would be the little magazine's one thousandth edition. Even Milo, despite his reputation as the office malingerer, had set his alarm early.

Fran was coming in to see the mag off with champagne and a speech, and Russell and Nikki would be there too. Sort of like a party, except he was going to have to work like a bitch and there was a real possibility that either Saffie or Tamara would end up walloping Nikki with the office copy of *Hart's Rules*.

He dislodged a couple of chihuahuas and reached over Christian to turn his alarm off.

'S'not time to get up, is it?' Christian muttered.

'It is today. Big day at work, remember?'

'Oh yeah, your thousandth edition.' Christian eased himself into a sitting position too. 'Congrats and all that. Was I supposed to get you a present?'

'No, a coffee'll do. And a bacon butty if you're getting up.'

Christian smiled. 'Pushing your luck to get breakfast in bed?'

'I'll always be pushing it to get something.' Milo leaned over to give him a kiss.

'Not in front of the dogs, Mile.'

'They'll have to learn the facts of life sooner or later,' Milo said, shrugging. 'Although after what I caught Bailey doing with one of your sofa cushions yesterday, I'd say he's way ahead of us.'

Christian nuzzled into Milo's neck. 'You know, I could always send them to the pictures if you fancy hitting snooze,' he whispered.

'That sounds good.' Milo sighed. 'But no, not today. I need to put some hours in before the big brass arrive. We're behind this issue.'

'How come?'

'Saf's gammy ankle caused a few problems. Not being able to get out to cover features. And Tam's... well, she's been a bit distracted since that barbecue, with Natalie staying at hers.'

Christian grimaced. 'I still feel really bad about your friend's ankle. And about you not being able to make your sister's barbecue.'

'It wasn't your fault.'

'It was my dogs that caused all the trouble.'

'Well, I'm your boyfriend. That means we share responsibility for them, so it's my fault as much as yours.'

'I like the sound of that,' Christian said, smiling. 'It was hard work being a single dad. I'll get you that coffee.'

Milo put a hand on his arm. 'Chris...'

'Yeah?'

'Chris, I... um...'

'What?'

Milo flinched. 'Oh, nothing. I'll tell you later.'

'Oh. OK.'

Milo watched Christian pull on a dressing gown and head downstairs.

I love you. It was only three words. One syllable each. Milo could sputter syllables by the gobful when he wanted to – or more frequently, when he didn't want to, dates being the optimal time for his mouth to detach itself from his brain. But try to summon one of the world's simplest phrases and he failed every time.

Milo looked at Chip the chihuahua, who was eyeing him hopefully, knowing that awake humans meant food would soon appear.

'I love you,' Milo told the little dog earnestly. Chip thumped his tail on the duvet, and Milo tickled his ears.

See, it was easy. He could say it to a chihuahua: why the hell couldn't he say it to Chris? Whenever he tried, he felt like his tongue had been double-knotted and his brain had forgotten every word it had ever learnt.

He felt it though, for perhaps the first real time in his life. After nearly two months' dating, it felt like time to take that next step. Milo wanted Christian to know he was serious about this – about him. But all those failed relationships – the ones Milo had killed in their infancy by steaming ahead too fast – were there in his mind: grabbing at his vocal cords and yelling 'not yet, you fool! Not yet!'

Christian was soon back with a coffee, which he presented to Milo with a kiss served on the side.

'Bacon's sizzling,' he said. 'You coming down? I need to feed the Bark Brigade.'

'Yeah.' Milo took a deep breath. 'Chris…'

'What?'

I love you. I love you. I love you. Easiest phrase in the world. *Just bloody say it, Milo!*

'Um… have you got any brown sauce?'

When Saffie limped into work, Tamara and Milo were there already. Today was a special day, thousandth issue deadline day, but Saffie wasn't in much of a party mood. Milo looked happy enough though, and as for Tam, perched on their spare desk with a cup of coffee…

'You're very smiley,' Saffie observed as she went to flick on the kettle.

Tamara didn't answer. She just carried on gazing into the distance with a little smile on her lips.

'What's with her?' Saffie asked Milo. 'I've got used to you coming in with a soppy look on your face, but our glorious leader usually has it pretty together.'

'It's worse than that,' Milo said. 'She's been humming.'

'Humming?'

'Yeah.'

Tamara roused herself. 'What are you two drivelling about?'

'You and your humming,' Milo said.

'You look worn out as well.' Saffie's eyes went wide. 'Oh my God!'

'What?' Tamara went to chuck her cold coffee down the sink, making what Saffie thought was a highly suspicious attempt to avoid eye contact.

'Tamara Horan, you got lucky last night.' Saffie held up

a hand. 'Don't try to deny it. It might've been a while but I can still spot the signs.'

Tamara smiled. 'I can neither confirm nor deny it in the presence of my baby brother, but there may have been a rather amazing date, yes. Not to mention an exchange of I-love-yous that I never saw coming.'

'Please God, tell me he didn't bring the bear.'

'Nope. For once there was neither bear nor kids. I had him all to myself.'

'I can't believe Harry the Ventriloquist turned out to be the one after all,' Milo said. 'You definitely had the most unpromising-sound match of the three of us. You'd never have swiped right on that guy, would you?'

'Not in a million years. More fool me.' She rinsed her mug out thoughtfully. 'I suppose that's why the agency doesn't tell you anything about appearance or jobs. Because Dr Sheldrake knows what shallow bastards we can be when it comes to unintentionally sabotaging our own happiness.'

'Milo's right, I did not see that coming,' Saffie said. 'The way you talked about him after the date, you made him sound like a complete dud.'

'I was in denial then. I didn't want you to know we'd made a genuine connection because I wasn't ready to admit it to myself. But it turns out Harry Hamilton is actually my perfect man – the one I never saw coming until he landed in my lap.'

'How are things at home?' Milo asked. 'Any progress on the Natalie situation?'

'No. She's still umming and ahhing about whether to talk to Andy,' Tamara said. 'I don't think she should, personally. I mean, I know she has to – he is her baby's father, more's the pity – but she shouldn't be getting worked up this close to her due date. It's not going to be the easiest of conversations, whatever she decides to do.'

'You want her to stay with you till after the birth?'

'It's up to her, naturally, but I'd prefer it. We've kind of got used to having her around. She feels like one of the family now. Strange, isn't it?'

'Very.' Saffie paused. 'But it's sort of nice. Women sticking together. I'm glad she's got you supporting her. Otherwise men like Andy would get it all their own way.'

'That's how I feel about it. But it's not really about him, or even the baby. I like Nat for her own sake too. She's strong and kind. Willow loves her. I'm glad we got to be friends, even if it has all been pretty traumatic for her.' Tamara shook her head. 'Try explaining it to people though. "Oh, is this your daughter?" "No, my ex-husband's much younger pregnant former lover." Just another day in the Horan household.'

'How about your love life, Milo?' Saffie asked. 'Still worried Christian's going off you?'

Milo sighed. 'I don't know. It feels like we're getting on great, but there's been no progress in the Three Little Words department. Even Tam's racing ahead of us, and we had a big head start on her and Harry. Chris won't say it, and I apparently can't. I've got a mental block brought on by West and the rest of them.'

'It'll happen. You just need the right moment.'

'Maybe.' He cast a moody look at the *Throstler* covers mounted on the walls around them. 'And now our work lives seem to be as complicated as our love lives. Are you still thinking about leaving us, Saf?'

'I... don't know. If Nikki keeps on down this path of turning the mag into another lifestyle clone...'

'I know what you mean,' Tamara said. 'I never thought I'd leave *The Throstler*. All I ever wanted was to do what Fran did, and keep this place going for the next generation. But now, with Nikki and Russell... I really don't know.'

Milo blinked. 'You're not saying you're going to leave as well?'

'I'm thinking about it. With Nikki pushing her own agenda, it feels like it's not my baby any more, you know? I won't be a puppet editor while Nikki turns my mag into something I don't recognise.'

'But it's not *The Throstler* without you.'

'It won't be *The Throstler* anyway, if Nikki succeeds in transforming it into a mini *Lifestyle North*.'

'Well, I'm not staying if you two are going,' Milo said.

A gloomy silence descended.

'Some thousandth-issue party, eh?' Tamara said with a weak smile.

'Are you and Russ going to manage to be polite to each other today?' Milo asked Saffie. 'This isn't just a flying visit; we'll have them here most of the day.'

Saffie felt her cheeks heat. For four out of five days this week she'd been working from home while her ankle healed, and she and Russell had been working closely together the whole time. She hadn't had a choice: her mobility had been severely limited, and she'd had to rely on Russell to fill in for her on some of the features she was due to cover.

The truth was that after reading his notebook, Saffie was finding it hard to maintain the level of pissed-offness she still felt he deserved. Whenever she looked at him, somewhere in his face she couldn't help seeing a shy, bullied, sensitive kid struggling to cope with the pain of knowing a loved one was going to die. He'd shared that with her; something so personal, so deeply painful, and he'd trusted her with it.

Several times she'd been on the verge of discussing the notebook with him, but something always held her back. It felt like it needed to be Russell who brought it up but he hadn't breathed a word, not even to ask for it back.

'We'll be OK,' she told Milo. 'I think we've reached an understanding.'

Tamara raised an eyebrow. 'Oh?'

'It doesn't merit an "oh", Tam. I meant "understanding" in a strictly professional sense. It's Nikki who's more likely to send me murdery.'

'Huh. Tell me about it.'

There was a knock at the door.

'I guess that's the VIPs,' Milo said.

34

Tamara opened the door and ushered in their guests.

'Well, are we ready to go to press?' Fran asked, holding up a bottle of something fizzy. Saffie had to marvel at the ease with which she took charge. When Fran was in the office it always felt as though, whatever changes had come and gone at *The Throstler*, for as long as she was alive she'd be the editor-in-chief.

'Not yet,' Tamara said. 'We're still playing catch-up after Saffie's injury. I'd keep the bubbly on ice for a few hours if I were you.'

'In that case we'd all better muck in, hadn't we?' Fran, looking delighted at the idea of being involved once again, claimed a seat at a spare desk. 'Pass me some page proofs and I'll give them the once-over. Russell, you've got your laptop with you. See if there's anything you can help Saffie with.'

Russell didn't seem to object to being bossed about by the magazine's erstwhile owner. He whipped off a smart salute and went to fetch his laptop from the car.

Fran turned to Nikki. 'You can help me with these proofs. I'll check the copy, you check the ads.'

Nikki curled her lip, as if such menial work was beneath her.

'Me?' she said. 'I'm the sales manager, not the proofreader. I thought that was Saffie's job.'

'One of them,' Saffie said, biting her tongue before she added anything else. She was trying to stay out of Nikki's way until she'd made up her mind about whether to apply for another job. She probably should – Nikki was unbearable to work with, she'd evidently taken a personal dislike to Saffie, and it was high time she took the next step in her career – but whenever she found something suitable on one of the job sites, something always held her back.

Russell came back in with his laptop and opened it on Saffie's desk.

'Saffie's working on layouts,' Fran said to Nikki. 'Roll your sleeves up and get to work, like the rest of us are. In my day, when we were on deadline no job was sacred. Everyone mucked in on what needed doing.'

Nikki lifted her chin. 'I don't mean to be rude, Fran, but that hardly applies to the magazine's owners. I shouldn't have to remind you that you are technically retired, and I am technically in charge.'

There was an audible gasp from the others in the room. To speak that way to Fran Cook, the legendary Fran Cook, in her own newsroom was a sacrilege Nikki clearly hadn't grasped. Nevertheless, she refused to back down, facing off against Fran with her arms folded.

Fran didn't react. She marked up a few errors on the proofs she was looking through before glancing up.

'So I see,' she said with icy calmness. 'I also see that "in charge" seems to be code for not wanting to mess up your expensive manicure with hard work, which on deadline day is no use to any of us. That being the case, I think you might be better off elsewhere until we're done.'

Nikki laughed. 'I'm sorry? Are you ordering me out of my own business?'

Russell stood up. 'Nikki, that's enough. That's my grandmother you're talking to. She made this place what it is and you'll give her the respect she's due.'

Nikki shook her head. 'I don't get this family! All I wanted was to help you evolve and grow. Isn't that what every business wants: to grow? And you've blocked me every step of the way. Always with you lot it's the past: the great and glorious past of *The Throstle's Nest*.' She laughed. 'That's right: trapped in the past, like the dinosaur it is.'

'The magazine's heritage is important,' Fran told her stiffly.

'You would say that, wouldn't you? You're part of the past as well. I'm the moderniser! I'm the one who wants to help! You all act like I'm the bad guy here.'

'You've got no one to blame for that but yourself, Nikki,' Saffie said. 'It's not the direction you've tried to take the magazine in – although I totally disagree with trying to make it into a lifestyle mag – it's the way you march over everyone. As if no one's opinion counts but yours. Did it never occur to you that after all the years we've kept this place going, our ideas might also be valid?'

'Your ideas? Your ideas are running this place into the ground! Where are your subscribers disappearing to? They're dying, Saffie, just like your stupid mag, and you're doing nothing to draw in a younger demographic.'

'We know that's an issue,' Tamara said. 'So why don't we

discuss it as a team? All you've just done is highlighted a problem – one we're all well aware of. You haven't offered a solution.'

Fran nodded. 'Well said, Tamara.'

Nikki practically stamped her foot. 'Of course I've offered a solution! What have I been saying to you all for months?'

'We know what you've been saying,' Saffie said. 'That we need to change the character of the mag. And when we've objected, you've tried to bully us into doing things your way. Because that's the only way you know, isn't it, Nikki – bullying? You're a brat. Too used to getting your own way to understand how to be a team player.'

Nikki stared at her, open-mouthed. Saffie regretted letting her mouth run away with her the instant the words left her lips, but she couldn't take it back. And actually, there was a certain satisfaction in seeing Nikki lost for words for once. It was obvious no one had ever dared speak to her that way before. Saffie steeled herself for the inevitable.

'Right,' Nikki said at last, in a voice so quiet it was almost a whisper. 'Saffie, you can clear your desk.'

Russell shook his head. 'Sorry, Nik, but that won't be happening.'

She turned to stare at him. 'I'm sorry?'

'You can't sack staff without my consent and I withhold it.'

Nikki laughed. 'I don't believe this. Did you not hear what she just said to me?'

'I did, and it was deserved,' Russell said calmly. 'I've tried to keep the peace by letting you have your own way far too often. I respect you as a businesswoman, but Saffie's right. The bullying behaviour's been getting worse, and it's high time I took a stand. It stops here, today, or me and you are done – both professionally and personally. Understand me?'

'Hear hear,' Milo muttered.

'I understand you better than you know,' Nikki said. 'Quite a pet of yours, that girl, isn't she? I do know about the two of you, Russell. I'm not stupid – or blind either.'

'What do you know about the two of us?'

'That date you wrote about. The scruffy, common girl with the blue hair and tattoos. I can add two and two as well as the next person.'

'Well, and what of it?'

'I just… thought you might…'

Suddenly, Nikki burst into tears.

Milo blinked. 'Whoa.'

'Fine,' Nikki sobbed. 'Have it your own way. Ruin the stupid magazine if that's what you want. I'm done.'

'Er, hey,' Saffie said, not quite sure how to respond to this unexpected turn of events. 'Sorry. I didn't mean to make you cry.'

She hadn't even realised the woman was capable of it. Until today, Nikki had given every impression of being the sort of person who extinguished cigarettes on her palm and would cheerfully impale parts of your body with a stiletto.

Russell looked concerned. 'Nik, what's up? What's all this really about?'

'Nothing.' Nikki took out a tissue and dabbed her eyes, smudging her mascara. 'Nothing you care about.'

He glanced at Saffie. 'I'd better drive her home. You guys get on with what needs doing. I'll be back in a bit.'

'Well!' Fran said when they'd gone. 'There's nothing like a bit of drama to mark a major milestone, I must say.' She clapped her hands. 'Now come on, everyone, back to work. What's the mag's unofficial motto?'

'Come light or darkness, rain or shine, *The Throstler* never misses a deadline,' Milo repeated dutifully.

Fran smiled at him beneficently. 'Very good, Milo. Let's jump to it.'

Saffie went back to laying out her feature, but her eyes kept flickering to the clock. It was nearly forty-five minutes later when Russell arrived back, although Nikki's place was only a ten-minute drive away. He looked sober and a little stern as he sat down at his laptop without a word.

'Er, hey. Is she going to be OK?' Saffie asked. 'I genuinely didn't mean to upset her. I mean, I knew she'd try to sack me but emotionally I thought she could take it. She always seems tough as shoe leather.'

'Don't worry about it. It wasn't your fault.'

'Did she tell you what the outburst was all about?'

'It's stress, I think,' he said vaguely. 'She's been burning the candle at both ends lately.'

'And, um… am I sacked then?'

He finally smiled. 'No. You're not sacked.'

She raised an eyebrow. 'Because you feel guilty about writing that feature?'

'No, because you're a bloody good writer and I don't want to lose you, Hildy.'

Saffie flushed at the reference.

'Nikki's going to be taking a step back though,' he said. 'She needs to get some rest. We've tentatively agreed that I'll be doing the hands-on management of both mags from now on.'

Saffie's feeling of relief was almost palpable. No more Nikki! Then she didn't have to go anywhere after all.

'That sounds like a lot of work for you,' she said.

'Yes, but I won't have the added stress of constantly appeasing people Nikki's pissed off, so swings and roundabouts. Shit!'

While Russell was talking, there was a sudden *fzzzt* and the room was plunged into gloom.

'What's going on?' Saffie said. 'My Mac's shut down. I hope it hasn't corrupted the layout file. Is everyone else off?'

Milo pressed the power button on his monitor, which failed to light up. 'Seems like it.'

Tamara peered out of the window.

'I think the whole street's down. There's not a light on out there.'

'Actually the whole area's down,' said Russell, who'd taken out his phone and was looking at breaking local news. 'Strong winds up in the hills have taken down a mast.'

'Bollocks! We need to have the print files away by five and there's the rest of the layout to do, plus two features to write. Does it say when we can expect power back?'

'Around twelve hours, it says. Maybe longer.'

There was silence as they all processed this.

'Then we'll just have to shut up shop and send the files tomorrow,' Saffie said at last. 'It's only a day. I'm sure subscribers will understand.'

Tamara shook her head. 'It'll be a three-day delay in delivery. It's Friday. Even if we all gave up our Saturdays to work on it, the printer couldn't set the presses going until Monday.'

'Well, what choice do we have? If the power's down, the power's down.' Saffie glanced at Russell's little netbook. 'I don't suppose you've got InDesign on there, have you, Russ?'

He shook his head. 'It's not powerful enough to run desktop publishing software. I really use it as a glorified word processor for typing up features on the go. Besides, I've only got about an hour's worth of battery.' He closed it to put it into standby mode. 'Have you got a laptop at home with the software?'

'Just a desktop.' She glanced around her colleagues. 'None of us have, have we?'

Milo shook his head. 'You know I try to avoid working at home unless absolutely necessary.'

'Not to mention at work,' Tamara observed, earning herself a punch on the arm from her brother.

'Then we can't do anything about it,' Saffie said. 'We'll just have to wait until we're hooked up again.'

'Oh yes we can.' Fran had drawn herself up to her full height. She was only five foot two, but somehow she managed to seem imposing even at that stature. 'In eighty-three years of production, *The Throstle's Nest* has never missed a deadline – not even in wartime. I'll be damned if it's going to miss one on my watch, especially not for the thousandth issue.'

'We need computers to produce a magazine, Fran,' Tamara said.

'Do we?' The old lady's eyes twinkled. 'And yet, *The Throstler* is considerably more ancient than any of the technology in this room.'

Russell's expression was somewhere between impressed and disbelieving. 'You can't be serious.'

'Young man, I am deadly serious. Did you know that once, during the war, my father heaved his Underwood typewriter down to the air-raid shelter so he could finish typing up a feature? If he could produce a magazine while bombs were dropping, I'm damn sure we can do the same in considerably less fraught circumstances.'

'But how?' Saffie asked.

'I'm glad you asked.' Fran rummaged in her handbag for a set of keys and held one up. 'This is for the loft storage at my house. Russell, take Saffie and drive over there. You ought to find what you need. Now, the completed pages—'

'They're not completed,' Tamara said, sounding dazed. 'They're uncorrected still. We haven't checked the proofs. Anyway, they're on the shared server, which'll have shut down along with everything else.'

'I've got a backup from yesterday,' Saffie said, taking a USB stick from her desk drawer. 'I got into the habit of doing one daily while I was working from home, in case anything went wrong with my remote connection to the server.' She nodded to Russell. 'Russ, how much charge did you say you'd got on your laptop?'

'It's at seventy per cent but the battery doesn't hold much. That's an hour at most – probably less.'

'Hopefully that'll be enough just to do corrections.'

'For what? I told you, it's not powerful enough to run creative software.'

'Maybe not InDesign or Photoshop but it'll run Acrobat. If Fran proofreads the completed sections, Milo can use your laptop to make minor text changes directly to the PDFs. The printer is in Manchester so I guess their power hasn't been affected. We can use my phone as a Wi-Fi hotspot to get them emailed over.'

'And what about the other pages? The ones that haven't been laid out yet?'

Fran handed him the loft key. 'You'd better see what you can find, hadn't you?'

35

'What can you see?' Saffie asked as Russell lay on his belly with his head sticking into the eaves storage, using his phone as a torch.

'Bloody hell, she's got all sorts in here,' came his muffled voice. 'Tam's old pram, my mum's sewing machine... Here, there's a box of 2000AD comics from when I was a kid.'

'Those aren't going to help us make a magazine, are they?'

He coughed and pulled his head out. 'There's three old typewriters too. I mean, *old*. I bet they were my great-grandad's.'

'Well, let's get them out.'

The typewriters weren't just old: they were bloody heavy. Saffie felt a newfound respect for Russell's great-grandad, who'd apparently managed to lug one of these down to an air-raid shelter. When they'd got them all out, she eyed them sceptically.

'I don't see how we can produce a mag on these,' she said.

'They did it in the old days, didn't they?'

'No, I mean we've got no ink for them. Or tape or whatever they used to use.'

'Oh. Hang on.' Russell crawled back into the eaves, emerging a moment later with a box labelled 'Underwood ribbons'.

'They'll be dried up though.' Saffie frowned as she opened it. 'Oh. There's a full bottle of ink in here for re-inking them. Does Fran keep it for just such an eventuality or what?'

'It wouldn't surprise me.' He turned to smile at her: the wide, warm one she remembered from their date. 'It's sort of exciting, this, isn't it?'

Saffie couldn't help smiling back. 'I know what you mean. It reminds me of playing at newspapers when I was a kid.'

'We're like Hildy and Walter. Intrepid reporters determined to file our copy in time for deadline no matter what the odds.'

'Complete with an awkward ex-spouse,' Saffie said, laughing.

Russell's smile disappeared. 'Mmm.'

'Sorry.' Saffie wasn't sure what she was apologising for, but she'd obviously said something to kill the mood. 'I hope she wasn't too upset before. I really hadn't meant to make her cry.'

'Don't worry about it. Like I said, it had nothing to do with you.'

He bent to pick up one of the typewriters, but Saffie put a hand on his arm.

'Hey,' she said.

Should she mention the notebook? This probably wasn't the time. Russell looked serious now their little moment of camaraderie was over, as if he was worried about something.

'Um, I just wanted to say I was impressed how you stood

up to Nikki,' she said. 'I mean, I'm sorry she got upset, but it was high time you told her off.'

'Yeah, you were right about that. There's only so far you can try to keep the peace before it all goes a bit... Chamberlain.'

'And thanks. For saving my job.'

'Purely selfish motives. I'd miss you.' He left the typewriters and looked at her. 'I have been thinking over what you said. It's true that mine and Nikki's relationship has soured recently, and I was refusing to confront the fact she'd changed. Not that she hasn't always been assertive, but her behaviour to staff crossed the line a long time ago. I was too concerned with keeping the business going and not rocking the boat when I should've been looking out for my staff. And my family.'

'I'm glad you finally realised that.'

He sighed. 'It shouldn't have taken you to point it out to me. My brain's been all over the place lately. I haven't been able to focus on anything except...'

'What?'

'Nothing.' He looked at her for a long moment. 'Nikki took a particular dislike to you. I'm sorry about the way she treated you. It was uncalled for.'

'Why did she take a dislike to me?'

'It was my fault.' Russell's voice was softer now, and he moved closer. 'I suppose I should've tried harder to hide it.'

'Hide what?'

'That I was attracted to you,' he said quietly. 'Nikki's not stupid, and she knows me well enough to tell when I like someone.'

He'd put his arms around her now. Saffie didn't push him away.

'Why should Nikki care who you like?' she said. 'You've been separated a long time, haven't you? She's moved on to someone new.'

'I don't think it's what you'd call jealousy. It's more... territorial. Once you've staked your claim to something, it's hard to let go of the idea it's yours.'

'You don't think she's still in love with you, do you?'

He laughed. 'Nikki? Definitely not.'

'But she used to be. Very much, once. And you loved her too.'

'I did. But not any more.'

'What went wrong?'

'I told you. We wanted different things. I know I've long waved goodbye to my salad days, but I haven't quite given up on that dream of having a family.'

'I reckon you'd be a good dad,' Saffie said softly.

'I'd certainly give it my best shot.' He looked into her eyes. 'If I ever meet anyone who wants to go halves.'

Saffie smiled and reached up to wipe a smudge of dust from his cheek. There was plastery powder in his hair, which was sticking up at one side. It was kind of cute.

'You look like a chimney sweep.'

'So am I forgiven yet? In case my previous apologies haven't made this clear, I'm really, really, really sorry I ever wrote that bastard feature on the dating agency; I'm sorry you were hurt and I'm sorrier than anything that I ruined my shot with you. I'm a miserable worm not worthy to squirm under your shoe and if you ever find it in your heart to give me another chance, I promise on my honour that I won't mess it up again.'

Saffie hesitated. 'Russ...'

'What?'

'I wanted to tell you... I read your notebook.'

He looked into her face. 'And?'

'And... I really think "Russell Rocketsocks: Space Adventurer" could've been a big hit, and I think Jason Schofield and his gang needed a slap for the way they picked on you, and... and I'm sorry about your dad.'

He closed his eyes. 'Thanks, Saffie.'

'It made me cry. The way you wrote about him. Why did you give it to me?'

'Because I wanted you to read it. To understand.'

'Understand what?'

'I don't know. Me. That there's more to me than just being that wanker who betrayed your trust for a feature. Am I forgiven then?'

'I think...' She took a deep breath. 'Yes. You're forgiven.'

He smiled. 'That's all I wanted to hear.'

Russell drew her to him, and a second later his warm lips were on hers. With a rush, Saffie experienced again what she had the night of their date: that spark, that rightness, that meant-to-be feeling she'd been trying so hard to resist while she'd been angry with him. But it was allowed now. She really had forgiven him, and it was all right to be here, in his arms, on his lips. It was *right*. He pressed her body closer, and she reached up to run her fingers through his curls.

'Phew,' he whispered when he drew back. 'Better for having to work for it. I hope that's the first of many?'

'Yes. But later.' Saffie gave him a last kiss and unwrapped his arms from her waist. 'Right now, we've got a magazine to produce.'

36

'What time is it?' Saffie asked as she pulled a sheet of freshly typed copy from the ancient, clunky typewriter and handed it to Fran for proofreading.

'Just gone four,' Russell said. Saffie's Mac had been stored under the desk to make room for their typewriters, and he was industriously typing up a feature opposite her.

The last feature. They were going to make it. They'd actually managed to produce a mag on deadline day, in the midst of a complete power outage, through sheer graft and resourcefulness. It was a rush like Saffie had never felt before. She felt, for the first time, like she was doing the job she'd dreamt of all her life.

'How much battery left on Russ's laptop?' Saffie asked Milo, who was using it to make the final corrections to the PDF pages.

'About seven per cent,' he said. 'And I have just... finished.' He hit Save and ejected the USB drive. 'Talk about the nick of time. I don't think it would've lasted another two minutes.'

Saffie nodded as he handed her the USB stick. 'Good job, Mile. I never knew you had it in you.'

'Had what in me?'

'Hard work.'

Milo held his stomach as he mimed doubling over with laughter. 'Funny lady. I'm the lynchpin of this magazine, me.'

Even Fran had to snort at that one.

Milo had excelled himself today, in fact, making good use of his more analogue artistic skills to create hand-drawn mounts for their typed copy. In fact, everyone had excelled themselves. Tamara had written a new editor's letter explaining how the plucky team had gone back to basics to get the magazine into the hands of its readers. She'd really played up the underdog triumphant angle, and the finished piece was, in Saffie's opinion, up there with Henry V's St Crispin's Day speech. Russell and Saffie had been hard at work finishing features and typing up copy, and Fran had put her still sharp editor's eye to good use checking page proofs with a bottle of Tippex to hand. OK, there'd be a distinctly handmade look to *The Throstler* come September, but their subscribers were going to love the story of how the quirky little mag had triumphed in the face of adversity.

'I can't believe we actually managed to *Cool Runnings* this,' Milo said. 'It gets the blood pumping, the odd crisis.'

Tamara came out of her office with a sheet of copy for him to mount. 'We're not there yet, Milo. We still have to get it to the printer's.'

Tamara's cheeks were glowing, and there was a light in her eyes that Saffie hadn't seen there for a while. The joy of a job well done.

'I'll drive to the printer's to deliver it,' Fran said. 'It seems fitting.'

Tamara smiled at her. 'Thanks, Granny.'

'Just this once I'm going to let that slide.'

Milo finished mounting the last couple of pages. 'Well, I think we're good to go.'

'Pass the finished pages here,' Saffie said. Fran handed them over, and Saffie gave them a cursory check to make sure they were all numbered. Then she put them in a card folder and gave them to Fran with the USB stick containing the previously finished pages. 'OK, if you give these to Tim at the printer's he can scan in the hard copy and set the presses running.'

'But before I go, we've just got time to toast it bon voyage.' Fran opened the champagne.

'I can honestly say we couldn't have earned this more,' she said as she poured them each a fluteful. 'What a way to see our thousandth issue off. Well done, all of you.'

'Speech!' Milo called, drumming on his desk. Fran laughed as she handed round drinks.

'I did have a speech I was going to give. All about the founding of the mag, my father's vision and such nonsense. But instead, I'm just going to say this.' She stood next to Tamara and raised her glass. 'Today, you reminded me what's at the heart of *The Throstler*: teamwork, graft and family. The family we're given and the family we find.' She smiled at Saffie, who flushed. 'Today you did yourselves proud, and I couldn't be prouder of you.' She took Tamara's hand and gave it a squeeze. 'And I don't know if I've ever said this, Tamara, but I couldn't have asked for a better successor as editor. You impressed the hell out of me today with that editorial. Well done.'

Tamara flushed deeply.

'You were right, Tam,' Milo said. 'I think she is mellowing.'

Fran grinned dangerously. 'Don't you believe it. You should've heard the speech I was going to give if you didn't make deadline.'

'So what's the toast to be, Fran?' Russell asked, lifting his glass.

'I think… to family,' Fran said. 'And to the next one thousand issues. May you all live to see your own grandchildren in these chairs.'

'To family,' everyone echoed, clinking their glasses.

'Oh!' Saffie blinked as the lights suddenly popped on. 'The power's back. Fran, you don't need to drive after all. I can scan the pages here and email them over.'

'Well, thank God for that,' Milo said with a low whistle of relief. 'Hey, we should go over to the pub for a proper celebration. We deserve it.'

'You guys go ahead,' Saffie said, finishing her champagne. 'I'll meet you there when I've sent everything off.'

Russell finished his drink too. 'I'll help you. You three go get a round in.'

Saffie tried to ignore the arch glances of her friends and their grandmother as she started scanning pages.

'What a day, eh?' Russell said when they were alone.

'I know. I never thought we'd make it.'

'I meant that kiss.'

She flushed. 'Oh.'

'I was impressed by the way you thrived under pressure though.'

'Thanks, boss.'

'I'm impressed by you generally. Professionally, I mean. I know I said this earlier, but you're a good writer, Saf. I never felt that more than today, watching you whizzing out quality copy like a machine.'

'You're not so bad yourself.'

He watched her as she scanned a page. 'I was going to ask if you wanted to come and work for me at *Lifestyle North*. We've got a massive subscriber base, and there'd be a pay rise and a promotion in it for you. I could do with a new right-hand woman now Nikki's stepping back.'

She looked up. 'Promotion?'

He nodded. 'Deputy editor.'

'Bloody hell, really?'

'Sure, you're more than capable. We make a great team, you and me.' He paused. 'Like I said, I was going to ask you that. But then I decided there was probably no point. Because I knew what you'd say.'

She frowned. 'Did you? That was presumptuous of you.'

'Well then? I'm asking now. Come and work for me, Saf. It'd be a significant pay increase and a promotion that'd see you heading up a team of ten. Everything you ever wanted. What do you say?'

She hesitated, glancing around at the naff granny-like scenes on the *Throstler* covers that decorated the walls. Her gaze came to rest on the old typewriters they'd used to produce today's issue, and at the ink staining her fingers.

It was funny. All her life, she'd dreamed of getting into 'proper' journalism. Not the sweet, quirky nonsense she produced for *The Throstler*, with its small but loyal readership of elderly people and conspiracy nuts, but serious features for a mainstream publication. But today, bashing away at the elderly Underwood, had really made her feel alive. It had made her realise how much she loved this place, this daft little mag, and the family Fran had told her she was now a part of. She loved interviewing the Golden Oldies, reading up on bizarre occurrences for the 'Stranger Than Fiction' section, visiting the supposedly haunted pubs and seeking out ever more phallic carrots for Novelty Vegetable Corner. She loved all of it.

'I... can't,' she told Russell slowly. 'I mean, it's mad. I've talked for years about moving on to bigger and better things. But I can't leave *The Throstler*. It's too much a part of me.'

Russell smiled. 'You see, I knew you'd say that.'

She shook her head. 'How? I didn't.'

'I knew though, all the same. It's in your eyes. Tam's got it, and Fran too. It gets to you, this little mag. I suppose that's why I bought it. I'm proud of everything I've done with *Lifestyle North*, but this is the family business and I guess genetically, I'm programmed to always have a little piece of my heart in it.'

'But I'm not family.'

'Not yet.'

She raised an eyebrow. 'What's that supposed to mean?'

'Oh, nothing. Just thinking ahead.' He leaned across the desk to kiss her. 'We ought to finish scanning these pages and go to the pub. Can we pick this conversation up later? I can come over to yours this evening.'

'I'd like that,' Saffie found herself saying. 'I'd like that very much.'

Saffie, Tamara, Milo and Russell were in the Mucky Duck when Russell glanced out of the window at a car, pulling into the side street that separated the pub from the *Throstler* offices. Fran had finished her sherry and 'left the young people to enjoy themselves'. As much as Saffie liked Fran, she was rather relieved when she left. The old lady's knowing looks as she glanced from Saffie to Russell had started making her uncomfortable. Saffie got the distinct feeling Fran was going to frogmarch them to the altar before another hour passed.

'That's Nikki's Audi,' Russell said, frowning. 'What's she doing back?'

'Maybe she came to apologise,' Tamara said. 'She said some pretty unacceptable things to Fran earlier.'

'She might be looking for me.' Russell glanced at his phone. 'She hasn't texted. I guess she thinks we're still in the office. She was pretty upset when I left her before; I should probably go see what she wants. Mind my pint, can you?'

He gave Saffie's knee a surreptitious squeeze under the table before disappearing.

'I saw that, Saf,' Milo said when he'd gone.

'What did you see?'

'Russ feeling you up. Something happened when you went to get those typewriters earlier, didn't it?'

Saffie shook her head. 'I hate it when you notice things.'

'Well, what happened? I didn't set up that whole A&E thing not to get results.'

'I bloody knew you set that up!'

'Tell Tam off,' Milo said, pointing at his sister. 'She was the mastermind behind the plan to get you guys together. She convinced me Russ was truly sorry and we should help him with his wooing.'

'You sneaky buggers. I can't believe you've been conspiring with him against me.'

Tamara smiled. 'Come on, we all know how you feel about him. He was genuinely sorry, you know. Came to me with his heart on his sleeve, begging me to help him because he was so hopelessly in love with you he couldn't function.'

Saffie frowned. 'He never said that, did he?'

'He said it with his eyes. Anyway, I know you can make each other happy.'

'What did happen at Fran's?' Milo asked.

Saffie glanced at the door. 'I'll tell you later, OK? He'll be back any minute.'

But ten minutes later, Russell still hadn't returned to claim his pint.

'What's he doing?' Tamara asked. 'Is he still out there talking to Nikki?'

'I'll go see what's going on.' Milo glanced at Saffie, who was frowning at her phone. 'What's that face for?'

'Oh, nothing. Kieran. He's asking if I want to meet him for a drink tonight.'

'Why?'

'He's been messaging me ever since I saw him at the speed

dating. Wanting to meet up, "just as friends". I keep putting him off but I'm running out of excuses.'

'You don't need an excuse, Saf. He's a creepy stalker and you're not obligated to be nice to him.'

Saffie sighed. 'He's lonely. I don't want to be cruel for the sake of it. I feel guilty enough over the wedding.'

'You need to get over that already,' Tamara said. 'It was years ago. You don't owe the guy anything.'

'Still. I don't want to hurt him.' She stood up. 'I'll go check on Russell. I need some air.'

She made her way outside, peering through the darkness for either Russell or Nikki.

'I just can't believe it,' she heard an excited voice say – Russell's voice. 'Oh my God, Nik, this is huge! I never thought you'd change your mind.'

Eh? Change her mind about what? Saffie made her way towards the voices.

Nikki was talking now. Her voice was trembling, as if with emotion.

'I know. I never believed I could have that maternal instinct,' she was saying. 'All my life I've told myself it wasn't for me, that career came first, and now I find suddenly I can't wait to be a mother.'

A mother! Saffie stopped in her tracks. She could see them now, standing in the car park at the back of the *Throstler* offices.

'I'm so sorry, Russ,' Nikki said earnestly. 'About earlier. I was just so... when I thought about you and her, knowing how much you'd always wanted to be a dad, it brought it all home, you know? I'd been trying to ignore it but

I couldn't any more. I've really been doing some thinking this afternoon.' She gave a wet laugh. 'Don't think I've ever cried so much.'

'Don't give it another thought,' Russell said softly. 'I totally understand. I just wish you'd told me what was going through your mind. I didn't realise there was more to it than plain jealousy.'

'Are you pleased then?' Nikki asked Russell, shyly.

'Pleased? I'm thrilled, Nik! God, I can't believe… and you'll be an amazing mum. I always knew you would be.'

'I'm just sorry I didn't realise it sooner.' She looked up at him. 'Thanks, Russell. For never giving up on me. I know I haven't always been easy to work with, or to live with. Or to love, I suppose.'

'Don't be daft. OK, I'll give you the first two, but you know I always found you very easy to love.'

And as Saffie watched, Russell picked Nikki up in his arms, swung her around and kissed her full on the mouth.

'You know, I don't think they're coming back,' Milo said when, fifteen minutes later, neither Russell nor Saffie had reappeared in the pub. He pulled Russell's pint towards him. 'I'm finishing this.'

'What do you think's going on?' Tamara asked. 'Do you think they've sneaked off together?'

'Or Russ has sneaked off somewhere with Nikki.'

Tamara shook her head. 'He wouldn't do that.'

Milo shrugged as he took a sip of his cousin's pint. 'She's

THE 24-HOUR DATING AGENCY

a very attractive woman, I should imagine, if you like that kind of thing. And he used to be mad about her. He couldn't keep his hands off her when they first got together. You remember?'

'They were young then.'

'She's always touching him though. I wouldn't be surprised if there are still some feelings there, at least on her side. If she made another play for him, do you think he'd be strong enough to turn her down?'

'That ship's sailed. She's got a new boyfriend now.' Tamara sipped her wine thoughtfully. 'I think Nikki's a bit like Andy: when he was squaring up to Harry at the barbecue. It's not that she wants Russ for herself – it's that having once had him, she can't bear the idea of anyone else getting him.'

'She obviously knows something happened between him and Saf. She said today she'd worked out about the date.'

Tamara felt her phone buzz in her pocket and glanced at her watch. It was six o'clock: the time Harry usually messaged her with some funny meme to make her smile. Despite her busy day and all the drama of getting the magazine finished in the blackout, he'd been on her mind. Every time she thought about their date – which had culminated in a pretty impressive night of passion that had made Tamara realise her libido had far from retired – she felt fluttery. It had been all she could do to hide her simpers from Fran, who'd nevertheless shot a couple of knowing looks her way.

'I think it's more than that,' she said to Milo as she slid out her phone. 'Nikki must've noticed Russ has got feelings for Saf – deeper feelings than plain attraction. I guess that rankles, especially when physically they're so different. She must feel like she's lost out to someone she thinks of as an inferior specimen of womanhood.'

'I wonder where the hell they've all gone?' Milo watched as she unlocked her phone. 'Are you texting Saf?'

'No.' Tamara stared at the screen. 'Shit! Milo, I'm going to have to go.'

'What is it? Are the kids OK?'

'It's not them, it's Natalie. She's gone into labour.'

37

Saffie kicked at the pavement with her good foot as she stomped home.

Russell bloody Foxton! That *bastard*! Oh, he'd really got to her this time. Saffie had sworn to herself she'd never trust that man again, but he had a way of getting under her skin. Reading her mind. It was bad enough he was her boss; constantly there in the office, where she couldn't get away from him. Then there was her sprained ankle (which he'd probably set up somehow, in cahoots with Bailey the chihuahua), forcing her to rely on him to get her to the hospital and work with him on features. And the notebook (forged, no doubt), making her feel sorry for him. Making her *care* about him! And he'd stood up to Nikki when she'd tried to sack her, and offered her a major promotion, and they'd worked side by side during the blackout, and he'd kissed her like he meant it and hinted at their future, when all the time... all the time...

Of course he'd never fully got over his ex-wife – no, sorry, his wife. There was no ex about it, and nor would there be, now. The reconciliation Saffie had witnessed had been too committed, too real. Now she thought back to all the times he'd talked about their relationship, both as Richard and

Russell, she could see it had always been Nikki he wanted. Even when he'd talked about their working relationship becoming difficult, it was with a wistful sadness that made it clear he longed for things to be different. It was Russell and Nikki who were Walter and Hildy, not Russell and Saffie. Of course it was.

Nikki was beautiful, glamorous, sophisticated; Russell had talked several times about the instant, passionate attraction between them, and the years of happy marriage before it had all gone wrong. Whereas he'd told Saffie right to her face that she wasn't his type: the tattooed, blue-haired scruffbag in the Docs and dungarees, looking like Worzel Gummidge's hard-up sister. How could she ever hope to compete with someone like Nikki? Plain, sarcastic Saffie Ackroyd, who punked it up to compensate for the fact she wasn't beautiful, and who'd never had an ounce of glamour in her life.

She knew, if she was being completely honest, that there was only one thing that had come between Russell and Nikki. Russell's desire to be a dad, and Nikki's determination never to be a mum, was what had ended their marriage. And now Nikki had had as thorough a change of heart as Ebenezer Scrooge on Christmas morning, and she and Russell...

Saffie found herself swallowing a sob. She'd actually let herself think, this time, that it was going to work out. That it was OK to let herself fall, because the boy in the notebook couldn't be someone who'd ever hurt her, no matter what stupid mistakes he'd made. But she'd only ever been the consolation prize. It was Nikki who was his first choice, and now the one thing that had stood in their way was gone, they could be together. They'd go back to being a perfect, beautiful couple and have perfect, beautiful children that Russell could play 'Beautiful Boy' to, to his heart's content. And she... what could she do?

She couldn't go back to the apps. Russell had ruined her for endless rounds of dates with tedious strangers. She'd just have to live and die alone, that was all. Or marry Kieran: that was another alternative. He was a nice guy, if a bit clingy. It wasn't his fault he'd had a sense of humour bypass at birth.

And he must love her, mustn't he? To still be hanging on to a hope of reconciliation, after all this time. Looked at one way that might seem creepy, but from another perspective it was actually quite romantic. Saffie would probably never find another man who'd love her as intently and earnestly as Kieran had – as he still did, apparently. He didn't see her as the runner-up prize because the woman he really wanted couldn't make the grade as breeding stock. That was the sort of love she ought to have in her life. And since Kieran was the only one offering it... Saffie had a good mind to text him and say she was available for that drink after all.

She was about to take out her phone and do so when she felt something soft rub against her calf. She glanced down.

'Nigel?' Saffie picked him up, and he gave a strangulated mew of appreciation as she tickled his ears. 'What're you doing out at this time, buddy?' It generally took a small earthquake and at least three foghorns to get the lazy old moggy to leave his spot on the sofa, and when he did go out he rarely ventured further than his designated toileting spot in the back garden.

She turned the corner on to her own road. There was a crowd of neighbours standing outside her house. Saffie put

Nigel down and approached the woman who lived in the house next door.

'Mrs Cavanagh?' she said. 'What's going on? What're you all looking at?'

'Saffie. Oh dear,' Mrs Cavanagh said, turning a worried face to her. 'Now don't worry, love, we rang 999 as soon as we realised. They ought to be here any moment.'

'But what—' Saffie stopped, sniffing the air. Smelt like… burnt barbecue. Her eyes widened as she spotted the thick black smoke drifting out through the sides of her closed windows.

'What the hell? Is there a fire?'

Mrs Cavanagh nodded to her electrician husband. 'Stephen thinks it was the blackout. That something must've surged when the power came back on.' She slipped an arm around Saffie's shoulders. 'Now, you just come along next door and let me make you a cup of tea. There's nothing you can do here. The fire brigade are on their way and they'll have it out in a jiff.'

Saffie was still staring, horror-struck, at her house. She couldn't see any flames, but there was a lot of smoke pouring out from the cracks now, and the smell of burning was getting stronger. 'But… my books… my furniture…'

'Don't think about that. Just be glad you're safe. You've got insurance, I presume, and there's nothing that's irreplaceable except a life.'

'Yes,' Saffie muttered, watching the smoke. 'Yes. That's… true, isn't it?'

She was about to turn, still in a daze, and let Mrs Cavanagh guide her into the house next door. Then her eyes widened.

'No!' she said. 'I have to go in there!'

Mr Cavanagh shook his head. 'Don't talk daft, lass. The smoke'll knock you out in minutes.'

'I have to! You don't understand. There is something irreplaceable in there. It's all he's got left of his dad, I couldn't let it...' Saffie shook off the arm around her shoulders, and before anyone could stop her, she'd run for the front door and let herself into her burning home.

Tamara unlocked her front door with fumbling fingers.

'Nat? Kids?' she called. 'Where are you?'

'We're up here!' Marcie's voice yelled from upstairs.

Tamara bounded up the stairs. Her daughter met her outside the spare room, where Natalie had been sleeping. Marcie's face was white and drawn.

'Mum, I think there's something wrong,' she said in a low voice.

'Wrong?' Tamara was alert at once. 'What can be wrong? The scans didn't show anything.'

'She's in a lot of pain – more than she ought to be, I think. I don't know how it works but Nat says it doesn't feel right.'

'Where are Dale and Will?'

'Dale's on the phone, trying to get an ambulance. I took Will round to Mrs Constable next door. She doesn't know there's anything wrong.'

'Good girl. You did well to keep your head. I'll go to Natalie.'

Natalie made an attempt to smile when Tamara went in. 'Tam. Thank God you're here.'

Tamara took her hand and gave it a squeeze. 'Don't worry about a thing, Nat. I won't let anything happen to you, or to Cody either.'

Natalie grimaced in pain as a contraction racked her. 'I didn't want to say anything... in front of the twins, but I don't think I'm dilating. Not as much as I should be. It feels all wrong down there.'

'Don't worry,' Tamara said soothingly, trying not to give in to her own panic. 'That's pretty common. They can sort it out easily once you get to the maternity ward.'

Tamara had no idea if that was true or not, but it seemed to reassure Natalie, who instantly accepted her word as an experienced birther of three. She flashed her a weak smile.

'Tam, please,' she whispered. 'I need you to do something for me.'

'Anything you want.'

'I want you to get Andy. Please.'

Tamara looked into Natalie's brown eyes, limpid with pain.

'Are you sure?' she asked softly.

Natalie nodded. 'This is his baby. I don't want to have it without him. I need him, Tam.'

'I'll... do what I can. Is that all?'

Natalie shook her head. 'I want you to promise me something too.'

'What is it?'

'If something does go wrong. If the baby survives and I... I don't. You know Andy can't cope. I don't want my baby brought up by a nanny or someone paid.' She met Tamara's eyes with a look so pleading, so earnest and filled with love and pain, that Tamara could only barely stop herself from crying. 'Will you raise him? Please.'

'Me?' Tamara didn't know what to say. 'But I... Natalie, I...'

'Please, Tam. Just promise.'

'But you're going to raise him. People don't die in childbirth these days.' Tamara attempted a laugh, but it sounded hollow even to her. 'It's just nerves. You don't need to be upsetting yourself thinking about things like that. You need to be focusing all your energy on bringing us a happy, healthy baby.'

'I will. Just promise first. Then I know—' She gave another whistle of pain. 'I know it'll all be OK.'

Tamara pressed her hand. 'I promise,' she whispered.

Natalie gave her a pained smile. 'Thank you. I knew you would.'

Dale popped his head around the door. 'Um, Mum?'

'Just a second, Nat. Hang in there.' Tamara left the room to talk to her son, who was lurking outside with Marcie, looking scared.

'Is the ambulance coming?' she asked him in a low voice.

'They said it might be a while because of the blackout,' he said. 'There's fires and stuff all over. They said it'd be better to get a taxi or drive her there.'

'Right. Then we'll drive.' Tamara was about to go back to Natalie when she paused. 'Can one of you ring your dad please, and tell him to meet us at the hospital?'

Dale scowled. 'Him? What for?'

'Because another of his babies is being born and this time he can damn well step up. And more importantly, because

Natalie asked for him and I promised we'd do what we could to get him to her in time for the birth.'

Dale lowered his voice. 'She won't die, will she, Mum? Or the baby?'

'No she bloody well won't. I won't let her.'

With a grim determination and a self-control she didn't know she possessed, Tamara marched calmly back into the sickroom. She seemed to be channelling Fran somehow. She hoped she was going to be able to keep it up for long enough to see the drama through.

'OK, Nat, time to go,' she said. 'We'll take my car to the hospital. It won't take us long.'

Natalie seemed to be in more pain now. Tamara gently helped her rise from the bed.

'Andy,' she gasped. 'Is he coming?'

'Yes,' Tamara said, hoping against hope this was true. She was getting horrible flashbacks to the day Willow had been born, when she'd lain alone and vulnerable in the delivery room waiting for a husband who never showed. 'He's… going to meet us there. Come on.'

38

Candles. Check. Romantic music. Check. Nice food and a bottle of red. Check.

Milo was all set. Tonight was the night, he'd decided: the night he was going to man up and finally tell Chris how he felt. Two pints of beer at the pub had given him a much-needed dose of Dutch courage, and now he was ready.

There was a knock at the door. Christian was outside, the five members of the Bark Brigade clustered around his feet.

'Well, here we are,' Christian said. 'What was with the sudden urge to make me dinner? I thought you'd be out celebrating with the other Throstlerees.'

'I was, but they all had to leave early.'

'Really? How come?'

'Russ and Saffie disappeared off for a quickie and Tam's had to go deliver her ex-husband's baby.'

Christian shook his head. 'Your family, mate.'

'Tell me about it.'

'So we're the runner-up company, are we?'

'Don't be daft. No, I, um... I missed you.'

Christian smiled. 'I suppose that's sweet.'

Milo stood aside to let him in. The dogs immediately gravitated to the various spots in Milo's living room they'd claimed as their own. Bailey cuddled up next to his favourite houseplant.

'Shall we eat at the table?' Milo said, gesturing to his kitchen-diner. 'I got us a spaghetti bolognese from Marks and Sparks.'

'Posh.' Christian frowned as he listened to the music. 'Is that... Barry White?'

'Er, yeah.'

He laughed. 'It's cute you still think you need to seduce me, Mile, but at this point you can just ask.'

'Just setting the mood.'

Milo wasn't sure why he felt nervous after so thoroughly psyching himself up for this. He never felt awkward around Christian except for those times he was trying to initiate a conversation about feelings.

'Come on through and I'll dish up,' he said.

The thick black smoke surged around Saffie, seeping through the thin layer of fabric as she held her sleeve against her mouth and nose.

She could make out flames now, an orange blur through her stinging, streaming eyes. In the kitchen: her homely, tiny kitchen with its white cupboards and blue appliances, so reassuring and domestic and solid when she'd left it this morning. And now... the flames licked around blackened, singed lumps that must've once been her kettle and toaster. Saffie let out a gasp that quickly became a cough.

The living room was filled with smoke but there were no flames, and through her blurred vision she could make out her things. The books on the shelves, including her pulp

face. 'Please try not to overthink this. As soon as we can tell you anything, we will.'

'Tam!'

Tamara looked round to see Andy hurrying towards her, white-faced and with his shirt hanging from his jeans as if he'd been halfway through getting dressed. Tamara felt a surging relief that he was here; that Natalie wouldn't have to wake up to discover, as Tamara once had, that her baby had been born while its father was off doing something more interesting. She didn't know whether to hug the man or slap him.

'Is she OK? How's the baby?' he demanded breathlessly.

'I don't know, they won't tell me.'

He turned to the nurse. 'Can you tell me? I'm the father.'

'You're the patient's father?'

Even through his worry, Andy managed to look affronted. 'I'm the baby's father.'

The nurse glanced at Tamara. 'Would you prefer to speak somewhere private?'

'No, that's OK. Tam's… a close friend of the family.'

In spite of everything else she had going through her mind, Tamara only barely repressed a snort at that description.

'Well, your wife—'

'Fiancée.' He grimaced. 'Ex-fiancée.'

'Your… the mother is experiencing posterior presentation, where the baby's head is facing towards her back. As labour was already quite advanced, the midwife judged it best to deliver by caesarean.' She smiled. 'And as far as we can tell both mother and baby are going to be fine, although Mum will be a little sore for a while.'

'Oh, thank God.' Andy sank into a chair by Tamara, laughing with relief. 'Thank God.'

'She'll need a lot of looking after for the next couple of weeks. No driving, no strenuous activity or heavy lifting.'

'That's fine,' Tamara said. 'I'll – we'll take good care of her. Thank you.'

The nurse nodded. 'I'll let you know once she's awake, then you can come in for a visit.' She disappeared back into the delivery room.

Andy was leaning back in his chair, white as a ghost, muttering to himself.

'I thought you weren't going to bother turning up,' Tamara said coldly.

He opened his eyes. 'I was at the gym. I came as soon as I got Dale's voicemail. He said she was asking for me.'

'That's right. When it came to the crunch, she decided even a dad like you was better than none at all.'

'She could've died,' he muttered. 'And I'd have been… I wouldn't have been…'

'No. You wouldn't. Again.'

'It's a judgement on me. Isn't it? I'm being punished for all my fuck-ups as a dad.'

'I don't think it works that way.'

He was silent for a moment.

'How's she been?' he asked at last. 'She wouldn't let me see her. Wouldn't even let me talk to her.'

'Is that surprising? When you pressed her to get a nanny she didn't want and flirted with another woman right in front of her?'

'That was nothing.' He turned to look at her. 'It wasn't, Tam, I swear it. I was stoking my ego but nothing else.'

Tamara shook her head. 'See, Andy, this is the problem. It's not whether anything actually happened: it's that you did it, right in front of her, when she was weeks from having your baby and her body image at an all-time low. You chose your ego over her need for love and reassurance. The fact you never actually cheated doesn't make you the hero you'd like to think it does.'

'She told you that?'

Tamara nodded.

Andy was silent as he thought this over.

'And then there was the nanny,' Tamara continued. 'When you told Nat you wanted to have another baby, to be a proper father, she really believed you meant it. Then suddenly you're outsourcing half the parental role to someone paid to care for your kid?'

He flushed. 'I never considered it that way. I just thought it'd help Nat out. We can afford it.'

'But she doesn't want help. She wants you and her to tackle parenthood together, as a team. The way most people do.'

'Yes.' He fell silent again.

Tamara left him alone with his thoughts while she texted Marcie and Dale to let them know Natalie and the baby were going to be OK. It would do Andy good to spend some time in his head. Maybe he'd even find some perspective in there.

'How are the kids?' he asked at last.

'Good. Excited about the baby.'

'I've been meaning to say thanks – I would've done, if I'd thought you wanted to see me after that stuff you said at the barbecue. Thanks for looking after Natalie for me.'

'We didn't do it for you,' she told him shortly.

'No. I know.' He stared at his fingers, splayed on his knees. 'Tam, I... I owe you an apology. And the kids too. I know it's a bit late, but—'

'You can say that again. But go ahead, if it gives you joy.'

'Tam, I'm sorry. I'm sorry for being a shit husband and an even shittier father. I'm sorry for walking out on you. And I'm sorry for turning up and disrupting everything by bringing Natalie and the baby into your lives.'

'We like having Natalie and the baby in our lives. It's you that's the problem. Anything else?'

'Yeah.' He rubbed his ear. 'I'm sorry I was a dick to your boyfriend at the barbecue. I was jealous, that's all.'

Tamara raised an eyebrow. 'Seriously?'

'Not of you – no offence. That's all water under the bridge. But the way he was with Willow, how she looked at him...' He sighed. 'I suppose it brought home all my shortcomings as a father. How I failed her. I took that out on him when what I needed to do was take a long, hard look at the man I am. I guess I haven't changed as much as I thought. But this, Natalie leaving, and then tonight when I was really afraid I might lose her and the baby for good...' He met her eyes. 'I want to do better, Tam. I really do.'

Tamara was unrelenting. 'We've heard this before.'

'When you said I only got back in touch because Nat told me to, that wasn't true. Perhaps she was the catalyst to start me thinking about what a failure I'd been as a dad, but it wasn't what made me want the kids back in my life.'

'Then what did?'

'I just... I wanted to get to know them. To do better. Make amends.'

Tamara relented the tiniest fraction of an amount. 'You were an absolute arse at the barbecue, about Harry and Eloise and a million other things, but I did regret screwing up what you'd started to build with the kids. For their sakes. It was so hard for them to let you back in, but once they did it meant a lot to them to have you in their lives again. Not that you deserved to be let back in.'

'You're right. I didn't deserve any of it. But I swear I'll give it my everything this time, Tam. If you'll let me see the kids, and if Nat just gives me another chance...' He paused. 'Do you think she will?'

'That's not for me to say, is it?'

'No.' Silence again. 'And you? Will you let me be a dad to Willow? Help me build bridges with the twins?'

'I... maybe,' she said. 'You'll have to really convince them you mean it this time though. You'll have to convince me. And to do that, you need to start by stepping up for Natalie. Whether or not she decides to give you another chance, that's your baby she's just risked her life having and you'd better bloody well be the best dad you can to him.'

'I will.' He looked determined. 'I swear I will. I've spent too much of my life despising myself for my failures. I won't fail again.'

'And just know that if she does take you back, Natalie's always got a family to come home to if you screw up again. She belongs to all of us now.'

'Right.' He turned to look at her, with just the flicker of a smile. 'You know, Tam, I've never met anyone quite like you.'

She smiled tightly. 'Probably for the best, eh?'

'You're so... I don't know. Sort of hard, and sort of soft,

and sort of everything in between. I never really deserved you. I don't think I ever really understood you either.'

'I know.'

'Harry realises he's got something pretty special, I hope.'

'He says so,' Tamara said, smiling as she pictured him. 'You don't deserve Natalie either. But just because you don't deserve her doesn't mean you can't work hard to earn her.'

They were interrupted by the nurse. 'Mr Horan? Ms Horan?'

They stood up.

'That's us,' Andy said.

'Your friend's awake. She's asked you both to come in and meet the new arrival.'

Natalie was groggy but smiling when they were shown into the delivery room. In her arms was a little pink mass of flailing limbs and huge eyes. He squinted at them as they came in.

'Oh God, Nat.' Andy fell to his knees and rested his head on her arm. 'I'm so sorry. I'm so, so sorry.'

'There'll be time for that when my drugs wear off,' Natalie said, a little slurred. 'First things first. Take Thomas for a cuddle.'

Andy took the baby in his arms, a wondering expression on his face as he ran his finger over the bridge of its tiny nose.

'Hello Thomas,' he said softly.

Tamara found herself welling up, and dashed away a tear.

'Oh, Willow's going to be so thrilled,' she whispered. 'She'll be busting to come down right away, Nat.'

'Then bring her, and the twins,' Natalie said. 'As soon as you like. I can't wait for Tommy to meet his big brother and sisters.'

'What happened to Cody?' Andy asked.

Natalie smiled at Tamara. 'Change of plan. I wanted to name him after his... well, I don't know what you are to him really, Tam. Stepmother doesn't sound quite right, does it?'

'Godmother,' Andy murmured, his gaze still fixed on the baby.

Natalie nodded. 'Yes, godmother. Of the fairy variety, I'd say.' She looked up at Tamara. 'I could've lost him if it wasn't for you.'

'Oh, nonsense. I'm just your wheels man.' Tamara gave Natalie's shoulder a fond squeeze. 'But I'm so relieved you're both OK,' she said softly. 'Well done, Nat. He's completely perfect.'

'Here.' Andy handed her the baby. 'Have a cuddle.'

Tamara took him in her arms, no longer bothering to check the tears running down her cheeks.

'You know, Thomas,' she whispered as she rested her head against his, 'I've got a feeling everything's going to be OK.'

39

Milo and Christian were finishing their spaghetti bolognese as Milo's special romantic playlist filled the air. It had moved on from Barry White and they were now being regaled with a bit of Marvin Gaye.

'This is the musical equivalent of oysters and Viagra,' Christian said. 'You've really pulled out all the stops, haven't you?'

'I just wanted to show you I appreciate you.' Milo reached for the bottle of wine. 'Top up?'

'No, I'm good.'

'Pudding? I've got chocolate mousse.'

'Honestly, Milo, I couldn't eat another thing.'

OK. It was time. They'd wined and they'd dined, they'd Barry Whited, the room was bathed in flickering candlelight and an incense burner filled the air with the intoxicating scent of sandalwood. Milo could wait a lifetime and never find a more appropriate moment to spill his feelings.

'Chris, um... I did actually have something I wanted to talk to you about.'

Christian sat up straight. 'Actually, I've been meaning to talk to you too.'

Milo felt a surge of panic. Shit! It was happening again,

wasn't it? Just like it had with West. 'We need to talk' – that came first, leading straight into 'it's not you, it's me' and finishing with a nice, patronising 'I hope we can still be friends'. God, he'd done it again. How hadn't he seen this coming?

'Christian, please—' he began, before he was interrupted by the buzz of his mobile phone.

'Who is it?' Christian asked.

'Text from Russell.'

Milo swiped to open the message, and felt the blood drain from his face.

'Oh my God,' he whispered. 'Chris, we have to go. It's Saffie.'

Saffie couldn't remember much after she'd fallen down the stairs. She remembered darkness closing in, and a strangely detached, academic pondering on whether this was the end for her as consciousness slipped away. What felt like hours later – although it might've been minutes, or even seconds – she'd drifted into a state of half-consciousness as a familiar shape had hoved into view, shouting her name. Then it had gone dark again, and the next thing she knew she was on a stretcher in the back of an ambulance.

Russell. He'd been there, she was sure of it. He'd been the shape in her house, and he'd sat by her in the ambulance. Or had he been a hallucination? All she knew was that she was waking up in a hospital bed.

'Wur,' she said, then stopped. It hurt to talk. Her throat felt like the Sahara, her head was oddly weightless and everything looked blurred.

'Ah, you're back with us,' a nurse observed. 'I am glad. We've got some friends of yours in the waiting room who've been worried sick.'

'Am I—' Saffie broke off into a cough.

'Now, try not to talk.' The nurse handed Saffie a glass of something pink and goopy. 'Here. This ought to ease your throat.'

Saffie drank a little of the soothing liquid then tried again.

'Am I OK?' she rasped.

'Well no, I'd say you're not OK. Walking headlong into burning buildings will tend to have that effect.' The nurse smiled. 'But there's no permanent damage. There's a minor concussion where you bumped your head, you've re-sprained your ankle, and the smoke inhalation is going to leave your throat and lungs rather sore for a while. But within a month, I fully expect you'll be right as rain. Now, are you up to having visitors? I've got a Tamara, a Milo and his boyfriend, and the friend who came in the ambulance with you.'

So Russell had been in the ambulance. But what had he been doing there? Not wanting to use her voice any more than she had to, Saffie nodded her consent for the visitors to be shown in.

Tam appeared first, carrying a load of chocolate bars. She dumped them on the bed.

'Sorry,' she said in answer to Saffie's puzzled look. 'I didn't have a chance to get you a proper present. These are from the hospital vending machine.'

Saffie cast a longing look at a Snickers, wondering how long it would be until her throat was healed enough to cope with peanuts.

'How did you—' she rasped.

'—know you were here? Milo texted. It didn't take me long to get here.' Tamara pointed to another part of the building. 'I was over there in the maternity wing. It seems to be the night for drama.'

Saffie shot her a puzzled frown, and she smiled.

'Natalie's baby decided to make an appearance. She's called him Thomas, after me, and Harry and me are to be godparents.' Tamara laughed at Saffie's expression. 'I know, it's weird as hell, but it feels... right, somehow. I think everything's going to be fine. I mean, I don't know how things are going to work out with Nat and Andy – she's going to give him another chance, and I believe him when he says he'll give it his all this time, but people can only change so much. But Nat knows she's got us now, so she'll never be without family.'

'Russ,' Saffie managed to gasp.

'Oh, Russ is the hero of the hour,' Tamara said. 'You know it was him who saved you?'

Saffie shook her head.

'It was all very romantic, throwing you over his shoulder and carrying you out of the house. Well, he might not've done that. I think he actually just dragged your prostrate form into the garden. But I prefer to imagine it the other way.' Tamara gave her a hug. 'Jesus, Saf, I'm so glad you're going to be OK. You're the second person I've had to say that to tonight.'

'Thanks, Tam,' Saffie managed to croak.

Tamara hugged her gently, trying not to press on any part of her that might be tender – which was basically all of her after her tumble down the stairs.

'Get well as quick as you can, Saf,' she said softly. 'I think life's about to take an interesting new turn for you, don't you?'

Saffie managed a laugh.

'I'll ask the nurse to show the boys in,' Tamara said. 'There's a maximum of three visitors at a time. They sent me ahead to fill you in on everything.'

Tamara disappeared, and moments later the nurse showed Russell to her bedside along with Milo and Christian. Saffie's mouth felt stiff and dry, but she managed to beam at them all.

'Hi,' she croaked.

Russell smiled. 'Hello, Batman.' He sounded slightly croaky himself, and his hair was singed at the ends.

'Russ. You—' She broke off, coughing.

'Don't talk if it hurts you.' He leaned over to hug her tightly. 'God, Saf, I thought you were a goner.'

'No such… luck,' she gasped.

'Well you look awful.' Milo hugged her too, holding on to her for some time. 'You bloody idiot, Saffie.'

She laughed hoarsely. 'Love you too.'

He turned to the lad at his side. 'You remember Chris.'

Christian gave her a shy wave. 'Hi.'

'We were just about to have pudding when Russ texted to tell me he'd had to drag my best friend from a burning building.' He took her hand and squeezed it hard. 'Seriously, thank God you're OK.'

'My… house?' she croaked.

'I spoke to one of the firefighters while you were being stretchered into the ambulance,' Russell said. 'It's going to be one hell of a clean-up job, but aside from the kitchen, he seemed to think most of what was in the rest of the house would be salvageable. Your books and things.'

Saffie's throat was starting to feel a little more accustomed to speaking. She tried a longer sentence.

'Why were you there?' she croaked.

'We had a date, remember? You invited me over to pick up where we left off at Fran's. I arrived just before the fire brigade.'

'You'll be staying with Nurse Milo until we can get your place sorted,' Milo told her. 'The doctor says you'll be here overnight, but you should be able to come home with me tomorrow. I'll get the spare room all nice and girly for you.'

'Sorry,' Saffie muttered. 'I'm a bother.'

'Bloody lucky to be alive is what you are, and I'm not letting you out of my sight for a good long while. Not until you've sworn a solemn oath to never give me a heart attack like that again.'

'Ruined your date,' Saffie said. She still felt dizzy; half in a dream. She wasn't sure if it was the smoke inhalation or the pain relief meds, but there was a floaty, fuzzy feeling in her head that was quite pleasant. She looked enquiringly at Milo. 'You… told him?'

'Er, no.' Milo glanced awkwardly at Christian. 'Sorry. I guess she's pretty out of it from whatever they've given her. This wasn't really how I wanted to introduce the two of you.'

Saffie waved an impatient hand. 'Milo!'

'What's she talking about?' Christian asked Milo.

'She's blathering drug-fuelled nonsense. I'd like to say this was the first time in our long friendship, but…'

Saffie took a drink from her bedside table. 'He... loves you,' she rasped. 'Can't tell... you.'

Christian blinked at Milo. 'Eh? Do you?'

Milo blushed deeply. 'Er... well, yes. Actually been trying to tell you for ages, actually.'

'Oh.' Christian was silent for a moment. 'Me too.'

'But then I could tell you were going off me so I—' Milo stopped. 'Hang on, what?'

'I've been trying to tell you the same thing. I just couldn't seem to find the right moment. I was worried you'd run a mile if I rushed it.'

'Seriously?' Milo laughed. 'Well that's classic us, isn't it? Spending months dancing round the same three-syllable phrase because we were both worried about scaring each other off.'

Christian looked embarrassed. 'So... shall we say it now?'

Milo shook his head. 'I can't do it with Saffie and Russell grinning at me.'

'Plus there's an old man down there having his catheter changed, which might kill the mood a bit.'

Saffie waved a hand, smiling. 'Go.'

'Good idea,' Milo said, making eye contact with Russell. 'I think you two probably need to talk as well.' He kissed Saffie on the forehead. 'Get better, Saf. I'll be back later.'

When Milo and Christian had gone, Russell pulled up a chair.

'What possessed you to run into the house like that?' he asked. 'No, don't answer if it's going to hurt your throat. I'm just glad you're safe.'

'Notebook,' she gasped.

He frowned. 'What?'

She looked at the nurse, who was hovering discreetly nearby. 'Notebook?'

'Yes, we have it. It's with your clothes in your locker. Here.'

The nurse unlocked the locker by Saffie's bed and handed the notebook to her. It looked a little black, but otherwise none the worse for its ordeal. Saffie wished she could say the same about herself.

Russell stared at it. 'This? You went in for this?'

Saffie nodded.

'But… why?'

'Your… dad,' she managed to croak.

He looked at her for a long moment. The nurse, with exemplary tact, went to busy herself elsewhere.

'You risked your life to get this for me?' Russell said softly. 'Because you knew these were the last memories I had of my dad?'

She nodded.

'Saffie, you stupid…' He laughed and hugged her again. 'Don't you ever, ever put yourself in danger like that for me again, you ridiculous, amazing girl.'

'Couldn't let it… burn,' she croaked.

'I couldn't let *you* burn. God, Saffie! If you'd died in there, I'd never be able to…' He let her go to look earnestly into her face. 'You really think the book matters more to me than keeping you safe? That there's anything more important to me than that?'

'Why?'

'Come on. If you don't know how I feel about you by now…' He took her hand and pressed it to his lips.

'But… Nikki,' she gasped.

'What about Nikki?'

'You and… Nikki. Kissing.' She reached for the glass by her bed and swallowed down some more of the liquid.

He frowned. 'What?'

She nodded vehemently. 'Kissing. She said… mum… changed her mind…'

Russell shook his head slowly. 'Wow. You've had quite a night, haven't you? Jumping into burning buildings, jumping to conclusions…'

Saffie tried to look severe, although it was tough with her eyes puffed up to golf ball proportions and her eyebrows singed off.

'Yes, Nikki did tell me tonight that she'd changed her mind about wanting to be a mum,' Russell said. 'What did you think that meant? That we were going to get back together?'

Saffie nodded.

'That was never the only issue between us, Saffie. And it's pretty obvious you missed the first half of the conversation.'

Saffie raised an eyebrow.

'Don't look like that,' he said. 'If you'd started eavesdropping five minutes earlier, you might've heard Nikki breaking the news that led me to swinging her around and kissing her – entirely platonically, I might add, because I was so thrilled for her. She's pregnant.'

Saffie spluttered, and Russell handed her the glass from her bedside table.

'That's what's been behind the mood swings recently,' he said. 'She'd been having a bit of a crisis. It was totally unplanned, and she couldn't decide what to do about it – especially when her boyfriend was adamant he never wanted kids. Today, after she broke down in the office, she finally decided that yes, she did want to be a mum. She broke it to Alex and was thrilled when he told her he wanted to go ahead with the pregnancy too. It turned out he'd just said he didn't want kids because he wanted to be with her. Just like I was once stupid enough to do. Anyway, she's taking a step back from the business while the two of them make a go of it as a family.'

Saffie groaned and hid her face in her hands. Russell reached out to pull them away.

'Come on, none of that,' he said softly. 'You didn't honestly believe me and Nikki were going to get back together, did you?'

'She's... beautiful.'

'Yes she is. But I'm in love with someone else, so it probably wouldn't have worked out.'

Saffie spluttered again.

'Sorry the idea upsets you so much,' Russell said. 'Oh, it's you, by the way.'

There was silence. Russell ran one finger over the sooty cover of his notebook.

'Well?' he said at last. 'Nothing to croak?'

Saffie nodded. 'Same.'

'Same?'

She nodded again.

'As in, you feel the same? Don't speak. Just do two nods for yes or one for no.'

Saffie smiled and nodded twice.

'You're positive? Because you can still get your money back from Alison Sheldrake.'

She shook her head.

'Can I kiss you then?' Russell asked. Saffie gave him another two nods, and he pulled her into his arms for a gentle kiss. There'd be plenty of time for passionate kisses, she hoped, when her throat had healed.

'Thanks,' she croaked when Russell drew away.

'For what?'

'Saving my life.'

'If that's what it takes to finally get you to forgive me for that stupid feature, Saf, I'd gladly run into a thousand firey infernos.'

'And thanks…' She drew a deep breath as she prepared for the pain of a long speech. 'For… helping me discover… there's something worth running into a burning building for. You.'

Epilogue

Nine months later...

The spring sunshine bathed the wildflower meadow with gold as Tamara, in a simple white suit, stood hand in hand with Harry under a floral arch. Harry, looking dapper, gazed proudly at his bride as they prepared to say their vows. Next to him, Dale was in a suit of his own as he performed best man duties for his new stepfather, although the way he kept tugging at his collar suggested he wasn't quite at ease in his finery. Beside him were Natalie, Marcie and Willow in their bridesmaids' dresses, with little Thomas in his mum's arms dressed in an incy-wincy pageboy outfit and cap. He looked like an infant recruit to the Peaky Blinders gang.

Saffie nudged Russell. 'You're not going to cry, are you?'

'Not today. I might when it's us.'

Saffie examined the engagement ring on her finger. 'If I go through with it. I haven't decided whether I want to do a runner to Scotland again yet.'

He shuddered. 'Don't even joke.'

'Don't worry. I'm feeling pretty good about it this time.'

'I've got a good feeling about this time around too.' He took her hand and kissed it.

'It's them before us anyway,' she said, nodding to Milo and Christian. 'And then Andy and Natalie. It seems to be a weddingy sort of year.'

'Glad you didn't get your money back on me?'

She smiled. '£500 is pretty steep for a date, but I'm ready to admit you were worth it.'

'That's the date doctor over there, isn't it?' Russell said, nodding to a woman a couple of rows in front.

Saffie squinted. 'Oh yeah. I didn't know Tam had invited her.'

'Makes sense though. It's thanks to her we're all here.'

They fell silent as the vicar started the ceremony.

'Congratulations, Tam,' Saffie said, giving her a kiss. 'Harry, you're a lucky man.'

He smiled at his bride. 'Don't I know it?'

Tamara gazed fondly back at him. 'From where I'm standing, I feel like I'm the one who hit the jackpot.'

Harry turned her around so he could give her a kiss, and Dale and Willow gagged in unison.

Marcie laughed. 'Come on, you two. It's their wedding day.'

Milo gave his nephew a nudge. 'Ready to do your speech, Dale?'

Dale tugged at his collar. 'No. Why did I have to be best man? You should've got the bear to do it, Harry.'

'Oh, you'll be great,' Harry said, slapping him on the back. 'I hope you've included your favourite embarrassing anecdote about the time you tried to teach me some skating moves.'

Dale grinned. 'Are you kidding? That's the whole speech.' He turned to his mother. 'Oh, Mum, can you fix a rip in my favourite tee before I go back to uni?'

Marcie shook her head. 'Dale, not today, for God's sake.' She grimaced. 'But, er, I did have something that needed a few buttons sewing back on as well, Mum. I mean, if you're doing his.'

Tamara rolled her eyes at Natalie. 'My supposedly grown-up kids. You'd better be prepared for this kind of thing in another eighteen years, Nat. Once the mum, always the mum.'

Saffie nudged Russell. 'I'm going to get us some grub from the buffet. Any requests?'

'Sausage roll and anything sweet,' he said immediately. 'Thanks, future wife.'

Saffie headed to the table where nibbles had been laid out.

'Sorry,' she said when she reached for a sausage roll at the same time as another guest. 'Oh. Hi, Fran.'

Fran smiled. 'I'm assuming you're raiding the pastries on behalf of my elder grandson, the sausage roll fiend?'

Saffie laughed. 'Naturally.'

'Actually, I'm glad I caught you, Saffie. I know it's probably horribly vulgar to talk about work at a wedding, but since it's good news, I don't think Tamara will mind.'

Saffie blinked. 'OK.'

She put down her paper plate and followed Fran a little way from the table.

Fran Cook, as it turned out, had not been enjoying her

retirement. The day they'd all come together to produce the thousandth issue of *The Throstle's Nest* had made her feel alive again, she'd said, and after all, age was just a number. So, when Nikki stepped back from the business to focus on her new family, Fran had bought her shares back. She was relishing having a finger in the family pie once again, and it felt right, somehow, that she should be at the helm for as long as she wanted to be.

Things had been going well for the little magazine since Fran had come back on board. She seemed to be chock-full of fresh ideas since her break, and then there was the thousandth issue. Saffie had been right when she'd reflected that it was the sort of feel-good story people could really get behind, and Tamara's rousing editorial had struck a chord with readers. For a while, they'd been a bit of a viral sensation. Everyone seemed to be sharing the tale of the plucky little mag that had beaten overwhelming odds to make its deadline. There'd been a surge in subscribers – people who would never normally have heard of them – and a corresponding surge in interested advertisers. They'd even been forced to take on more staff, with Saffie now heading up a team of three feature writers.

Fran, as always, got straight to business.

'I haven't discussed this with Russell but I have discussed it with Tamara,' she said. 'Not that I think he'd object, but frankly he's far too biased in your favour to make any sort of objective decision. But you've been a brilliant little worker for us for a long time now, you're an excellent journalist and I can't think of anyone I'd rather see sitting in the chair. After all, you are family – soon to be officially so.'

'Fran, I don't understand.'

'I want to offer you a promotion,' Fran said. 'You've proven yourself more than worthy, and I know you turned down a far better job to stay with us.' She smiled at Saffie's expression. 'Yes, Russell told me. He's abnormally proud of you, you know. Anyway, if you'd like the position of *Throstler* editor, it's yours.'

'Editor!' Saffie stared at her. 'But... Tam's the editor. She's a brilliant editor. She's not leaving, is she?'

'She's moving on to better things, but she'll still be part of *The Throstler*,' Fran said. 'This Russell does know about, although he's been sworn to secrecy. From now on, we've decided the *Lifestyle North* team and my little rabble at *The Throstle's Nest* are going to be working more closely together. Russell and Tamara are going to jointly hold the position of Editorial Director, with responsibility across both mags, so they can pool their resources more efficiently.' She looked at Saffie keenly. 'Well? What do you say?'

'Well, I...' Saffie felt dizzy. 'Yes. I say yes. I mean, I'd be honoured.'

'That's how I knew you were family. Because when it came to that little mag we all love, you never wavered. Congratulations, dear.'

She disappeared, leaving Saffie staring after her.

'Is this yours?' a voice asked.

'Hmm?' She looked around. Alison Sheldrake was at the buffet, pointing at her abandoned plate. 'Oh. Yes.' Saffie went back to claim it.

'Um, how's it going with the agency?' Saffie felt awkward in the presence of the woman she owed all her happiness to, remembering how she'd unceremoniously accused her of being a fraud last time they'd met.

Dr Sheldrake shrugged. 'It's gone. Closed down. Well, there was no money in it. Are you going to eat that brownie?'

'Er, no.' Saffie absently handed over the mini brownie. 'That's a shame. About the agency.'

'Not really. I did what I set out to do.' Dr Sheldrake popped the brownie in her mouth and gave Saffie a shrewd look. 'I'm taking stock of my assets at the moment, so if you want that refund I suggest you apply for it now.'

Saffie flushed. 'No, that's OK. It, um… it worked out between me and Russell. In the end.'

Dr Sheldrake smiled. 'I thought it might.'

She was about to go when Saffie put a hand on her arm.

'Why did you do it? Set up the agency?' she asked. 'You must've known it couldn't work as a business.'

'As a business? You're right, I did. But it worked for you, didn't it?' She glanced at Tamara and Harry, blissfully happy as they chatted to their guests. 'And for the others I signed up. Money isn't the only reason something's worth doing.'

'All right, but… *how* did you do it? None of us have ended up with the people we'd have picked. If we were left to ourselves, I mean.'

Dr Sheldrake smiled. 'And how had that been working out for you? Being left to yourselves?'

'Well, we were all single and miserable.'

'So you were. There's your answer then.'

Saffie felt a pair of arms wrap around her waist, and turned to face Russell. Dr Sheldrake melted into the crowd.

'Where've you been?' he whispered, kissing her neck. 'I missed you.'

'Mingling.' She turned to look for Dr Sheldrake, but couldn't see her. 'Alison Sheldrake closed her agency.'

'I bet she lost her shirt.' He nuzzled his nose against her. 'Not that I'm complaining. I did pretty well out of it.'

'We all did.' Her gaze fell on Christian and Milo, holding hands as they separated off from the other guests to take a walk, and on Tamara and Harry. 'Not the partners we would've chosen, but the ones we needed. I wonder how she does it.'

'She's a witch. Only explanation.'

'It did all feel a bit magical. I should write us up for *The Throstler*'s "Stranger than Fiction" feature.'

'We'd get letters complaining it was too far-fetched.' He shook his head, 'Always it's work with you.'

'That's why you love me. Boss.'

'True enough. I am definitely the Walter to your Hildy.' He lifted his face from her neck to smile at her. 'I think that was when I realised, you know – that I was destined to fall for you. An hour into our first date, watching your eyes shining during *His Girl Friday*.'

She smiled too. 'I thought you didn't believe in love at first sight.'

'No.' He looked at the other happy couples on the meadow: Milo and Christian, oblivious to everyone but each other, and Tamara and Harry forming a little family group with Willow, Marcie, Dale, Natalie and Thomas. 'But love in twenty-four hours seems to have a pretty good success rate.'

'Couldn't have put it better myself.' She lifted her lips to him for a kiss.

Acknowledgements

Huge thanks have to go to my agent, Laura Longrigg at MBA Literary Agents, and to my amazing editor at Aria, Martina Arzu, for all their hard work bringing this book to the world. Not to mention the rest of the team at Aria who have all done such a wonderful job once again.

Big thanks too to all of my talented, supportive writer pals: Rachel Burton, Victoria Cooke, Rachel Dove, Sophie Claire, Jacqui Cooper, Kiley Dunbar, Helena Fairfax, Kate Field, Melinda Hammond, Marie Laval, Katey Lovell, Helen Pollard, Debbie Rayner, Rachael Stewart, Victoria Walters, Angela Wren, and many others. Thanks as well to the Romantic Novelists' Association for being such a wonderful and supportive organisation.

As ever, thanks to my supportive family and friends – my partner and long-term beta reader Mark Anslow; friends Robert Fletcher and Nigel and Lynette Emsley; Firths, Brahams and Anslows everywhere. You're all brilliant.

And finally, a special thank you to Sara Ainsworth, the winner of a competition on my Facebook page to choose a name for my new heroine. The name suits her perfectly – it's hard to imagine now that she could ever have been anything other than a Saffie!

About the Author

MARY JAYNE BAKER grew up in rural West Yorkshire, right in the heart of Brontë country… and she's still there.

After graduating from Durham University with a degree in English Literature, she dallied with living in cities including London, Nottingham and Cambridge, but eventually came back with her own romantic hero in tow to her beloved Dales, where she first started telling stories about heroines with flaws and the men who love them.

Mary Jayne's novel *A Question of Us* was the winner of the Romantic Novelists' Association's Romantic Comedy Novel of the Year Award 2020. She also writes uplifting women's fiction as Lisa Swift, and World War II sagas as Gracie Taylor.